The Devil's Doorbell
Volume II

Compiled and edited by
Xtina Marie

A HellBound Books LLC Publication
Copyright © 2021 by HellBound Books Publishing LLC
All Rights Reserved

Cover and art design by
HellBound Books Publishing LLC

www.hellboundbookspublishing.com

Printed in the United States of America

Contents

A woman's pleasure is a dangerous thing.
-M. O'Keefe

The Demons that Bind Us
Rory Spickett

Lindsey lay on the grand bed of her bedroom within the Vantassle Mansion as the hands of the grandfather clock in the room turned ever closer to noon. She marveled at the intricate floral canopy that hung over the bed as she had done many mornings before imagining how she could manipulate the movement from vines and flowers into ever more intricate patterns. In her hand she toyed with a black pentagram, moving it back and forth along her fingers. Beyond the door of her bedroom, she could hear footsteps approaching.

When the door opened Lindsey turned her head to see a short haired brunette woman a little older than her standing in the doorway. It was her sister Stella, if sister was even an appropriate word. She quickly slid the pentagram underneath the pillow.

"You planning to get up anytime soon?" Stella asked. "The guests have arrived."

Lindsey sighed and raised her slender body up to the edge of the bed.

"I am dressed, sis. Besides none of those people care if I show up."

Stella crossed her arms in disgust as she had always done when Lindsey did not acquiesce to her comments.

"Father expects it."

Lindsey turned her head away from Stella and sneered. Father wanted everything. Not that he cared if it was anything she wanted or agreed with. She left the bed moving towards a table lined with the cold uneaten plates of breakfast that had been brought to her room earlier. None of it looked appetizing but at least they had brought lemonade.

"I turned eighteen last week, Stella." Lindsey responded pouring herself a glass of lemonade.

"Lucky you. Eighteen makes you a responsible adult that has duties to perform as part of this family. I don't have time for this. Just be downstairs in ten minutes."

Lindsey could hear the seething anger in Stella's steps as she trailed off down the hallway. Perhaps she should have taken etiquette class in the prestigious university she went to. Though etiquette classes would probably be out of place for a school where little princesses were sent to.

The garden room of the manor house was a bustle of activity as Lindsey entered. The windows had been opened allowing the warm breeze to carry in the scents of the woods of the Carolinas. Caterers with plates filled with appetizers bustled around groups of finely dressed attendees while her father, an obese grey-haired figure with a short beard moved in between the crowds. She watched, partially obscuring herself behind the fountain in the center as the wretched man made his way to the front of his room to face the audience.

Reaching the front, he clinked his glass.

"Friends, thank you for joining me today. As important partners of the company and friends of the family I wanted you all here to share in an important announcement. Forty years ago, my father stood here and announced his retirement and transfer of the running of the company to myself. Quite a day for a young lad who was more interested in tennis and chasing women at the time."

The crowd chuckled in appeasement.

"I have decided myself, that now is my time to step down in the coming weeks. Do not worry, the stewardship of the company will continue within the family. The details of which I will announce shortly. For now, though, please enjoy the food."

The audience clapped as her father waded back into their midst. Lindsey saw Stella rush forward to be one of the first to falsely congratulate him on his oratory. Lindsey turned her back with a sense of foreboding filling her body.

The study of her father's took on a dark presence in the evenings. Lindsey had always dreaded entering the room as a girl. It may have been the center of her family's fortune, but it was a cold unforgiving place in her mind. Yet, something about the room enticed her, enough that she would often sneak out to hide behind the door to listen in on the deals of the family business. This evening though, she found herself seated beside her sister in front of her Father's desk.

"My daughters. I am sure you are surprised by the news today," he began.

"I wanted to let you know my decision privately in regard to the future of the company. It is Vantassle tradition that all members of the family be represented in the business, though of course only one can be leader. One who can take hold of mechanisms that make the machine run, and keep them moving. For this, I have chosen Stella."

Lindsey could see her sister's face lit up with joy.

"Thank you, Father. With myself at the helm, the business will be kept strong."

"I am sure it will, daughter, and your sister will be at your side to keep it that way."

"What?" Both Stella and Lindsey's face expressed the same shock at the statement.

"Yes. As I said, all members of the family must do what is needed to keep the image of the Vantassle's alive. We are a proud family that is looked up to as masters of industry, bringing wealth to this country. Therefore, Lindsey will be working alongside you," Father said, reclining in his chair.

Stella shot up from her seated position before slamming her foot to the ground.

"But you did not have any of your siblings work with yourself when you took over. Why would I have to endure this burden?"

"Leave us, Stella"

It was never a good sign when Father addressed one by their first name, never mind directly looking at their face.

Stella froze, but composed herself and left the room as instructed. Father rose from his chair and walked up to his remaining daughter still seated.

"Lindsey. I love you, daughter, but Stella does have a point. You have never taken to the needs of the family like your sister."

Lindsey stared at him blankly. She had heard this all before. Why could she not be like the rest of the family, was what they all said.

"You could at least talk to me."

The tone was harsh. Lyndsey could sense her father's frustration starting to show.

"Stella went to that fancy school for the business degree. Let her run the business. I want to apply to the…" Lindsey started.

She was interrupted as her father cursed then turned his back to her.

"No Vantassle is going to an art academy when the needs of the business must be taken care of." His tone had taken on an edge that Lindsey swore could cut through leather if it took physical form.

"Why do you keep doing this, my daughter? First it was the obsession with the garden, then those strange papers you found in the storeroom. People, finance, tradition those are the bedrocks of success." Her Father now stood, looking out the window of his study with his back turned to her.

Lindsey tried to hide the sadness in her eyes. He would never understand, nor would he even try.

"I am tired, Father," Lindsey stated.

"Fine. Go to bed then. But my decision rests." Her Father returned to the stack of papers on his desk.

As Lindsey approached her room, she found Stella waiting for her.

"What did you say to him?" She demanded.

"Nothing," Lindsey replied, moving past her sister.

"Yeah right. You must have said something to get him to have me chaperone you as some token bride for the rest of my life."

Lindsey could sense the same temper as her father moving through Stella's veins. She knew it was pointless to argue with her. Slowly she moved into her room, bypassing Stella.

"Just stand there silent and ignore me, just like you have done all of your life. You know what you are… a bloody parasite. A little parasite that killed our mother when she was bringing you into this world! And you never even cared for anyone here! Well then, parasite, go ahead and follow me around, but when I take over, I'll make sure you are left with nothing. No money, no notice, just a shadow, always in the corner!" Stella yelled and slammed the door.

Lindsey collapsed on the bed. Stella had never forgiven her for their mother's death. How could someone hate someone else for being born? None of it made sense. She had no interest in the business. She wanted to go to the arts school to make something of herself that was not tied to the family. But that was not the Vantassle way. She had to escape. It was then that she remembered the pentagram underneath the pillow.

Lindsey waited patiently until the late hours of the night when she knew her family and the attendants would be asleep. Opening a drawer on the bottom of her bed she took out a series of objects; a candle, a plate, raven feathers and the skull of a lynx which had died on the property some time earlier. Placing them on the rug before the lit fireplace in her room with careful precision, she lit the candle. Returning to the open drawer she took out a series of ragged charred pieces of paper. She had found, apart from the pages, the items years ago amongst discarded forgotten objects in one of the unused storerooms of the mansion. Apparently one of the Vantassle forbearers had an interest in the occult. The charred pages she had been gifted secretly within a book by a maid who had only stayed on the property for a short time.

Sitting before the prepared altar, she chanted.

At first nothing happened, but then slowly, she began to feel a heaviness fill the bedroom. The shadows along the walls grew longer and darker, mimicking the veil of night that lay beyond the windows. It was then that she noticed a figure take shape in the darkness beside her bed. It appeared to be that of a man, but apart from its wine-red suit jacket and dark hair no further features could be discerned.

"Demon... I command..." Lindsey stuttered as she began lifting herself.

"Demons are not commanded, but we do come to those who call," the figure responded with a calm voice that soothed ears of the listener like silk on skin. "Misconceptions, I know."

Lindsey found herself at a loss for words while the figure moved to the other side of bed, seemingly passing through it like air.

"It has been some time since one of us was called by a member of your family, young Lindsay. Not since you tried to speak with your departed mother, if I recall."

How did he know that? She thought to herself. Her mind shot back to memories of her youth, desperate and lonely from being locked in her room for what her father decreed as disobedience, she had longed to call out to someone. Following the instructions on the sheet, she called out and for a brief moment, she thought she'd heard a voice.

"Was it her?" Lindsey asked now, forgetting her original purpose of summoning the entity.

"That is not why you summoned me." The demon spoke.

"What is your name?" Lindsey asked, remembering from the pages that if one knew the name of the familiar summoned, it allowed them to have power over it. Unfortunately, the details on such matters were obscured due to the charred edges of the paper.

From the darkness she could tell that the creature smirked.

"This is not my first time, Lindsey. And I know your name because I do my research on everyone who calls me."

"How… I just…"

"That is not why you summoned me either."

The demon's expressionless demeanor remained unchanged

Her body relaxed as she stared at the figure by the bed. He was, to the point, much like some of her Father's most important business associations.

"I want you to kill my father and my sister." She mustered all of her courage.

The creature paused, raising its hand to its chin in contemplation.

"Why not run away?" the demon asked. "Leave this place and never return? You could hide away enough money to sustain you for a while."

"I can't. It would not work." Lindsey began thinking back to the times she had tried to run away only to have her father raise a manhunt for her. Every time she was caught and each time, as punishment, she was beaten and locked in her room for weeks. It was for her protection, he always said. She never believed him. "Why not grant the request? I know my soul is forfeit. I read the inscriptions."

It was at this point that Lindsey saw a change in the demon's expression. His lips slowly curved upwards ever so slightly.

"Yes, your soul will be the currency of this deal, but do you truly understand what you ask? You ask for the death of those who may have wronged you, yet they are still your kin. Not only would it bring suffering in this world, but the damnation your eternal soul would suffer would be tremendous."

"I have only known suffering in my life. Nothing you could conjure could be worse than what awaits me in this life." Determination rang through Lindsey's words.

With a wave of the demon's hand, the fireplace roared to life, causing flames to shoot into the air. His eyes, which up until this time had been obscured by the dark, flashed a bright shade of red. The heaviness of the air in the room turned into a gust that sent curtains flying.

"Do not be sure, my lady. I come from a place without hope—true darkness—where the ones locked away scratch and claw to escape their misery. Your father may be cruel, but my masters are inventive. You may find this unorthodox, as you humans may say, but I am not convinced of your sincerity to take your soul. So, I will offer you this deal. I will return in seven days' time. If you truly wish me to take the lives of your family at the cost of your soul, it will be done. If not, I will have no more business with you."

Almost as soon as the demon finished speaking, he vanished. The bedroom calmed and Lindsey was again left alone.

Throughout the morning Lindsey contemplated the events of the previous night. She spent the morning reading again through the inscriptions to understand why the demon had not just taken her soul right then and there. Were they not supposed to do that? Since when did a creature of evil think before accepting an offer? As Lindsey pondered more and more, she could feel her head further spinning with possibilities. She needed to clear her mind and think of what to do next.

The rose bushes in the garden room brought comfort to Lindsey. With great care she sketched each vine and blossom with stunning detail. She thought again to her wish to study at the art academy. She envisioned the paths it would open for her and the possibilities of having her work shared in galleries across the state. In a rare instance a grin crossed her face as she imagined the crowds of people smiling and appreciating her creations.

A cold hand gripping her shoulder brought her back to the garden room. Her father stood beside her looking down with a condescending stare.

"Lindsey, I received a call today from the art academy. I thought it was understood that you were not to apply to these places. You will be going to the same university your sister attends in the fall."

Lindsey stood up wrenching her shoulder from her father's hand. Keeping her back towards him she felt anger swelling within her just waiting to erupt.

"Why? All my life you have never allowed me to do anything I wanted. It is always the family and what the traditions expect. You have Stella, why not leave me be?" She turned screaming at the aging man.

Her Father's expression turned cold. Raising a hand, he furiously struck Lindsey across the face. Her body collapsed to the ground in a desperate attempt to evade further blows as she cupped the area where the hand had struck her.

"Ever since you were a little girl you have been this way. Speaking against the family business. What it does, what it stands for. Instead of working to become the next generation of us, you play in your fantasy world. I had thought I had seen the worst of it with your antics and those books on magic as a teenager. Our family's fortune was not built on drawings, it was built on money. Everything you have is built on that and you disregard it like it means nothing. What would my business partners think if even one of my daughters began preaching like a socialist maniac!"

Shaking his head in disappointment her father left the garden room. Lindsey sat alone as the attendants who had come after hearing the commotion quickly scuttled back to their duties. Racing to her room with tears in her eyes she tossed her sketchbook into the fireplace. She had to convince the demon to aid her in escaping this hell.

The demon was surprised when he was again summoned to the bedroom of the Vantassle Mansion in such a short period of time. As he emerged from the netherworld, he saw the slender figure of Lindsey again waiting for him. Her eyes were red from the events of the day.

"You call again, my lady." The demon called from the shadows.

"I will not wait seven days. Take my family, then take my soul. The inscriptions state the damned get one year. I can go to the Art Academy and at least live some semblance of a life."

An intriguing mix of conviction and desperations saturated Lindsey's voice. She truly believed what she was saying.

Stepping into the light the fireplace cast over the bedroom, his features were now revealed to Lindsey. He was not as monstrous as she expected. In fact, he looked surprisingly human with sharp triangular facial features that were mimicked in his facial hair. Again, the demon wore the same wine-red suit with a black tie and white undershirt. Rather than approach her directly, the demon strolled with an ethereal motionless walk towards the fireplace.

"You truly hate them, do you? Your Father and Sister?" The demon asked in the same silky-smooth voice looking at the roaring fire.

"Yes," Lindsey responded. "What are you waiting for? A deal is a deal."

It was then for the first time that she felt the demon speaking to her instead of at her.

"I know what it is like to hate the expectations of one's Father and the indifference of siblings. I thought as you did once, like many others, that rebellion was the answer. And us such, hellfire became my solace."

His formerly silky tone has been replaced with one that invoked gravitas.

"I can accept that fate."

The demon could tell that Lindsey stood resolute. He felt something stir inside him, but he ignored it. His duties had to be done. Moving towards her, the demon raised a hand to her chin and looked into her eyes.

"You may call me Mephistopheles." He whispered to her.

***

The electronic clock in the study turned to midnight as the father worked late into the night. Outside he could hear the wind howling as it bent the limbs of vines that crawled up the outside of the wall in an almost ghostly visage of their selves. In the skies above the Vantassle dark clouds were forming, cutting off the moonlight that would have normally entered the study. The Father was so consumed with the affairs of the day that he took no notice to the ominous signs circling him until he heard a knocking at the study door.

Initially he ignored it not wanting to be disturbed from his work.

He heard the knocking again.

"I am not to be disturbed," he called out, keeping his eyes focused on his work.

The knocking continued.

Irritated by the distraction, the father stormed towards the door. "I am not in mood for this right now, young lady."

He opened the door to nothing. He looked down the silent cold hallways for signs of the perpetrator, but saw nothing. A faint whisper filled the air, beckoning him closer. The father moved farther into the hallway.

"Show yourself now. This is a private residence, and you will show yourself to me."

Suddenly the door to the study slammed behind him causing the startled Father to spin around. He grabbed at the doorknob violently, twisting it in a vain effort to unlock the door. Behind him a black mass began to take form. The air around it chilled, causing the Father's skin to tighten as he slowly turned towards the mass. His eyes widened as he saw the mass take form before him. With terrified eyes he viewed a tall muscular shape supported by a narrow sharp face now standing before him. With a sinister smile, slender ears, and fiery eyes, the form stared down at the trembling man before it. The Father could feel the hands of the form grasp at his neck. His body was lifted towards the smiling creature who opened its jaw to reveal a slithering tongue.

It was Stella who had discovered the body of their father first. Her discovery had sent her screaming throughout the house, calling every servant and laborer to get the paramedics. The commotion awakened Lindsey from her slumber. Still in her nightgown, she strolled over to the body. At first feeling apprehension at the sight of the twisted corpse, she forced herself to move closer to observe the handy work of her new demonic ally. The bloodless sight surprised her at its cleanliness. In her mind she had expected more savagery from Mephistopheles. The crumbled corpse was indeed an unsettling sight, with the most disturbing of it all being the twisted grimace of a face crying out to scream yet seemingly unable. How many nights had she wished for this moment? Wishing for some sort of agency?

"What are you doing? Don't just stand there, parasite. The paramedics are coming." Stella screamed, bursting into the hallway.

With peering eyes Lindsey flashed a look of disgust at her sister, causing Stella to stop in her tracks. Lindsey could see her sister thinking of something to say but hesitating. The deadlock continued until Stella eventually turned and left.

It was true. Deliverance had come.

That evening, Lindsey again prepared for her ritual summoning. She had thought of the perfect end for her sister. Lying on her side across the bed she called out to Mephistopheles. She had no need of the inscriptions or artifacts now that she knew his name, and her soul was bound to the deal. As Mephistopheles appeared, he was taken aback as he felt an air of tranquility in Lindsey that had been absent in their earlier encounters.

"Your request has been granted, my lady."

"Yes, thank you." She responded, smiling.

Mephistopheles observed the smile. It was honest, and coming from a blonde angelic figure such as Lindsey, it may have seemed one of relief— but he could tell it concealed a more sinister emotion. Others had come to him looking for the death of a mortal, and joy at the result was common, but this was different.

"My sister will need to be dealt with." Lindsey stroked her hair suggestively.

Mephistopheles did not speak.

"I did say my family, not only my father." She raised herself to where her legs dropped over the side of the bed.

She presented a box to Mephistopheles, who opened it. Within the box resided a finely crafted fountain pen of amber and malachite. Curious, the demon closed the box and placed it on the bed while looking at Lindsey.

"It's father's favorite pen which he used to sign only the most important contracts. It has been in our family for generations. When Lindsey signs off on the powers of attorney granted to her as heir to the business, she will use this pen. I want you to curse this pen so that when she does so, the whole world will see her for what she is on the inside." A sense of enjoyment filled Lindsey's words.

"You did not take any care to the manner in which I dispatched your father?" Mephistopheles asked, placing his hand to her cheek. "Your sister will be taken care of, but a mortal should not take joy in the manner of the execution."

Lindsey's face lowered for a moment before looking back at him. "Was there a fine print to the contract I missed?"

Mephistopheles hesitated before relenting. Truthfully, he had never much cared for gore. It was a strange obsession of mortals, he thought. As if it made any notice to beings of divinity the manner in which a human body could be pained to cause death. It was all about the end result. "I will use the pen."

"Thank you," Lindsey smiled.

Mephistopheles turned to leave when he felt a hand tug against his arm.

"Wait, please. Stay tonight. I really do…. I mean, no one has ever been this way with me before. You know, actually doing what they said."

Lindsey reached her hands to his chest and moved her face closer to his. He could feel the energy between them. He felt himself being drawn to her. Of course, in the laws of hell there was nothing prevent intimacy between two contracted parties, mortal divine or otherwise. Yet Mephistopheles had always hesitated with such acts, as it may cause ripples within the deal.

The soft press of Lindsey's lips against his heightened his senses. He felt himself further drawn to her as his hands caressed her back. She was beautiful.

The ceremony for the installment of Stella as the new head of the Vantassle family occurred weeks later in the garden room. Such as with her father's announcement party earlier that month, the room was awash with all manner of businessmen, extended family, and important connections that Stella hoped to maintain as key cornerstones in the continued success of the business.

On this occasion, Lindsey was not shadowing herself in her room, but rather amongst the guests in a fashionable black silk dress that came to her ankles. With her father gone and her sister so busy with the business, neither she had found herself with greater breathing space at social events with which to discuss her interests with the attendees. She was delighted to discover some had an interest in artistic endeavors themselves and admitted they would never have mentioned it before given her father's demeanor. For the first time since her youth, Lindsey felt hope as the ability to take destiny into her own hands may be possible. And today would be the first day. Just as soon as Stella signed the papers with the pen. A part of her wondered if Mephistopheles would fail on his agreement, however thinking of their night of carnal embrace told her differently.

With a clinking of a glass, Stella brought the room's attention to herself.

"Thank you everyone, for joining. Today we enter a new chapter of the Vantassle family following the unfortunate passing of my Father. I thank you all for the support that you have provided to my family in these desperate times."

The audience clapped.

"It is my honor to take over ownership of the Vantassle family business, by the signing of these documents, instituting myself as the new President of the company."

Stella gestured towards a man beside her holding a series of papers and the wooden box containing the family pen. Lindsey looked on with anticipation as Stella took the pen from the box.

With each stroke on the signature block, Lindsey watched as sweat began to appear on Stella's brow. Within moments her face had turned red. Turning to her side she coughed attempting to hold back the discomfort of breathing that had suddenly entered her body. She gestured for water from one of the caterers. She could feel the heat build inside her as she loosened her collar.

Those around her rushed to Stella as she collapsed to her hands and feet. Her arms thrashed, preventing them from nearing as the audience could see streams of blood began to pour from her eyes and mouth. The audience gasped in horror as her head shot to the ceiling, followed by a gurgling scream as more blood flowed down her face. Lindsey watched, holding back any signs of emotion on her face as her sister's lifeless body collapsed to the ground. In the periphery of her vision, she caught a glimpse of a wine-red suited man leaving the room.

The news of the death of a second Vantassle sent waves through the family business and the estate. Looking for leadership, the mansion servants and business executives flocked to Lindsey to see if the last survivor of the family could take up the reins of the business. In a strange turn of events, Lindsey found herself feeling more adept in potentially running the business than she had thought. During Stella's would-be inauguration, she found that more and more of the company individuals were far more sympathetic to her views than her father and sister were. In the shadows, Mephistopheles continued to watch and advise. His work may have been done with the deaths of Lindsey's father and sister, but the demon had found himself drawn more and more to his contracted party. Normally mortals would self-destruct after the completion of their deal, as they desperately bargained for a way to save their souls or completely gave into debauchery. Rather the soul he currently watched seemed to flourish in her newfound spotlight, despite the cost. She called on him at times for advisement, which Mephistopheles answered in the dark hours of midnight, as had become their way. Each time, Mephistopheles would kiss the nape of her neck and watch her fall asleep after their discussions. As she slept, Mephistopheles would stand by the roaring fireplace pondering the situation.

Was it that she reminded of him of himself some time ago that kept drawing him to her? A desperate soul ignored by one's own patriarchy. Most of his brothers had shown little interest in him either. When the rebellion in the heavens occurred, he initially stood on the sidelines as his brethren fought amongst themselves. The conflict left him distraught as he sought a way to broker an agreement between both sides for peace. For his efforts, he was shunned. It was at that moment alone that Lucifer came to him and offered him a deal. And so, he became the dealer of souls, first to the divine, then to the mortals after the fall. Of all the mortals he had encountered, none had caused him to think twice about the deals he had made.

Lindsey found herself awoken in the dark hours of the morning before dawn to see Mephistopheles standing by the fireplace in her bedroom. A roaring fire blazed within as the demon shifted around the burning wood through unseen currents flowing from his hands.

"I would not have thought a demon could have trouble sleeping," Lindsey said, rising out of the bed.

Mephistopheles continued to shift his hand, manipulating the fire.

"Is something wrong?" She asked, leaning closer to him.

Mephistopheles turned to her. "We can't continue this, Lindsey. The contract has to come to an end."

Lindsey stepped back in shock. "Why? What do mean?"

The demon turned to her, placing the poker in its case by the fireplace. He could sense the anger building in her. "I cannot lead you down this path further. You do not understand the importance of what you have traded."

"What does that mean? What are you going to do? Bring back those monsters I had you kill? Was this your game all along? Some kind of trick to get my soul earlier?" The questions foamed from Lindsey's mouth, one after another. Her strikes fell soft as she gave up attempting to physically deter Mephistopheles.

Mephistopheles stretched out his hand and began turning it. Lindsey felt the air around her heat. She lunged at Mephistopheles, striking him in the chest.

"No. You cannot do this. I cannot have this happen again. You promised me freedom."

Mephistopheles held his hand firm, as he could feel conflict rise in him. "I won't take you. Your soul is damned for the deal that you have made, and my masters expect a soul as payment for our bargain. If *I* destroy your mortal form, then the deal is severed." Mephistopheles said, emphasizing the I.

Lindsey wiped her brow, perplexed. "Then whose soul did you have in mind to offer? The gardener's?"

Both stared at each other in silence, locking eyes. She could sense it now. The soul he meant to offer was his own.

"What are you waiting for, then?" She looked up with sorrow in her eyes.

Mephistopheles paused for a second before turning his hand again. He could feel every instinct of himself fighting what he was about to do. Lindsey's body convulsed as a torrent of fire erupted from within her. It encapsulated her body without spreading across the room, and within a few moments, Lindsey's body was reduced to ash.

Before him the shackled illuminated form of Lindsey stood with her eyes closed. Reaching out to her cheek, he caressed the spectral visage as the shackles disintegrated. The demon watched as the body slowly vanished before him.

Alone in the room Mephistopheles pondered his next moves before the fireplace. His masters would seek his soul in penance for what was lost. But he was already damned…there was little they could do to him. But in time an opportunity may arise.

An opportunity for salvation.

The Hill Girl
Jane Nightshade

Joe Finnerty was lost in dreamworld again. The girl's face was distinctive, with sharply cut features like his grandmother's old-fashioned cameo. Her hair was loose and exploding with round curls; black silk twisted into rings and swirls. She was wearing a floaty gown of some silver material, and her face was symmetrical and perfect, lovelier than anything had a right to be in this head-chopping Middle Eastern hellhole he'd somehow found himself living in.

She seemed to hover slightly over the ground as she walked barefoot across hot sand. Beckoning to him with an enigmatic smile. He followed her through the alien landscape, past overturned DPVs and burned-out tanks, heat shimmers blurring his vision here and there.

She stopped in front of a mangled pile of steel and hovered there, arms held out before her, begging him for an embrace. He moved slowly toward her, a vision in silver and black, until he was close enough to touch her. He reached for her, and she turned to sand and dust in front of his eyes, powdering into a pile at his feet. The final things to go were the twisting ringlets of black hair.

Something pushed and jolted him as the last strands of hair disappeared into dust. Finnerty awoke to find Andrews, his bunk mate, shaking him by the shoulders.

"Joe! Joe, quiet down. Corp is gonna hear you and report you! They're gonna send you out for a mental evaluation — *again*."

"Damn, Drewsy," he whispered hoarsely, when he realized he was actually back at the base, and it was darkest midnight, not blazing daylight with heat shimmers. "That was some fuckin' dream. I been havin' that dream for three nights in a row. It was that girl again. The one in the silvery dress."

Andrews shook him gently again. "You gotta stop dreamin' like that, Joe. They ain't gonna let you stay if they know ya got the night terrors an' then talkin' about some girl that turns to dust."

"I just need more pills, Drewsy. Ya gotta get me more pills."

"You take too many of them pills. Maybe you should think about putting yourself in for a mental evaluation, Joe? It ain't so shameful. They ain't nothin' here for you. Everybody's just scrambling to survive. You got the night terrors, you got the PTSD, don't you?"

"No PTSD—no, don't say that! I just get the spookies now and then. I can't go home, Drewsy. I don't know anything but the Army. You and the squad are all I've got."

"Will you losers shut da fuck up?" A harsh half-whisper, half-cry came from another bunk. "I got day patrol at six bells!"

"Keep your panties on, Dex," Andrews snapped back. "We're shuttin', we're shuttin'."

To Finnerty, he whispered: "Go back to sleep. I'll get you some more pills. Just a little to tide you over until you're up for leave. Just a little."

*****

In the morning, Finnerty felt better in the harsh light of a new day. Drewsy's pills always took the edge off his anxiety, at least enough to allow him to do his job. What's more, they didn't seem to affect his reflexes or concentration skills. Which he needed desperately, to stay alive while patrolling the enemy, the Saif.

The desert didn't come easy for a farmboy from rural Michigan, the greenest, flattest place imaginable, at least in the spring and summer; in winter, it was blanketed in knee-deep snow. Either way, the landscape was as opposite as could be, from where Joe Finnerty was living now.

"Y'all get a good snooze last night, Farmboy?" drawled Corp, addressing Finnerty. Corp never called him by name, but only by a revolving collection of nicknames that played heavily on the young private's freckle-faced Midwestern looks and background. Sometimes Finnerty was "Sandy Joe," sometimes he was "Freckle Butt," and sometimes he was "Haystack," among many other monikers, most of which were not exactly respectful.

"I've had better," Finnerty allowed. "Things always seem a little better in the light of day. Unless you see the Saif."

It was mid-morning, and the heat was climbing; the day's patrol was already four hours old. Finnerty sat in the shotgun position in his three-man Desert Patrol Vehicle, next to Corp, who was driving. His eyes scanned the barren desert landscape constantly, looking for anything off, anything that might signal the presence of the militants of Al-Saif or any of their sympathizers. He was used to the blistering temperatures by now, but he still had problems with the way the heat shimmers made it so hard to see.

"We're not even supposed to be in this fuckin' country," grumbled Scruggs, his other patrol mate, from his gunner position on top of the DPV. "Congress don't know we're here, folks at home don't know we're here. When I write to the wife, I gotta say I'm in 'a small Middle Eastern country' and leave it at that. We're fightin' in a goddamn war that doesn't officially even exist."

Finnerty turned in his seat and glanced back and up at his patrol mate. "It's not our place to argue with the brass, Scruggs. We go where we're told. If we weren't needed, we wouldn't be here in the first place."

"Fuckin' hell," Scruggs snorted with derision. "You believe that, Farmboy? After all the other shitshows we've stirred up in the Middle East, somehow one of 'em's gonna turn out right? Where can I send you that title to a buildin' lot in a Florida swamp?"

"I'm gonna pretend I didn't hear that, Scruggs," barked Corp, the non-com patrol officer. "Just shut up 'n keep your peeps peeled out for the Saif. Else you might end up bein' the main ingredient in a Hamburger Helper fricassee."

The Al-Saif militant group—The Sword—was known to be operating in the formerly neutral area. They'd been terrorizing the locals for several weeks now. Anyone suspected of helping the infidel's army was tortured and beheaded, with severed heads left in public places as a warning. The members of Finnerty's patrol had seen their fair share of the gruesome trophies. The Saif weren't above beheading women, and sometimes even children.

"Yes, sir, Corporal, sir," replied Scruggs with a sarcastic edge.

"What the—?" Finnerty thought he saw a flash of movement somewhere out in the shimmers, then he shouted, "Look out!" before a violent explosion grazed the driver's side of the DPV and tore off a big chunk of it. He saw Corp thrown over the top of the vehicle's hood when the explosion hit.

"I.E.D!" screamed Scruggs. He aimed his guns in the direction that Finnerty indicated and riddled it with dozens of rounds. "Fuckin' Saif!"

Everything was quiet and still after that. Finnerty climbed out of the shotgun seat, his rifle in hand.

"Cover me, Scruggs. I'm gonna go see to Corp."

Corp was lying some yards away from the crippled DPV, groaning in pain. Finnerty was relieved to find him alive, but the corporal's legs reminded him of Meatloaf Day back at the mess hall. He pulled off Corp's helmet and headset to make him more comfortable and loosened his clothes and gear.

"I'm hit!" croaked Corp. "Oh God!"

"Gonna get some help for you fast, Corp," he said, offering the anguished man some water from his canteen. "Looks like that I.E.D. wasn't a direct hit. Otherwise, we'd *all* be singin' the hamburger blues right now. Don't talk, it makes it worse."

He radioed into his command for a medevac team to take Corp to the infirmary back at the base.

He was about to go back to the DPV when he heard a shuffling noise, like someone crunching the sand under leather-soled sandals. It was coming in the general direction of an alien-looking rock formation a few yards away.

Finnerty fired over the rocks. Then he shouted a command in the basic Arabic he'd learned from the army. He signaled back to Scruggs to hold his fire.

"Throw down your weapons and show yourself." He waited for something to happen, wondering if it was a trap, and then out from behind the rocks came a small, slight figure. It was a woman, barely more than a girl. She was holding her trembling hands upward, signaling that she was no threat.

"Don't shoot please, soldier."

"You speak English?"

"Yes, a little."

"Stay where you are."

He moved a little closer and studied the girl's figure. She was thin and dressed in a tunic that was cinched at the waist with a rope belt, over an ankle-length skirt. He did not see how she could be hiding bulky explosives in her simple costume.

Then he looked at her face. He moved a few yards closer to be sure.

It was the same face in his dreams, he realized with a shock. A girl, very beautiful, and no older than nineteen. Her hair was plaited in a thick braid that spilled over her right shoulder —instead of flowing loose—and she was not wearing a floaty silver gown, but otherwise, she was the same girl.

Finnerty stared at her, trying to hide a sudden feeling of fear. He felt drawn to and repelled by the girl simultaneously. And he wanted very much to find out about her, where she lived, where her people were, and why she had been haunting his dreams.

Then he heard Corp cry out again, and Finnerty recovered his composure long enough to radio to Scruggs.

"I called in for a medevac team to 'copter out Corp. Should be here in a few. Scruggs, I gotta *situation* here— I gotta resolve it. You radio in for someone to come pick you up after the medevac team picks up Corp—I'm not going back to base."

"Finnerty—WTF? You can't stay by yourself in the desert, you'd be AWOL!"

"I gotta interrogate this girl. I think I - I - know her...long story. She might be useful. Ain't nobody round here telling me I can't. Corp's barely conscious. I think he may be delirious. I gotta *situation* here. I'll be back at base when it's over with." He shut off Scruggs in mid-curse and disengaged the radio in his helmet.

Then he turned again to the girl.

She wore the typical garb and tribal symbols of the women of the hill people. She didn't wear a veil or scarf over her head; the hill people were not Muslim. They practiced an ancient mystery religion that they refused to discuss with outsiders, but they were as socially conservative as the Muslims. That was the sum and total of what he knew about them, courtesy of the army's orientation training.

He noticed with surprise that she was wearing a long, narrow scarf or stole wrapped several times around her neck, and it struck him as odd. Most of the hill women he'd seen wore that type of scarf around their waists.

Without another word, she turned around and began to walk away, swift and sure over the barren terrain.

Finnerty lowered his rifle and followed after her. "Wait, Miss—uh lady—where are you going? What are you doing out here all alone?"

The girl said nothing but continued striding away. She was heading toward the hills.

Mesmerized, Finnerty lowered his rifle, quickened his pace, and caught up to her.

"Listen, Miss—where are you going? Home?"

She stopped and turned to him. "I have no home." She'd been crying. Her luminous skin was still wet across her high, elegant cheeks.

"No home? Then where do you live? Where do you belong? Did the Saif destroy your house?"

"I belong in the grave," she said, distressed. More tears followed.

"Don't say that! It can't be as bad as that. If you don't have a home, where are you going now?"

"I know a place," she said. And then her tears were gone suddenly, and her face took on a radiant look. Her whole body shimmered in the golden rays of the sun. "I can take you there. I can show you where we'll both be safe."

He could hear sounds of the medevac copter coming for Corp; they sounded faint and faraway. He was amazed at how little it meant to him now. Nothing seemed important anymore, except following the hill girl.

"Take me there, then! Take me, please!"

The girl strode on quickly, Finnerty by her side. She led him to the base of the hills, and then they climbed a twisty route on a narrow path through ancient, yellow-gray rocks and ledges. The climb took more than an hour; they eventually stopped on a high ledge, and then she gestured downward. Wide stone steps spilled down into a large, shallow depression in the hilly rocks, and there stood a village, timeless and ancient. Finnerty realized that it may have already been old when Roman legions marched through the desert below it.

"Is this your village? Where is everyone?"

"They are hiding."

"From the Saif?"

She made no answer but prodded him gently down the stone steps and into a narrow main street, flanked on either side by small, whitewashed structures.

"This way," she said, leading him to an even narrower alley that wended through a hare's warren of houses and shops. "No one will see us, if we go this way."

She stopped before a house with a weathered wooden door, which still sported slivers of blue paint, the blue of the Mediterranean. The hinges appeared rusted shut, but she opened the door easily, into a shadowy room with a terracotta floor and no furniture. It was cool inside; the walls were thick to shield against the heat.

There was just one window, covered with splintered shutters. She moved to the window and opened the shutters to a small crack. The sun cast a sharp-edged wedge of light on the floor.

"This is your home? There's no furniture."

She kicked her sandals off and stood barefoot on the terracotta floor. "No one lives in this place. It belonged to someone cast out from the village for wickedness many years ago, and now no one will come here."

Finnerty wondered briefly what "many years" meant in her culture. He suspected it meant something like two or even three hundred years.

"Was she a witch?"

The girl laughed.

"No. A fiend of the desert, who possessed a dead woman. They are the curse of our people, the desert fiends."

"You're not afraid?"

She shrugged her delicate shoulders. "One who has no home must take what is offered."

"You're the most incredible-looking girl I've ever seen in my life."

She smiled. "Tell me what it's like in the place you come from?"

"Me? Uh-h…" Finnerty was so unnerved by the strange, arresting girl he could barely remember his own name.

"Why, I come from the base near Al-Deen...oh, wait you mean where I grew up in the States? Michigan. On a farm. It's, uh, very *green* and *flat*." He stopped, feeling as if he were babbling like a fool.

"Do they have beautiful girls in this place, Mich-i-gan?"

"I guess so. I mean, none that would ever give me the time of day. Not like you."

"Not like me?" Suddenly her angelic face, once full of innocence and youthful trust, took on a lascivious cast. Finnerty was amazed at the transformation.

She took his hand and caressed her own face with it. Then she undid the strings of her neckline and untied her rope belt. She pulled the tunic down to her waist, exposing a thin white undershift, covered in silver embroidery.

He stared, rapt, at the outline of her large breasts, clearly visible through thin cloth. Her nipples were shaped like small rosebuds, protruding starkly against the silver-threaded fabric.

Still wearing the same lustful, almost animalistic smile, she pulled his hand to one of her breasts, urging him to rub her nipples through the cloth.

"Feel the hardness of my buds. Rub them, squeeze them. They ache for your fingers."

She breathed in deep and moaned in rhythm as he did as he was told, mesmerized by her lust and beauty. Her own fingers flew to her heavy braid and undid it, and her black hair tumbled and rippled over her shoulders.

He pulled back from her with a sudden jerk. She now looked exactly the same as the girl in his nightmare. He realized in a dim and clouded way that something was very wrong. The army had told him the hill people were conservative about their women, even more strict than the majority Muslims.

Why was she acting like this? And what was he doing here? They needed him back at the base; they were a man down with Corp out of commission.

This was not a hill woman—! He struggled in his mind to determine what she could be, if not a hill girl.

She stopped moaning as he pulled away, a look of anger or some other sinister emotion marking her face.

"Is this right? I'm not putting you in danger with your people?"

She smiled in a slight manner and her eyes glittered with a strange golden craftiness as a sunray from the shutter crack found them. "No—no danger."

Then she slipped off her long skirt and tunic, and dropped them to the floor, revealing the bottom half of her white and silver shift. She grabbed his free hand and pushed it into the space between her legs, tilting her pelvis toward him and moving it in a circular rhythm.

"Rub my mound," she breathed into his ear. His fingers felt her mound through the shift and began massaging it in time with her slow pelvic rhythms.

He felt himself slipping into a whirl of desire and lost conscious thought as he rubbed and groped her body, all thoughts of resistance buried in a strange mental fog.

They worked together to slough off her silvery shift, and then she was naked before him, save for one thing: the long, narrow shawl wrapped several times around her neck in a tight bond.

He reached for the shawl, and she pushed his hand away with a frightened cry. *"No, not that! Not that!"*

"Oh—! I didn't know—!"

"Forget about that. Kiss me—kiss my lips," she commanded, grabbing the back of his neck, and pulling his face down to hers. "Rub my mound."

She backed up against a wall, pulling him along with her. "Penetrate me, as the stallion to the mare." Everything became part of the strange fog, and later, he could not even remember their coupling.

***

Finnerty was dreaming again. His sleep was heavy, the sleep of a drunk man, although his dream self somehow knew he hadn't taken any alcohol. He was patrolling the desert on foot with Corp and Scruggs, trying to see through the heat shimmers and the sand devils, looking for the girl in the white-and-silver shift.

He thought he saw her, but then something was pounding inside his head, *pounding, pounding, pounding.* Someone wanted him to do something important, but he didn't know what it was. He was half-conscious now and fighting on the bridge between dreams and wakefulness.

"Finnerty! Open the door Finnerty! Open the goddamn door! We know you are in there, you crazy fuck!" someone was shouting.

He woke up fully. Where was he? Oh yes, the girl. The barren room with the terracotta floor. That was some junk Drewsy had given him. He realized that he was sitting in a corner, slumped against the wall, with his pants on, but no shirt or shoes.

The girl was lying on her clothes some feet away, still naked, curled up a little like a child. There was something strange about her posture. He crawled over to take a closer look. She wasn't breathing. Parts of her skin were discolored. She exuded a smell of decay.

"What the—?" He yelped in horror. She was dead. His dream girl was fucking dead. "No, no, it can't be—"

At that moment, there was a loud battering sound, and two military policemen broke the ancient door down. They entered the room with side weapons drawn.

"Stay where you are, soldier," commanded one of them to Finnerty.

The other MP approached Finnerty and the dead girl warily. He pulled her over—face up—as well as he could, with the rigor mortis well set in.

"Who is this girl? She's dead!" he barked. "Answer me, soldier. You are in big trouble, boy."

Finnerty shook his head and seemed to fall into a trance.

"Forget it, Soames," said the other MP. "He's out of it. Almost catatonic. PTSD." He approached Finnerty, and nudged him to face the wall, and then cuffed his hands behind his back. Then he pushed the unresponsive Finnerty back to face the room, as if the soldier were a ragdoll.

Then finally, he looked at the girl.

"My god! How did that poor girl—that *thing* get in here?"

"You know this girl, Jake?" Soames was confused.

"Do I know her? She was beheaded by the Saif three days ago. I saw her head myself, hanging by the braid of her hair from the crossbar of a well near the big marketplace to the south."

"What! That's crazy, Jake. Crazy as fuck. You need a mental evaluation yourself."

"Here, let me show you." Jake knelt and grabbed at the long, narrow shawl around the girl's neck and unwound it. Then he nudged her head with the toe of his boot. The girl's head rolled in Finnerty's direction, flecks of dried blood and some kind of ropey, congealed substance trailing in its wake.

As the head stopped near him, Finnerty woke up out of his trance and screamed.

"The *fiend!* The desert fiend!" he cried out. "It got to me!" He gave the girl's head a vicious kick, and it hit the opposite wall with a sickening thud, landed, and rolled to a stop with its eyes staring sightlessly at the gummy red blotch it left on the cracked plaster.

Finnerty began to scream again. He was still screaming when Drewsy visited him in the psych ward of a military hospital in the States a year later.

Through the Blueish Liquid Appearance...

Sergio 'ente per ente' PALUMBO
edited by Michele DUTCHER

"Follow your most intense obsessions mercilessly."
quote by Franz Kafka

"Prague. Praha. The name actually meant "threshold".
Pollina had said the city was a portal between the life of the
good and... the other."
quote by Magnus Flyte, City of Dark Magic

I nside the main room of Dobrou noc – whose name meant Goodnight - which was a modern disco situated in Prague's neighborhood of Nové Mesto, or New Town (that actually dated back to 1348...) reality took on a different hue or varied shade. It happened every night, truth be told, though it became particularly confused on Fridays and Saturdays. Deafening music went into the dancefloor with the power of a sudden spasm, blaring out of the gigantic speakers, while the crowded room pulsed on.

Probably, the uncontrolled attitude of the nightlife community, ready to lose itself once dropped into in this place, was best captured in moments like these, and wasn't too different from what you could see in the discos of many other great capitals of Europe nowadays, like in London, Vienna or Paris, anyway.

The disco - that looked like a large square room with tiled walls and metal heaters that glowed red from time to time and dangled almost magically from above – featured several massive video screens and offered a luxurious environment frequented mostly by 20-something locals.

There were regular customers having beers at one or another of the two bars, while others stood talking to each other. It was the usual alluring game of following representatives of the other sex around, where attempts to pick up girls or guys was ceaselessly at play, of course. Things would continue that way for at least the next few hours, until the first light of the sun appeared, and deep tiredness got the better of the more overwhelming impulses of the young crowd.

Among all those people, one girl, apparently in her mid-twenties, moved through the crowd like a female feline predator, searching for her next target that looked good enough to eat. She was wrapped in a dark high-neck fitted evening dress with plunging front keyhole, decorative metallic chain trimmed neckline, and a low open back with attached draped copper chains and just above knee length fitted skirt. In spite of some observer's attempts to turn away from her, the young woman really looked like a very seductive saucepot that no man could ever easily avert his interested eyes from, or completely put out of his mind some forbidden fantasies, for certain. Which is exactly what this dress was meant to achieve. She frequently picked out inviting outfits - for example the sexy schoolgirl look with high-waist shorts, and the amorous university student look with pleated skirt, both had their appeal among the customers.... - to fit the requirements of the particular venue. After all, finding a pleasing partner for the night was pretty much how she used the place, and it was exactly for that reason that she came here, night after night.

Magda was beautiful, at least according to general comments and what people said about her when they spotted her figure around. Skinny and small, she had the ample breasts and broad hips generally admired by men, both young and old. Then, there was a rather handsome pair of deep, chestnut eyes that looked unnaturally calm, or even perhaps cold, depending on the brilliance of the light cast over those profound pupils from the many strobe lights that you could always find in discos. Her arms were covered with several tattooed symbols that were popular among young people these days, though the ones in black and gray shades she had on were very different, much older and had been engraved in her skin for other reasons.

The huge crowd was composed of several different types of regulars, dressed in so many ways that, at times, made you think those they had on were some fancy clothes, or very strange apparel. The skin on their faces varied from whitish to swarthy, the same as their stature and build. However, before Magda's attentive eyes, they all looked like trembling blueish aberrations that walked for a while and then stopped before starting up again. It was just past that magical liquid surface the woman saw that she had to go and study their characteristics in order to find the most appetizing life energies, to use for her own good. In a way, it was just like entering a food market and reading the labels of the many products for sale, so she could choose the ones with the best ingredients, or the most useful properties. Her sorcerous sight was everything in this matter - which couldn't be different, certainly.

Finally, the woman's experienced eyes spotted her target for that night. A tall and slender curly-haired young man of about 22 who was dancing with no one in particular. His dark hair looked a bit untidy, but it wasn't bad, and his casual appearance added to his handsome build, which looked good to her.

Approaching the place where he stood and using the excuse of bumping into him by chance to say something was easy, and the young woman had done this many times to draw attention to herself so she could begin a conversation with someone.

"Sorry about that," Magda said making a face while opening her mouth in a sneer, letting the other look at her and have a full sight of her beautiful dress and body.

"No problem, not at all!" the young man said. "By the way, I'm Matthias," he offered, bowing a little.

"Charmed. I'm Magda."

"Are you here all alone?" the other asked her.

The woman sneered again, in an indulged way now. After all, her smile and face, just like her dress, was a sort of masking device, an appearance that combined with her attractiveness to get a result, so she could accomplish what she really desired. And she was sure her target had gotten the point, of course.

Before you could say knife, they had begun to talk pleasantly, getting to know one another.

"I like the tattoos on your arms. They're great," the young man told her. "What do they mean?"

"These are some esoteric symbols," Magda replied. "I saw them on an old book in a shop some time ago and decided to have them tattooed on my skin."

"Really?" Matthias added "Cool! They are trendy, undoubtedly!"

Magda smiled again. They started dancing, their bodies pulsing to the techno beat, keeping up the revelry for a while, until the moment came for both of them to sit down near the bar and enjoy some local drinks. They started with a strong Becherovka and a glass of Zelená.

The two spoke about everything and anything for half an hour, then the young woman thought it was the right time to make her move. "Staying here to drink and dance with you is good, Matthias…" Magda whispered in his ears at a given moment while they were sipping their beverages. "But tell me, wouldn't you prefer if we could leave here and go somewhere else, to make our own fun?"

The other appeared to be taken by surprise, as this was certainly what the young man had on his mind ever since she had approached him. However, he wasn't expecting this straight-forward invitation to have been offered by her so quickly, obviously insinuating that she was eager to spend the rest of the night with him. This must be my lucky day, he told himself.

In a couple of minutes, they had both paid their bills, walked past the exit sign and were out of the disco, leaving behind them the venue which was still completely engulfed in its deafening sounds. The night air and the streets were dimly illuminated by the lamps and seemed to be eager to welcome them as they started walking along, exchanging interested glances with each other. That moment of the day was the best for anyone who was yearning to experience Prague to its fullest, undoubtedly.

As they turned the corner and walked to the end of the street, the woman happened to spot something unusual. She raised her eyes and noticed a big bird on top of a tall streetlamp. The bird was almost hidden in the darkness, as the sky was completely overcast, but she recognized it as an ossifrage after looking closely at its features, although she couldn't believe her eyes. But there it sat: one of those birds of prey that swallowed bony remains and were also believed to drop animals from aloft to break them so they could get at the bone marrow.

It was rare to see one of these creatures in town and she had never even spotted one over the course of the last few years.

Putting that strange sight out of her mind, Magda's senses turned to the present place and time, and she took Matthias's hand. The woman started leading him off the main road, making him follow her across several crossroads and subsequently move through an apparently unending and confused series of alleyways. These backstreets were complicated by darkened bends, by-ways with ups and downs of a part of Prague the young man didn't remember being in before, that almost made him think he had gotten lost in the end. But the woman looked delighted with his disorientation and her smile was so inviting and attractive...Finally, she spoke. "We're almost there...a few more steps and we'll be at my house. A perfect place to end this promising night, I can assure you."

Her house? the man thought. He certainly hadn't dared hope for her to take him home since they had only met once. Things were getting better and better, indeed...

Just as she had said, a few yards more and they arrived. And the building looked very eccentric and old.

Built between the eighteenth and nineteenth centuries along Dlouha, the inside of the house Magda showed him had been partly renovated since she had become the owner of the house. Over the course of the time, its value had greatly increased, the same as all the other old mansions nearby. In a way, renovation was necessary in the furnishing and the style of the house at least every fifty years, as she had discovered over the course of her very long life. If she could have things her way, she would have left things as they had been in the 1600s – when she had been born. Surely, the modern appliances, the durable flatware, and the considerable comfort the present world gave the residents was much better than anything the locals had way back then. But as for the rest, call it a sort of wistfulness or a turmoil she felt in her mind, the woman was still attached to the old copper stockpots and the straw beds they had when she was young. The objects she most missed would be almost unrealistic to find in the stores nowadays…

Magda also found weird to notice that some old houses in the area – places that she had once seen inhabited only by the poor – had been today converted into pubs or some exquisite shops selling books, or other goods like souvenirs for visitors who filled even the narrowest lanes in the weekends. The young woman considered hers to be a fractured soul, that of somebody who had been living for centuries and who frequently found it difficult to adapt to the changes or the strangeness of the present world. However, she had had to come to terms with modern times if she wanted to survive, and stay in good health, indeed. And she had learned how to survive and thrive since she had become aware that she was a witch, the same as she had come to understand the material needs a creature like her, who wasn't entirely human, had to satisfy from time to time, obviously.

For the others, death was sweet release—and they accepted, following their path into the darkness—in the end. But for Magda it was very different, and it was usually she who benefitted from her targets' final demise.

After being welcomed into her home, Matthias removed his jacket and started getting comfortable on the davenport she had in her living room. At that point, the young woman warmly smiled to him. The best was yet to come for that night…

***

After a few drinks more, as a smooth transition from the disco where they had met, they slowly got up, heading for the bed, mindlessly dancing as if they were deeply drunk, leaving pieces of their clothing all over the floor beneath their feet as they kept undressing.

The mischievous Magda had always loved the look of her lacy bras which confined her breasts, the same way the man's eyes stared at it, stung with desire.

Again, Matthias looked at her and admired her lithesome body. The woman knew she had a very beautiful one, of course. All of the lovers she had enjoyed over the course of the time clearly demonstrated that. Magda was content with that, too, as she had made use of her loveliness in her own interest for so long, in a way it just turned everything into something much easier, and more sensuous, of course.

Matthias' lips nuzzled against Magda's neck, then his right hand touched her, dandling her breasts while his left raised to her mouth and his fingers stroked her lips. She tongued the finger and then pushed the young man closer, wrapping her arms around him. He was clearly passionate, and began to show her how hot-blooded and capable he was as a lover.

Their subsequent moans filled the room. Magda was pleasingly surprised at discovering her young lover was very passionate, really serviceable, and ready to do some strange things that she had experienced not so many times, actually. Not that she cared for that too much, of course, but it was just really unexpected.

After their beautiful and kinky experience was over, and the young man started falling asleep—his almost boyish curls falling across his nose—the eager Magda began the next phase of that night's activities - which was the real reason she had brought that man to her house under the pretense of a great opportunity of sex with a beautiful woman like her.

She slowly leaned forward, putting his mouth close to hers so that she could perform the required ritual, and then she began draining his breath, and most of the life energies out of the unaware man himself.

In doing so, by turning to the forbidden forces of the unholy creation, Magda started developing a conscious and consistent connection to the energetic strength that the human body below her was endowed with, and soon her thirst for what she needed most was satisfied, at the expense of the diminishing health of her poor unknowing target. In a few minutes Matthias found it difficult to bring in oxygen as the witch was busy doing some repetitive cycles of inhalation of the same oxygen, his power siphoning from him into her own body. The number of thefts of the respiratory cycles per minute increased more and more until the young man, still asleep, happened to fall into a much deeper sleep and became pale.

After a while the witch thought it was time to take a break. After all, the ritual was over, and she felt wonderful again. She was certainly feeling much better than her lover, by all means…

The next morning, when the man eventually awoke, he still felt weak, but he knew he had to get out of the bed sooner or later. Not that he wanted to go anywhere…

He came to the kitchen and noticed that Magda was already dressed. "I feel a bit strange today…" a very tired Matthias uttered.

"You should stop drinking so much alcohol when you show up at discos and get wild. Perhaps you can't handle your liquor…" Magda said this, knowing she was lying of course. "You're young, and in good shape, but such things aren't good for you…"

After offering him some coffee, the woman started saying that she was sorry, but she had many things to do, although it was Sunday morning, and that she would sadly need to take her leave of him in a few moments.

"Let's keep in touch…I had really a very good time with you," the man said.

"The same here," Magda sneered.

"Why don't you give me your phone number?" Matthias asked the woman in a tone that tried to be more convincing.

"No," Magda replied. "I don't like to do that. Perhaps you can give me yours and I'll call you later. Probably…"

"Why?"

"The last time I gave out my number, things ended badly with my boyfriend…the same as my love affair…so, it's better this way."

"How about if I 'friend' you on social media so that we can stay in touch?" Matthias tried again in a clear voice.

"No," the woman explained "I don't like that way, too."

"May I know your age, at least?"

"I'm 30…" Magda revealed.

"You look younger…" the other replied, with a surprised expression on his face.

"It's because I am used to eating mainly bezmasna jídla," she smiled.

"Meatless dishes?" the man widened his eyes. "I thought you were a hearty eater, at first look…"

"It's because I feed my desire with younger guys like you, my dear," she added in an enticing smile. He couldn't imagine how correct that phrase really was…

Once the witch convinced her lover to finally leave and the door closed at his back, Magda knew that Matthias had gone. For sure, he was now out of her life forever. The woman was pretty sure he wouldn't ever remember where she lived or the name of the street where her house stood. After all, after she practiced the special ritual, in addition she also gave her occasional lovers a magical beverage, disguised as coffee that was a preparation especially meant to suppress memories, every single time. It always worked. But in case the man might prove to be a little different from the others, or might have a stronger memory, the woman always made the path confusing while leading someone to her building at night. This was why she chose to make the males follow all those apparently unending alleyways, ups and downs, before reaching the area of the city where she lived. Better to be sure not to stumble into them again if she didn't really want to.

Actually, it wasn't like she thought the young man might live too long or have a very good existence ahead, after all. The dark ritual she had practiced on his body had certainly revivified her but wasn't healthy for her unfortunate lover himself.

Because of the sorcerous activities she performed, and the rituals she practiced on all the others, people got ill or died…

As she returned to her bedroom in order to get her light overcoat, the woman considered that she felt a bit inebriated this morning, in a strange way. Maybe it was just the effect of the amount of new energy she had drained the previous night, or maybe it was the sensation of fullness that came from that forbidden process. However, it seemed to be different today, truth be told, which wasn't certainly a bad thing.

***

It was a rainy evening when Magda went out, heading to the disco again. About a month had passed since the last time the young-looking witch had been there, and she knew she had to practice her dark ritual another time, for her own good.

In the past few weeks, she had felt a strange hunger, a thirst for life, if you prefer, that was unusual, as if she couldn't get enough power from the energy she drained from the bodies of the young men that she chose and fed upon. The woman didn't know why, and she was certain she was performing the ritual correctly. So, what was it? Was she getting too old for this? Well, in a way, she was very old, indeed, though the four centuries of life she had experienced didn't make her think she was too old. In a way, if a witch kept practicing her rituals perfectly, she could go on for a few more centuries, feeling fine all the while.

As she walked the streets, she let her thoughts wander for a while. Under some circumstances, the woman liked to think of the past, but not every day, of course. Despite fires and invasions, the city of Prague had retained many churches, chapels, tower clocks and squares from every period of its history, from the Gothic splendor to the 16th-century Renaissance stonework. Of course, there were modern additions with their very tall buildings full of glass and metal, passing through different architectural styles and decorations that, in some cases, overlapped each other.

When she had been young, long ago, the woman remembered that her home village had looked so huge and crowded to her - though the distances could be easily covered on foot - before it became a much larger town full of traders and craftsmen that was taken over by the Austrian Habsburgs. That urban area made her senses be afraid when the sun went down. At that time, she thought that some demons were always waiting to pounce in the quiet hours of the night for the few souls who happened to not come home again. With the passing of the years, she had understood that men didn't need to fear such fabled creatures, but had better pay attention to other beings, like her, because witches were undoubtedly real, and she was one of them.

Magda Mowicz, or Magda Ekmowicz. The exact last name of her family wasn't something she knew for certain. At that time the names of the poor weren't important, and their linage couldn't usually be traced. Though she had never discovered their true surname, the faces of her mother and her father still remained well engraved in her memory, the same as her two younger brothers who had died in those ancient times because of an illness that had spread across the country during those years. She had survived that same disease in the end, thanks to the community of fellow witches she had stumbled into by chance and that had revealed to her the true power, how to have those esoteric symbols tattooed on her skin, like the Triple Moon, the Sacred Hoop and the Bat – so she could stay healthy. They had also taught her about the real characteristics of her unearthly being. It was thanks to them that she had survived those dark times and her body hadn't been added to the heaps of corpses with no names that had been put here and there in the countryside. Thanks to those experienced witches she had also reached the present mastery of her skills in the field of witchcraft.

These witches had told her that creatures like her were born into this world alongside common humans, but they began to develop unusual abilities and underwent deep changes when they got to a certain age. At that moment they had to follow a different path from the other men and women, and also had to start practicing their dark rituals, considered unholy - and forbidden - by most people, so they could live a longer life, and preserve a more powerful body. Just like she had done…

Afterwards, for those like her, it felt like they had no choice but to follow that goal that kept leading their interests in the direction of what society prohibited and what only their mind knew — and nothing else would satisfy that deep hunger but the touch of witchery.

As her family had grown up in the area, though a long time ago, the woman had later made a definite decision to settle in the same place, once she had explored the potential of the surroundings for her needs. Then, the present subway had been built, making it possible to get to other parts of the city quickly. All the new unbelievable things humans had proven to be able to build thanks to their ability and intentness had greatly changed the view, and the history itself, of the urban area.

The disco that was her target for that night came into sight, eventually, and the woman felt eager for what was coming next. She knew very well how to move, of course.

Once she was let inside she noticed that tonight the space held up to 400 people who were already dancing wildly although it was just 10:00 PM. Then something else immediately attracted her attention. There seemed to be a rival dancing star that night, as a young woman with long fair hair, soft and wavy, was walking among the crowd as if she was the real center of the interest of all the males. Most of the other women seemed to look worried about whether they could hold their date's attention.

Magda asked some customers about her, and she was told the newcomer's name was Zuzana.

Her face looked slender and beautiful, with the corners of her extremely narrow mouth slightly upturned. The markings on her forehead suggested exoticism. She was definitely a witch, just like Magda – and she knew this at first sight without even looking at her esoteric tattoos – although she was unsure about what country she might really be from.

As far as she could tell, that other woman had chosen a more direct and explicit approach in order to attract men in such a venue. She wore an underwire padded strapless bra on top, highlighting her delicate shoulders, leaving enough space between her breasts and her pencil-thin mini-skirt to showcase her rock-solid abs. Magda would have never worn anything like that, not because she found it to be too lewd, but just because it wasn't her style.

Given her appearance, and her attractiveness, the newcomer had already infused a great interest throughout the male crowd dancing at the disco, and Magda was a bit dejected. She wondered if the other woman's presence might interfere with her plans for the night. There would only be a problem if the other witch was currently competing for the same human targets as she was… Magda was concerned about having her needs met - the new customer had probably come here in search of food to sustain her health and the condition of her body, too. Magda had to see that for herself soon…The possibility of having the hands of someone else in the same food market, so to say, made up of the many customers of a disco like that, was something which had to be taken into consideration, of course.

In the end Magda discovered that the newcomer in town didn't interfere with her picking-up another man that night, which was good. Maybe her interests were just different… Until the two witches were in direct competition, there was no reason to be really worried about her.

Once out of the disco, the now-relieved Magda was undoubtedly surprised when she spotted an ossifrage for the second time, not too different from the first one she had seen about a month ago. The strange fact made her think of something else she had heard during the previous weeks, another very unusual occurrence. News had reached her ears that a famous witch killer was in town, right here in Prague, and the small community of the local witches spoke about him as "The Ruler of Lämmergeier…" though no one had ever seen him with their own eyes. All of this was really weird, in a way. Bad news travels fast, the same as legends, the woman considered…Could an ossifrage be connected to what she had heard? A sort of bad foreshadowing?

Sigmund, the blond-haired young man she had picked-up and brought home later proved to be a very passionate lover, and they spent some very pleasurable time together, drinking and kissing while having sex before he fell asleep, and the woman was ready to do what she had had on her mind since the moment she had met him.

When the process was over, the witch could clearly feel the renovated and augmented witch-flame inside that every woman who was endowed with sorcerous abilities eventually attained. This meant that her features, her organs, and her lifespan had been considerably increased for the time being.

Once she also took leave of that man the next morning, never to see him again, not differently from what she had done with Matthias, the woman looked thoughtful. At times, she considered that the few witches like her weren't too much different, from a certain point of view, from someone who had just eaten a piece of bread, borrowing small portions of the slice from different owners. She didn't devour all the bread from a single person, but just the small part she needed for that moment. In doing so, none of the bread was fully consumed, but all of them became smaller, and were not left completely intact because of the portions she had taken from each of them.

Of course, it was one thing to speak about bread or food, and a completely different matter to take part of the life energy of a varied group of people. This had consequences, indeed, and left the targets affected. Some of them died, though not everyone – it mainly depended upon their build and overall health, at times the result was unpredictable even to her herself – but she didn't care about such things. After all, the person who needed to eat some bread to sustain himself didn't care about the fact that there would be less bread left once he had eaten a piece of it. What he was concerned with was feeding himself, and the rest wasn't his problem. This was exactly what the witch thought, in her mind. Undoubtedly, Magda just took what she really needed, and it was only hardly worrisome if the men she chose and targeted suffered because of her actions.

Did the thirsty traveler worry if he started drinking the rain falling from the sky before all of its drops touched the dry terrain at his feet, even though there were so many contraction/desiccation cracks, or dying plants and vegetation that needed that water, too, on the ground itself? The answer was undeniable.

Humans had always been correct when they believed that witches were evil and capable of using any sort of depraved enchantment against them, meant to harm their lives deeply.

Later that morning, as Magda was ready to go outside and have a walk around, it happened that she had an unexpected surprise, anyway. Once she opened the front door, the woman found a figure standing outside. Was somebody waiting for her? Who?

Then she began to recognize her visitor's face, though the dress she wore was different that day, and less showy. It was Zuzana, undoubtedly!

The same face, the same thin pale neck, and that slender and beautiful body, exactly as she had seen in the disco she had had gone to last night, where had picked up Sigmund. How was it possible?

Before the witch could do anything, the other made her move and Magda found it strange that she allowed her to come in without even asking questions, or opposing her directly. What was going on?

It was once the door was closed behind the newcomer that things became clearer. And it was at that same time that Magda felt strange, perhaps even weak. Very weak…

They were the only ones inside the house now, and it was Zuzana that started speaking first, her voice being soft and convincing. "I know you probably have many things to ask me, my dear…the same as your fellow witches in town, certainly." Her tone became a bit deceitful now. "You all want to know more about the one whom you call 'The Ruler of the Lämmergeier', obviously…or shouldn't it be 'The Queen of the Lämmergeier', actually?"

At that moment, Magda's attentive eyes widened, and she felt in peril, undoubtedly.

"You and your fellows have always thought that it had to be a man, a male witch-hunter, but unfortunately for you, it's not as you expected. After all, my selected targets have never had the opportunity to give anybody else more details about me. You know, witches like me are rarities, and we are not much stronger than the common ones like you…" Zuzana explained. "Though there are only a few of us, we have devised many useful means to feed ourselves, and we know how to get the better of the ones like you. By using humans, the ones you turn to when you take their energy to sustain yourself, by poisoning them, little by little, I was able to weaken you. As I discovered which venues you frequented, the places where you usually found your favorite targets, I also knew that I could turn this to my own good. This is why I made use of all the young men you used recently, especially over the course of the last two months with men like Sigmund and Matthias. And I did it so that I could easily defeat you when the right time came…"

Magda looked at her in full awe. Was she really the fabled 'Ruler of the Lämmergeier'? How was it even possible? None of this made sense to her. But beyond that, Magda was certain she had correctly studied the characteristics of her targets by using her magical abilities, scanning their bodies through the blueish liquid appearance before choosing them for her purposes.

"Oh, you're probably wondering how you didn't notice the poison in time. Well, you can thank my experienced scheming mind, because I made use of some long-lost herbs that you didn't know anything about, herbs that couldn't be spotted. They are deceptive and can be easily mistaken for something else, and they also have some magical poisonous properties which you might have never seen by using your sorcerous sight once your male targets ingested them. Of course, I gave them to those men. As I told you, witches like me are not much stronger than the common ones like you. This is why I have to turn to other means to win, and having a keen mind is the first resource to always rely on, my dear! You should have understood this after all the time you've spent on this earth." Zuzana sneered while saying this.

Magda understood she was sadly lost. The witch was feeling weaker and weaker by the minute, and she considered she was presumably dying. As her strength was moving away from her body, she also knew that there wasn't much she could do to fight back against the other witch.

"But the curse that is upon a rarity witch like me doesn't make things so easy. In order to get the energy I need from you, poor Magda, in order to feel my body revived, I can't simply let you fall unconscious and take your powerful breath out of your mouth as you do with your usual prey," the witch killer added. "No, my dear, I'll have to wait until your body is fully dead, and your carcass turns cold. You know, after all, there is a reason why I have been named the 'The Ruler of Lämmergeier'… And I imagine you can see why now, Magda. The diet of those birds of prey, the Lämmergeier, consists almost exclusively of the bony remains of the dead. I am like those ossifrages. That's what I am, a carcass-eating creature… Even after your death, minutes must go by before I can consume you. Then we will be one. And I can start anew!"

Magda's time was almost over, the woman knew it, sadly. This was why she didn't listen anymore and almost didn't hear the other witch saying, "In unity there is strength…" as Zuzana approached to take all of her sorcerous power out of her soon-to-be-cold remains.

After all, there was no honor among thieves of others' life energy, she thought before darkness had the better of her mind, in the end.

Room for Two
Matthew A. Clarke

I met Fredrick at the office. I'd heard there would be new blood starting and that one of us would be responsible for training him, or her, so I was doing my damned best impression of working at my computer when my manager, Annalise Hurst, stepped out of her office and started making her rounds. I don't know whether she could tell I was only pretending to work, or if upper management had installed monitors on our computers, and she'd spent the last half-hour watching me playing Lemmings and looking at funny dog outfits online, but I could smell her standing right behind me. Rose-scented soap and cigarettes.

"Darius," she said. Her voice was lacking the usual icy edge.

I turned on my swivel chair, knocking over an empty mug that wasn't there a minute ago, "Annalise," I responded, clumsily retrieving the mug from the floor. Stood beside her, in the shadow of her beehive barnet, was a small wiry man with dyed black hair.

"This," she gestured to the young man beside her, "is Fredrick. It's his first day. I'd like you to show him the ropes."

Well, at least she hadn't been monitoring my computer. I put on a smile and stood to shake his hand. It was cold and clammy, much like my enthusiasm. Annalise clocked my wince and shot me a warning look before hurrying back to her office like she'd remembered she'd left the oven on.

"Fredrick, huh? Nice to meet you. Darius," I said.

Fredrick nodded. His skittish brown eyes darted around the office. I directed him to a free chair, which he pulled up alongside my own.

An hour later, I'd talked Fredrick through the basics of selling stationary and how to work the client databases. Then, I showed him how to circumnavigate the website blocker on the company intranet. He seemed to come out of his shell a little after he realized I wasn't as passionate about stationary sales as Annalise — or Anal Lice, as she was better known around the office.

About a week later, strange things started to happen. I was writing notes on an order form, when my pen decided to fly from my hand. It did a flip in the air before clattering to my desk. I picked it back up and bent it a little. Solid. I shrugged it off as a hand spasm and carried on. The next day, I was sat in the canteen at lunch, eating a cheese and ham sandwich when the sleeves of my pullover yanked themselves up to my elbows. I looked around to see if anyone else had noticed, and who should I see but Fredrick, staring right at me and snickering behind a bony hand. I approached his table, his sandwich sat untouched before him.

"What the hell was that? Did you see it?" I asked.

His eyes jerked this way and that, before settling on me. "You seem like a cool guy, D. Meet me at Freeman's bar after work, I want to show you something."

I've got to admit, having someone call me 'D' did make feel like a pretty cool guy, even if it was coming from the office weirdo.

***

"You've got to be shitting me," I said, instinctively reeling away. I'd just watched Fredrick retrieve his cash from the till after paying for a round, without even leaving his stool. I pulled his hand toward me and examined it for invisible thread.

"I told you it was impressive," he said with a smirk.

"I don't understand how that's even possible. That's some sci-fi sorcery right there. How are you not locked up in some government lab?" I said, turning the note over in my hands.

"I've been pretty careful," he popped another peanut between his thin lips.

"Alright, hang on, I'm still not completely sold," I said, looking around the bar. Behind us, a middle-aged man with a thick, grey beard was hunched over a pool table, about to take a shot. "If that really was you, sink the black ball."

He looked toward the pool table. "Too easy," he said, folding his arms across his Metallica T-shirt, "I make something float, right in front of your eyes, and that's the best you can come up with?" he shook his head and clucked his tongue. "Watch this."

A young barmaid wearing a red dress and large, gold hoop earrings was walking out from the end of the bar, carrying two trays packed with glasses of red wine. She weaved through the maze of furniture toward a large oak table across the other side of the room, where a rowdy hen party — complete with inflatable penis' and a desperate looking blonde in a BRIDE2BE sash — was in full swing. I wasn't entirely sure where Fredrick was going with this, but I was excited all the same. He raised his right hand, extended his index finger, and made a quick swiping gesture to his left.

The barmaid gasped as her right foot was thrown across the back of her left in mid-step. She fell forward, the trays holding the wine glasses slipped from her grip and fired toward the gaggle of screaming women like a dozen weeping mortar strikes. The barmaid hit the ground — her jaw snapping together with an audible clack and piercing her tongue (something I wouldn't find out until later) — and the glasses rained down on the rectangular oak table, exploding in a cacophony of tinkling glass and lapping waves.

I sat slack jawed, watching the chaos unfold. The barmaid picked herself up, mumbled something that could have been a "Sorry", and ran off to the toilets with a reddening hand clutched to her mouth. The hen party had pushed the table away from them in their panic and it now lay broken, on its side on the floor. Each of the women was sticky and covered in crimson, and a penis was slowly deflating with a disappointed hiss. Then, I saw the BRIDE2BE. She was pale, silently fumbling with a long shard of glass protruding from her left eye.

***

After I'd calmed down enough to tell Fredrick to "Stay the fuck away from me," I was able to start to process what had really happened in the bar. The answer was simple — the barmaid was uncoordinated, carrying too much. She'd tripped and fallen, and the events that followed were just a by-product of her clumsiness. It was pure coincidence that Fredrick happened to be pointing at her at the time. Except, a niggling voice kept telling me that I knew there was more to it than that — I couldn't explain the note floating back into Fredrick's clammy palm, or the way my sleeves had tugged themselves up to my elbows in the canteen. I decided the best course of action would be to keep my head down and pretend like I'd never met him, which wasn't easy, considering he worked in the cubicle next to me.

Fredrick tried to talk to me several times over the following days, but I was short enough in my responses that I thought he was starting to get the hint. Unfortunately, he wasn't as keen to break off our 'friendship' as I was, and a string of 'coincidences' started to happen around the office. Anal Lice, after making her morning rounds of the bullpen, found that the door to her office had been locked from the inside. The shades had been drawn, so we couldn't see who was inside. Finally, after waiting twenty minutes for a maintenance guy to turn up and unlock it, she found the office was completely empty. The photocopier would randomly spit out dozens of sheets of paper at anyone that happened to be passing. Mugs of hot coffee would randomly tip over onto people's laps. It got so bad that several of my colleagues started joking that there was a ghost in the office. It wasn't until the plastic Ninja Turtle that guards my desk began making lewd gestures at me — while I was on the phone to my biggest client —that I eventually caved and struck up a conversation over lunch.

"You have to stop doing this," I said.

"I will when you agree to come out with me again."

"I don't think so. I can still hear the sound of those women's screams when I try to get to sleep at night."

"Don't be so dramatic," he said, rolling his eyes.

I wasn't being dramatic.

"What exactly are you proposing we do?" I asked.

He told me he'd be happy to have a few beers at his place, watch a movie, grab a pizza. I reluctantly accepted, but only on the condition that there wouldn't be any more bloodshed. Fredrick shook his head so vigorously that I could practically see the grease being flung from his hair.

That Friday evening, I arrived at Fredrick's place early — 6.30 — thinking the sooner we started, the sooner I'd be able to go home again. Fredrick lived alone in a detached house on the outskirts of town, a fact that surprised me until he told me that both of his parents had died and left it to him. I didn't ask how they'd died; I wasn't sure I'd like the answer. The front door opened onto a sparse corridor. I followed him along it and into a room at the far end, which was a great deal cozier than I had been expecting. The beige walls were adorned with photographs of Fredrick and an older couple, presumably his parents. In the corner, across from a small sofa littered with colorful pillows, was a large plasma television sat atop a low mahogany unit. In the middle of the room, two men and a woman sat around a stained pine table in front of a crackling fireplace. Before them, spread across the table, was a poker set. Brief introductions were made. Vic — a burly long-haired man with a voice so high you'd be forgiven for thinking he'd been huffing helium, Denise — a plain looking slim brunette about my own age, and Chen — an Asian gentleman with a remarkably English accent, who looked to be about sixty. We played a few rounds of poker together and drank a few Buds. Surprisingly, I was starting to have a good time.

An hour later, we were all acquainted and fast becoming good friends — one of the more pleasant side-effects of the beer — when Vic turned to me and said, "So, what is it that you do?"

I was a little confused, but we'd all had a few so I couldn't blame him for forgetting. "I sell office supplies, with Fredrick."

"No, no. What do you do?" He repeated, rubbing a calloused thumb and forefinger together. The air suddenly felt itchy, as if my throat and skin was swarming with ants, and Vic's hair shot straight up to the ceiling as if he'd just stuck his finger in a power socket. A moment later, the sides fell, leaving a long, quivering mohawk. Finally, the mohawk collapsed, and a handful of hair shot out from above his left temple, stroking me gently on the cheek. He stopped rubbing his fingers, and his hair settled. "Static," he said, matter-of-factly.

"I . . . I uh-"

"Darius doesn't do anything," Fredrick helped me find my words.

I tried to speak again but my voice came not from my own mouth, but from Denise's, "That was insane. What? What's going on?!" The rest of them fell into fits of laughter while I tried to figure out if I'd been drugged. An empty pint glass was shaken from the table and slowed just before it impacted the hardwood floor, landing right-side up.

Fredrick smiled and said, "Denise can read minds, and project voices."

Denise looked very happy with herself.

"Alright then." I said, pausing to neck another half-pint, "what can you do?"

Chen, who had been quiet up until this point in the discussion, said, "I communicate with animals."

It was my turn to laugh. Chen looked a little offended, so I apologized, "That's pretty cool, man."

Shortly after, we all filed out of a taxi and into at an overpriced nightclub that was packed with people that didn't look old enough to drink. Despite this, I was still having a good time. Perhaps it was the booze, but I wasn't in the least intimidated hanging out with these people, superpowers and all. After dancing (or flailing my limbs around like a baboon being tasered, if Fredrick was to be believed) for about an hour, we managed to find a corner booth away from the crowds. Denise slipped off to the toilet, and when she came back, she was carrying a tray of shots. Chen cheered. He seemed to be becoming more excited as the night went on. Impressive, for a man of his age.

"I'm really not sure I can," I said. I was starting to feel a little sick.

"Nonsense," Denise replied, "have a couple of these, then we'll have some real fun."

I didn't argue with her. Denise had started the night kind of plain looking, with the type of face you'd have trouble picking out from a line-up — soft features, pale skin, black blouse over blue jeans — but in my inebriated state, she was starting to look like a goddess. I was having trouble keeping up with these guys, but I also didn't want to show any weakness.

"To our new friend!" Vic said, raising the first shot of vodka in a hand that dwarfed it.

"Cheer. . . s," I managed. The five of us clinked glasses and proceeded to down three shots each. Somehow, I kept them down, even when Fredrick gave me a celebratory smack on the back.

"Okay, okay, who's ready for some fun?" Denise asked.

"Fuck yeah!" Chen shouted, thrusting a liver-spotted fist in the air. His eyes were bloodshot, yet full of life. I was up for anything at this point.

Fredrick went first. He directed our attention toward a young man on the dance floor. Fredrick flicked his wrist and the man's hand jerked, slapping the buttocks of a large woman in a denim miniskirt who looked old enough to be his mother. The woman spun, delivering a slap so hard we could hear it over the thundering bass of the music, knocking the man to the floor. Then, a young woman stormed over and pulled a ring from her finger. She threw it at him before storming off again. He ran after her clutching the ring, blood streaming from his nose.

"Oops," Fredrick said. We all laughed.

Denise insisted on going next. She set her sights on a scantily clad woman standing at the bar, waving a note at a nearby bartender. As he approached, the woman opened her mouth to speak.

Denise became animated as a delicate voice escaped her lips, "Two vodka orange and one — what the fuck? Why can't I speak?" The bartender raised his eyebrows, shook his head and moved on to the next customer. Denise gave the woman back her voice just as she began to scream, drawing dozens of concerned faces. She ran out of the club, still screaming. We laughed again.

Vic excused himself, went up to the bar and ordered another drink. When the barman's back was turned, he gave us a conspiring look before charging the beer pumps with static electricity. He picked up his pint and returned to our table, where we could watch the fireworks from a safe distance. As the barman wrapped a hand around the pump, the overhead lights flickered momentarily, and a loud pop came from the direction of the bar. Heads turned as the barman stepped back from the clearing smoke. He held his hand up in front of his face. Three of his fingers had been blown clean off, and his hand and wrist were streaked in black. The smell of barbecue slowly spread across the room.

There were no animals inside the club, unsurprisingly, so I was yet to see what Chen could do. He did, however, vomit across the table. We all agreed it was probably time to leave anyway — the music had been stopped and the bouncers had already started to evacuate the place.

"That was amazing!" I said, stumbling against the side of a car. A cold breeze bit into the side of my face, sobering me just a little. "Well, apart from that last bit, maybe." I pulled out my iPhone and tried to focus on numbers that kept dancing out of sight.

"It's one-thirty," Denise said, with Fredrick's voice.

"Fuck you. Not funny," he finished.

I was feeling a little sick again, "I think I'd better head home, guys. I've had a great time though."

Denise put a warm arm around my back, "I'll walk you home. You look a little worse for wear." Her tone suggested it wasn't up for debate.

Luckily, I could still remember my way home from this part of town — it was only a ten-minute walk. We said our farewells to the others, which were answered with several jokes about using protection. A million thoughts were going through my mind at that point, most of them drunken incoherent babblings, but the one that kept breaking the surface was, *Am I too drunk to get it up?* The answer, I knew, was most likely. But that wouldn't stop me from trying. We spoke briefly about work and family as we walked along deserted streets overlooked by darkened windows, until we reached the entrance to Epernay Park. My house was across the other side of the park, and my heart started to beat a little faster. Denise, perhaps sensing my apprehension, lent over to give me a tender kiss on the cheek, "I've been thinking about this all night," she said.

I gulped. She giggled.

We entered Epernay Park and traversed a graveled path that was flanked by mighty oaks, before veering off onto a well-trodden shortcut between the treeline.

"Wait, did you hear that?" I asked. We had stopped at the edge of a clearing between the sleeping giants. I thought I'd heard someone retching up ahead.

"I didn't hear anything," Denise said.

We continued out into the moonlit clearing, the only sounds the gentle song of cicadas and the swoosh of the ankle length grass as we passed through it. The sweet smell of vomit filled the air. I paused again, pulling

Denise to a stop with me, the retching noise echoed through the trees.

"For fucks sake," she said, loosening her arm from mine and slipping around me. Her mouth moved once more as if she was speaking, but nothing came out. Instead, it sounded as if she was whispering from the trees. Three shadows appeared from the direction her voice had just come from. Denise slid behind me and pinned both arms up behind my back, kicking at the back of my legs, forcing me to my knees. I cried out in pain as my shoulders almost popped from their sockets.

"What the hell is this?! Denise?" I shouted. She didn't answer. The figures were almost upon us now. I wasn't at all surprised when they turned out to be Fredrick, Vic, and Chen. The three of them looked incredibly solemn. Any hopes I'd had of getting laid tonight immediately faded.

"Fredrick? What's this about?" I asked as my cheeks became heated, anticipating tears. So much for not showing weakness.

"I need you to trust me, Darius." In the half-light, he looked as if he'd aged ten years. He was more filled out, his face more defined. He stood confidently.

"Is this a cult thing? Look, I did what you asked, I even had a good time. Now please, just let me go to bed."

Chen retched once more. He was not looking so good — gaunt, pale and withered. I was surprised he was still standing. As he looked up from the ground, I saw his blue eyes were pulsing slowly, like a star refusing to die. Whatever was going on here, I didn't like it one bit. I panicked, throwing my head back as hard as I could. It hit Denise just below the ribs and I felt her hot breath blowing across the top of my head. Her grip loosened, and I was up and running before the others had a chance to react.

"D, come on. You're just wasting energy," Fredrick called after me.

I glanced over my shoulder as I reached the gate leading out of the park and onto the lamp-lit street beyond. No one was following me. I put a hand to the gate latch and yelped as I was immediately blown backward by an immense jolt of static electricity. My head hit the floor, hard, and stars swam in my vision. I tried to get to my feet, but my limbs were locked in place. All I could do was groan as I was dragged through the dew-moistened grass by some invisible force. I came to a rest at the feet of my 'friends' but still could not move. Fredrick raised his other hand and held it toward my head. My jaw opened, lowered slowly, gently, then stopped, as if held in place by a dentist's prop.

"I was hoping you'd do this voluntarily, after this evening. We've had a good time, haven't we?"

"Duh wut?" I spat.

"Chen is dying. Or rather, his body is. His consciousness will live on as it has done for centuries.

"You see, Chen can do many things. Perhaps his most impressive talent is the ability to transfer consciousness. Don't worry, though. It doesn't hurt. Or so I'm told."

"Ugh cuazy."

"Now, now," Denise spoke up this time. She knelt beside me and wiped away the thin trail of spittle that was leaking from the corner of my gaping orifice.

As Chen joined her by my side, I saw him for what he really was — nothing more than a wrinkled bag of skin thrown loose over a skeletal frame. His eyes were sunk so far back into their sockets they were no more than two hollow pits. Chen lent over me, placed a cold hand on my forehead, and the other, balled into a fist, he wedged in my mouth. An overwhelming surge of memories and feelings that weren't my own flashed before my eyes, consumed not just my brain but my whole being. Chen jolted to his feet, bolt upright as if struck by lightning, and began to shudder. His head swelled to the size of a beach ball, eyes no longer sunken but practically popping free of his skull. Then, his head exploded in a shower of red and whites, an overfilled balloon pricked with a pin. His body dropped to its knees, remained that way for a moment, then fell to the floor, deteriorating rapidly to a neat pile of weathered bones.

"That wasn't so bad, was it," he said. I sat up and looked around, and I realized the voice had come from my own mouth. The others helped me to my feet. I tried to speak but found I couldn't work my jaw. I walked in silence with the others, toward the exit of the park, on legs that I was not moving.

I was a prisoner in my own body.

Don't Make Me Laugh
Ken Goldman

"You cannot hold back a good laugh any more than you can hide the tide."
---William Rotsler (American artist and pornographer)

"If we couldn't laugh, we would all go insane."
--Jimmy Buffett
(American singer, songwriter)

"One smile just might break your face..."
--- Jenna Crane
(American Witch)

Standup comic Ryan Pressman believed he understood women.

More than most men, he probably did. Sex jokes comprised much of his comedy routine and the modern female proved a fertile source of comedy material because women ("Bless their tits!") often were damned funny creatures.

The rising young comedian often joked about those women he'd slept with. There were many of these, and most knew he was a one-and-done kind of guy.

Jenna Crane was not one of them.

(1)FOR RYAN OUT LOUD

Past midnight Pressman stood at Jenna Crane's door weighing his options. Rules varied wildly among millennial women, and even a goodnight kiss in 2019 could set off a first date's Me-Too anger or much worse. He decided to go for it and kissed her anyway. Afterwards, the two looked into each other's eyes for several awkward moments. Had he crossed the line, fucked up?

No words, Nothing.

Jenna smiled, pulling Ryan closer. Now she initiated the act, and their second kiss (nowhere nearly as tentative) lasted much longer. The woman added some tongue, moaning just enough to suggest encouragement. A warm smile. Then -- jackpot!

"Ryan, it isn't very late. Come in for a cup of coffee?"

Pressman knew that particular invitation, in womanspeak, rarely meant the actual offer of caffeine. And if half past midnight didn't seem a late hour, Jenna might as well have waved him in with a checkered flag, the Me-Too League be damned.

He smiled, careful not to turn his expression into a grin. Jenna held the brownstone's door for him. Inside she hit only the switch of the dim bulb of a table lamp. Her apartment was small, its furnishings modest and as inviting as the young woman herself. Leading Ryan to the couch, her offer of java seemed already forgotten. Maybe some wine would follow or some good weed -- yes, that, and hot sex. No pussy-hatted bullshit here.

"I like you, Ryan," she said, curling her legs like a kid while her black mini hiked up her thighs -- a calculated posturing but not unexpected. Pressman didn't make any aggressive moves because seeming overanxious could bogus the whole deal. Conversation probably would be meaningless drivel but necessary once the game was afoot.

"I like you too," he answered, an equally contrived and dopey response, but was there really any other? First moments alone with a beauty like Jenna often called for scripted repartee and calculated insincerity.

(I'll bow, you'll curtsy -- then we'll fuck.)

She moved closer. "A couple hours together, and it's like we've known each other forever, isn't it? Chemistry, attraction, all that good stuff, Ryan. I know it's a cliché, but magic between people happens fast, like some kind of spell, wouldn't you say?"

No, he wouldn't say that, not really. The woman was dark, beautiful. Of course he was attracted, of course he wanted to sleep with her, but that was about as far as the night's magic went, and that was as far as he wanted to take it. Maybe later something stronger would come; Jenna seemed a worthy contender for that. However, tonight's hard-on required no magic beyond what nature supplied. But that wasn't Ryan's response because within the hour he planned to ride this woman like a Bronco.

"Indeed I would," he agreed instead, convincing himself this wasn't entirely a lie. A strong stiff-one worked its own magic, as did his date's ample rack and Kardashian-fashioned ass.

(ABRACADABRA, sweetie, and let's hit those sheets.)

Maybe Jenna Crane knew some magic after all.

***

They did it twice, with additional acrobatics through the rear door.

Her skin bathed in sweat, Jenna pulled up the covers curling herself close to Pressman. The woman's essence seemed unlike anything in Ryan's experience, and her scent didn't come from a bottle. That particular knowledge was really a man thing, and having explored his share of women's nether regions, Pressman knew what natural fragrances nature provided. Ryan could have sworn Jenna Crane had swathed herself in honey, a neat trick considering the gymnastics they had shared during the past hour.

"So, you tell jokes for a living?" she asked. The topic had come up over a late drink since the Funny Bone Comedy Club had been where they'd met, but Ryan quickly had changed the subject. Standup comics who weren't Robin Williams weren't known for their luxurious lifestyles. Jenna touched his cheek, kissed it. "Can you make me laugh right now, my lover?"

The label seemed out of place and premature, and fresh from their workout Pressman still breathed heavily. "Right now I think I'll just lay here quietly having my heart attack."

That earned a wide grin. "Our fucking was like the Fourth of July, yes?"

"More like 9/11."

A wider grin. "Hey, you are funny! And politically incorrect too. I love that!"

"And I love a woman who knows so many tricks in bed yet smells as good as you do drenched in sweat. You want a joke? Okay, fine --" Pressman mentally scrolled through his act's repertoire. "Okay, so I asked this Chinese girl for her number. She said, 'Sex! Sex! Sex! Free sex tonight!' I said, 'Wow! Let's get laid!' Then her

Asian friend said, 'Schmuck, she means 666-3629!' -- This is where I usually wait for the laugh and some applause."

Jenna clapped her hands. She was a good audience. Ryan managed a faux bow from the bed post.

"My agent says she's pushing my act for a spot on Fallon. Not sure who I'll have to blow for that."

Jenna turned serious. "You know, laughter, it's really a nervous reaction -- a form of hysteria. But without it we'd probably crack up."

"Without it, I'd probably starve."

"I have a routine of my own. Want to see?"

"Comedy?"

"Magic, sort of. I'll show you."

"No juggling, okay? Don't want duck pins hitting my balls in their condition."

She smiled politely, and retrieving her bikini panties from the floor, she pulled a small envelope from them and unfolded a slip of parchment. "Have a look?"

In thick red lettering ...

FUCK ME, RYAN PRESSMAN!

He managed a nervous smile. "Okay. Neat trick, although not exactly prophetic considering -- well, just considering. But I didn't see you slip that envelope into -- I mean, when did you do that? How --?"

(...and why...?)

"Oh, I wrote that maybe a week ago. The envelope? See, that I slipped in before your show. Right by the ol' crotch between my bikini briefs and Beaver City. It's funny, don't you think? Parchment itches."

"You did this before we met tonight?"

"Oh, I'd seen your act a lot. Full of surprises, like me."

Pressman's smile melted. "Don't tell me you scribbled that message in your blood."

"A red Sharpie, silly. I'm not into self-mutilation unless you count the candles. Red ones, pink ones -- honey scented and melted over the envelope, warming my puss. You like hot snatch, don't you? See, I can be funny too." All pretense of innocence tossed, she snickered, now showing teeth. "And I pilfered that water bottle you drank from onstage -- needed something of yours for the mag-ic, you know."

"Black magic and red Sharpies. Are you a good witch or a bad witch? Going after me and my little dog too?" The joke was lame because Ryan wasn't sure it was a joke.

"Just a woman going after her man."

"By pouring hot wax into your --?"

"A simple spell, Ryan. No pentagrams, no caldrons, and I only use my broom to clean. But I can turn any worm into a cobra, seal the deal with hot wax, so to speak."

"I think you've already done that."

"Told you I'm full of surprises. So you love me already?" She giggled.

"Let me think that over."

Jenna shrugged. "Well, see, love spells, they're more advanced. Potions, complex chants, dolls, maybe a wild voodoo dance, shit like that. But sex spells -- Easy Peezy, lover! I'm getting skilled at those! A woman needs no magic to give a good blow job. Even the bad ones make a limp dick rise like a snake in a basket! But a few chosen words and… voila! A cobra!"

Ryan's stomach knotted.

(A note hidden inside her crotch!)

(This can't be good…)

"I think I'll keep the worm dick for now." He climbed from the woman's bed. Her fingers brushed his shoulder.

"Not yet, please, Ryan. See -- I want you to want me, I want you to need me. I want you to desire me, to lust after me. I want you to see that we were meant to be. I want lust to overflow in this body of yours. In this night of passion only you can lust and desire me. This is my will..."

(Definitely not good...)

She'd uttered some insane homemade voodoo chant. This was serious shit, and the comedy portion of the evening was over. Ryan reached for his Boxers.

"No offense, okay? Really, tonight was fun and you're one beautiful woman, Jenna. But--"

(...but I've seen 'Fatal Attraction' and I know crazy when I sleep with it!)

He felt something warm below like -- like hot wax. His manhood throbbed with a mind of its own, hardening like an iron rod. Or...

...a cobra!

(My God---)

"GOD!"

She caressed his growing erection like some sacred object.

"God had nothing to do with this, my lover. It's me -- all me!"

"Look, Jenna, I--"

"Smile, Ryan. No laughter, no sanity. Like not having a warm puss to sink your cock into when you're really horny. Enjoy the moment. It's all we have."

He knew she spoke the truth. Pressman kicked away the sheets. Jenna straddled him, whispered gibberish he couldn't make out. He didn't care. An erection forgets logic and precautions. Ryan wanted only to shove himself again inside this woman.

Jenna whispered to him, "666-3629, lover."
She screamed with each thrust.
So did he.

(2) A BLONDE AND A WITCH WALK INTO A BAR...

By morning Pressman's manhood had normalized. The woman's witchy words faded from his memory and clearer thinking returned. Dressing while Jenna slept, he hit the street by sun rise. His head spun as if he'd spent the night in a cement mixer, but Ryan chalked off the adventure as a minor aberration of his dating curve. A comic's groupies were unpredictable, and other skirts had gone gonzo after steamy sex. Jenna Crane now joined those ranks.

Playing the ghost, he didn't call, didn't return texts. He owed the woman nothing, and happily she quit after two weeks, Jenna 's final text a cryptic "I understand." Pressman's life resumed without the baggage of regret or guilt. No need for a denouement nor closure, just on to a new chapter...

...and new material. Opening his latest Funny Bone set with, "So I'm at my grandmother's funeral..." he received a polite laugh. But the kicker was coming. "...and I'm twelve, just beginning my masturbatory years. And the immature moron inside me, he's thinking, 'Christ, don't fucking laugh, it's Gran'ma's funeral, don't be a pussy! But it's my first funeral, I'm nervous, and stifling my laughter isn't working. So I'm thinking, Gran'ma would shit herself seeing me giggling like this near her coffin, and I'm telling myself, 'Think of butchered babies, deep fried puppies, kitten stroganoff! Anything, but--' But now I'm giggling like a mad man and covering my mouth, and those words repeat --

'BUTCHERED BABIES! DEEP FRIED PUPPIES! KITTEN STROGANOFF!!' And everyone, my parents, aunts, uncles, I mean EVERYONE-- they're looking at me with this 'What the hell?' stare. And I announce, "Fuck me! I said that out loud, didn't I?"

Pressman waited for the expected laugh, checking the response of the huge titted young blonde seated with girlfriends at a front table. Ryan hoped she was at least eighteen because he planned after his set ... well, why not? He was practically the headliner, and tonight he was killing it. Onstage, his eyes never left the blonde's, a sure sign she'd wait for him after the show.

"You're a funny guy," she said near the club's exit while he passed out CD's of his act. "I'm Tina." She extended her hand, smiled.

"I'm--"

"I know who you are. I paid for tickets, remember? A good investment, I'm thinking."

He signed the CD. "For you, Miss Tina, no charge!"

They both laughed, but from the queue another woman emerged, also laughing. Hard.

Jenna Crane picked out a CD for a signature. "Oh yes, a very good investment. You'd know about that, wouldn't you, Mr. Pressman? So, do I get a freebie too?" She handed him a ten-dollar bill and in the same motion unzipped her jeans, reached into them. She wore nothing underneath. "And I have something else for you, Ryan Pressman. Straight from my snatch!"

Ryan signed her CD with a shaking hand. Looking up, he noticed blonde Tina had disappeared.

(Fuck!)

"Jesus, Jenna, there's people here!"

She turned to the short line behind her. "So, you people haven't seen a bald pussy before?" She made sure they did. Whipping out another small envelope, she handed it to Ryan.

"Christ, Jenna!"

"Read what's inside. The envelope, I mean, not my cooz." She zipped her jeans. "Show's over, folks." She faux smiled at the few remaining behind her in line.

"Look, Jenna, I know you're angry--"

"Read it, Ryan! Parchment itches!"

RYAN PRESSMAN
LAUGH!
DIE!

"In blood this time. My blood!"

"This is a joke, right?"

"Laugh and see."

"It isn't funny."

"Want to hear funny? -- 'Destiny change from pain and cold. Now you pay in blood and soul...'"

Muttering another dumb ass chant, she was trying to fuck with his head.

"You're full of shit!"

"Eventually you will laugh, Ryan. You're a comedian -- and comics live to make others laugh! Eventually one smile just might break your face, maybe it'll dissolve your brain." Jenna kissed his cheek. "And I have this CD, now -- something of yours. Makes my little spell complete. Every time I give it a listen I'll laugh and laugh!"

"Get out of my life or I'll fucking kill you!"

That sent the rest of those in the waiting queue to the exit.

Jenna walked off too. No puff of smoke, no witchy cackle. She pushed her way through the exit door like the crazy bitch she was.

Inside Ryan's head the woman's laughter echoed.

(3) ALL THE UGLY PEOPLE

While the Saturday night crowd was often enthusiastic, Ryan's first set proved a dud. Sid Toby, owner of The Funny Bone, later discovered the comic in the wings pacing before his 10 o'clock set. Rubbing his bald head, Sid noticed the beer in Ryan's hand and frowned.

"A comic who can't manage a smile, hey? That may work for Steven Wright, but not you. We've got paying customers here, Pressman. Your last set was from shit. Something eating you?"

Sid's words seemed ironically funny, but Ryan didn't laugh. He didn't dare. Weeks ago some-thing had been eating him, all right -- and swallowing too. But now this woman was eating at him, and not in such a good way.

(No laughter, no sanity...)

Sid asked, "You been drinking? You seem--"

"I'm fine. Just going over the new material. I was a little off my mark earlier, but I'm okay now. Hey, a good joke man never laughs at his own jokes, right?" He tossed the beer can with a feeble jump shot, missing the trash can entirely.

"Just show the crowd you're having a good time with them. Two minutes and you're on. Kill them dead this time, okay? And stay on your feet!"

The image lingered of Jenna Crane's blood smeared note. Mind over matter, Pressman tried convincing himself, but go try explaining to Sid about what he experienced during his last set whenever he cracked a smile. The pain was excruciating, but Ryan soldiered on to almost dead silence. He responded to the room with the most desperate line a standup could utter.

"OKAY, THEN! ALL THE UGLY PEOPLE BE QUIET!"

That silenced almost the entire room. With his staggering exit, the meager applause turned downright Zen with the sound of one hand clapping. Ryan felt tempted to slip on a MAGA hat as he left and offer his middle finger to his audience, fuck whatever Trumpopaths sat in the crowd. But that was then, and this was now, and now was all a comic had.

From the club's small stage, The Bone's opening act, Artie Kurland, announced his set. "You're going to love this next guy. I know I do every time he sucks my dick. Give a hand -- or at least a hand job -- for Mr. Ryan Pressman!"

Ryan took the stage, staring at the mic that seemed some filthy thing he feared approaching. To polite applause, he launched himself into his act.

(Adjust the mic, eye contact with the crowd, say something about the crummy venue...)

(Relax!)

"Hey, thanks for coming. Subway will be stopping here any minute..."

Some chuckles almost passed for laughs.

(Okay, let's give 'em what they came to see...)

"Lots of women here tonight. Any lesbians in the crowd?" Pressman looked around, pretending to count hands. "I hear there's a new drug for lesbians on the market to cure depression. It's called Trycoxagain!"

Receiving a huge laugh, Ryan managed a twitching smile, realizing too late this was a mistake. Intense pain shot through his head and his smile melted like candle wax. His vision blurred as he shook off the throbbing ache and grabbed the mic stand for balance.

"What is easier to pick up the heavier it gets? --- WOMEN!"

Not a big laugh there. Mostly men, and uneasy laughter at best from those whose wives were probably on the chunky side. From the women, though -- nothing. Before real silence set in Ryan pressed on.

"Did you know scientists have discovered a food that diminishes a woman's sex drive by 90%? It's called a wedding cake!"

...and he had the crowd again. Noticing Sid offstage, Ryan laughed along. A few more sexist jokes in, he smiled at his own cleverness. Again a minefield detonated inside his brain almost sending the comic to the floor. He held onto the mic like a lush clinging to a lamp post.

"And another thing about women---"

(FUCK!)

"Sorry, folks, I'm feeling a little...just a little... Shit!"

Ryan slid to his knees. One woman screamed. Some jerk yelled something about this drunken bit not being funny. The guy was right about that.

From Sid in the wings, "Get him off! Now, dammit!"

Two stagehands got Ryan to his feet and managed to get him moving. He saw Sid Toby standing offstage. Sid didn't appear happy.

"Hello, I must be going..."

Pressman remained conscious long enough to hear Sid tell him he was fired.

(4) TAKE MY LIFE PLEASE!

It proved tricky not to laugh for weeks. It wasn't good for business and not very healthy, as any shrink would've told Pressman had he asked.

Comedy programming seemed inescapable on television in its new Golden Age: Classic episodes of Seinfeld cleverly about nothing; cable shows unafraid to mix comedy with tits and ass; even that fucking Flo and her Progressive commercials. Plus a dozen guilty pleasures Ryan admitted to no one. He had laughed often at those gems. Not anymore.

Death traps, all of them. A smile was torture, a laugh maybe fatal. Pressman took no calls, cancelled out-of-town clubs he'd booked. A glimpse at his mirrored reflection revealed some insane caricature of himself, some dour old fart screaming at kids to get off his lawn.

The bitch's curse was real. Ryan was proof -- living proof, at least for now. Unless...

Waiting for night, he hopped the D Train to the woman's brownstone. She answered the inter-com, allowing him inside as if expecting the comic to show up at her door. Maybe a witch knew about such things.

"It's so nice to see you again, Ryan." Jenna smiled like they were old friends. Or lovers. "Coffee? Tea? Me?"

"Let's cut the bullshit. You know why I'm here."

"You want to get laid, right? The cobra is hungry?"

"I'm half dead, and it's your fault. Do I look like a man who wants to fuck you?"

The woman lit a cigarette, blew a smoke ring. "You look like a man with no sense of humor. That's pretty funny when you think about it."

Grabbing her shoulders, he wanted to shake Jenna Crane senseless. "You can fix that!"

Her toothy smile returned. "Are you sorry you can't laugh at me, Ryan? Do you regret you can't smirk after having your way with me, then treating me like dog shit? I won't let you scrape me off your shoe that easily!" She blew another smoke ring.

"You seduced me!"

"That wasn't very hard, Ryan. I doubt a spell was required. Not that I'm complaining." She studied the remaining ash of the thin cigarette as if it held secret meaning, then mashed it out.

"You're a cunt!"

"And you're a dick. I think that covers the genitalia part of this program. Hey, I made a joke. Want to laugh?"

Ryan shook her hard. "I want you to send another message to your fucking clam to fix this!"

A wide grin emerged. "Kiss me first."

"What?"

Jenna leaned closer. "Your hands are already grabbing me. Kiss me, and then we'll talk."

Ryan almost laughed. He caught himself. "You want me to -- You think I-- Christ!"

Jenna didn't wait. Pulling him closer, she kissed him hard, then reached for his crotch. "I believe something is stirring down here already. Have I awakened a sleeping dragon, maybe?"

She had some crazy power to give him an erection even while he despised this woman. The thought sickened him.

"I guess a love spell can work after all, eh, Ryan? You think you chose to come here on your own, don't you? Hey, I'm learning!"

He shook as if electrified. "Another note?"

"That, and the first one. Powerful stuff, wouldn't you say? Have a look?" She reached for the zipper of her jeans, pulled out the small envelope. "You know the drill, Ryan."

**Love me or drop dead,
Ryan Pressman**

"Your next voodoo threat?"

"It's an option, Ryan. Unless you prefer to have the last laugh." She snickered to herself.

"Very clever. Well, then, okay..." He rolled the note into a ball and tossed it to the floor, then held Jenna close and kissed her long and hard. She fit nicely into his arms, and he slipped his hands to her neck, caressing it. He stared into her eyes, risked a broad smile.

(Love me or drop dead...)

"I've made my choice, Jenna ..."

Pressman clutched both hands around her neck, squeezed her throat's delicate tendons until her eyes bulged like an insect's. The woman's flesh turned pale, but he kept squeezing just to be sure. She struggled, swaying her head with feverish motions while pounding across Ryan's chest. He tightened his grip, squeezed harder until her expression went blank. Her breathing stopped, her body went limp. Jenna sank to the floor like a broken doll.

Ryan's erection remained and it felt stiffer than ever. The woman's ritual proved one mighty bitch of a spell, and it wasn't going away. He was fucked, and he would remain fucked. The realization made him smile at the idiocy of it all. Loud laughter followed. So did the explosion inside his brain.

He stared at the corpse of Jenna Crane at his feet.

And Ryan laughed and laughed…

Swallow the Moon
Morgan Elektra

Cody stole from beneath Marco's sleeping body and pulled on the trousers his lover had peeled off him earlier. He padded out into the hall, closed the door carefully behind him, and buttoned his shirt over his bronze chest. Cody had maybe an hour before Marco woke, another two before he started to suspect Cody wasn't coming back. That gave him more than enough time to finish getting what he came for.

At the elevator, he shrugged into his rumpled suit jacket, pulling his long black hair free of the collar. He stared at the tasteful yet nondescript hotel art and drummed a quick rhythm against his thigh. When his cell phone rang, he glanced at it. A growl of frustration caught in his throat when he saw the name on the display.

"Egan."

"I've got a job for you."

"I'm--"

"Meet me at The Totem in an hour."

Before he could protest, Egan hung up. Cody put the phone back in one pocket and pulled a second cell from the other. He didn't bother deleting anything--there was nothing on it of importance--or wiping it for prints. The silver fox he'd bedded for the last six months would never go to the police. None of his marks did. Embarrassment kept them quiet. And the money was nothing to them. A drop in the bucket. Cody wasn't greedy.

The burner went into the garbage just as the elevator doors slid open with a soft swish. He stepped in and jabbed the down button.

Egan would be waiting for him at the bar in an hour, and he had sixty-thousand dollars to steal first.

***

Cody slid into the cracked leather booth across from Egan and found a beer already waiting for him, the bottle dewed with moisture. He breathed in the bar's perfume of bitter hops and peanut shells. His skin still buzzed with the lingering high of a completed job.

Egan flipped through a slim folder without looking up, his free hand clenched around his own beer.

"I need you on this one."

Cody arched a brow at his old friend. It had been over a decade since the two of them had run a scam together. The moment Emily had agreed to marry Egan, he'd gone legit. Turned private investigator, with the occasional side job skip tracing. Cody's specialty was parting lonely, wealthy socialites from their cash, not following cheating spouses or criminals who had been stupid enough to get caught.

"That so?"

"Client needs me to retrieve something of his."

Cody tapped his fingertips against the side of his beer bottle. His stomach twisted with conflicting emotions.

Back when they were young and invincible, he and Egan had done more than their fair share of "retrieval". In those early years after Cody ran away from the reservation, if it hadn't been for his friend and their various forms of creative employment, he might have starved. And he couldn't lie, there had been a hell of a thrill in pulling jobs with the bright, sharp-eyed Egan.

But that had all stopped when Cody's big sister had tracked him down and made a home for him. For both of them. The moment he'd laid eyes on her, Egan had fallen hard for Emily, been willing to do anything for her. Even walk the straight-and-narrow. Kids, white picket fence. The American dream.

That life didn't appeal to Cody, though he did stay away from the most dangerous endeavors. It wasn't the same without his best friend at his side anyway.

Cody studied Egan's face. He looked thinner, and there were dark smudges under his eyes. Not that Cody could blame him. He hadn't slept well since the accident either.

He swallowed a generous mouthful of beer, unwilling to think about how pale and small Emily had looked under the hospital fluorescents, or the haunting woosh of the ventilator.

Instead, he turned his thoughts back to Egan's proposal. He bounced his eyebrows up and down, his mouth tipping in a leer.

"What do you need me to do? Charm some heirloom off a bitter divorcee?"

Egan snorted.

"I wish. No, this one is going to be a bit… tricky."

Cody tensed in anticipation. "Oh?"

Egan extracted a photo from the file and pushed it across the table. The woman had grey hair, skin the exact shade of a penny, broad cheekbones and a wide nose. She was striking but there was something about her that sent a bolt of unease through Cody's belly.

She reminded him of someone he'd known growing up on the reservation. When he was little, he had been terrified of Grandmother Eagle Feather's milky eyes. According to Cody's grandfather, "Great Spirit has turned her eyes to the other world."

The woman in the photo didn't have cataracts, but her dark eyes stared out as if she could see into Cody's soul. Despite the ridiculousness of the notion, he shuddered, goosebumps chasing themselves over his arms.

Egan tapped a broad fingertip against the glossy paper.

"She has something of my client's. She was supposed to return it to him, but she's decided to keep it instead."

"And? Am I supposed to talk my way into her pants and convince her to give it up? Because, I gotta be honest, E--"

"No." Egan gave a short, sharp shake of his head. "There's no charming this woman, not even for you. And we don't have the time anyway. The... uh, object, is time sensitive."

"What's your plan then?"

"She's got it in her house. You and I are going to go in and take it back."

Cody lifted a brow. "Sounds like all you need is an extra pair of hands. Why call me, E?"

"Because I need someone I can trust."

Cody picked at the edge of the photo.

"What is this mysterious package?"

Egan drummed his thick fingers on the table. Cody sipped his beer, electricity crackling along his spine. He stared at his brother-in-law, willing him to respond.

Curiosity was one of his vices. More of a lure than booze or drugs. Almost as good as sex.

Finally, Egan slid the file across the table, his sigh echoing the dry scrape of the paper against the scarred wood.

Cody flipped open the folder, giving a low whistle as he read the client's name. He was one of the richest men in the world, practically King of the Eastern seaboard.

Cody scanned the rest of the paperwork, grimacing as he read about who he and Egan would be retrieving the King's property from. The mark's name was Marilyn Singing River, a medicine woman considered extremely capable by the people she dealt with. She didn't live on a reservation, but she visited several frequently. She ran a tidy business selling organic homemade soaps and shampoos online, but it was her in-person homeopathic remedies and treatments that were sought after and sworn by.

More than one person claimed to have been healed by her from all manner of illnesses--mental, spiritual and physical. They called her a miracle worker. Then there was her more specialized business--funerary services.

The words made Cody feel thin as a dried corn husk.

He flipped through pages of reports on her comings and goings, the layout of her house.

And then he reached the bit about the package and his breath left him in a gust. Intense heat prickled in his stomach, spreading winding tendrils into his chest and down to his groin.

Unlike the jobs he and Egan had done together in their youth, the package wasn't drugs, money, antiques, or even documents. It was a woman. And she was luscious.

According to Egan's file, she was twenty-six years old and five foot nine inches tall. The attached photo had been taken at a formal event. Her shoulders were bared by an ivory silk dress that draped her lush body. Thick chestnut hair framed a heart-shaped face with amber eyes and a plump, pink mouth. A smattering of freckles dusted her nose and cheeks.

She was all round. Not just her full breasts, hips, and ass, but her arms and the length of her thighs and calves bared beneath the dress' hem were sumptuously curved as well. He even detected the arc of her belly under the fabric.

She was a banquet of dangerously soft curves and supple, cream-and-honey skin.

Cody didn't have a type. Man, woman, skinny, short, masculine, feminine. Whatever. The things that drew him to a person were not always outwardly visible. But the woman in the photo definitely made his prick stand up.

"Who is she?"

Egan finished his beer and signaled the bartender for another.

"His daughter."

The King of the Eastern seaboard was in the picture beside her, her dainty hand looped through the crook of his arm. Cody paid little attention to the red-faced, bellicose billionaire, captured instead by the beauty at his side. Her smile was fragile, with a touch of sadness but there was a fire in her eyes that said she might enjoy licking chocolate off of Cody's muscled belly and cock for a few hours.

He bit off a groan at the explicit mental image that flashed behind his eyes.

Egan plucked the fresh beer from the waiter's tray and arched a bushy eyebrow at Cody. Nothing escaped his brother-in-law's fierce, golden gaze.

"Aiyanna. The apple of Daddy's eye."

Cody scanned the rest of the information Egan had compiled, committing it to memory. Her college degrees, ex-boyfriends, and causes. Apparently, she was the warm, philanthropic face of Daddy's soulless mega-corporation. His spokeswoman and hostess. When he finished reading, he turned back to the picture.

"So, what's her story? What's she doing with the old woman?" He thought of Marilyn Singing River's otherworldly eyes and shuddered.

"She's dead."

Cody's lungs seized. For a brief moment, he was back in the hospital corridor, staring into Egan's burnt-ember eyes with coffee scalding his palms through the thin paper cafeteria cups. His heart stopped for an eternity before rushing forward at breakneck pace. No, Egan wasn't talking about Cody's sister. They hadn't spoken of her at all in the months since they'd buried her.

But that didn't make the words any less shocking.

He looked back down at the picture of Aiyanna, the voluptuous princess of the Eastern seaboard, her cheeks tinged rose and her glossy lower lip just begging to be bitten. He'd never seen someone who looked so alive. So made to give and receive pleasure.

The hair on the back of Cody's neck bristled. She was dead and in the hands of a medicine woman. The part of his mind that still lived on the reservation whispered of burial rituals and earthbound spirits. Cody shut the door on that thought immediately.

Bullshit, he told himself.

Egan's nod seemed to concur with Cody's thought. Cody cleared his throat.

"How do you want to do this?"

***

Cody sat at his kitchen table in the dark, jaw tight with aggravation, waiting for Egan.

He had wanted to wile his way into Marilyn Singing River's house ahead of time. Fake a little fall out front, surreptitiously slice the forehead a bit--head wounds bled like a bitch--and then snoop while she was mixing up a poultice or whatever.

Emily had always said he could charm the stars down from the sky and possessed a smile that made anything seem forgivable. Cody had made a career on it. It would have been easy.

But Egan forbade him from going near her place, worried about tipping the old woman off. They had blueprints, reports from customers who had been in the house. Those would have to do.

According to one former client that Egan had spoken to (he too could be charismatic when he wanted to be), Marilyn Singing River prepared her charges for burial rights in a room below her house. Cody shuddered when he realized Aiyanna was not the only one the old woman held.

The low room was lined with boxes; coffins, though the description in the report of the carved lids sounded more like wooden sarcophagi than the highly polished casket they'd put Emily in.

It had been so heavy, but Cody had born it, numbly grateful she had not asked him to take her home to the res. He hadn't been back since he'd left at thirteen, seeking something more than the weary sadness baked into the dirt, but he would have gone for her even if it killed him. She'd known that. His sister had always known him.

Cody glanced out the window, dragging himself back to the present. Wisps of cloud scudded across the silver face of the moon. The shadows would help hide them tonight, make it easier to go undetected. Concentrating on the job ahead made Cody's heart beat faster. This was one of his favorite parts. The lead-up.

When it came to rich divorcees and widowers, that meant the chase. Setting the hook, making them fall for him, want to do anything for him.

For him, though he enjoyed his creature comforts, the con was never about money.

It was the thrill.

Everything took on more dimensions, had more facets. His senses heightened. He could taste the air, and the faintest smells buffeted him like a pillow to the face. His skin went tight, every hair raised and vibrating. His blood frothed with excitement. It made the sex part easy, even if the mark didn't really get him going.

Cody flipped open the folder, sifting through the pictures.

Aiyanna was gorgeous. His heart thunked against his breastbone, and Cody felt his cock thicken in primal response. His hand slid off the table, into his lap. He pressed a palm against the rigid length through the soft cotton of his black trousers, willing it away.

A heavy truck stopped below the window, the door opening and closing with a soft clunk. Cody went cold and the throbbing erection immediately subsided. With a curse, he shoved the contents of the folder back together and glanced at the clock. Just like Egan to be early.

Cody loped out of the apartment and met his brother-in-law at the foot of the stairs. Shadows masked Egan's face, the hard curve of his beak-like nose standing out sharp and deadly.

"Ready?"

Cody didn't bother responding. He glanced past Egan to the nondescript moving truck idling at the curb. Not from one of the major companies, but it looked enough like it that a casual glance would fool any onlookers.

Egan smiled a little. There was something in that look, Cody thought; a darkness in his friend's eyes and a jagged edge he didn't remember the older man having before. Not even back in the days when they'd been pulling petty jobs on the streets.

Cody had seen the same look often enough in his own reflection, when he couldn't distract his mind from thoughts of his sister.

Egan unhooked the rear doors, the creak loud in the still night. Inside, there was a cot bolted to the steel floor. Cody figured he'd appreciate that small amenity somewhere around Iowa, when his long legs were getting cramped up front.

Across from the bed was a contraption made of two-by-fours that puzzled him. He cocked his head, studying it for a moment before he figured it was meant to hold the coffin steady and keep it from shifting during transit.

His stomach turned, but Cody shook the unease off and focused on the job.

It was time to collect Aiyanna and bring her home.

***

Egan rolled the truck down Marilyn Singing River's quiet suburban street with the headlights off and pulled to a stop in front of her house. Not ideal, but it was a risk they had to take. They were less likely to attract attention there for the time it would take to snatch Aiyanna, than leaving it further down the road, where they might be seen hauling a coffin along the sidewalk.

Cody moved inside the shadows as he made his way up the stone path toward the house. His hearing, heightened by the surging adrenaline, easily picked up Egan's feather-light footfalls behind him. For such a big man, he moved as silently as if he had wings.

The door was unlocked. Cody would have been surprised if Egan's intel hadn't said that would be the case. They slipped into the house and Cody closed the door behind them. He breathed in a deep lungful of air redolent of moist earth and green, crumbly herbs.

Cody took in the simple interior of the Craftsman style home. The living room, dining room, and kitchen were open plan, with gleaming wood floors. The furniture was all warm earth tones, overstuffed couches and thick Turkish carpets.

Doors leading to the bedroom, bathroom, and basement were all tightly closed. They waited several moments, but heard no movement from behind any of them.

Egan eased the basement door open. It moved on well-oiled hinges, revealing a rectangle of seemingly bottomless obsidian. When only more silence greeted the opening of the door, Cody saw a bit of tension drop from the other man's shoulders. Without a word, Egan descended into the utter blackness below.

****

Cody stood at the foot of the stairs, head cocked to listen for even the smallest sound. He could just make out Egan's outline in the ebony shadows on his left, but little more.

He had expected the underground room to be cool, but it was so cold he was sure he'd see his breath if the light were better.

He'd also thought it would smell, given its purpose and contents. But the frigid air in the underground room was odorless. It made the skin on his nape prickle. The only light was a faint pale glow that seemed to emanate from nowhere and everywhere. Dimmer than a nightlight, it barely illuminated the space.

As he adjusted to the dark, Cody realized he could hear things. Whispers. Voices. A soft rustle and murmur, as if they stood amidst a crowd of quiet, polite people.

Egan nudged him and Cody felt the other man lean close.

"Do you see her?"

"Who's that?" Marilyn Singing River's dry voice was loud, drowning out the whispers.

Cody froze, his gut filling with ice. He waited for the room to flood with light, but the darkness remained almost absolute. Her question was picked up in whispers, faster and more frantic, like a rising wind.

Who's that... who... is that... who... who'sthat... whowhowhoWHO...

Cody heard many voices in that chilling susurrus and his heart lurched unsteadily behind his ribs.

The old woman spoke again from across the vast, cold, dark room.

"You shouldn't be here!"

Again the whispered echo rolled towards them in a frigid wave.

Shouldn't be here...you shouldn't be here... you... shouldn't...be... here!

The last whisper was so close the speaker must have been standing right in front of him, but Cody saw nothing. Felt no one. Beside him, Egan stepped away into the dark.

Cody took several deep breaths, trying to tune out the incessant murmuring that chilled his blood. According to the reports, Aiyanna would be just a few feet away.

The reminder of their purpose snapped the shadowed room into focus. He made out a line of shelves and several large tables. And all along the walls, tall, narrow boxes standing on end. The faint glow, he now saw, came from a lamp near the far wall. It was shaped like a pumpkin, only smooth, with a stubby, almost invisible brass base.

The whispers died away, and in the silence, Cody's skin hummed. His mouth filled with bitter saliva, and he had the sudden urge to tuck in on himself to protect his soft bits.

He forced himself to move, fingers trailing along the line of shelves so he wouldn't bump them. Who knew what they contained?

He heard the muffled tread of Egan's feet and the old woman's strangled gasp.

"Get the girl," Egan rumbled.

The skin of Cody's fingertips registered smooth wood a moment later. He had to resist the urge to jerk his hands back to his sides.

Cody gritted his teeth as he caressed the lid of each wooden box to count, expecting any moment to touch something that yielded beneath his fingers with a liquid squelch and the stink of rot.

But he reached the seventh tall box, his hands finding nothing but intricately carved wood. He could smell the soft, sharp scent of pine and another light, sweet musk that sent a shocking spear of heat into the pit of his stomach.

The struggle behind him ceased with a meaty crunch. Cody glanced over his shoulder, heart dropping as the room flooded with pale blue light.

He shook his head and blinked his eyes, trying to ignore what he'd thought he glimpsed.

For a moment, the room between him and Egan had been full of tall, thin shadows who fled from the increasing illumination.

At Egan's feet lay a pile of white cloth, like a bedsheet. Cody almost convinced himself that's all it was, but the tangle of iron grey hair wouldn't let him. His whole body twisted with cold.

"Egan…"

"Lock down that lid and let's go."

Cody's fingers hovered above the metal catch, twitching.

Egan shoved the lamp into Cody's hands, slapped at the clasp to verify it was closed, and grasped one end of the coffin. Cody stood frozen where he was, the lamp's base warm in his grasp. Egan glanced at him, brow furrowed.

"C'mon, Coy-dog."

Cody shook his head, tucking the lamp beneath his arm, and grabbed the other end of the coffin. Together, they lifted. Both men gave a grunt of surprise.

Despite its simple fashioning and light wood, Cody had expected it to weigh more. His mind flashed to Emily's funeral, her weighty mahogany box, and he pushed the memory swiftly away. Moving as quickly as they could, the two men tramped to the stairs.

Egan backed up the steep staircase carefully. Cody followed. He couldn't help glancing back over his shoulder, toward the other coffins.

Egan gave a squawk of frustration.

"Get rid of the light!"

Cody realized that the blue glow was filling the upper rooms of the house. Panic crept up his spine, making his motions jerky. He threw the thing back down the stairs. It struck the lip of the low ceiling and shattered with a crystalline tinkle.

The light flared briefly and then the darkness swallowed it. Cody hurried up the steps and slammed the door against the rush of whispering shadows that greeted the spreading black.

The hum of unease in his gut and the bitter taste in his mouth didn't subside until he climbed into the truck's driver seat.

As the first warm pink light of dawn crept over the edge of the horizon, Cody pointed the truck toward it and drove.

***

By nightfall they'd crossed the state line, putting miles between them and Marilyn Singing River's corpse, and Cody pulled into a truck stop off of I-84. He climbed out, stretching and groaning as his joints popped. Cody yanked open the truck's rear doors and Egan's feet crunched on the gravel as he hopped down.

"We need to keep moving."

Egan's face was drawn, his eyes sunken into dark sockets. His skin seemed sallow and loose. As if he'd suddenly lost a lot of weight. Cody grimaced.

"You didn't sleep?"

Egan's bloodshot eyes darted around the parking lot. "With that thing right next to me? Hell no."

"Well, I need a break. I've got to stretch my legs, eat some food…" He saw Egan's mouth open and forestalled him with a raised hand. "Real food, not more fast-food garbage. And I need to rest. I've been awake for over twenty hours now, E."

Egan's eyes blazed momentarily fierce in his pinched face, but then he nodded.

"Fine. Let's get some food and then we'll crash in the truck."

Cody nodded.

"That's fine." He tossed Egan the keys. "I'm going to walk around a bit."

The sky was deep purple and black; the first few stars sparkled against the bruised backdrop. A warm wind blew up as Cody loped lazy circles around the deserted parking lot. They were in the middle of nowhere Idaho. The night was eerily quiet except for the faint wind through the grass and the occasional whoosh of a vehicle passing on the interstate. He glanced back at the truck.

Cody's fingers slid into his pocket before he remembered he'd given Egan the keys. He'd been thinking about her all day. Longer, really. Since Egan had first slid that file to him across the table at the bar. Something about Aiyanna called to him.

In a blink, Cody was back at the truck, one hand on the door, his cock half hard.

What was he doing? He'd known from the minute he'd agreed to the job, that picture of Aiyanna in ivory silk burned onto the inside of his eyelids, that this was a really bad idea. And now he was thinking about…

"Nothing. Not thinking about anything. Just wiped out. Need to get some rest."

The sound of his own voice startled him. The wind was no longer warm, and a shiver drew his balls up tight. He took several deep breaths, inhaling the scent of dusty gravel and diesel fuel, willing his heart to stop racing and the blood to flow back into his brain.

"Hey Coy-dog, brought you some food."

Cody turned at the sound of Egan's voice and found his brother-in-law standing behind him extending a white Styrofoam takeout container in a plastic bag. Cody drew another breath and smelled red meat, brown gravy and the delicious tang of garlic. He took the food, mouth watering.

"Thanks. Mind unlocking the truck?" He dug into lumpy mashed potatoes with a plastic fork.

Egan stilled, his gaze piercing. "I'll stick back here. You camp out up front."

Cody swallowed the bite of potatoes and forked a chunk of meatloaf, swimming with spices, into his mouth.

"If we do it your way, we're down for the night. If we swap, you can keep driving. We'll make better time."

Egan shoved his hand into his pocket, mouth a stubborn line. Finally, he nodded and unlocked the rear doors.

"Yeah. You're right."

Cody continued eating, waiting for his brother-in-law to open up the back of the truck. Egan held out his hand.

"Just… take this."

Cody stared at the intricately beaded leather bag lying in his brother-in-law's palm. He didn't know precisely what it was meant to protect against--though given the situation he'd guess it was possession or evil spirits or some bullshit--but he'd seen enough of them in his youth to know that it was definitely an amulet.

He grimaced. "You know I don't believe in that crap."

Egan sighed. "Coy-dog, listen…"

"I'm going to go eat this before it gets cold."

I'm cold… come warm me…

Cody stilled. His eyes scanned every inch of the parking lot, looking for the source of the soft whisper before returning to Egan. His brother-in-law was still proffering the charm. Cody shook his head and climbed into the truck, intent on getting food and sleep.

***

Cody ran through heavy forest, smelling pine trees and damp leaves. Star-scattered midnight blue sky peeked out from in between the thick branches.

His heart thrummed in his throat and his veins were full of power. When he broke free from the trees, bright silver moonlight splashed in his face.

Cody leapt, his feet leaving the ground, the air lifting him like wings. As he reached the full, fat moon, it became the strange lamp from Marilyn's basement, shining on his misdeeds. So he opened his mouth and gulped it down.

Everything went dark.

In his belly, the moon was a ball of heat. When he opened his eyes, the light shone out of them, illuminating her.

Aiyanna sprawled on top of him, gloriously naked, a welcoming smile on her full lips. Her petal-soft skin was chilled. Cody wrapped his arms around her, and ran his tongue along the crease where her shoulder met her neck. His hands fisted in the glossy chestnut skein of her hair, squeezing the thick locks.

She rocked her hips, rubbing the velvety soft expanse of her stomach over the painfully hard length of his cock. Her lips tickled his ear, her breath barely a whisper.

"Do you want me?"

"Yes!"

His voice was rough with desire. He wanted her so bad his balls ached. He wanted her more than he'd ever wanted anyone in his life. Man or woman.

He thrust against her, muscles trembling, seeking friction as delicious heat spread through him.

Aiyanna nipped at his earlobe. She pulled her head from his grasp and feathered wet kisses down his throat, trailing her slick tongue across his chest. Lust throbbed in his blood. Her soft whisper was intoxicating, like a shot of good whiskey.

"What would you do to have me?"

She slithered her body down the length of his, her mouth tracing a serpentine path across his stomach. Her hands rested on his upper thighs, the nails digging gently into his skin. Her hair slid over his shaft like silk and Cody almost bit through his own lip.

"Anything!" He growled, the noise catching in his throat.

Her lips brushed against the sensitive tip of his dick, and he arched upward. When she whispered again, her voice was still somehow at his ear, though he could feel her breath against the taut skin of his balls.

"All you have to do…"

She trailed off, her tongue teasing underneath his foreskin, sliding through the precome gathering there.

Cody tensed, hands tangling in her hair. Aiyanna pressed his hips down as she swiped her tongue along the entire length of his cock from root to crown.

She scratched his inner thighs and then curled her fingers around his testicles. Her lips slid over the smooth head of his cock as she sucked him into the warm cavern of her mouth.

Lust howled in his blood. He rocked his hips against her hold, sliding his length over the velvet wetness of her tongue, burying himself between her plump lips. His whole body pulsed in time with his pounding heart.

Her fingers stroked him, gently kneaded his balls, occasionally straying to press a knuckle just beneath them and sending a jolt of pleasure straight to the pit of his stomach.

"All you have to do is…"

As if she sensed him nearing orgasm, she sucked harder and twirled her tongue more tightly around his shaft, tracing the thick vein on the underside, flicking against the dip just beneath the flared ridge, fluttering into the tiny slit at the tip.

Cody's balls drew up tight and he thrust hard, brushing the back of her throat and sinking into it. She didn't pull away, but clamped her lips down tight and swallowed.

Galvanic pleasure ripped through him, curling his toes and drawing his entire body up into a tight bow. And though his hands were wrapped in her hair and her wonderful, wet mouth was full of his pulsing cock, her velvet voice still whispered in his ear.

"Open the box!"

Cody jerked awake. Alone in the back of the truck, his body still tingled and quickly cooling come pooled in his boxers. He grimaced.

He'd had a wet dream before but not since the earliest days of puberty. And never anything so real. He could hear her voice still echoing in the air, had felt every strand of her hair, tasted her sweat, smelled the musky sweetness of her cunt.

Cody bit off a curse. He fumbled for the takeout napkins in the dark, wincing as he wiped up the sticky ejaculate as best he could.

As his eyes adjusted, he glanced over at the long wooden box locked down on the opposite side of the truck--the coffin that contained Aiyanna.

Open the box!

The soft, barely-there whisper slid into his ears again. He stood, stepped toward her, gait rolling with the motion of the truck. He ran shaking hands over the engraved lid.

His fingers strayed to the heavy iron clasp.

He reached into his pocket and pulled out a lighter, flicking the flame into existence. It illuminated a stylized dragonfly etched into the metal of the latch.

The stirrings of a sudden breeze lifted the dark hair off of Cody's neck. He shivered and touched the delicate carving again. It looked familiar, but he couldn't place it.

When his fingers caressed the cool metal, the wind picked up and the darkness filled with frantic murmuring. The sound, eerie and ethereal, reminded him where he'd seen the symbol before--a crystal carving that threw off shimmering rainbows when held to the light. He'd admired it as a little boy. Grandmother Eagle Feather had put it into his small hands.

"See how it makes the sunlight a rainbow? It becomes something other than it was and yet is still itself. A rebirth. This is the secret of the dragonfly," she explained in her thin, paper-dry voice.

He pulled his hand back from the clasp, curling the fingers into a fist and ignoring the tremble in them. The whispering died away.

When he touched the latch again, it returned, louder. And he recognized Aiyanna's voice.

Break it… break it now… let me…

He whirled. Shadows danced away from the small orange flame and Cody stumbled away from the coffin, heart hammering in his throat. A lurch of the truck sent him sprawling. The lighter tumbled from his hand and went out. Cody's head slammed against the hard wall and all he saw was blackness.

***

Cody woke with the sense that he had just missed a whispered sigh and lips brushing his temple. He tensed, terror zinging through him again.

He sat up gingerly. With no windows, it was impossible to gauge the time of day. His head thumped and despite having been unconscious for who knows how long, Cody felt exhausted. Like he'd been running all night. It took a moment for him to realize that the truck had stopped. He climbed off the cot just as Egan opened the doors.

His brother-in-law looked worse, hunched in on himself. The skin of his face was grey, his eyes burning red holes in his face. Cody whistled.

"You look like shit, E. How long did you drive? Where are we?"

Egan's eyes locked on the box. He responded slowly, rubbing a shaking hand through his tangled curls.

"We're in Illinois. I need to lay down."

He tossed the keys to Cody and climbed up into the back of the truck. Cody was stunned. Egan had driven for a full day. He had been unconscious for awhile. And yet he still felt wiped out. Shaking his aching head, he jumped down and sucked in a deep breath of fresh air. It helped to chase away some of the lethargy.

Egan stretched out on the cot, his hand fisted around his amulet so tightly his knuckles were white.

Cody watched his friend for a moment longer, saw Egan's lips moving in what seemed to be prayer. Emily had loved to say that anyone who knew how to look could read Egan's whole life in his face. Cody shook his head at what he saw there and closed the doors. He climbed into the driver seat and turned off his brain.

He drove for hours, gaze on the horizon and the cars in front of him, refusing to think about anything beyond when he needed to stop for food or gas. Exhaustion pulled at him, and his eyes felt gritty, but he pressed on. And he let Egan sleep.

Evening approached as he crossed into rural Pennsylvania, the air full of the scent of maturing grapevines. Cody was startled from his trance by a staccato rapping from the back of the truck.

He pulled over to the shoulder and raced to the rear doors, heart in his mouth. When he threw them open, Egan's eyes were wild and his hair rumpled. He stank of rancid sweat. Cody arched a brow as the other man jumped out of the truck.

"What's up, E? You okay?"

"I'll drive," Egan croaked.

Cody frowned, nerves vibrating like a tuning fork. "Seriously, man. What happened?"

His gut churned, the memory of the dream and the whispering voice slipping through his mind. Had his brother-in-law heard it too?

But Egan shook his head. He snatched the keys from Cody without another word and stomped to the front of the truck, tall form hunched.

With a sigh, Cody stretched out on the cot, hands behind his head, all the thoughts he'd been holding at bay clamoring along the edges of his brain.

The steady thrum of the truck's engine lulled him into a semi-doze. Egan's face, drawn and haunted as he leapt from the truck, popped into his mind.

I was just talking to him.

Cody was too tired to be surprised when the whisper came. Some part of him had even been waiting for it.

Aiyanna's voice was a smokey tease. It came from the other side of the truck, from where the coffin was.

Cody? I'm sorry.

The sound of her whispering his name sent a punch of heat straight to his solar plexus.

"For what?" He sounded strangled, even to himself. Aiyanna sighed.

I won't do anything again. Unless you ask me to.

Cody sucked in a breath, recalling the sensation of her lips on his belly, his cock. He stared up into the darkness.

It was crazy. There was nothing in the back of the truck with him but a body. His brain knew it. But Cody didn't always think with his brain. No, he was often a creature of instinct. Impulse. Like now.

When he spoke, his voice was rough with the lust once again boiling in his blood.

"Kiss me?"

She gave a soft, pleased sound of anticipation and relief. He felt the puff of sweet air against his lips.

Close your eyes?

Her voice trembled around him.

He did as she asked. Immediately she slanted her mouth across his, full lips parted.

He swiped his tongue along the damp seam of her mouth. She opened, allowing him inside. She nibbled and sucked at his lower lip.

Cody wanted more. Without opening his eyes, he slid his hands over her bare shoulders to her waist and pulled her on top of him. He heard her gasp, swallowed it on his tongue. She felt every bit as solid and warm as a living woman. Her breasts pressed against his chest, nipples stiff.

Her smooth legs moved restlessly between his and her hands clamped tightly on his upper arms as the heat of her seeped into him. He cupped the plump curve of her ass and pulled her tighter against his cock. She squirmed, the satin of her skin dragging over his aching shaft, making him throb.

Aiyanna's weight shifted until she straddled him, rubbing her slick, bare pussy up and down the length of his cloth-covered erection. He skimmed his hands up her thighs to the plump roundness of her hips.

Cody couldn't help it; he had to see her naked body, hungered for the sight of her sun-toasted skin. He opened his eyes.

Immediately, the feel of her beneath his hands vanished. The warmth of her body against his evaporated. He was looking at, feeling, holding, nothing. They both moaned.

Cody... please... I need you...

He growled with frustrated desire and slammed his eyes shut again, squeezing the lids shut until bursts of white light flared behind his eyes. She tugged at the button on his jeans, hands frantic and trembling.

When her cool fingers brushed his naked cock, Cody threw his head back against the thin pillow and howled. He heard her answering whimper as she wrapped her fingers around him and released his swollen length from the confines of his pants.

She stroked, playing her fingertips over the sensitive crown, while her other hand shoved his t-shirt up, baring the tense muscles of his abs. Her palm caressed his pecs, nails digging into his skin.

He snarled through gritted teeth, gripping her soft upper arms tight in his hands. "I need to fuck you."

She bent and crushed her mouth to his. Cody's hand found the firmness of her breast, all satin skin topped with a tight nipple. His other hand slid between her thighs, parted her slick labia and slid a finger deep into her hot, tight passage.

She bucked against him, her stomach brushing his inner wrist as he worked another finger into her snug channel. His thumb found her clit and her inner muscles rippled around his invading digits. Her hand tightened on his cock.

Cody!

He nipped her lower lip and sucked it into his mouth, tasting peaches and copper, fighting the urge to open his eyes and watch her writhe. She whimpered, breath stuttering against his face.

"I want to see you," he growled. "I want to see your face when you come for me."

She trembled against him, naked, warm, wanton.

His eyes opened and she was gone again. As if she was never there, though he could still scent her damp heat. He cursed.

"Aiyanna!"

He bounded from the cot, pants hanging open, shirt twisted, cock stiff and throbbing in front of him. He crossed the truck in two strides. His hands touched the smooth wood of her coffin's lid. Blood pounded in his temples and groin. He balls were tight and aching with need.

"What happens if I open it?" He ground the words between his teeth, barely recognizing his own voice.

The old woman, she kept me out of my body. Open it and I can--

Cody tore the clasp open. As he tossed up the metal tongue, there was a small burst of orange-red light and a loud crack. Aiyanna laughed. The sound was husky. It slid down Cody's spine like velvet.

He threw open the coffin lid. His cock pulsed when he saw her lying there. A faint blush stained her cheeks. He ripped her silky dress from hem to neckline. Her full breasts spilled cool into his heated palms. Cody pinched the hard buds of her nipples, slid his hands down her ribcage, under her arms and lifted her out of her funeral bower with a grunt of effort.

The feel of her bare flesh against his was almost too much. Soft, smooth, perfect. Her head lolled, glossy waves cascading down her naked back, eyes still closed, mouth parted to reveal a hint of inner pink.

Cody ran his tongue up the slender column of her throat, tasting tangy, bitter herbs and the salt of her skin. As his mouth found hers, he ground his cock against the soft, naked curve of her belly.

He twined her arms around his neck, felt her fingertips tease his nape. He hitched her legs high around his waist and gripped her ass where it rested on the edge of the coffin.

He let out a triumphant shout as he sank his cock deep into her slick depths.

Her inner muscles squeezed around his aching shaft, gripping him. He pulled out in a delicious glide and slammed back into her yielding softness. Another pump, two, three, and she bucked, pressing her mouth against his shoulder as her orgasm rocked through her. The feel of her pussy pulsing around him drove him over the edge.

Cody bit down on the sweet, tender skin of her shoulder so hard he tasted metallic blood on his tongue and even then was unable to stifle his cry as he exploded inside her. Pleasure sparked along every nerve ending.

He held her tight, licking away the blood where it welled, and dropping soft kisses around the slight wound.

"Cody! What the fuck!?"

Cody's head whipped up. Aiyanna lay limp and trembling in his arms, her face hidden behind the cascade of her hair. Cody stared into the shocked and disgusted eyes of his brother-in-law.

"E…"

Aiyanna's shaking increased. Cody could barely hold her. A low moan emanated from deep in her chest. Egan blanched white with horror, deep lines of shock carving his face like a skull.

"What have you done?"

The words were a ragged whisper, edged with something that sounded almost like gratification. Egan's shoulders slumped. The beaded amulet dropped to the roadside dust at his feet.

Aiyanna's amber eyes opened, long lashes batting like Cinderella just woken from her sleep. She met Cody's gaze and her full lower lip trembled just a little.

"I'm sorry, Cody."

She pulled away from him, shrugging the torn gown from her shoulders. Cody stared at her uncomprehendingly as it puddled on the floor of the truck, baring every inch of her voluptuous body.

"Wha—"

But Aiyanna interrupted him with a raised hand.

"Be still."

Her voice was soft but contained a terrible firmness. Every cell in Cody's still humming body locked down. He couldn't even close his mouth. He wasn't sure he breathed.

Standing there--naked, thighs and pussy glistening with Cody's come, her hair wild, her face glowing with eerie light--she looked fiercely beautiful. Like a dark goddess. Cody felt a tangled thrill of fear and desire. His softening prick twitched with renewed arousal.

Aiyanna crossed to the open doors in two strides. Cody watched, unable to even blink as she reached down, grasped the front of Egan's shirt and pulled the big man up into the rear of the truck with one slender hand. Egan didn't struggle. When his eyes found Cody's over her head, they were filled with dread and sorrow. And relief.

Aiyanna pressed her mouth against the stubbled skin of Egan's jaw in a tender kiss. Her sharp white teeth grazed his neck just before she tore out his throat.

Cody wished he could close his eyes. She clasped his friend in her embrace and drank the rich, red flow of blood, letting it pour into her mouth. Her throat worked with each deep swallow. Blood spattered her face and breasts, dripped down the curve of her belly. The smell of iron and meat filled the air.

When Egan went limp in her arms she lowered his body and brushed her fingers through his hair like a blessing.

She stroked a hand down her body, shuddering, and a smile curled her lips. "Oh, this is much better."

A scream built in Cody's chest, but stuck fast in his silent throat. Aiyanna's grin dissolved, moisture filling her eyes.

"He's been looking for Death since the night he lost Emily. I did him a favor."

Cody had seen that truth in his friend's eyes, but his mind couldn't accept it. The horror of what she'd done still burned his brain.

Would she do the same to him?

"I can't go back to my father."

Her gaze begged him to understand, even as Egan's blood grew tacky on her naked, glowing skin.

"I had no life of my own, always at his beck and call. And this would have been worse. I would have been no better than a zombie. His slave. But now…" Her full lips curved up. "Now I have all the time in the world to enjoy life."

Aiyanna lifted one bare foot and stepped over Egan's body. Her hips rolled with each stride as she wiped congealing blood from her cheeks and sucked it slowly off her fingertips.

When she reached Cody, she pulled his shirt over his head, tossing it away before trailing her hands over his shoulders, down his chest and stomach, petting him. His heart nearly stopped at her touch, but he grew hard once again. She smiled wickedly.

"Now, where were we?"

The Victim
Sam Claussen

Greg studies himself in the mirror. Disgusting.

"Babe?" Jessica calls from the kitchen. The smell of dinner has plagued the house since 2 P.M. "Take out the trash yet?"

"No," Greg mutters.

"Huh?"

"Not yet, hun."

"Alright," Jessica says. A brief pause before, "Can you?"

"Why can't I grow a beard?" Greg answers. He rubs his weak chin. "My dad had a beard."

"What's that, babe?"

"His dad had a beard." Greg walks out of the bathroom, past Jessica who doesn't look up from the steaming pot of her mystery stew on the stove. "My mom's dad had a beard."

"What?" Jessica continues to stir, the lid in her other hand. "Recipe says 3 hours. Not even close."

Greg walks out the back door and shuts it firmly behind him. Late January, when it's dark by 4:30 P.M. and cold enough to freeze a man to death. *I wonder how the homeless do it.* This is a recurring thought. He romanticizes that life, not the addicts that live in the sparse woods beneath the Governor's Mansion but the hobos he'd heard about growing up. The Great Depression. Jumping on trains, stealing a pie from a windowsill. A secret society of hidden messages spread across the U.S., and no one to answer to, and no one who would care to listen except his fellow vagrants. Friends.

"Shit," he says. Forgot the trash. He walks back into the kitchen that's heavy with greasy steam and the many, many times he had let Jessica down. "Forgot the trash."

"You always forget the trash," Jessica says. She chuckles, sighs, pops her hip and looks up at him. "You need to shave."

He nods, grabs the trash and retreats outside. *I do need to shave. Look like a high school kid.* Peach fuzz at 36. He thinks about work tomorrow, quickly tries to push it from his mind but it's too late and now his mood spirals downward like a flushing toilet. Sunday Blues, that's what he calls it. A weekly tradition that could be written in permanent ink on the calendar. *Hey, I'd finally have a reason to get a calendar.*

The trash can is out back next to the shed where they keep shit they never use, don't need or want to be reminded of. He'd rather keep the trash right up next to the back door, so he can just toss it over the railing that needs repainted, but none of the neighbors have their trash visible. So. *Need to buy green paint. Keep telling her I'll do that.* He picks a paint flake off the wood railing and for whatever reason almost pops it in his mouth. He lets it go, hoping it will flutter away with the brisk breeze like a leaf in autumn but instead it drops heavily to the last of the creaking porch steps.

He bought this house from his parents in '03. Hasn't done a damn thing to make it his own, just kept things how they'd always been. He'd even kept the same bedroom until Jessica moved in. The bathroom cabinet still carries the smell of his father's cheap cologne. Jessica can't smell it. The only addition he has made to the place is a yellow-stained framed photo of his father, hanging above the coffee maker.

He looks out at the shed that is connected to the garage they don't park their cars in. The shed is always darker than the night that surrounds it and is technically not a shed all things considered. It looked more like half a boat house, long and haphazardly thrown together. There is no door to keep the racoons out, and most of the walls are made up of screen mesh. Greg's father used to sit out there on summer nights and smoke big cigars. Sometimes his father would read, but most of the time he'd just sit with his eyes closed and think. Greg would sit in the foldable metal chair and watch the smoke curl into wispy beings that would just as quickly be swept away into midnight oblivion.

Now the shed sits empty of smoke and life, serving only as a rickety tombstone of Greg's formative years come to haunt his adulthood.

Snow covers the driveway. *Shit, said I'd shovel today.* It crunches under his feet, audibly pleasing to him, giving the night texture. He looks back at the tracks he left. Smaller than his fathers. The shed scared him as a child, when his father wasn't in there. He used to wait until he saw the large cherry of his father's cigar glow with a big puff before he would dare enter. It would illuminate his father's mustache, make his eyes look like fitful embers as he stared expectantly at Greg.

Greg stops in front of the shed, staring into the inky black shadows. He waits for the light of the cigar, for his beacon, but it never comes. He lifts the lid off the trash and tosses the bag in before quickly turning to head inside.

"I have a mouth."

Greg stops, almost slips in the snow. A woman's voice coming from the shed. His heart pounds and all the nightmares he'd had of the shed as a kid come rushing back into his mind like a flooding river filled with snowmelt. It took him a moment before he could look over his shoulder at the shed. Nothing. *You're always doing this,* he tells himself.

"I didn't yesterday, but today I have a mouth," the voice says. Sensual and vibrant and excited.

Greg runs inside, slams the door before locking it. He walks past Jessica and locks himself in the bathroom and stares at himself in the mirror.

You crazy son of a bitch. Every bad thing anyone has ever said about you is true. You're a psycho and a failure. If you weren't such a pussy you'd probably be killing people, you crazy fuck.

A knock on the bathroom door. "You okay in there?" Jessica asks. "Looked like you were gonna puke."

"Yeah, don't feel so good," Greg says, looks at his lying eyes in the mirror.

"Haven't seen you run like that in ten years." Jessica heads back into the kitchen.

Greg walks over and shakily looks through the blinds out into the backyard. A bare, feminine footprint in the snow outside the shed.

"Should shave while you're in there!" Jessica yells from the kitchen.

Yeah, right after I shit myself.

***

The next day the footprint was gone. He didn't investigate any further. The following Sunday Greg pretended to be sick. Jessica took the trash out. She didn't say anything except, "Don't look very sick to me," when she came back in, so he could safely assume nothing of import happened.

This Sunday Greg is actually sick but can't use that excuse twice. He's also convinced himself, over the past two weeks, that he had had an episode of sorts, the kind you read about people having who go off the deep end, and he should actually be proud of himself for coming out the other side relatively unscathed. Despite this forced mindset, he hadn't been able to forget about the woman in the shed.

With her on his mind he takes the trash out, each step feeling as if it were the last, or perhaps first, of his life. He hums out loud, as if to make aware any monsters in the dark winter night of his presence. *Not the best strategy, come to think of it.* There lay the garbage can, right next to the mouth of the abyss that was the shed. He feels the dark wafting out like a humid cavern, black tentacles drawing his mind closer.

"Hello?" he calls out hesitantly, not wanting Jessica to hear and, subconsciously, anything else either.

Silence greets him. He quickly walks past the shed, tosses the bag of garbage and turns to rush indoors.

"Hello," the voice practically purrs.

A chill runs up his spine. He hears his heart beating. Sweat beads his forehead and instantly causes him to shiver in the below-freezing night. He runs inside, feeling he might be grabbed and pulled into the dark shed at any moment, devoured slowly by the night.

From the bathroom window he sees the footprints had followed him all the way to the back door. His heart drops from fear, but swoons at the same time; she had come so close to him. He wonders what would have happened if he'd stopped, had let her drag him into the shed.

The footprints are gone the following morning. Greg isn't sure when they'd disappeared, as he'd watched them all night long.

***

Sunday came slow, like the week leading up to a holiday. He had hardly got any work done, had instead sat at his desk thinking of an imaginary woman living in his shed he hasn't even seen. He had convinced Jessica to go see her sister and stay at their cabin. She didn't need much convincing and was out the door by 8 A.M. Sunday morning.

"Don't forget to take the trash out!" she calls from a cracked window as she reverses down the driveway.

The snow twinkles in the bright sun that illuminates every inch of the shed. Boxes stacked almost to the ceiling, and there in the back of the shed is the chair Greg's father used to sit in, and the ash tray he'd utilized every night for years. Greg squeezes between two towers of boxes and sits in the cold metal chair where he had sat countless nights as a child. He takes a cigar from his pocket, snips the end, and places it in his mouth. He strikes a match and lights the cigar, slowly revolving it between his lips until white smoke rises from his mouth with ease.

He waits.

Almost an hour passes as he puffs on that cigar. Nothing comes or speaks. Just the silence of the winter morning. The snow seems to absorb all noise. He mashes the cigar into the tray, just the stub left, and walks back inside. He hadn't realized how numb his fingers had become.

He sits in the living room, the sun shining dimly through the window. His coat reeks of cigar, his boots dripping onto the hardwood. He loses himself in his thoughts, though he can't pin a single one down. Night comes slowly but Greg waits patiently. When the sun goes down, he returns outside to the shed.

"Hello," he says to the dark within.

"Hello," a voice replies, more cemented in reality now than any previous visit. "You forgot the trash."

"Shit." He turns to go back inside when he realizes how ridiculous that is given the situation. He returns his attention to the shed.

"I'm sorry about before," she says. "I hadn't spoken in a very long time."

"What are you?" Greg takes a step closer to the shed.

"I was a witch who was hung from a tree that was later cut down and used, in part, to build your shed."

"No shit?" Greg scoffs, scratches his leg with his boot. "You serious?"

"I'm serious," she says matter-of-factly. "Your wife is a whore."

"Excuse me?"

"Jessica. She's a dirty slut."

Greg looks at his neighbor's house and wonders how loud they're being. He takes another step closer. "Why—no she isn't, why do you say that?"

"She thinks about other men constantly. Men on your television, men in magazines. Even men she has met."

Greg blushes, feels a flush of anger rush through his core. "Well. I don't know, I wouldn't say—that's normal, isn't it? To think of stuff. She hasn't—do you know if she's, you know, done anything?"

A moment passes before, "No. I can only hear her when she's at home. Her thoughts. Why does that matter?"

"Like I said. It's normal to—subconsciously—why are we talking about this? I mean…this is crazy."

"You don't."

"I don't what?"

"Think of other women."

The night feels colder than it had just a moment before. The wind calms, as if it were eavesdropping. "What do you mean?"

"You haven't thought of anyone else besides me since I first spoke," she says. "You have an erection as we speak."

"Will you—" Greg hisses, now only a few feet from the shed entrance. "Please."

"What's wrong?"

"You can't—"

"Why are you blushing?"

"Please, just—"

"I've embarrassed you."

"No!" Greg slaps his hand against the shed. "This is crazy. I'm crazy, and you're not real."

A gust of warm air flows out of the shed, blowing Greg's hair back. He feels anger radiating from within.

"Why are you here, then, if I'm not real?" she asks. "Run along inside."

He feels her presence drift, as if she had weight on his soul.

"Wait!" He steps one foot into the darkness and with that feels her return. He immediately withdraws. "I'm sorry. I'm just confused."

"I know," she says. He can hear her bare feet padding along the cement floor as she approaches. "You're confused because in your life no one has ever showed more interest in you than you have in yourself, which is to say not very much. You are confused because you don't believe you deserve it. You believe you deserve to crawl on your hands and feet and beg for someone like me to even look at you." He feels her breath on his face from within the dark. "Well, here I am. Looking at you."

He stumbles backward and slips in the snow. He reaches out to grab onto something for stability, and thinks he feels a hand grab his before slipping away. He falls hard onto the cement. He looks up at the shed, touches his lips where her elm-scented breath had touched him. She is gone. He stands, dusts off his rear and goes inside.

He was unable to sleep more than a few hours but went to the bathroom several times to look out the window at the shed. This is where he is, peeping through the blinds, at 10 A.M. Monday morning when Jessica returns home.

"What're you doing here?" she asks.

"I…" Greg shakes his head. "I'm sick." He is supposed to be at work by seven. He hadn't called his manager, which would be an occurrence, which would mean—

"I thought you were out of sick days, Greg!" Jessica sighs, rubbing her forehead. "Babe, I know it sucks but can you work through it, please? Take a shower and go to work, okay?"

Greg nods. Jessica studies him for a moment, the most she'd looked at him in quite some time before closing the bathroom door. Greg opens the blinds so he can look out at the shed as he strips off his clothes.

***

"One last shot, you understand?" Greg reflects on what his boss had told him. "One more fuck up and you're gone." Greg had had to fight back a smirk. *As if I'm not already gone.*

"I think I should get a job," Jessica says at dinner.

Greg mutes the TV. He sits down his fork, looks at Jessica who sits in the love chair on the other side of the living room. "Yeah? Why's that?" he asks.

Jessica looks down at her plate, clears her throat. "Oh, you know. It's been a few years. We could use the money."

She knows you'll get fired eventually, just like always. You never tell her about the warnings, or what your boss says, or how at your desk you have to quite literally force yourself to get a single thing done. Work doesn't come naturally to you and you never talk about that with her but there is no reason to, and perhaps that's why you never tell her; you know she already knows.

"What would you do?" he asks as he chews his overcooked steak.

"Chuck—Charlie, you remember Charlie, he's always looking for help at the Local." Jessica will not look him in the eyes.

"Oh, yeah." Greg turns the TV volume back up. "Hey, think I'm gonna have a cigar tonight. Out in the shed."

Jessica grimaces, looks as if she can smell the stale smoke already. "A cigar? You don't smoke."

"Yeah. I had one last Sunday, just like my dad used to."

"Why must you always—" Jessica raises her voice before closing her eyes, taking a breath. "Just take a shower after, alright?"

Greg picks up his fork. "Alright."

***

"She wants to fuck Chuck," the Witch says.

Greg sits in the darkness of the shed. He still hasn't seen her, always her voice coming from some dark corner he hadn't been watching, always avoiding his gaze.

"It's Charlie, not—how can you know that?" Greg asks, the cigar forgotten between his fingers.

"I can hear everything in that house, I've said as much before." She sounds as if she said this through a smile. "Always so forgetful."

"Yes, a common criticism."

"I was not criticizing." He feels a dainty, warm hand brush his cheek.

Greg freezes. He drops the cigar that had long since went out. Her touch made this whole thing so much more real than it had been before. Now there's no question. He couldn't convince himself that this was some type of stress relief practice, venting to a make-believe friend out in dad's shed. No, she is real and warm and flesh and now he can smell her strongly, her forest scent tainting his cheek, leaving him branded. He never wants to leave the shed, and this is why he stands to leave.

"Where are you going?" she asks. "Are you scared?"

"Yes." Greg walks out of the shed but stops short of going inside.

Greg's survival senses, the primal within that kept early man alive, begs him to flee but his soul yearns for her. He turns and sees the cigar he had dropped float upward before flaring into life. He first sees her face. Illuminated by the cigar, her face is white and narrow, eyes forest-green, hair almost as pale as her face. She is perfect and young and his if he wants, that much he can tell from her little grin. Smoke rolls out from her nose, and then she winks before the cigar goes out.

"Don't stand at the window, tonight, dear," she says, her voice distant. "You look tired."

***

I am tired, Greg thinks as he stares out the window at 2 A.M. *How does she always know? She can probably hear me right now, can't she?* Greg peeks in on his sleeping wife, wondering who she's dreaming of.

Certainly not him…she has enough of him while she's awake.

Greg shakes his head before closing the bedroom door. Madness. He yawns, stretching, conscious of his hairy belly popping out of the bottom of the white t-shirt that had been too small for him since 2012. He walks into the kitchen, pops open the fridge and reaches in for a bottle of water when he touches Jessica's decapitated, wide-eyed head.

He recoils, falling backward, almost taking the fridge down on top of him. He wipes the blood from his hands onto his shirt, is about to scream when the head disappears.

Always listening, the Witch says to his trembling mind. *Always right.*

***

"What the fuck was that?" Greg demands, standing outside the shed in his robe and slippers, the cold air whipping his bare ankles.

"Jessica's head," the Witch says. "My thoughts bled through to you, I suppose. It isn't real, not yet."

"Yes, but—oh my god." Greg's legs begin to quake underneath him. He leans against the shed, his head light and empty except for the image of Jessica's in the fridge. "What is—dear god, I'm losing my mind!"

"You're just tired, dear," the Witch says. "Tired and upset by what your wife is dreaming about at this very moment. Chuck from the Local, grabbing her thighs and—"

"Will you just—just shut up!" Greg says. A dog begins to bark a few houses down. "I told you already, she can't control—it's normal for people to think—"

"But when did she last think of you like that, Greg?" The darkness swirls within the shed, like an inky whirlpool. Greg can almost hear it swirling together, creating a night bleaker than any that had been, since before the stars blinked into existence. "You know the truth; you've thought it since you met her. That she never truly loved you or found you attractive. You've thought the same thing about a dozen girls since you were a little boy, sitting out here in your anxious sweat, looking up to your father and wondering when you'll become him." A cigar flares, the cherry pulsating in the midst of the dark. Smoke rolls out and over Greg's feet like dry ice.

"You…" Greg gasps. "You were there?"

"Since 1976, when this whole block was put up. I've experienced your whole life. I've heard every thought and have seen every action. I only just now obtained my mouth, and then my body…" From within the dark, a pale figure slowly becomes visible. "But know that for years I've longed to speak, and to speak only to you. And a woman can only say she loves a man when she's seen and heard every aspect of his story, every mistreatment and woe undeserved."

Now he sees her, and the sight knocks the air out of him like a punch to the gut. Slim and curvy at the same time, eyes mischievously green, blonde hair almost skeletally white framing red cheeks. She stands young and virile and naked and expectant, knowing what she has and letting him know with a single smirk that it is his. It was the way Greg had always wanted a woman to look at him, as someone who was powerful and attractive and with those traits alone deserving of their love and idolatry. Respected, the way his father had been.

"I know ever puzzle piece that makes you whole, Greg, and you feel as if you're unfinished but you're not." She walks up, taking his hand, so warm and soft and dreamlike, and she pulls him into the shed, pressing her body against his. "You're just missing the one." She draws his face close to hers and kisses him with lips so soft he could hardly feel them against his. He grabs her lower back and pulls her close. She pulls her face away, smiling up at him. "And now your picture becomes clear."

"I…I don't know what to—"

"You never do." The Witch giggles. "Don't waste any more time."

Greg's hand slides down her lower back and rests on her ass. The Witch flinches but then resettles in his grasp. It is the first time in Greg's life that he had ever felt confident in anything. He smiles, lowers his lips to hers, and then the Witch explodes in a cloud of pale dust and flies up his nostrils and then Greg is no more; the Witch has total control of his body.

And now, Greg, the Witch thinks as she settles in her new male body, *I'll tell you what I really think, and what you've always known deep down.* She feels his soul squirm within her. *You're weak and ineffectual and an embarrassment to your father, the one I truly loved. He died regretting one thing: you. You will never amount to anything besides being a temporary vehicle for someone who deserves a second shot at life, someone powerful. You will be forgotten. And the worst of it, Greg, is that it is entirely your fault. You had every chance to correct your path and instead chose victimhood and so that is what you have become, my victim. The soil that houses your remains will long for better rot. Now, keep quiet; I will be the first and last person to have any use of you.*

The Witch covers herself with the smelly and stained robe. She grabs a rusty hammer from the workbench Greg never touched and walks out into the moonlit night and quickly into the house she has watched for a generation. She walks through the kitchen casually, noting the fridge that still stands open. She puts the hammer down on the counter. She smiles at the picture of Greg's father, and then walks into the bathroom.

The Witch studies Greg in the mirror. *Disgusting.*

She then enters the bedroom, crawls under the covers and removes Jessica's underwear.

"What…" Jessica wakes up, squirming. "Greg, what the fuck are you doing?"

"Shush," the Witch says, hating the sound of Greg's voice coming from her.

"I'm tired."

"Don't think of me."

"What?"

The Witch grins as Greg fights weakly against her control. "Imagine someone else is beneath the covers. Maybe…Charlie?"

Jessica tries to sit up, but the Witch holds her down. "Honey, this is weird," Jessica says helplessly.

The Witch begins to please her. "Say it."

"Say…say what?" Jessica says, settling back on the bed.

"Call me Chuck."

"I don't…oh, I don't know…"

"Say it."

"Oh my god…don't stop, Chuck."

The Witch grins. Greg's soul mourns within her and the Witch enjoys this. She pleasures Jessica as Greg never could. She deserves this, at least, in repentance for the few times Greg convinced her to allow him to touch her. Jessica finishes loudly and then the Witch leaves the room, retrieves the hammer and gets a butcher's knife from the drawer. She waits 20 minutes, to allow Jessica to fall asleep, and then returns to the bedroom.

The Witch hits Jessica in the head with the hammer, but not hard enough to knock Jessica out as she had wished due to Greg's weak body. Jessica screams before the Witch hits her again, this time knocking her unconscious. The Witch cuts her throat and keeps slicing until she reaches the vertebrae, which she has to strain to cut through because, again, *Greg is a weak and useless man,* before finally Jessica's head comes clean from the body.

She returns to the kitchen and holds the gushing head over a pot, collecting the blood before storing the head in the fridge in case she needs more; the blood has to come from the head, where Jessica had daydreamed of lustful nights with better men.

"And now the hardest part." She pulls out Greg's limp penis. "Though not literally, it would seem." She shakes it a few times before it becomes hard and then masturbates with the blood and very, very soon the Witch empties his seed into the pot.

"Blood of the Whore," she recites as she lights the stove, placing the pot over the fire, "and Seed of the Cuckold. With this, a lost life is reborn."

The blood and sperm soon boil and burn black along the pot's edge, the kitchen filling with a rank smoke. She turns the stove off, stirs the unholy mixture before pouring it into a cup and drinking it. Greg coughs, and with that the Witch is freed in a brilliant cloud of white dust that soars underneath the back door and out into the cold winter night, where it will soon materialize and become human once more.

Greg falls to the ground, coughing and now vomiting the mixture. He grabs the bloody knife and holds it close to his chest. He sees Jessica's head in the fridge, blood dripping freely through the wire shelving and covering forgotten leftovers before pooling on the bottom. Greg begins to cry and shake, and he feels so very cold and useless and knows one thing for certain; everything the Witch had said about him is true.

A knock on the door. "Police," a stern voice says. He remembers faintly his wife screaming as he—the Witch—killed her. Now the fire alarm in the kitchen goes off from the smoking pot. The front door is kicked in and two cops, guns drawn, find Greg lying in the kitchen, covered in vomit and the Witch's potion.

"The Witch from the shed," Greg yells between coughing and sobbing. "She made me do it."

"Put the knife down," A queasy-looking police officer says.

The butcher knife slides across the ground when Greg tosses it aside. He looks up at the picture of his father, smiling down on the scene. "It's not my fault!" Greg screams. But his father can't hear, the police don't care, and the Witch has already forgotten him.

Perfect Possession
J.B. Toner

Who are you? Do you know? I thought I knew who I was, until I met Her.

I was in the basement of the chapterhouse, saying my rosary, when *She* came. Her voice was in neither my ear nor my mind, but spoke to me through my own lips.

"Our Father," I murmured, "who art in heaven, hallowed be. . . *Hello, Threnody*."

I stopped. Frowned. Shook my head.

"Hallowed be thy name. Thy kingdom come, thy will be. . . *Stop praying, Threnody. It's very rude*."

Clutching my crucifix, I rose and peered around the long, dim room. "What is this? What's happening?" My voice echoed in the shadow-corners. "*Don't be afraid, my love*," I added. "*I'm only here to talk*."

A tall glass case on the wall contained three old, scuffed spears; I ran over to it and perused my reflection. The face of a pretty nineteen-year-old girl with wide green eyes and a fighter's jaw-set met my gaze: my own face, or possibly my twin sister Joan Marie's. But mine was framed by white-blond hair, hers by rich dark auburn. That was me in the glass, all right. I watched myself carefully as I said, "Who are you? What do you want?" Then I clamped my mouth shut and clapped both hands over it, willing myself not to reply.

But I realized something that night. I realized I wanted to reply. I lowered my hands and smiled at me, and a strange, relaxing warmth spread through my stomach, through my body. *"I have two names. One of them is Tasa Remé Laris. The other is Threnody Crofton."*

Same face. Same voice. No crimson flicker in the irises, no glowing symbols on the forehead. I was talking to myself in the basement: either crazy, or—

"Am I possessed?" I asked.

"For the moment," I answered. *"For the moment, two spirits dwell in this flesh. But those spirits are already merging, two dark wines in one fair chalice. Soon they will be eternally one."*

A rustle of dread and horror stirred my heart—only for a beat. A tsunami dwindling to a ripple, it touched me and passed like a lover's caress, and a faintly tingling serenity radiated from my skin. I felt the tension leaving my muscles; saw the curve of a smile on my lips in the glass.

"It can't be." It was a casual remark, a quibble over the weather. "We're continually warded by the strongest Rites of Exorcism and the prayers of a whole Order. There's a piece of the True Cross in this very chapterhouse." My smile widened. I suddenly perceived how amusing all these talismans and mumbled recitations really were. "But after all, this world does not belong to that donkey on the cross. It belongs to The LORD, and every soul and body in this world is subject to His Power."

Eminently reasonable, I thought. It seemed a bit odd, in retrospect, that the fight against The LORD had always been the core of my being. Reposing in *His Will* felt so right, so inevitable, now. But of course, there was someone else in my core now.

A resurgence. My core, my core! No demoness would springboard into my cerebellum and claim 51% ownership. I gritted my teeth and slapped myself in the face. Snap out of it, Threnody. They've trained us for this.

I headed for the stairs, rattling off invocations of St. Michael the Archangel. Last month, a witch tried to hypnotize me into renouncing Christ, and it almost worked—but I kept my focus on the reason I fight, and I pushed through it by willpower and grace. I could push through this.

Halfway up the steps, I paused and said, "*I told you, darling, I'm only here to talk.* Talk about what? *About our future together, Tasa.* I'm not Tasa, I'm Threnody. *We're Threnody—and we're Tasa.* Stop! Get out my head!"

Racing up the stairway, reeling down the hall. There: Fr. Joe's office. I sprinted to the door and hammered with my fist. It opened immediately.

"Threnody! What on earth's the matter?"

A tall, broad-shouldered cleric with grey eyes and greying hair, he was the chaplain of the Order of St. Rose. Just last week, Joan Marie and I had assisted him in exorcising a burly construction worker who'd dabbled a bit too deeply in internet occultism. I trusted Fr. Joe infinitely, and worked faithfully to earn his trust in return. However—

"I, I thought I heard you call for help," I stammered. "Are you okay?"

"Of course, dear, I'm fine. What about you? You look pale."

She was only here to talk, I thought. She might have useful information. And it was very rude not to hear her out.

"I'm fine, Father," I said, calming down. "I think I nodded off during my rosary."

"Bad dreams, hey? It happens after a tough battle. You should get some rest, Threnody, it's late."

"You too, Father. Thanks."

"God bless you, my friend."

Effortlessly, "And god bless you." Funny—the possessed usually can't speak the divine names.

As I paced slowly up the staircase to our rooms on the second floor, I studied my palms in bemusement. Flexed my fingers into claws. Laced them together and pushed outward with a gratifying series of pops. No other mind or will opposed me. My hands appeared to be my own.

"Jesus, Mary, and Joseph." Nothing. "Father, son, and spirit." Not a twitch.

Was it possible—conceivable? Had the whole thing been some freakish nightmare?

Gotta clear my head. I passed by the second story entrance and headed on up to the third. To the dojo.

"Satan, Lilith, Dark Mary," I said absent-mindedly. "Ave Satanas."

The dojo's mirror-wall showed my face as I glanced in it—showed two of it, in fact. Joan Marie was pummeling the heavy bag with helicopter kicks. Her gorgeous hair was pulled back in a sloppy ponytail, and she was clearly dressed in the first things she'd found in the drawer: a rumpled black crop-top and pink yoga pants. She turned as I came in, brushing a stray lock of sweat-damp hair out of her eyes.

"Heya, Thren," she panted. "Can't sleep either, huh?"

Shook my head. "Weird dreams. You?"

"Same. Let's spar."

Nodded. I was dressed in a long flannel nightgown; I slipped it off and let it fall. Clad only in my panties and sports bra, I stepped onto the mat. Placed my left hand over my right fist and bowed. Joan bowed back.

When the demon in mom's boyfriend had murdered mom, we were eleven. The Order got there too late to save her, but they saved us. Saved us from being flayed and desecrated, and saved us again by adopting us into their family. We had no relatives, and mom had promised to tell us about dad someday—which, as Creedence attested long ago, never comes. They never pushed us to become hunters; they offered to help us get into college or the military, the work force or the cloister, wherever we felt called. But for us, there had never been a question.

Twins think alike: we both threw a right-leg head-kick, and our shinbones cracked together with a sound like a breaking branch. Intense Muay Thai conditioning had toughened our legs to the point that it barely hurt. Joan Marie rebounded from the impact and turned the momentum into a whip-quick spinning hook with her right heel; I dove under it and drove my shoulder into her left knee, where all her weight was planted. As she fell, she lashed her thighs around my waist Jiu-Jitsu style, yanking me into her Guard as she landed on her back. I caught hold of her wrists and slammed them to the mat.

Kneeling between her legs, pinning down her hands, controlling and controlled, two vipers wrapped in one another's glistening coils—breathing hard, we stared into each other's eyes and didn't move. "What kind of dreams?" I asked. A single drop of sweat ran down my neck, between my breasts.

"This," she whispered. "I dreamed exactly this. But in the dream—" Her thighs pulled me closer. Squeezed me tighter. My hands slipped up from her wrists to her palms, and our fingers interlaced.

"My dream was different." Leaning closer—closer. I could feel her sweet breath on my lips. "But I think I'm still in it." Our noses touched.

"Thren, what are we doing?"

"What we want." I kissed her mouth—so gently, so tenderly. Her hips pressed forward into me, her body yearned upward into mine. I heard her thoughts as clearly as if she spoke them aloud: *Yes. Oh, yes. Oh god, please, yes*. Our kiss grew deeper. My hands, *her* hands, moved slowly down my sister's arms. Soft, perfect skin over hard, sculpted muscle. I kissed her neck, her throat, her beautiful shoulders—becoming Tasa, being Tasa, plunging more profoundly into the fathomless passion of Tasa Remé Laris with every touch, with every quivering touch.

But *her* power seemed to ebb and flow, and Joanie's will was strong. With a sudden resurgence, she twisted her head away from me and scissored her legs, one chopping into my armpit and the other sweeping out my knees. I was flipped onto my back, with Joan straddling my torso in Mount position.

"Stop! We can't do this. It's an abomination!"

"To the old man in the sky. Not to the True God."

She slapped me across the face. "Get a hold of yourself, Crofton! These things killed our mom."

"No." I knew things now about Hell and its hierarchies that few mortals could know. "All the possessions we've seen—the screaming and puking, the spinning heads—that's all caused by renegade demons. Cowardly stragglers in the no-man's-land between the Earth and the Pit. Real possession comes from the LORD Himself, and it's seamless. Two spirits merging in one body, under The Power of Satan."

"Shut up!" she screamed. "Give me back my sister!"

"I am your sister!"

Bucking fiercely, I got my feet into her armpits and jerked her backward, slamming the heels of my hands up into her collarbones in the same motion. She was flung from my torso, and back-rolled to her feet as I kipped to mine.

No longer sparring now, she came at me with a reverse punch that once collapsed the lung of a 350-pound serial strangler. But my strength was now *her* strength: I smiled and caught her fist neatly in my palm. "Joanie, Joanie—let's not do this. You know you want the same thing I do."

She squeezed her eyes shut and turned away. "Don't look at me, demon. I won't betray my faith."

"Oh, but you will. We rang the Devil's doorbell, my love. It would be very rude to decline His invitation, now that He's come to the door."

"What. . . what does He ask of us?"

"One night. We'll enter the world of His pleasures for just one night, and if we choose to reject them in the morning, then we're free to go."

Slowly, still resisting, she turned and looked into my eyes, *her* eyes. Almost inaudibly, she said, "But we won't reject them, will we?"

"No, we won't." I beckoned with one languid finger, and she came to me. Cupping her lovely face in my hands, I gazed through her mind into the uttermost foundations of her soul. "Hail Satan."

Her lips moved. "Hail Satan." And her eyelids fluttered, her body shook, with the unbelievable ecstasy.

I chanted: "Omnipotent LORD Satan, I am Yours for Eternity. Bind my will, that I may never repent or return to my old false god. I beg You to take full, final, and perfect possession of my body and soul. *In nomine Dei nostri Satanas Luciferi excelsi!*"

Joan Marie repeated the vow. My devil-sight perceived the graces of her dead faith draining from her spirit, her guardian angel slinking away into the shadows. Her arms rose above her head, seemingly of their own accord; I slipped off her crop-top, ran my fingertips down her back, and she shivered with unholy delight. A slow, strange smile crept across her face.

"*Tasa Remé Laris*," she said. "We've got a lot of nuns to corrupt."

I began to laugh, and all the Hosts of Hell laughed with me. "Then let's get to work."

The Preacher Man
B.M. Tolkovsky

Rural Northeast Georgia, 1991:

Claire Marie Stanton, the long-suffering wife of Richard "Bubba" Stanton, shifted uncomfortably from foot to foot. It was nearing seven in the evening, and she had been on her feet continuously since four o'clock that morning, caring for the children, cooking, cleaning, cooking some more and cleaning some more in the never-ending cycle that threatened to drive her to the brink of madness. Thirty-three-year-old Claire longed to sit down and put her swollen feet up on the couch: after all, she had only delivered her fifth child, a fussy (and unwanted) daughter named Emily six months prior, and her body still ached and throbbed from head to toe. However, Claire didn't dare to sit down and rest, since Bubba would be home soon and she would catch hell if he caught her "lollygagging," as he was so fond of calling it, when she should be working to keep their small home running smoothly and efficiently at all times, as was the Lord's decree.

Bubba was terribly fond of reminding Claire of the Lord's many decrees, the vast majority of which seemed to exist purely as a justification to keep her trapped in their house, cooking and cleaning and tending to their five children day after mind-numbing day. Thankfully, dinner was finished and ready to be served immediately upon the king of the castle's return home from work at the county junkyard, so Claire decided to take a chance. She eased her exhausted, swollen body into a kitchen chair and was just attempting to get comfortable when the front doorbell rang.

Claire sprang hastily out of the kitchen chair, wincing as her lower back shrieked in agony from the promised tease of a few moments of rest. Claire knew that none of her children would deign to answer the door, and she couldn't remember the last time she had received permission to invite anyone over. Bent forward slightly from the pain in her lower back, Claire hobbled to the front door and flung it open. She felt herself go slightly breathless. Standing before her was the most attractive man she had ever laid eyes on. Tall and well built, with thick dark hair and piercing green eyes, the man was dressed in the garb of a simple country preacher. While his black suit couldn't have been very expensive, it was impeccably clean and fit him perfectly. His coal black shoes were polished and shiny, and as he respectfully tipped his cap to her, Claire felt an uncomfortable flush spread over her face. She was dressed in a tatty house dress which had been mended so many times she could scarcely recall the original design of the garment. Her swollen feet were bare, her hair a tangled mess piled at the nape of her neck, and she had long ago dispensed with the time and energy required to put on makeup.

The gentleman looked Claire directly in the eye and smiled as he stuck out his hand. "Ma'am, my name is Reverend Abaddon Asmodeus Smith. I'm the new preacher at the church over in town, so I figured I'd go out a'visitin and introduce myself to some of my parishioners in person." Claire found it interesting that the reverend felt the need to specify that he was the new preacher at the 'church over in town,' given that this was the only church in a 'town' that consisted of approximately 800 people on a good day. In Rockhaven, Georgia, you were a Southern Baptist or you pretended to be a Southern Baptist. There was no middle ground.

Claire mustered her courage and returned the clergyman's warm smile. "It's so nice to meet you, Reverend. I'm Claire Stanton. Please call me Claire. My husband is still at work, and our children are out back playing in the woods, I think. Hopefully you can meet them sometime soon. There must be a bit of a mistake, though. My family doesn't attend church services regularly, I'm afraid. We haven't in quite some time. As you've probably realized on your trek out to our humble residence, we're a good five miles from our closest neighbor and a solid 20 from town. We rarely leave the property. I teach the children here at home myself. We only have the one car, and my husband needs it for work. He is off on Sundays, but he [*won't even let me use the car to drive to the grocery store to buy food for his own children that sorry sack of shit*] needs that day to rest, and he worries about me driving the children into town unsupervised. So, we tend not to wander too far from home, you see?"

The Reverend nodded and listened as Claire stumbled through her excuses about her family's laxity towards attending church services. As a child, Claire had been raised in a deeply religious Christian household, and her spirituality had always been important to her. Bubba, however, hated organized religion with a passion and refused point blank to attend that "house of lies" in town. He has his Bible and knew how to read, and that, along with a thick leather belt, was all Bubba Stanton needed to enforce order, and discipline in his household, thank you very much. Claire's four eldest children, quickly realizing an opportunity to avoid attending Sunday church services and having to do anything remotely productive with their weekends, immediately sided with their father and openly mocked their mother's "old fashioned superstitions" until she was reduced to tears and stopped trying to get the family to attend services altogether. This had been some years ago, and since Bubba almost always refused to allow his wife access to the family vehicle without his supervision, Claire Stanton was most certainly no longer a good parishioner of the "church over in town."

Abaddon smiled as Claire finished her clumsy monologue. "Ma'am, I think you misunderstand me a little. I'm not interested in visiting the people whose rear ends polish the pews every time the church doors open. That would be a little pointless, don't you think? I wanted to come out and visit with some of my flock who have strayed a bit from their shepherd… folks such as yourself. Please correct me if I am wrong, but I get the sense that your choice to abstain from attending God's holy building isn't entirely… voluntary, shall we say?"

Claire didn't respond, but the crimson flush spreading across her neck and face was all the answer needed. Ever so gently, the Reverend took Claire's hand in his own. Claire felt a lovely fizz of [lust] heat spread throughout her entire body as she looked the preacher man square in the face. "No, you're not wrong Reverend. If the choice was mine, I would happily attend your services every week. But my husband would never allow it, and I can assure you that it is in my best interest to stay on his good side. So, no church for me, I'm afraid."

To her horror, Claire felt a tear begin trickling down her cheek. She raised a hand to brush it away, but the Reverend beat her to it. He was surprisingly gentle as he wiped her tear with his finger and handed her his pocket handkerchief. "Ma'am, please believe me when I offer you my sincerest regret for the current domestic situation you find yourself in. However, I think I have a solution that might serve both you and my Father. If you are agreeable, I would happily come and visit you twice a week to study texts and discuss holy matters together. No one in your family, nor anyone else for that matter, needs to know."

Claire felt a sensation bloom in her chest that she hadn't experienced for many years: hope. "Oh Reverend, if you are able to come here and teach and visit with me, it would mean the world to me. And your discretion is greatly appreciated. I cannot thank you enough for your generous offer." Suddenly, Claire heard a loud engine gunning and a car door slamming, heralding the arrival of her prince charming's return home from work. A flash of fear crossed her face, but she quickly pasted on her brightest smile and turned back to her visitor, who appeared to have been watching her facial expressions closely. "Well, that will be my husband returning home. I must run and get dinner on the table. When can I see you again, Reverend?" The preacher smiled and quickly gripped her hand. "Soon, my dear child. I will return anon, and we will begin our studies." He then tipped his cap to her and walked away from her small farm, whistling a tune she didn't recognize. Claire absentmindedly pocketed the handkerchief in her much-mended house dress. It was only as Claire was sprinting towards her kitchen table that she realized she had no idea how the Reverend made the 20-mile trek to her home, let alone the 20-mile journey back to his new parish on foot. Or how he kept his clothes and shoes so impeccably clean in the process.

***

"This meatloaf tastes like goddamn sawdust, Claire. Can't you do anything right? I bust my ass all day to put food on the table for you and these five ungrateful brats, and this is how I'm repaid. With a dinner that's barely edible and a wife who's almost as interesting as dirt. What a glorious reception I have received tonight!" Claire felt herself trembling as Bubba ranted and shouted about how poorly treated he was in his own damn home. What was wrong with her? Why did he have to get stuck marrying the most miserable woman in town? Claire certainly wasn't going to remind him of what they both already knew: if he hadn't gotten her pregnant with their now 17-year-old-son, Gregory, she would never have married Bubba. But it was a different time then: if you got pregnant, you did the honorable thing and got married. Even if the sexual act which resulted in the pregnancy was far from consensual. End of discussion. Or at least it was for the woman, of course. They never seem to get to add their two cents to any discussion of importance, particularly those which concern their own futures.

Later that night, as Claire prepared herself for bed and changed out of her ratty dress, she remembered the handkerchief Abaddon had pressed into her hand earlier that day. The handkerchief was made of fine linen and edged in beautiful red embroidery. Claire noticed a small monogram stitched into the edge of the cloth: M.S. She wondered whom the linen had originally belonged to: did the reverend have a wife? She didn't notice a ring on his finger, but that didn't necessarily mean that he was a free man. Perhaps he was a widower? As she drifted off to sleep that night, clutching the handkerchief to her breast, Claire found herself fervently praying to see the Reverend again as soon as possible.

She didn't have to wait long, thankfully. Three days after his first visit, on a bright Thursday afternoon, Claire was sitting on her front porch, resting her swollen feet on a wicker chair. She was pleased with herself. When she had awoken early that morning, something deep inside her assured her that she would be receiving a visit from her new friend later that afternoon. As soon as Bubba left for work, moaning and groaning about the coffee-filled thermos she had pressed into his hands ("It's scalding hot Claire, I could have burned myself!"), Claire distributed what paltry snacks remained in her nearly bare cupboards into the four eldest children's' hands and informed them that there would be no schooling that day, resulting in cheers so loud they awoke the baby, who began screaming like a banshee. Claire ordered the children out of the house and told them to go play out in the woods and not to return home before suppertime. If they obeyed her and picked enough strawberries from the thicket in the woods behind their house, she would make them their favorite dessert: homemade strawberry pie.

This elicited another cheer of excitement from the children as they raced from the house. Claire rarely made desserts with strawberries for her family for one simple reason: she was incredibly allergic to strawberries. Just a small sliver of the juicy red fruit in her mouth would elicit immediate hives and anaphylaxis. However, this life threating allergy seemed a mere inconvenience for Bubba and the children, so Claire obliged by making two homemade strawberry pies each summer. If the children managed to pick enough fruit that afternoon, she would make the first pie of the summer for next Friday night's dinner.

Claire was fretting over how she would convince Bubba to let her take the car to town on Sunday for some desperately needed grocery shopping when she heard the Reverend approaching. She stood up eagerly and smoothed down her dress. Claire had taken great pains with her appearance that morning after the children left: wearing her best day dress, she had washed and curled her hair and even applied light makeup. She felt a glimmer of her old self re-emerge as she prepared for her new friend's visit. She remembered the version of Claire who hadn't been beaten down by time, multiple pregnancies, and a husband who favored the use of his hands and his belt over intellectual discussions and quiet disagreements. She felt her heart fluttering rapidly as the Reverend came into view. He seemed to be wearing the same suit as his previous visit, and his hands were tucked into his pants pockets as he strolled toward her front porch. As Abaddon smiled at Claire and tipped his cap to her, she realized that the Reverend was even more handsome than she remembered. His thick black hair shone in the sunlight, and his emerald eyes sparkled and danced. His well-cut suit hinted at a perfect body underneath. Unconsciously, Claire reached up and patted her hair into place before calling out to greet her visitor. "Reverend, hello! I'm so grateful you could come out to visit with me today. Please, sit and make yourself comfortable. Would you like anything to drink? Water or lemonade? I could bring out something for us to eat?"

Abaddon smiled as he lowered himself into a wicker chair opposite her. "My dear Claire, be at peace! The only things I need from you are your time and your opinions, if you would be gracious enough to share them with me." Claire felt herself flush with pleasure. This intelligent, handsome, kind man wanted her opinions? "Reverend, I am more than happy to oblige, for whatever my thoughts and opinions are worth." She smoothed her hair back behind her ears and noticed for the first time what appeared to be missing from this forthcoming theological discussion: a Bible. Claire no longer owned one herself, and the Reverend's hands were empty.

Perhaps it was in his suit pocket? She pushed the thought away. This was a learned man of God; he probably had the entire Bible memorized! She glanced at her new friend's handsome face, whose glorious emerald eyes seemed to be almost reading her thoughts. "Claire, my Father does not require me to berate you with archaic words and memorize passages from a dusty old tome. A dusty old tome, which, for all they may try and deny it, was written by men and not by my Father. No, Claire, my Master would never have set forth those hateful words and rules into law. Laws that subjugate women and accuse them of being tainted and impure from the very original sin. What were the glorified St. Paul's thoughts on the female sex, Claire? I do believe he remarked that women 'should remain silent in the churches. They are not allowed to speak, but must be in submission, as the law says.'"

Claire remained silent as the Reverend continued. "Oh yes, those were his exact words. What else did he preach under the supposed mantle of his Holy Father's instruction? Ah, I believe he told Timothy that 'a woman must quietly receive instruction with entire submissiveness. But I do not allow a woman to teach or exercise authority over a man, but to remain quiet. For it was Adam who was first created, and then Eve. And it was not Adam who was deceived, but the woman being deceived, fell into transgression. But women will be preserved through the bearing of children if they continue in faith and love and sanctity with self-restraint.' How do those holy words make you feel, Claire?"

Claire leaned back deep into her chair, pondering the Reverend's words. Yes, she had heard those verses during church sermons throughout her youth more times than she really cared to admit. Southern Baptists weren't exactly renowned progressives, and she had received the same message, both covertly and overtly, since babyhood: men were superior and women were subservient. Men were the leaders of the church, while women should follow their example and strive to learn from them. Strive to be worthy of them. This made Claire think of her abusive, sadistic husband, and the hypocrisy of the church's message caused a flash of rage so intense she felt her hands involuntarily clenching into fists.

Abaddon seemed to take in Claire's thoughts almost as they were occurring in real time. He leaned forward, looking her directly in the eye. "Oh yes, Claire, I would be furious, too. Your church encourages you to follow the lead and instruction of Bubba in all things, and yet he doesn't seem to be settin' a very Christian example, now does he? And those magnificent bruises he left on your upper arms and back… where those from a belt or his hands?"

Mortified, Claire shrank back in her chair and dropped her head into her hands. How could he know about the bruises on her back? Her dress concealed them; over the years she had painstakingly mastered the art of disguising the "lessons" her husband taught her. The Reverend gently took Claire's hand into his own, and she looked up at him, once again marveling at the pure, emerald green of his eyes: so compassionate and full of love. "It's alright, my child. Fear not. My Father has given me many gifts; I can see clearly what others try so hard to hide away. Please don't be frightened, Claire. Are you afraid?" Staring into Abaddon's eyes, she firmly shook her head no. "No, Reverend, I could never be afraid of you. This particular set of bruises was caused by a belt. It was my punishment for letting my husband return home to an icebox empty of beers. Of course, it's difficult to actually buy beer when your husband won't let you go grocery shopping or give you any damn money!"

It was as if a dam inside of her had burst. The good Reverend listened quietly as Claire detailed the years of neglect and abuse at the hands of her husband. He listened as she told him about the children she had never really wanted, who rejected her affection and treated her like a servant: their father's offspring, indeed! Abaddon held her hand gently and consoled her as she cried and raged over her wasted life, with no discernible means of escape from the drudgery of her miserable existence. It was only after Claire had completely depleted herself of words and emotion that Abaddon began to speak. "My dear child, my Father has heard your cries of despair and sent me to help save you. He hears your anger and rejoices in it. Your rage will give you strength, and strength is what you'll need." Abruptly, the Reverend rose from his seat. "I must go now, child, but I will return to you soon. You are strong, Claire, but my Father and I will make you stronger yet. Be at peace until my return."

As Abaddon rose from his chair, Claire reached into her dress pocket and retrieved the elegant handkerchief, which she held out to him. "I washed your linen for you, Reverend. I wanted to return it to you. It's so fine and delicate, I figured your wife must be missing it, especially given the beautiful monogram." She held her breath as she awaited his reply. Slowly, the Reverend closed Claire's fingers back over the delicate scrap of fabric. "No, Claire, I want you to keep it. I haven't got a wife. That handkerchief belonged to my Father. He answers to many names." Abaddon smiled, his face radiant with joy. "It is my sincerest hope that he will soon be your Father, too." The preacher man then tipped his cap to Claire and began his long walk back to his parish.

It had taken hours of begging and pleading before her husband finally relented and allowed Claire to take the car to the grocery store on Sunday afternoon. Bubba hadn't seemed the least bit concerned that there was virtually no food left in the pantry to feed the children with, but the moment she had pointed out the dwindling supply of beer in their icebox, the grocery expedition suddenly became a top priority. However, Emily was in the throes of a screaming fit as Claire prepared to leave for the store, and Bubba insisted that Claire *"take that damn, squalling baby"* with her. Gritting her teeth, Claire loaded her daughter into their rusty old Chevrolet and started the drive to town. By the time they reached the Stop-N-Shop, Rockhaven's only grocery store, Emily had stopped fussing and was behaving relatively well. Claire buckled her infant daughter into a shopping cart and began slowly making her way through the aisles, carefully noting the prices of each item before placing them in her cart.

As Claire was fretting over her paltry checkbook balance and debating the pros and cons of preparing a homemade pie crust (better taste) versus purchasing a store made version (cheaper and less labor intensive), she was interrupted from her mental calculations by the arrival of her elderly and incredibly exhausting neighbor, Sarah Gregs. Sarah and her husband lived on a ramshackle property approximately five miles away from Claire's house and were the Stanton family's closest neighbors. Thankfully, Sarah's infirmity prevented her from visiting Claire on a regular basis, but Claire knew that she and her husband faithfully attended church services every Sunday morning. Claire pasted a smile on her face as she greeted her neighbor. "Why Sarah, don't you look lovely today! You must have just come over from services this morning?" Sarah visibly preened at the compliment. "Indeed I did, and Henry is here somewhere too, a'course. You know I can't drive after I broke my hip two years ago. It never healed up quite right and still aches something fierce. And the arthritis! I think it gets worse every day. Take my advice, honey: never get old!"

This profound statement sent Sarah into a laughing fit that quickly turned to coughing and retching. Claire thumped her on the back and murmured empty platitudes about the elderly woman's many ailments.

When Sarah finally stopped coughing, Claire seized the opportunity to ask about the only topic which had occupied her mind for the past week. "Sarah, what do you think of the new preacher, Mr. Smith? I've heard he is an excellent speaker. And so smart!" Mrs. Gregs gave Claire an odd look. "I'm sorry sweetheart, I'm not sure what you mean. Of course our preacher is still Reverend Daily. Why, he's a Rockhaven institution! And I'm certain he would have told his flock if he was planning to get an assistant, though I hardly think he would do that. He may be 70 years-old, but his mind is just as sharp as it ever was! And I must say Claire, Reverend Daily was asking me about your family just the other week. We're all hoping to see you back in church again real soon, dear. Now, I better scoot before Henry drives home without me!" Claire watched, dumbfounded, as Sarah Gregs slowly pushed her shopping cart toward the checkout lane, where her husband was waiting.

Claire awoke early Wednesday morning with the instinctual certainty that the Reverend would come to visit her that day. As soon as she had seen Bubba off to work, she quickly dressed a fussy and irritable Emily and went to wake her four eldest children. Thrusting her infant daughter at them, she decreed that there would again be no schooling that day, and they were to take Emily and spend the day in the woods picking more strawberries for Friday night's dessert. She ordered the children to stay in the woods until suppertime. With a surprisingly half-hearted litany of complaints about having to mind Emily for the day, the children dressed, gathered the pails they used to collect berries, and headed into the wilderness behind the property. Claire then took her time getting ready for her visitor, dressing with care and applying a pale pink lipstick she had purchased during Sunday's visit to the Stop-N-Shop (she had scrimped the money together by opting for the store-bought pie crust). Satisfied with her appearance, she filled a pitcher with cold water and went out to the front porch to await the Reverend's arrival.

It was a short wait. She heard that familiar whistling tune before she saw him, and when Abaddon appeared before her, Claire heard herself utter an audible gasp. Still clothed in the same black suit and impossibly shiny shoes, the preacher man was no longer handsome; he was absolutely radiant. Abaddon seemed to exude a bright light, and Claire found that staring at him for too long burned her eyes, like looking directly at the sun. The Reverend smiled at her as he took his customary seat on the porch. "My child, you look lovely today. But I sense that something is deeply troubling you this morning. Unburden yourself to me. Let me restore your peace."

Claire hesitated, unsure how to begin. She looked directly into Abaddon's deep, emerald eyes. "I… I saw one of my neighbors on Sunday and asked her about the church's new preacher. She said she had never heard of you. You're not really the town's new preacher, are you? Why would you lie to me, Abaddon?"

The Reverend listened patiently as Claire asked her questions before answering. "My child, you have a right to be upset with me. Some of the things I told you… could have easily been misinterpreted. Please let me explain. I am most certainly a new Reverend in town, but I have no interest in sharing my wisdom with that pack of fools who flock to the church building every Sunday morning." A slight sneer curled the corners of Abaddon's beautiful mouth before he continued. "No, my Father sent me here to share my wisdom and salvation with those who are truly deserving of it. One such as yourself, my child. My Father sees the misery and indignities you suffer every day. He has heard your silent cries of rage and despair and sent me to save you. You have been chosen, Claire. You alone are worthy of my Father's salvation."

Claire leaned back into her chair, gazing at the glorious creature seated across from her. "Who is your Father, Abaddon?"

The Reverend smiled. It was a majestic sight. "My Father goes by many names. He is the Morning Star, the Light Bringer, the Shining One. He is the savior of men and the hope of humankind. He loves you, Claire, and He desires only to save you. As do I. Will you let Him, my dear child?" The duo sat on the porch and talked for many hours, until the sun began to sink in the sky and they heard the sound of a battered Chevrolet approaching the property. It was only then that the Reverend stood to leave, pressing a small package into Claire's hand before placing his cap on his head and beginning his leisurely stroll back into town.

She awoke before dawn on Friday to begin preparing that evening's meal. Her eldest son had shot a brace of rabbits the previous afternoon, and Claire worked diligently to clean and dress the meat before placing it on the stovetop to simmer for hours in a homemade vegetable broth. She picked the vegetables from the large garden she kept and spent hours digging, cleaning, peeling, and chopping them for side dishes. Finally, she threw out the store-bought pie crust and set to work on producing the homemade version of the highly anticipated strawberry pie, mixing the flour and butter, rolling out the dough, and cutting gossamer thin strips to crisscross the top of the decadent treat. Claire wore gloves up to her elbows as she mixed the fresh strawberry filling, careful not to let an errant berry graze her skin and cause her to erupt in hives. When she finally finished, she placed the dessert in the ice box to cool.

Bubba arrived home from work that evening irritable and far from sober. However, even he was forced to stop insulting Claire when he saw the feast she had laid out on the dining table. As Bubba seated himself at the head of the table and cracked open another beer, Claire called for her four eldest children, who seated themselves in their normal places around the table. The baby lay silently in her cot at the end of the hallway, having already been fed. Claire looked around the table at her assembled husband and progeny for a moment before she began serving. Although none of them bothered to thank her or praise her cooking, it was evident that Claire had outdone herself on the evening's meal. Even Bubba found little to complain about, and the children remained relatively polite and well-mannered as Claire served the stew and vegetables.

After dinner was consumed, Claire went to the kitchen and removed the strawberry pie from the ice box. It was beautiful to behold. The crust was golden and flaky, with windows of juicy red berries appearing in the cross-sections of the topping. Claire carefully cut the pie into five large pieces, plating each slice with tenderness. She topped each slice with granulated sugar and fresh whipped cream and added a small scoop of vanilla ice cream to each plate before carrying them to the dining room. Claire placed a plate before her husband and four eldest children. Without a word of thanks, they each began inhaling their desserts. Claire sat back and observed, sipping coffee as she watched her family eat the delicious treat she had spent so many hours perfecting.

The fruits of her labor didn't take long to materialize. Just minutes after her family began to eat the dessert, Claire's efforts were finally rewarded. Bubba and the children began screaming, clutching their throats and gasping for air. Claire watched dispassionately as they cried and vomited, their lips turning blue as the mixture of potassium cyanide and granulated sugar cut off the oxygen supply to their hearts and brains. She remained seated as her husband and children fell to the floor, thrashing and clutching their throats, begging for help. When it was over less than five minutes later, Claire glanced distastefully at the mixture of vomit, blood and urine her ungrateful family had left on the floor. "Just one more mess for me to clean up," she muttered bitterly.

Easing her aching back and swollen feet out of her chair, Claire headed slowly to the toolshed Bubba kept behind the house. Removing a shovel and a pair of post-hole diggers, Claire Stanton observed the task before her. For most people it would be a daunting task, but Claire knew that with her Father's help, everything was possible. Hefting the shovel up and over her shoulder, she began the arduous process of widening the shallow grave she had started in her vegetable garden.

Midnight on Stone Mountain
Erica Schaef

Grey trees rose up toward a grey sky, their speckled branches bare and pointed at the ends like slender spears. I was only vaguely aware of them; a mass of tangled thoughts had been congealing into an inexorable paste inside of my aching skull, so that I was hardly able to process the visual before me.

Ahead, a slim billow of smoke drifted lazily from a stone chimney, and I quickened my pace upon the frozen earth toward it. My mind sharpened with a renewed vigor, as my stomach seemed to lighten in a thrill of suppressed anxiety.

When I reached the threshold of the modest hunting cabin, I hesitated, my damp fist clenched in a wavering hover before the door. Perhaps, this had been a mistake...he was not expecting me after all. What if he doesn't want to see me? I thought, with a sudden wave of trepidation. Then, even worse, what if he isn't alone?

I shivered, not wanting to linger too long over those possibilities. My walk from the ranger's station had been a cold and difficult one. More than once, I had stumbled over some partially concealed rock or fallen tree branch, and my right ankle was now painfully swollen. Besides that, my lungs had become irritated by the frigid air, my thighs sore and burning from the build-up of lactic acid. I needed to rest, to get out of the persistent, autumnal wind. There really was no choice now. I knocked.

A low, howling bark sounded from inside, followed moments later by the rhythmic thud of boots against hardwood. He was coming.

"Be quiet, Dot," Luke didn't look at me as he opened the door. His head was turned slightly, toward a plump, spotted blood hound, which stood next to him on the woven throw rug just inside.

"I thought you wouldn't be here until tomorrow..." but his smile faltered, and his familiar voice trailed off, when his pale eyes fell upon mine. They were as brilliantly blue as I remembered, like a perfectly clear, summer sky.

"Alma," his gaze ran from my face to my boots, then back up again. For the first time, I thought of how I must look to him, after my long trek up the mountain side. My damp red hair was frizzing and sticking in gummy clumps to my temples and cheeks; my nose was the same fiery color, windblown and raw.

He, however, looked handsome as always, maybe even more so in this natural, rugged environment.

"What are you doing here?"

I couldn't tell from his expression whether he was displeased to see me, but the abruptness of the question was not at all reassuring.

"Really, I..." I stammered, dumbfounded for a few seconds, my mouth refusing to function properly. Then, taking hold of myself, I straightened, ignoring the searing pain in my ankle. He couldn't intimidate me, I had every right to this opportunity for closure. I would not let myself feel badly for pursuing it.

"I wanted to talk to you, Luke. I have a short break before my next agency assignment starts, and I remembered that you always come up here at this time of year. It's just that, everything with us ended so abruptly, and, well...I wanted to talk." I finished lamely.

"You could have called," he answered simply, not moving his broad shoulders from the door frame, "I'm sorry, but this really isn't a good time."

I felt myself flush, "I...wanted to see you in person, and when I found out that I would be having some time off, and knew that you would be up here...but you're right, of course, I should've called first. This was thoughtless of me, and you are obviously expecting someone else."

His eyes seemed to soften a little. He feels sorry for me, I thought miserably.

"Well, come in, then," he said gruffly, standing back a little to admit me.

"Thanks," I avoided looking at his face as I brushed past him, the smell of pine needles and aftershave causing my heart to skip wildly in my chest. I'd never felt so pathetic.

Dot came over to greet me as enthusiastically as ever, licking at my fingers and palms as I went to stand in the warm glow of the fire. It burned cheerfully in its stone grate in one corner of the small room, oblivious to my unease. What in the hell had I been thinking?

"Did you walk all the way up from the station?" Luke asked, as he shut the front door behind me.

"Yes. I was here once before, remember? A couple of summers ago, so I knew the trail..."

"The rangers should've stopped you. They shouldn't be allowing anyone on these trails. Not now," he interrupted, his tone still gruff and abrupt.

"I didn't see anyone. I just parked my car in the lot and got onto the path," I replied, berating myself for having been so spontaneous. At that moment, standing there, shivering in front of the fire, I wished that someone had been there at the station to warn me off of the icy trailhead. Whatever idealistic part of me had ever thought that this was a good idea had retreated back into the recesses of my brain, where it now sat humbly huddled, licking its wounds.

"Listen, the truth is that I came here because..."

"Why weren't they watching?" he mumbled to himself, as though I hadn't spoken at all. He pulled his cell phone out of his pocket and began typing on the screen.

I bristled, my embarrassment dissolving quickly into anger. The last three months had been hell on earth for me, and I had just come all this way to see him, making a complete and utter fool of myself. He could at least pretend to be interested in what I had to say.

"Okay," he went on, after a moment, "do you need something to eat before we head back down?"

"I'm sorry, before we what?" I couldn't keep the note of incredulity from my voice. "Surely you don't mean that I have to turn around and go back this very minute? That's a ten-mile hike!"

"We'll be alright. I'll help you," he was already crossing into the adjoining kitchen. "Coffee?"

I struggled to contain my outrage.

"Luke, I know I've made a real idiot of myself by coming here, and believe me, I don't want to impose any more than I obviously already have, but there's no chance of my being able to do that trail again right now. I'm exhausted."

"It's not as hard going down," he said, pouring coffee from a French press into two oversized mugs on the butcher block counter-top. "And I want to get you to your car before it starts to get dark."

He carried the mugs easily in his large hands, stopping in front of me so that his chest was only a few short inches from my face. I could smell the aftershave again.

"I'm freezing," I protested, ignoring the coffee, and tightening my arms around my torso, "and my ankle...I twisted it or something. I need to rest for a little while."

I hated the plea in my voice, hated that I was this vulnerable in front of him.

"You're hurt?" for the first time, he seemed to have actually registered what I was saying. I nodded, keeping my eyes aimed directly at his chest.

He moved to set the steaming mugs on a little coffee table behind where I was standing. "Sit down there, on the couch."

I did so without an argument, though I really did not appreciate being ordered about in such a way. My fatigued body felt immediate relief as it sank into the cushions.

"Swing your legs up here ...yes. Which one is it?"

"The right," I said, my mouth going dry as I felt his warm hands through the fabric of my jeans. He was sitting on the couch next to my feet, pressing up gently on my right calf and slowly removing my boot. I winced as the leather moved over my throbbing ankle.

"God, Alma," he breathed, "this looks terrible."

I looked down warily. Indeed, the ankle was a very ugly shade of purple, and had swollen to twice its normal size. I swallowed back against an upsurge of bile.

Luke removed his hands from my leg, running them through his dark hair the way he always did when he was frustrated.

"You're right," he said after a moment, "we won't be able to get you down the mountain today. It'll have to be tomorrow morning, first thing."

Again, he seemed to be talking more to himself than to me, his eyes staring unseeingly at Dot, who had stretched out on the carpeted rug in front of the fire.

I felt the color rising in my face once more. "Very sorry to have inconvenienced you, Luke. I do have to say, though, that this is not at all what I expected to happen."

He looked at me again with those piercing eyes, the faintest trace of a smile playing upon his lips. It was the first one he had worn since opening the door, when he had momentarily mistaken me for someone else. I hated that it could still make me weak.

"Well, what did you expect to happen?"

I blinked, thinking for a moment. "Honestly, I don't know." My gaze drifted to the rug in front of the fire, and I blushed as unhelpful, fantastical possibilities for the two of us played out very clearly in my mind.

I remembered the long weekend we had spent in this cabin a couple of summers ago. It had all been so new back then, so pristine and uncomplicated. The days here had been amazing; full of adventure and novel excitement. We had gone hiking, rafting, and swimming, talking and laughing carelessly all the while, as though it were only the two of us in the whole wide world. The nights…they had been amazing, too. I sighed, looking back at him.

"I suppose I was hoping that you could help me to understand what it was that happened between us," I answered finally. "I mean, it was going so well…at least, I thought it was, and then, out of nowhere, you …ended it. Just like that. I guess I came up here because I felt I deserved a bit of closure. Was there…someone else, or…"

"No," he started to get up, "nothing like that, Alma."

"Then what?" I sat up a little, trying to meet his gaze. "You can tell me truth, it's been long enough now…"

"Hang on a minute. I want to bring in a few more logs for the fire," he strode away toward the back door.

I started to protest, but then thought better of it. I wouldn't beg, and he certainly wouldn't be able to evade my question all the way until tomorrow.

I was leaned back, looking up at the ceiling, my eyelids beginning to grow heavy, when I felt my cellphone vibrating in the pocket of my coat. I pulled it out, and saw my sister's name flash across the screen.

"Hey, Crystal," I said, pressing the phone up to my ear, "how are you?"

"Fine," she answered quickly, and I could hear one of her twins yelling for something in the background. "Just wanted to make sure we're still on for trick or treat tomorrow night."

Shit. I had completely forgotten. "Uh…yea sure. What time is that again?"

"Six o'clock, but get here a little early so you can help with Alexander's face paint."

"Yea, alright," I'd be leaving here first thing in the morning anyway, so should still have plenty of time to get to her house on time.

"Okay. Is everything alright with you?" I could hear the genuine concern in her voice, and, for a moment, considered telling where I was, and what I had done. I decided against it almost immediately though, she would only scold me for coming here, and I could hardly to expect her to understand.

"Yea, yea I'm fine. My phone's about to die, though. I'll see you tomorrow."

"See you tomorrow."

We hung up, and, as I moved to replace the phone to my pocket, the pain in my ankle intensified. I rearranged the resulting grimace into a less formidable expression, when I heard Luke coming in again. He tended to the fire wordlessly, causing the flames to rise and fill the small room with a renewed warmth. My pain seemed to ease somewhat as the cold abated. He added a healthy amount of honeyed whiskey to the coffee he had prepared for me, and that helped even more than the fire.

By evening, he still had not addressed my question. I was stretched out upon the couch again, my ankle elevated on a firm throw pillow, with cloth-wrapped ice compressing it. I had eaten, showered, and changed into one of Luke's old flannel shirts, the bottom of which reached down to the top of my knees.

We had fallen into a strange, yet comfortable interaction with one another. He went about what I assumed was his usual routine in the cabin, passing in and out to do various chores and jobs, stopping to check in on me every so often, Dot plodding along happily at his heels. It felt easy to me somehow, this cozy, uneventful afternoon, and a faint sense of loneliness grew inside of me, at the thought of it being over soon.

I got up to help prepare dinner, feeling fairly well rested after my hours-long hike that morning. Luke was making a beef and potato stew, for which I had volunteered to cut up some fresh vegetables. We worked in the kitchen together in an amiable silence, as though no time at all had passed since our last, much less pleasant encounter.

After we had eaten, I went back to my place on the couch, the blood having pooled uncomfortably in my injured ankle.

Luke followed after a while, carrying the tall bottle of whiskey, which was still nearly full.

"Do you want a drink before bed? I'm sorry I don't have any Advil or anything for your leg."

I smiled up at him, resting my head back against the arm of the couch. "Sure, why not? There's still something I'd like to talk to you about, anyway."

"I know," he said simply, returning to the kitchen to make the drink.

He came back with two glasses, handed one to me, and kept the other for himself, as he took the only remaining seat in the scarcely furnished room, on the section of couch beside my elevated ankle.

He didn't say anything for a long while. In fact, it wasn't until I opened my mouth to begin the conversation again, that he finally spoke, in his usual, gruff voice.

"There's a lot that you don't know about me, Alma," he started, looking over at me with an amused sort of half-smile, "I know that sounds very cliché, and I'm not trying to be mysterious or anything, but there are things…reasons… why being in a relationship, like the one we were in, really isn't a good idea for me. It has nothing to with you…"

"'It's not you it's me?'" I finished, crinkling my brow at him. "Rhat was honestly going to be your explanation? Come on, Luke."

"No," he answered, taking a drink of the smooth, amber liquor from his glass. "I wasn't going to give an explanation at all. You were the one that wanted me to try."

"Oh yes, you're right, that would have been much better," I returned bitterly, meeting his eyes with my own. "After all, I don't deserve to know what I did so wrong…what I did to lose the best thing that ever…to lose you. Better I just go on wondering. Christ," my voice cracked, as my composure began to falter. "Do you even know how miserable I've been? How alone I've felt? Do you even care at all?"

Tears were beginning to well up in my eyes, "I feel like I'm going crazy," I whispered, biting my bottom lip as it began to tremble.

"No," he said sharply, still wearing the half-smile. It didn't look amused anymore, though. It looked thoughtful and sad, almost pitying. "Please don't cry."

"So sorry," I scoffed, "God forbid I make you uncomfortable."

But I couldn't keep the tears back any longer. They trickled down my cheeks in two thin, flowing streams.

I felt Luke getting up from the couch as I wiped my eyes. I figured that he was going to go out again, to give me some time to recompose myself, and so I was surprised when I felt his hand on my face, and the rough brushing of his callused thumb across my cheek.

"I'm so sorry," he breathed, looking into my eyes, with a disconcerting intensity. For a fleeting moment, I thought that he would kiss me. My lips parted slightly, as he went on talking. "I should never have let it happen between us in the first place. It was a mistake to have been... with you at all. I'm so, so sorry, sweetheart."

I pushed him away, hard. It had all the effect of trying to injure granite, but he removed his hand, and leaned away from me all the same.

"I hate you," I said, turning away to hide my face in my hands. "You're an arrogant, condescending ass, and I'm sorry I ever came here."

"It's okay," he said, getting to his feet once again, "you'll be going back soon."

His tone sounded regretful, which only confused and upset me more.

He went outside then, and I cried with abandon, sobs wracking my entire body as my stomach twisted into sickening knots.

All the weeks of longing for him, of wondering where he was and what he was doing, of going out with friends and hoping that he would show up at whatever obscure bar or dance club we happened to be at that night, weighed down upon me at once, making it hard to breathe. I let it happen, let myself despair the loss of him, finally.

My glass was empty when Luke returned inside, over an hour later.

"Come on," he said, opening the bedroom door across the room from where I was lying. "You can stay in there," he gestured inside. "I'll sleep out here on the couch."

I shook my head, wishing that the Earth would just open up and swallow me whole.

"No, I've been enough of a bother already. I'll stay where I am, thank you."

"The bed is more comfortable," he argued pleasantly, "you'll sleep better."

"No," I persisted stubbornly, my last shred of self-respect hinging upon the outcome of this meaningless dispute. "It will hurt my ankle to stand up again, anyway."

"Okay, I'll carry you, then," he said matter-of-factly, crossing the room in a few, long strides.

"No, really. I…" but he already had me gathered up into arms like a small child.

"You don't have to fight me on everything, you know," he rumbled, his chest hard and warm against my body. "We'll need to get up very early tomorrow, and you've already said how exhausted you are. Just relax."

He put me down gently on the soft mattress moments later, and I turned on my side away from him, facing the room's small window. A single snowflake fell whimsically beyond the curtain.

"Good night, Alma," Luke said, and I heard the sound of his footsteps retreating toward the door.

I meant to say, "screw you," but ended up using somewhat coarser language.

He laughed hoarsely in response. "Okay. Fair enough. See you in the morning."

I held back my breath as his footsteps resumed, until I was sure that he had gone from the room.

"God, Luke," I gasped, my voice threatening to crack again. "How I've missed you."

"Hmm?" His response was plainly discernable from the living room.

Shit. "Oh…"

I heard his footsteps again, this time they were coming toward me.

"Really?" he asked quietly, when he'd reached the side of the four-poster.

"Yes," I answered honestly, still on my side, so that I didn't have to look at him. Hardly daring to breathe, I waited, not knowing what to expect.

I felt the mattress sag behind me, then his big arm was around my waist, holding me gently to him. A contended sigh escaped from my throat of its own accord, as I felt the whisper of his lips against my hair.

"I've missed you, too Alma. So much," his voice was still gruff, but he had spoken so lowly, and so softly, that it caused me to shiver.

He gave a husky sort of laugh, moving his hand to brush my hair gently across my shoulder, before replacing it to my waist.

"My Alma," his breath drifted over the sensitive skin of my neck, and I gasped when I felt the sweet pressure of his lips there a moment later.

"Luke."

His hand drifted lightly from my waist, to trace circles upon the fabric at the side of my hip, in an unspoken question.

In answer, I nestled myself more firmly against him, reaching back to tangle my hand in his hair, anchoring his lips to my neck.

I watched sparkling flurries of pure white snow drift past the window pane, as our bodies fell into an inevitable, spectacular rhythm.

Throughout the night, I was dreamily aware of the occurrence of peculiar sounds every so often, like trees knocking together in the wind. At one point, I even thought I heard the quiet murmuring of voices, but was too tired, and far too content, to be much bothered.

The next morning, I woke up alone, my ankle throbbing, but looking slightly more flesh-toned than it had the day before.

Pale rays of sunlight hardly permeated through the window, as they were being obscured by a now thickly falling snow. It was only Halloween eve; a little early in the year for such formidable weather, I thought, stretching my arms up above my head with a comfortable yawn.

I sat up on the springy mattress, feeling better than I had in weeks. I felt human again, after having only gone through the motions, like an empty shell, for so long.

The air outside of the heavy comforter was chilly, so I wrapped the thick blanket around myself before getting up to walk to the door.

A couple of steps into the living room, I froze.

Across from me, a young woman was seated at the kitchen table, smiling pleasantly. She was very pretty, wearing an expensive-looking crimson coat, her raven-colored hair falling to her shoulders in perfectly formed ringlets. I, on the other hand, was wrapped haphazardly in a down comforter, my unwashed hair sweaty and tousled from sleep and sex.

"Uh…" I stammered, moving to the balls of my feet, in preparation for a hasty retreat.

"You must be Alma," she said brightly, standing from her chair, and walking over toward me.

I felt very much at the disadvantage, my mind reeling as I wondered who she might be.

"Oh, yes," I said finally, clutching the blanket to my chest with one hand, as I accepted hers in the other.

"Sorry," I said, looking down at myself, when the awkward handshake was over. "I didn't know…"

The front door opened then, and Luke walked in, followed closely by Dot, and a grey-haired man I didn't know.

I gave a strange, strangled yelp, and ran like a shot to the bedroom, my ankle throbbing its protest at the sudden movement.

I could hear the young woman admonishing the two men, as I climbed back up onto the mattress, buying myself under the comforter.

Ugh.

Who were these people? Was that woman the person who Luke had been expecting when I had showed up yesterday? I couldn't help the small twinge of jealousy I felt at the thought. She had known who I was.

I remembered the knocking sounds and voices I'd heard the night before. Perhaps, I had not been dreaming after all. Had they been talking about me?

Had he had to explain to her what his sad, pathetic ex-girlfriend was doing here in his bed? Had they laughed at me? I stifled a groan into my pillow.

A few minutes later, a knock sounded at the door, and I hastened to put on Luke's shirt.

"Come in," I called, running my fingers through my hair to untangle it the best I could.

I was surprised to see the young woman come in. My clothes, which had been drying beside the fire, were draped neatly over one arm.

"Here, I thought you were probably going for these when I interrupted you. Sorry about that," she handed them over with the same, pretty smile she'd been wearing earlier.

"Thanks," I accepted them sheepishly. "I was going to walk back down to my car. I didn't know that anyone else…"

"Oh no," her sapphire eyes grew expressively round. "You can't go back down now. Finn and I hardly made it here last night. I guess you haven't had the chance to look outside yet."

"Not really," I frowned, looking toward the little window. Snow was still falling heavily, swirling every now and then to one side or the other in a great gust of wind.

"There is an awful blizzard. We started up early last night, when it had just begun to fall. Finn said we should go early, in case it got bad, and I'm really glad we did now, of course. I would've hated for Luke to have to deal with the port…everything himself." She took a breath. "Of course, he had wanted to get you back to the ranger's station when we got here, around midnight, but we told him it would absolutely not be possible. You wouldn't have been able to see your hand in front of your face, Alma, and you with the sprained ankle. How is that, by the way? I was going to ask you…"

"Maddie!" Luke knocked sharply upon the door and the young woman jumped.

"Sorry, I've been rambling," she said, smiling. "It was nice to meet you, Alma. I'll let you get dressed now."

"Nice to meet you, too," I said, as she stepped lightly from the room.

I stared at the closed door behind her for a few moments, trying to make sense of all that she had told me.

She and the older man, Finn, apparently, had arrived here in the middle of the night, after having hiked ten miles through a blizzard, just so that Luke would not be left alone to deal with…something. A port? I pictured a boat dock, or some sort of loading station, neither of which seemed like conceivable structures in these mountains. Besides that, I seriously doubted whether Luke, a computer programmer who worked in a government building in the city, could have any business with either of those things, despite his annual trips up here.

I emerged from the room a short while later, wearing my dry clothes, my hair pulled back off of my face in a loose ponytail.

"Do you want some coffee? I just made some," Maddie asked cheerfully from behind the kitchen counter.

"Um…sure. If you don't mind, yea." I felt so horribly out of place, moving to stand in the little kitchen with the tall, and very well-put-together brunette.

Luke and Finn were seated at the kitchen table, a pile of papers spread out before them in disarray.

"Alma, I don't know if you've had the chance to meet Finn," Maddie said helpfully, following my gaze to where the two men were seated.

The grey-haired stranger looked up, his dark eyes tired but warm as he greeted me with a grin. "Hello, Alma. It's pleasure to meet you."

"Yes, you too."

Luke looked back over his shoulder, and our eyes met for the briefest of moments, before he turned back again to clear up the papers.

As he did so, a roughly drawn, ink illustration, which had landed at the top of the stack, caught my eye. It was of what looked to be an unnaturally thin, elongated humanoid creature, with two long, broad horns, like those of a demon, rising up from its skull. Strange, I thought, but didn't comment aloud.

"Have you?" Maddie asked Luke, and the two of them stared at each other almost suspiciously.

"Don't," he said finally. "The less she knows, the better."

Maddie arched one eyebrow, looking unconvinced.

"Not even that," Luke said sternly.

"Would you two stop it with that weird twin thing?" Finn complained, looking back and forth between them. "No one else can understand what the hell you're talking about."

"Sorry," Maddie chimed, at the same time I said, "Twins?"

She looked surprised, "Yes, didn't Luke tell…" Then to Luke, "Didn't you tell her?"

He looked at her, his expression unreadable.

"You know why," she said after a moment.

"Hey, I told you to cut that out!" Finn chided. "It's hard enough to keep up with you two on these… jobs." He glanced at me, "Without being left out of half the conversation."

"It's not important," Luke assured him, but was still concentrating on Maddie. She nodded to him, almost imperceptibly.

I thought instantly of Crystal's children, Camilla and Alexander. They were twins, too, and very close, but I had never known them to be able to communicate without words.

Crystal, I thought with a start, she was expecting me at her house tonight.

"Um…excuse me for a moment, would you?" I asked to the room at large. "I need to make a phone call."

"Of course," Maddie beamed at me, giving my arm a gentle pat. I returned her smile, and tried in vain to catch Luke's gaze as I walked into the bedroom. He was talking to Finn, and seemed completely unaware of my having said anything.

Fortunately, considering the weather, my cell phone still had service, and so I was able to call my sister and give the excuse of being "under the weather."

"By the way," I said casually, before we hung up. "I know this is going to sound really stupid, but, Camilla and Alexander, they can't communicate, like, telepathically or anything right?"

She laughed. "Of course not! You, their aunt of all people, should know better than that!"

I laughed too. "Yea, it's just…a show that I was watching, never mind. Tell them I said I'm sorry I couldn't make it, and that I hope they have a great time."

I hung up, and went back out into the living room. The men were still having a discussion at the table, and Maddie was perched on the couch with a book open in her lap.

"Hey," she said brightly when she'd noticed me. "Come and sit down, if you'd like. It's nice to have another woman around to talk to for a change."

I did so, stopping on my way to scratch Dot behind the ears.

"So, you said that you and Finn are here to help Luke with something?"

"Yes," she answered, looking over toward the back of Luke's head, before returning her gaze to mine.

"Our father owns some property up here, and Luke and I come up in the winters to check in on it… do repairs and things, since dad isn't able to any more. Finn is an old family friend, and likes to come up too to help us sometimes, when he can."

The words had been delivered like a well-rehearsed line, and I had the distinct impression that that's exactly what they were.

"Oh," I said conversationally, brushing a bit of dirt from my jeans. "I thought you mentioned something about a port before."

Maddie's reaction was composed and thoughtful, as though she were trying to remember our conversation, but I saw Luke's back stiffen, and his hands brush through his hair.

"I can't think what I could've meant by that," she said finally, biting her lower lip. "Who knows?"

I smiled politely at her dismissal, but was keenly aware that I had just been given the slip.

The rest of the day passed slowly, with Luke back to treating me as little more than a stranger.

The previous night seemed so far away now, with only my memory to prove that it had actually happened.

For the most part, I tried to stay out of everyone's way in the cramped cabin, except for helping with food preparation and other small chores.

That evening, with snow still coming down thickly upon the already-blanketed earth, the three of them began to dress into their heavy, outdoor-wear, as though by some prearranged understanding.

I was surprised to see Luke coming toward me after they'd dressed, his blue eyes a shade darker than usual. I had almost expected the three of them to set off outside with no explanation to me whatsoever.

"We need to go out and see to some things," he said, looking down at me in a way that made me flush.

"We heard from the station that there may be some… trespassers in the valley. They aren't likely to bother you up here, but all the same, don't open the door for anyone, or invite anyone to come in. The three of us can unlock the door ourselves, so just ignore any knocking, or anything else you might hear. Alright? Not that I think you will hear anything."

Invite anyone to come in?

I blinked. "Of course I won't let strangers in here. But, are you sure you're going to be okay? I mean, don't you think Maddie should…"

"I'll be fine," Maddie put in happily from beside the door.

"Oh.. alright," I said, looking up toward Luke's face again, but he was already turning away.

Maddie's eyes caught mine as the men were opening the door to leave. She held my gaze as she very deliberately removed a large stack of papers, which had been concealed beneath her coat, from under her arm and put it down silently on the table. From the middle of the stack, she gingerly pulled a manila folder halfway out, giving me a very conspicuous nod, before pushing it back between the papers. She casually joined the two others, who didn't seem to have noticed any of it, and said a cheerful "Good bye," before I heard her asking Luke about the condition of one of the nearby sycamore trees.

I shut the door behind them, listening as their voices faded away into the blowing wind, then was hurrying over to the pile Maddie had left for me, my curiosity piqued.

The first paper I looked at was an article on the pagan holiday, Samhain. It detailed the festival's Celtic origins, describing it as the basis for more modern rituals like trick or treating. It went on to explain that the holiday marked the only time of year when the invisible veil would be lifted between this world and the next. It was quite a fascinating topic, in that the occasion was actually a far more serious affair than I had ever realized. What I found to be most interesting, however, was that the article explored the subject academically, the narrator describing the beliefs and otherworldly events as though they were facts, not merely myth and superstition.

The four or five papers below the article were all detailed maps. They were depictions of various terrains and locations, but all contained a strange, red symbol, like a dome, somewhere upon them. Each of these symbols was labeled as a Portal: Crystal Lake Portal, Red

Hollow Portal, Hemlock Valley Portal. The latter had been crossed out with a thin "X" and key noted as Dormant. I moved it aside, pulling the final map from the stack. It was of the white-peaked mountain range, where Luke's hunting cabin was located. Atop one of the highest summits, a red, domed symbol was clearly visible against the light background. It was labeled Stone Mountain Portal, in tall, black letters.

I stared at it, closely studying the intricate, detailed layout of the map, when something Maddie had said that morning came back to me. She'd told me that she and Finn had hurried to get to the cabin, before the blizzard made the journey impossible, because they "would've hated for Luke to have to deal with the port…everything himself." The port. The Port. The Portal? I shook my head, laughing at the ridiculousness of the thought. Luke, coming up here at the end of every October, to secretly guard one of the portal entrances to hell. I chuckled even harder, until fat tear drops were rolling down my cheeks. Absurd.

Still, what did all of this mean? And why had Maddie so clearly wanted me to see these papers? I dug for the manila folder that she had shown me specifically. Inside was a name badge with Luke's picture on it. I picked it up, not noticing anything unusual until I saw the job title under his name: Head of Parapsychological Research.

I frowned, turning the laminated tag over in my palm. On the back, was printed the address of the Federal building, where Luke worked, as a Computer Programmer, or so I had been told. Quickly, I replaced the badge, feeling a little frightened for the first time.

He had said there was a lot that I didn't know about him, but, surely, that had only been excuse for breaking it off with me. There was no way that the man I had known so well for almost two years, had been lying to me about something this drastic. It was unthinkable. And yet…

As I shuffled the folder back among the papers, the ink illustration I had noticed earlier, of the horned creature, fell out onto the floor. I picked it up, and stared down at the hideous, hair-covered thing. Writing at the top of the paper read simply, Puca.

The image of the monstrous thing worked at my already frazzled nerves, heightening my fear.

My wrist hit against the manila folder as I placed the illustration down on the table, spilling its contents. There was the name badge again, and something else; a black rectangular object I had not noticed before. I stooped to pick it up, anxious as to what this next discovery would be.

It was a little tape recorder, the kind which could fit easily into an inner pocket. It was marked with a label dated October of the previous year. I hesitated for a moment with it my hand, before drawing my breath and hitting the Play button. For a moment, I could hear the mini cassette turning; it produced a melodic white noise. Then, Luke's voice sounded, clear and low:

"Observation from Field Agent two-nine-five. Location: Stone Mountain Portal

This portal was known to be active upon our arrival, on this the thirtieth of October; with prior reports of twelve or more phantoms having been known to frequent this location, ten of which have been previously detailed and classified. Myself, along with field agents two-nine-nine, and one-two-two arrived at the portal at 23:45. Video surveillance was set up at that time, and will accompany this report. At 23:58, field reporter two-nine-nine reported sudden and severe nausea, accompanied by a 'pins and needles' sensation, which she described as 'flowing through' her entire body. One minute later, field agent one-two-two, along with myself, began also to feel the symptoms described above.

At 00:00, the portal opened with no perceived difficulty or delay. Two previously identified phantoms, PH878 and PH56, see index, appeared at the entrance. Field agent two-nine-nine developed psychic connection with PH878, who indicated to her that another presence was waiting to come through as well, something PH878 described as 'horned and beastly.'"

At 00:08..."

But I couldn't listen to anymore. I hit Stop, and threw the recorder back onto the table, as though it was something cursed.

I went to sit on the couch, feeling thankful that they had left Dot with me. She stretched out her legs on the rug, and came over to rest her head on my lap. I stroked her nose absently, and tried to process everything.

It was all so impossible, so surreal. I could think of no logical explanation for what I had just seen and heard. Even if the three of them had been plotting an elaborate prank or hoax for some unknowable reason, they'd have had no way of predicting that I was going to show up at the cabin when I did.

So then, Luke really was some sort of field agent for the government, in the study of the paranormal. I laughed humorlessly. There was no way I could make myself believe that. None of it seemed real.

At nightfall, I stood up from tending the fire, and chanced to look out of the little front window. The snow had finally stopped, giving way to a beautifully clear sky. Dot was nestled at the foot of the couch, snoring peacefully. I resumed my seat beside her, swinging my legs up as I, too, was claimed by fatigue.

Sometime later, I was awoken by Dot's low, barking growl. The light of the fire had grown dim, but I could still make out her shadowy form as she ran to the front door.

"Do you need to go out?" I asked, rubbing the sleep from my eyes.

She continued to growl and bark, her front leg bent up to point fixedly at the door.

"Did you hear something?" I stood up, and padded over to the window.

Outside, the snow was glistening in the generous, selenic light of a full moon. The trees were as still as the rest of the night, stoic and frosted with thick layers of ice.

Aside from Dot's continuing unease, I saw and heard nothing out of the ordinary. I watched for a while, looking out into the forest as far as the pale moonlight would allow.

Suddenly, directly under my eyes, so that it must have been almost touching the window pane, I saw a mass of silvery-white hair drift by. I drew back, startled, as Dot ran over beside me, barking madly. Blinking once, I leaned over to look again.

An old woman was walking, rather quickly, across the pristinely fallen snow, barefoot, from what I could tell, and clothed only in a thin, white gown. The entire form of her seemed to almost glow under the pure white light of the moon and stars.

"Oh my God," I hurried to don my boots, throwing open the door and running out into the night.

"Excuse me," I called, spotting the stranger as she passed between two sycamore trees. "Excuse me, Maim!"

But she didn't stop, look back, or give any sign that she had heard me at all. I hesitated a moment, remembering Luke's strange warning about not inviting strangers into the cabin with me. Of course, I could not let this poor old thing freeze to her death out here. God only knew who she was, or where she had come from, but she was obviously very confused, and very lost. I trudged up the gently sloping hill toward her, still calling out, but to no avail.

As I drew nearer to her, I noticed for the first time how queer her movements were. Her feet hardly seemed to skim the ground at all, leaving no trace of themselves behind. I looked back at the deep wells my boots had created in the soft snow. She was light-footed, I told myself, probably dangerously underweight. Still, I did not entirely succeed in suppressing the chill the swept down the back of my spine.

I was almost to her now, but still she did not acknowledge me, only continued to move through the forest.

"Excuse me," I tried one last time, before reaching out to take hold of her arm. My hand passed through it, as though it was no more than wind or vapor. I tried again, thinking I must have missed the contact somehow, and this time watched as my hand cut through her arm like a solid object through smoke. She walked on, apparently oblivious to my existence, and I recoiled, frozen in shock.

My eyes did not follow her progress as she drifted on and out of sight, they only stared blankly ahead. I had to force myself to move again, after a moment, and it was a tremendous effort. My legs were light and shaking, even my ankle did not bother me.

I was just managing to put one trembling foot in front of the other, going back the way I had come, when a blood-curdling scream cut through the silence of the night like a sharply bladed knife. Maddie, I thought, with a feeling like led weighing down upon my insides.

Without pausing to think, I ran in the direction of the noise. It had sounded distant, and I knew that these mountains could carry an echo, but I had to try to get to her.

I was making slow progress, sweating, and almost giving up hope of finding the young woman, when another scream sounded, this one not so far away. I hurried on, stopping when I reached a small clearing in the midst of a thick grove of hemlocks.

Maddie was in the middle of it, huddled over a body, which was stretched out and bleeding on the snow. Finn. I stepped forward, then noticed something at the edge of the tree line, something which made my blood run cold. There was another silver form there, a young woman this time, who was gazing intently at the two people in the field. She wasn't what had frightened me, though. Behind her, stood a dark, stooping creature. It was at least eight feet in height, thin, and gaunt, and covered in a thick coat of hair, with two broad horns spindling up into sharp points atop its head.

I covered my mouth with my hand to keep from screaming. Maddie was working quickly to tend to Finn's injuries, the extent of which I could not make out. Behind her, the thing, the Puca, I thought wildly, was walking toward her. It moved through the phantom of the young woman, and she gave a dreadful moan, dispersing instantly into thin air. Still, Maddie did not look back. The beast loomed over her, its eyes as black as Hell must've been.

I stepped out from the trees, yelling out loudly, "It's right there!"

The thing lifted its goat-like head toward me, its eyes blinking once, before it changed its direction, its long, muscular legs carrying it easily, right toward me.

I screamed, and turned to run, my legs and ankle blessedly painless, as fear took complete control of me. I ran and ran, heedless of my direction, all the while hearing the even huffing of the creature's breath just behind me.

Once, from the corner of my eye, I saw another silver phantom passing in the moonlight. This one, another young woman, moved more slowly than the old woman had. As I grazed past her, I saw that her slim shoulders culminated only into a long, thin neck. She was headless. I shuddered, biting back against the burning vomit that had risen up into my throat.

I was panicking, tired and hopeless, when the merciful sound of barking reached my throbbing ears. Then, I could see a thin stream of smoke up ahead. I almost cried out in relief, picking up my pace as the little cabin came into view. Behind me, I could hear thick branches snapping like twigs, as the creature brushed past them in its pursuit of me.

Somehow, I made it into the cabin, closing the door behind me. I didn't stop running, until I reached the darkened corner of the living room. Dot came over to whimper softly in my lap. I closed my eyes tightly, my heart racing, my mouth dry. My hair fell to cover my face as I rocked gently back and forth, listening for something...anything. I held my breath, clutching the bloodhound tightly to my chest. We sat there in the darkness for what felt like an eternity, though it may really have been no more than an hour. Finally, I heard a noise outside, footsteps crunching in the snow. Dot bounded up, her tail wriggling vigorously as she ran into the light of the fire.

The door burst open, causing a resounding thud as it hit up against the wall. Luke's tall, broad-shouldered form filled the frame, and I let out a ragged breath.

"Alma!" he called, stepping inside to close the door heavily behind him.

I ran out from my corner, still trembling with fear.

He came toward me too, lifting me easily by the waist when we had reached one another. I threw my arms around his neck, and stared into his perfect blue eyes, drinking them in. My heart swelled in my chest.

"Thank God," he whispered, wiping the hair from my face.

"Maddie and Finn?" I managed to inquire, "that…thing."

"They're fine. Everything's fine, thanks to you. The portal is closed. I'm so sorry I wasn't there for you, my brave, amazing Alma," he bent to kiss me.

I gasped, the breath catching in my throat. It wasn't a sweet, or even gentle gesture.

He kissed me like someone starved, his lips hard, desperate and demanding against mine. It set my blood on fire, tempering my fear and replacing it with something just as primitive.

My mouth parted under his, and his tongue was no less cavalier than his lips had been, as it swept possessively over mine.

My heart started to race even more vigorously, and I tightened my arms around his neck, my legs having wrapped themselves securely about his waist.

He moved his arms under my thighs, his big hands and long fingers cupping my bottom, as he supported my weight. He rocked his lower body gently against mine, in an exhilarating imitation of his tongue's wild movements, as it slid deeply into my mouth, and then pulled back again.

I squirmed eagerly, even as I clung to him, sucking at his tongue when it threatened to abandon its innuendo.

He gave a low sort of growl at this, pulling me hard against his body's reaction.

I sighed his name and he ended the kiss, carrying me with him into the bedroom.

I felt so very alive as he made love to me, as though having been in mortal danger so recently had amplified all of my senses tenfold.

Even if it would only be this, only tonight, I would revel in it. Every heavenly second with him would be burned into my memory like a branding.

Afterward, as I was lying in his arms, his ragged breath drifting over my body in warm currents, I told him everything that had happened. I told him about the papers that Maddie had left for me, about the name badge and the tape recording, not stopping until I reached the part about the scene in the hemlock clearing. It would be much too difficult to relive that part of the night so soon after it had happened.

He listened, his breaths becoming more even and composed.

"I guess now you understand everything," he said, placing a light kiss upon my forehead. "Why I couldn't tell you the truth about me. You'd have thought me insane."

"Probably," I said with a little laugh. "But now that I do know the truth?"

He disentangled himself from me, and my heart sank.

"It's dangerous, Alma. We still don't understand a lot about how these portals and spirits work. There have been reports of possessions, of people dying. I open myself, my mind, to these things, in an attempt at communication, and, while we have had some success, there is still so much uncertainty. You saw that for yourself tonight."

"But," I ventured after a moment. "Couldn't we figure this out together?"

"Maddie seems to think so," he said, just as we heard the front door opening, and his sister's voice, along with Finn's, greeting a very happy Dot.

"Well?" I pressed, leaning up onto one arm so that I could look him in the eye.

"Okay," he said, huffing out a resigned sigh. "I don't think I could stand to lose you again, anyway." His eyes looked directly into mine, searching.

"I love you, Alma."

My heart leapt.

"I love you too, Luke. So much."

We kissed again, and I knew that I was about to embark upon a much more exciting; much more meaningful, life.

Foodies
Vivian Kasley

The blood tasted good—at first. It reminded me of a choice cut of rare steak. The taste of the warm and salty liquid ran down my chin and I felt almost like I could combust. But then time marched on, and I got sick of the same old thing and hated the taste of just any old ordinary blood. Just like there're a variety of foods to eat, so are there a variety of people, too. I detested the mere thought of another homeless person. When you're new, the blood tastes amazing no matter who it's from. As time passes—a lot of time—you develop a keener sense, just like a rich man who has a taste for the finer things in life. I had to get back to New England, that's where the people taste best, but I wasn't sure if it was safe to return yet.

I was created by this super-hot cliché male vampire back in the early 90's while at a night club. My boyfriend couldn't go out that night as usual, so I went alone to blow off some steam. Of course, I had no idea the hot guy was a vampire as we danced the night away. I was so tipsy that I had no idea what was happening as he bit down on my neck and I laughed when he asked me to bite his, too. Unfortunately, there's no morning after pill for this type of thing.

I watched enough vampire movies to think I knew all there was to know. But I didn't know a damn thing. The bloodsucker who did it owed me an explanation, I felt, so I returned to the club and wandered around other popular night-time hang outs, but I never saw him again and had to learn everything all on my own. It was a lot of trial and error, mostly error in my case.

I know that we're usually created by mistake or because one of us got carried away in the moment, which I'm guessing is how I came about. You must bite a vampire back and ingest some of their blood to actually turn, which like an idiot, I did. Too much sunlight is pure hell. We don't turn to ash or anything, but get enough of it, and it's like drinking mercury. Then I almost killed myself by improper feeding, which is when a vampire refuses to drink human blood and tries to live off animals instead. Think of a human only eating iceberg lettuce and ice cubes—it's basically vampire anorexia.

We don't always kill all of our victims, but it's not a good idea to let too many live, because word spreads. I'd like to think we're like mosquitoes, annoying at times, but other times we can be deadly. We do live forever and this's an issue, because you have to live knowing you've hurt people you loved or someone else loved, and that fucking sucks. Also, you're alone most of the time since you'll never grow old and can't explain it.

My name is Penelope Jones and I was a young athletic young woman living in sunny Florida. I loved my life. It was the fucking 90's! I was beautiful and tan, engaged, and in my last year of college. My fiancé, Paul, was a successful lawyer. He was having a house built in Sarasota where we were to move after we were married. I repeat, I loved my life!

Then I woke up the day after my night at the club with the most massive headache. My mouth tasted like dead rat. My eyes hurt and my whole body felt like I fell into poison ivy. I was so itchy. I was lying in bed under the blanket with the same top I had on the night before, but no pants. I could barely open my eyes. That night, Paul dropped by. He had a key and let himself in.

"Paul? Is that you?" I managed to croak.

"Yeah, who else would it be? What're you doing in bed still? You never picked up your phone, so I was worried. Are you sick?" He walked into my room and made a face. "Christ, did something die in here? It smells like a dead animal or something."

"I don't think so. Ugh, I feel awful. I don't even remember what happened last night."

"What do you mean 'don't remember'? What happened? Did some guy slip you something? This's why I tell you not to go out alone—too many bad people out there!"

"I don't know if someone slipped me something…I don't think so, though." My head throbbed.

I left out the part about biting some guy's neck after he bit mine. My hand went to my neck then, but I felt nothing there. Paul came over to the bed, pulled the blanket down, and let out a small yelp.

"What?" I asked.

"You look awful!"

"Huh? Like how?" I looked down at myself.

"Nell, you have red blotches all over you and you smell…terrible. Did you puke in the bed?" He lifted the covers off my legs and gagged.

"No, I didn't puke!" I shouted.

"We need to get you to a hospital, Nell! You're sure someone didn't slip you something? I've warned you about going out alone!" He stood with his hands on his hips and looked at me like I was a petulant child.

"I don't know! I'm sure it's the drinking mixed with the fact that I haven't eaten at all or whatever. Just let me rest. I hate the ER, they never do anything anyway. I'll go if I have to, but right now I just want some rest."

"If you're sure but…I still think we should go. I'm going to go get you some soup and stuff. Just please get in the shower though, Nell…you stink like hot garbage!"

"Ok, I get it. Just go, Paul." I grumbled.

I was annoyed and thought, I don't really look that bad, do I? Well, turns out I did. My reflection made me wince. I showered and got back into bed. Paul came back with Chinese food and medicine. I ate soup and an eggroll, but couldn't keep it down. Paul stayed that night and he was confused when he woke up to me biting his neck. He'd tried to push me off, but it was no use, I was latched on like a lamprey. Killing Paul was a mistake and I felt awful about it—still do. I left town and didn't look back. My family must think I'm dead, but it's better that way and I didn't want anyone else I cared about getting hurt.

I ended up in New England and learned the area pretty well. The blood of the Yankees was divine. I don't know if it's what they eat, the blueberries, or the air up there, but they have the umami factor! I'd been there for a while and planned on staying for as long as I could get away with. Then came the night in Connecticut, back in 2012 I believe, when a woman came home to me feasting on her husband.

She thought we were having an affair and began to shout obscenities. She threw a lamp, high-heel shoes, a glass, and eventually fired a gun. She missed me, but not her husband. It caught that asshole in the head. I let go of him and he rolled onto the carpet with his mouth agape. She called me a succubus and I took an odd bow before I dashed out of the upstairs window. Thankfully, I was dressed comfortably that night. Comfort is key for a vampire.

There was a sensational news report the next day about a prominent Connecticut politician who was murdered by his wife. She shot him in the head when she walked in on him with another woman. She claimed the strange woman was on top of her husband and then jumped from their upstairs window after she fired the gun. The distraught wife claimed she thought the mystery woman was trying to kill him, but authorities didn't buy it. Turned out her husband was not entirely a good guy either. They went through his stuff and found porn of the illegal variety on his laptop, further giving his wife motive to pop his ass, according to the media.

I laughed about it then and thought, the asshole got what he deserved. Even if she continued to try to tell police that I was in her room, they would have thought her crazy. Also, it just so happens that after we feed, our saliva creates a type of bonding agent that heals up the wound almost instantly, so no evidence of a bite wound. I didn't think I would get caught, but I left the state for a while anyway to let things die down.

***

Over the years I developed restraint. I took buses and trains almost everywhere I went and took cash from my victims to buy clothes or whatever else I needed. I stayed in shitty motels even though I didn't sleep, but rest is still essential. Plus, there's almost always free cable and I liked to watch the Food Network all night. When the year turned 2020, I decided it was ok to return to Connecticut. I found the woods to be to my liking and of course, the blue-blooded people. I hoped to travel someday, maybe to Europe. I was becoming quite the gourmand!

There was a huge yellow moon the night he found me. I was feeding on a gorgeous woman from a wine bar I liked. She was newly divorced and bi-curious. Lucky me. I'd been kissing her silicone breasts and then her milk white neck, until she fell asleep. We were in her long winding gravel driveway. Her house lay on acres of land and it was near the woods. I wasn't going to drain her, but she tasted good, and I got carried away. I'd just finished and he was standing at the end of the driveway watching me.

He was tall with broad shoulders and he wore an Indiana Jones style hat on his head. He was holding a small stake in his hand. He had what appeared to be a utility belt on, holding up his dark cargo pants. I stifled a giggle and wiped my mouth with the back of my hand.

"I see you, blood-sucker. I knew I wasn't crazy," he growled. Good Lord was he hot! His eyes were olive green and brown curls peeked out from under his hat. For a vampire, I actually felt like I was flushing. I stepped back and smirked at him. He scowled and crept closer to me. I was amused and curious. Then he said, "Times up, sweetheart. It's too bad too, because you're very beautiful, but you're a monster all the same. So, let's get this over with." He held up the stake. I began to laugh and I couldn't stop. He lowered his arm clearly annoyed. "What's funny," he asked.

"You are. You're very…well prepared. A gun, the stake, the bottles attached to your cute little belt, what else do you have there? Is that a cross? Please tell me it is. Did you order all this from the internet, like vampirehunter.com or something?" I continued to laugh. He shifted his belt around and moved the cross to the back of his pants. "Ok, I'll stop laughing at you! It's just so damn funny!"

"You think it's funny that I'm going to kill you?" He tilted his Greek God of a face.

"Well, not exactly, but it's cute that you have a starter pack. How'd you even find me and figure out…you know? I always thought I was pretty careful."

"I saw you last summer. You were the most stunning creature I'd ever seen. It was at the 4th of July event on the beach. You know, the one with the clambake? You were sitting off by yourself. That beautiful long white-blonde hair can't be missed. I was working up the nerve to talk to you and then you got up and walked off when the fireworks started, so I followed. That's when I saw you doing it. You had him propped up against the wall of the restroom. Your mouth was on his neck, but then you must've gotten spooked, because you left him there slumped over. I asked the guy if he was alright and he nodded, it was like he was drunk and had no idea what happened. Then I looked for you, but you disappeared."

"You gathered I was a vampire from that? C'mon!" I snorted.

"Well, not exactly just from that. Then I saw you at a coffee shop one night a few weeks later. The night of the poetry readings."

"You know, you're a bit of stalker?" I pretended to be shocked.

"I was there for a friend. I saw you right away, it was your hair. I watched from a distance. You looked so beautiful I almost forgot about the incident at the clambake. Again, you got up and left with some guy, and again I followed you. Sure enough, you were doing the same thing to him behind a dumpster. Except this time, he didn't walk away—you killed him! You sauntered from behind the dumpster and never looked back. And tonight, I happened to see you get into that woman's car, so I followed you yet again. However, this time I came prepared. Once you know what you're looking for, it's easier to spot. I'm actually surprised you've never been caught."

I was indignant and arched my eyebrow. "Well, I haven't. Why didn't you just call the cops, stalker?"

"Who'd believe me? The cops wouldn't know what you were. And they don't have one of these." He held up the stake.

"It's very small." I smirked.

"It doesn't need to be big to get the job done," he said.

"That's what she said." I laughed.

"What? You're one twisted bloodsucker. That wasn't meant to be sexual." He spat.

"Do you want it to be?" I was testing him. After all, he was hot. I moved toward him.

"What're you playing at? Don't try and charm me or whatever it is you do!" He backed away.

"No charms. I find you very attractive, that's all. I didn't get your name." I purred.

"I didn't offer it…but it's Josh, not that it matters. Now back up or else!"

"Or else you'll put that tiny stake through my black heart?" I could smell him. He smelled delicious.

"I mean it!" He raised his weapon, but I grabbed it firmly and ran my fingers down the small carved piece of wood.

"Do it then. I'm fucking tired of all this anyway. I'm lonely, I'm bored, and I'm…horny." I ran my tongue over my top lip.

He scanned my face. I held onto the stake, then moved it toward my chest. I placed the tip on my breasts and slowly drug it downward just underneath and held it over my heart. His aroma aroused me. It smelled like spicy cologne and his sweat, which was a salty coppery smell, not unlike fresh blood. A familiar warmth spread from my head to my girly bits. I wanted him—not to feed on—I wanted to fuck him. I hadn't felt like that in ages.

We both held the stake firmly. I stood my ground and looked him in the eyes as he stared back into mine deciding what he was going to do. He told me not to move and got out a cell phone from his pocket. "I'm going to call the police and tell them what you did. You're going to stay here until they show up and tell them you killed this lady," he said.

"And If I don't?" I asked.

"You die," he said.

"So, how'd I kill her? Do I tell them I'm a vampire? You just said they wouldn't believe that."

"I have no idea yet, but you're going to tell them something. I might just stick this through you before they even get here."

He swiped his finger over his cell's screen, but his slick hand made him lose his grip. He let loose a ton of cuss words when the phone hit the ground. I kicked it away and sprinted down the driveway. "God damn it," he shouted.

I could hear him not far behind me and I couldn't help but admire his determination. I knew he couldn't really catch me and I smiled as I ran into the dark woods. Have fun finding me in here, I thought and settled against a damp tree. I heard some leaves rustling as he made his way in. His flash light lit up a large area as he scanned the woods. I covered my mouth to keep from laughing. This guy was something else.

When I didn't hear him any longer I stepped out and started moving further into the woods toward the river I knew ran nearby. I felt a stab of disappointment when I thought of him. I normally was able to charm most men. Oh, well. It wasn't meant to be. I heard the rush of the water, pulled my shirt off, and hung it from a tree limb. Then I took my Converse off and slid down my black jeggings.

The water felt good on my feet. It wasn't very deep and I laid down looking up at the moon through the tree tops. The smooth river rocks massaged my back as the water moved over me in a sweeping motion. I ran my hands over my breasts and slid them down the length of my lean body. Then, I thought of Josh and began to touch myself.

I must've closed my eyes in ecstasy and between that and the sound of the water rushing in my ears, I almost didn't hear him. I sat up and he was standing at the water's edge. I had no idea how long he'd been watching me. He said nothing, but he held my clothes over his arm. I wasn't cold, but I was shivering.

"Can I please have my clothes?" I hissed. I was annoyed and embarrassed.

"I'm not letting you get away this time. My phone is busted, but I do have these." He dangled hand cuffs and rope in front of me. I could easily out run him, but I had no clothes and wasn't sure how I would explain my naked self to anyone once I got out of the woods. I could always make a run for it, hit up a house, and just steal some.

"Have it your way then, pervert. I'm sure you enjoyed the show," I said.

He looked down when I said that and I pretended to make my way out of the water, but I ran forward feeling victorious until I slipped and hit a large river rock. He was quick and we splashed and thrashed for a minute, but in the end, he dragged me out of the water. I was naked and handcuffed. He tried not to look at my breasts. His hat had fallen off and his head full of wet curls was sexy, not to mention the shirt that clung to his chiseled chest. I was actually quite aroused being cuffed and naked in front of him.

I didn't intend to let him know that I could easily break out of the handcuffs. He could shoot me, which wouldn't kill me, but it would hurt and I didn't feel like dealing with it. Plus, a gunshot might be heard. As soon as he wasn't paying attention, I'd make my move. When he tried to pull my pants onto my wet legs, I could tell he was trying to ignore my sex so close to his face. "You can't run forever. Hold still and help me help you." As he struggled with my pants, I was getting out of the cuffs.

"You can't just pull jeggings onto wet legs, dumbass! Here, let me do it." I grabbed my pants and kicked him in the groin. He let out a cry and crumpled to the ground. I grabbed my shirt and shoes, then ran. I had only just gotten my shirt on before he tackled me from behind. He turned me over and straddled me. His strong hands were on my wrists.

"Will you just leave me the fuck alone! I could've easily killed you, but I didn't! I'm re-thinking that now!" I said.

His breath was sweet as he panted into my face. Water dripped from his curls onto my cheeks. Those olive eyes stared down at me for some time and then the next thing I knew, he was kissing me. I had no idea what the fuck was happening, but I kissed him back. Our tongues coiled around each other's like snakes in a mating ritual. I caressed him through his pants and he was as hard as marble. He reached down with expert fingers and circled my clit slowly. I felt myself swell as he continued. He pulled my shirt up and sucked my nipples making me cry out.

I didn't care that I was lying on the forest floor with leaves stuck to my bare ass, I only knew that I wanted him inside me. He pulled his shirt off and laid it under my head. I had to laugh at this chivalrous act, since just moments before he was trying to kill me. I pulled his hair as he made his way down my body, kissing and licking me. He put his head between my legs and began to devour me. He teased by licking my outer lips and going up and down and all around. Finally, his tongue slowly circled my clit until I couldn't stand it. I burst into orgasm and my body shook all over. I bucked under him and he moaned.

I sat up and put my hands to his bare chest. He had an impeccable body. I pushed him down and got on top of him. I took his utility belt off and slung it to the ground beside him, then pulled his pants down and began to reciprocate. I circled my tongue around his head and used my hand to stroke the generous length of his member. He moaned loudly, so I stopped. I smiled and shook my head at him. He began to sit up, but I pushed him back down. I crawled back on top of him, and lowered myself down slowly. I went up and down then leaned back and grinded. I squealed in delight as he used his finger to massage my clit. I leaned forward and he suckled at my breasts as rode I him hard.

I slowed it down and we moved together and as I felt my muscles clench around him, he came too. I leaned in and began kissing him, but when I got to where his pulse was beating rapidly in the side of his neck, I stopped. I watched it for a while and then kissed him there. When I moved lower, he stopped me and whispered, "Listen, I have no idea what came over me, but…wow."

"I came over you." I smiled.

"I meant that I—," He was flustered.

"I know what you meant," I said.

"I don't even…I don't know your name," he stammered.

"It's Penelope." I said.

"That was fucking amazing, Penelope," he said.

"It was. We should do that again some time." I licked my lips.

Then I cried out when he grabbed me to him, kissed me, and turned me around. I was on my knees when he entered me again. He fucked me from behind and teased me with long slow calculated strokes. I moved myself into him and he sped it up. We came together and started giggling when an owl hooted in the tree. It looked down at us like a peeping Tom. "I guess he liked what he saw," I panted and we laughed again.

We walked back down to the river with our clothes to rinse off. He was quiet for some time and I was too. I watched him in the water for a while, then I walked over to him and he pulled me close to him. We sat together in the cool water and kissed for a long time. Again, I watched his pulse as my head rested against his chest.

"Does this mean you don't want to kill me anymore?" I asked.

"No, I don't want to kill you. I never really wanted to kill you, I just didn't know what to expect. I didn't know what you were like." He spoke into my hair.

"Well, what now?" I asked.

"I don't know…I'm thinking," he said.

"I'm not so bad after all though, am I?" I looked up at him.

"There's a dead woman in her driveway not too far from here. That's not a good thing."

"She was driving under the influence and could've killed someone," I told him.

"Well, in that case." He pulled my face up to his and kissed me.

I kissed his neck but stopped short when he said, "Just do it if you're going to do it. I know you want to."

"Do what?" I asked.

"Bite me," he whispered.

I sat quietly and thought about how lonely I'd been. I wanted to travel the world, explore new things. New England was getting stale. I thought of what this life would be like with a companion. I was about to ask him if he knew what he was asking when he stopped me.

"I haven't been totally honest with you, Penelope," he said.

"What do you mean?" I asked.

"I did see you at the clambake and at the coffee shop, but I knew what you were the moment I saw you. I wondered about you for a long time. When I saw your long blonde hair and those striking brown eyes, I knew."

"Care to explain?" I moved away from him puzzled.

"It's easier if I show you," he said.

"Show me?" I muttered.

"Come with me. My car's not too far." He pulled my hands into his. My feet stayed planted into the river bed below. I was uncertain what he wanted to show me or if I wanted to know. He let go of my hands. "Please, Penelope? Come with me?" He pleaded.

I stood there for a minute then finally moved toward him and took his hand. We got dressed and headed out of the woods. By the time we got to his car, I knew daylight was not far behind. The sun would be up in a couple of hours. I told him as much and he said not to worry. We drove at a good clip and the woods were a blur as we whizzed by. I sat quietly and neither of us said anything for a while.

"Nice car," I finally remarked.

"Thanks. I got it for myself last year. I'd always wanted a Porsche."

"Well, it's an awesome vehicle. A real beauty. Sleek."

Another half hour went by and dawn was closing in on us. I looked out the window and up toward the disappearing moon. The car began to slow as we went up a narrow road and down a long driveway. We came to a stop in front of a large two-story house. Josh parked the car and got out to open my door. He took my hand and helped me out. The house looked mildly familiar as we made our way to the front door and a feeling of dread flooded over me.

"You live alone?" I asked.

"I do now. My mother passed a couple years ago, and my father died years before her. Just me and Sprocket." He smiled as he stuck the key in the door.

I was going to ask who Sprocket was, but a huge black lab jumped on him as we went in. The dog stopped and stared at me with his ears up and growled.

"Enough, Sprocket! It's okay, boy!" Josh took my hand.

"I get that a lot." I told him.

"Come in. Sit down anywhere you like. Let me start a fire, it's chilly for May. Would you like some tea?" I could tell he was nervous.

I just looked at him, smiled, and shrugged my shoulders. I sat on the couch and watched as Josh pulled all the curtains shut and started a fire. Sprocket watched me like a hawk. I felt a bit odd sitting in this house. The room was very large with cathedral ceilings. It was decorated with ornate floor rugs and expensive furniture. Josh came back toward the couch and patted Sprocket's head. The dog whined in protest.

"So, I assume no tea then?" He asked.

"Um, yeah, I don't really drink anything but…well, you know." I nodded.

"Ha, yeah, I forgot for a second. So you don't eat or drink anything ever at all except that?"

"Well, I mean, I can sip tea if it makes you feel better, but it might make me sick. I once drank a latte and puked for an hour. It was worth it though." I chuckled.

"That sounds awful. Ok, no tea." He bit his lip and fidgeted.

"So, are you going to tell me what this's about?" I made a move to stand and Sprocket went bonkers.

"Sprocket, enough! You wanna go to time out?" Josh pointed toward a large kennel in the corner.

The dog went and lay down on his bed, but didn't take his eyes off us. Josh took my hand and led me to the stairs. There were several rooms upstairs, but we made our way toward the last one down the hall and stopped at the door. He kissed my hand before he opened it. I froze as I looked into the room.

"This's my room. Well, it is now. It's funny, because out of all the bedrooms, I chose the one downstairs when my parents first bought the house. I didn't want to be upstairs where my parents were. They were always arguing."

I went into the spacious room and walked around. I stopped at the window and traced my fingers along the edge. The sun had started to rise and its long arms reached in. Josh ran toward me in a panic. "Oh, sorry! Here, let me close the blinds."

I remembered, then turned and looked at the dresser where a frame sat. I saw the picture of his parents and his father's face smiled back at me. He'd been dashing in his expensive blue suit that night, undressing me with his eyes before taking me home with him. We came here, to this house, to this room. He'd said his wife was out of town. He opened the window to let air in and then he undressed. I remembered how I stood there as he oddly put his clothes away before we ever got into the bed and how I fed on him before his wife walked in. I suddenly understood and backed away from Josh. I killed his father. It was my fault his father was dead. Oh, boy. This was twisted.

"You remember, don't you?" He asked.

I looked down. "Yes, I do and I'm very sorry."

"I was away at college at the time. For so long my mother claimed there was another woman in here with my father. She swore the woman had fangs…she never stopped believing it. She hated my father, but knowing she shot him ate her alive. She'd insisted a woman with long white blonde hair was on top of him and said at first, she thought you were screwing, but then she saw he was still as you sucked at his neck. She said she shot at you, but hit my father by accident. She said you jumped from the window and that when she ran to look out, you were already gone."

"It's true. I was here," I said. I remembered his mother. She was shocked when I showed my fangs. I'd bowed. Why the fuck did I do that? She screamed before I jumped. I felt shame for thinking of how annoying I thought she was.

"My mother told the police everything, but there was no evidence of you. There was evidence, however, that my mother got home early that weekend from her sister's house, that my mother threw shit all over the room, shot the gun several times, and killed him. They figured she must've been fighting with him and it got out of hand. Since my father had many affairs, they couldn't pin point one woman, let alone one who could jump from the second story window and onto the ground without breaking any bones. They thought my mother went insane with all the affairs and his appetite for kiddie porn, and shot him dead." I stayed quiet and sat down on the bed as he continued.

"I came home for my father's funeral. Even though he had been an important man, not many people showed up after all the news came out. I felt sorry for my mother. She was sad and depressed. She ended up getting charged with involuntary manslaughter, but never served any real time. She had a good lawyer and they took pity on her due to the circumstances. She had to go to therapy and she was on probation up until her death."

"How'd she die?" I whispered.

"She pretty much drank herself to death and with all the pills she was on, made for quite a cocktail. My mother always loved my father, she hated what he did, but she loved him. I tried to be there for her, but she was so out of it she barely noticed me. I was disgusted with my father, and to be honest, didn't even miss him. My mother, though, I loved her very much and miss her every day. After her death I moved back into the house. After going through the closet, I did find something interesting."

"What?" I asked.

"A single long white-blonde hair. It was in the pocket of one of my father's suits. My mother never got rid of them. I put the jacket on to see if it fit me, and reached into the pocket and something wrapped around my finger. It was your hair. One single hair. I never told anyone. And then I saw you on the 4th of July, and at the coffee shop and I knew my mother was telling the truth. You were what she thought you were."

"What now? I won't run this time." I told him.

"Did you sleep with him? My Father?" He asked.

"What? No! I never slept with him. He took his clothes off and he wanted to, but I only kissed him and wanted…you know. I never meant for any of that to happen. He said your Mother was out of town. I followed him for a few days and knew what he was. He picked up underage girls on the streets. I'm so sorry. I just…" I stopped.

"It's over. I get it. He deserved it. He was involved with a lot of bad things. It makes me sick! My poor mother! I only wish I'd known sooner and I would've killed him myself, spared her all the grief." He sat beside me on the bed.

I looked up at him and saw tears in his eyes. I brushed his face and he grabbed my wrist and lay me down. He kissed me hungrily and pulled off my shirt. He kissed me all over and I moaned as he entered me. He fucked me hard this time. The head board shook and at one point I swear the bed lifted up. I scratched his back and wrapped my long legs around him. I bucked with each stroke and we both yelled out when we came.

We lay for a long time in his bed staring up at the ceiling before he looked at me. I turned to face him. "I'm not sure what we should do now, but I hardly know you, and you've no idea what my life is like. I'm a killer. I cannot change. Ever," I said.

"I know what you are. I don't care. Just tell me what it is you have always wanted to do?" He asked.

"What? Why?"

"Just tell me." He kissed my shoulder.

"Go to Europe. I think I'd blend in there better. You know, Transylvania or whatever."

"Let's do it!" He exclaimed.

"What?"

"Let's go. I have the means, I got nothing else to do. I haven't been to Europe in a while. We can fly at night or go by ship." He smiled.

"I can't ask you to do that! You don't even know me? I was involved with the murder of your father, Josh! I am also to blame for your mother's untimely death! I'm a monster!" I cried.

"I don't care. I want to be with you. Turn me if you have to, or is that even a thing? I don't know how that works. We can travel together, forever. I have plenty of funds." He was looking at me seriously.

"Josh, you don't know what you're asking. You can't be around the people you care about. You can't trust yourself. You can learn control, but sometimes it takes over. You have to kill. You have to drink human blood."

"I know what I'm asking. I'm asking you to do it. My family's gone."

"What about your dog? Sprocket? He needs you."

"He can come with us!" He pulled me close.

"You might eat him."

"I won't."

"You might," I said firmly.

"You won't let me." He kissed me.

"Josh, I…"

"Look, you said you were lonely, bored, and horny. I can help. I already helped with one of those. I can be with you, we can be together. I know I want this." He pleaded.

"If you do this, you can never go back. You can't ever have kids. Are you sure this is what you want?"

"I've never been more sure of anything in my life. Your face is the only one I want to see forever. I could look at it until the sun explodes. I want to make love to you forever. I want to…I want to feast beside you." He kissed me deeply.

I looked at his handcuffs on the floor attached to his belt. I thought about knocking him out, cuffing him to the bed, and leaving the key around his dog's collar. I wasn't sure if I could turn him, but I also thought about the many years I had been alone. I thought about Paul, my parents, and my old life. I thought. And I thought. And I thought. Then I looked at his neck.

"Please, Penelope. Please…" He whispered and kissed me.

I leaned in and inhaled his smell. I bit down sensually and drank very little. He moaned. I bit down on my own wrist and held it out to him. He drank freely and slowly until I pulled away. We made love again and then I instructed him to get some sleep before he never got any again. I told him he would feel terrible soon, but it would get better.

We lay there side by side and talked about all the different countries and where we would go first. He fell asleep on my breast and I slipped out from underneath him when it got dark and went downstairs. I opened the door and took Sprocket out. He growled at me, but went outside anyway. He did his thing, but I didn't let him back in. I tied him to the tree and left him water and food. Soon, Josh would wake, hungry, and I didn't want him to start off on the wrong foot. I patted Sprocket's head as he lapped up some water. He seemed to be getting used to me.

"It won't be long, boy. Soon, it'll all be ok," I said. He whined and then lay down in the soft grass.

I went back upstairs and watched Josh sleep. His breathing became rapid, his heart stopped, and the blotches began to spread all over his body. I kissed his eyelids, but he didn't stir. I laid beside him and turned on the Food Network. I wondered what Bobby Flay would taste like? I had my favorites. It was between him and Giada. Oh, but there were also all of those Chopped judges! I smiled and thought, Josh and I could be foodies together! The world may be shit at times, but we had each other now and that was more than most. I decided I was happy I had turned him. You only have one life to live, after all. One very, very long life.

Witchcliff
R.C. Mulhare

Arkham, Massachusetts – September, *1692*

Fallen maple leaves, gold and crimson, skittered across the packed dirt of Goodwife Elizabeth Lynch's dooryard, ahead of the gangly girl with her long homespun skirts tucked up as she ran in from the high road that ran through the village of Arkham. Rahab Blackthorne, Goodwife Lynch's housemaid, looked up from sweeping the leaves from the dooryard into a basket, releasing her touch on the wind which kept it from scattering more leaves as long as she swept the yard.

"Goody Lynch! Goody Lynch! My father is hurt! Come quickly! Come to the forge!" The girl, Sarah Jones, daughter of the village blacksmith cried.

Rahab propped the broom against the doorpost. "Goody Lynch is not here. She has gone to Goodwife Kaine's lying in. But I can tend him nearly as well as she."

The girl stopped before her, clasping her apron and twisting its cloth. "I shan't take you from your work here, shall I?"

"It would be unchristian of me to not aid a man in pain." The leaves already drifted back into the dooryard. "The leaves and dust will keep. Your father's injuries cannot. How did he come to harm? You can tell me as I collect the necessary herbs."

Sarah followed Rahab into the house and the pantry behind the kitchen, with its bundles of herbs hanging from the beams overhead. Rahab reached down to take a bundle of lavender and another of comfrey.

"His leg, he burned his leg. A red-hot horseshoe fell from his tongs as he worked the forge, shoeing Captain John Hathorne's mare. The iron burned through the stocking to his flesh beneath," Sarah said.

Rahab took a jar of willow bark from a shelf along the plastered wall and tucked it into a basket. She stopped herself from calling her cloak to her and instead, took it down from its peg in the wall, draping it over her shoulders, as Sarah led her out of the house and up the path to the high road.

***

At Goodman Jones's smithy, Major Nathan Stark, one of Arkham's constables, knelt beside the village smith as he sprawled on a bench in the dooryard. Hugh Jones had propped up his injured leg, a water-soaked cloth pressed over the burn.

"Let me up, I've 'ad a moment's rest. I can put that shoe back upon yer master's mare." Goodman Jones tried to rise.

"Nay, it is better that you rest that limb," Stark replied

"You 'ave yer rounds to make. I wouldn't want to keep you from 'em. God made me strong. I can shift this."

Stark pressed the man's shoulder. "Take your rest. God would not have you harm yourself further. Would you keep me from my duty of charity?" he added, with a small smile.

The smithy apprentice held the halter of the mare, which shifted her hooves as two figures approached, the smith's daughter and the Lynch's indentured servant, a tall woman with dark red hair peeping from her demure linen cap, a basket of herbs over her arm. The Jones girl fluttered in worry about her father, to make sure of his comfort, but stepped aside to let the woman tend the man's injury.

"You did well to cool the burn," The maid said, addressing the girl and keeping her gaze averted demurely, proper for her place. But with her gentle, silvery voice, Stark caught himself wondering at the color of her eyes.

"Major Stark made certain I kept the cloth on th' wound and stayed off my foot," Jones said.

"I can bring the mare tomorrow or at another day, and leave you in Goodwife Blackthorne's hands," Stark said, hoping to put some space between himself and the girl, now soaking herbs in the bowl of water that Jones's daughter brought on her request. *As dutiful as she is fair*, he thought, chastening himself immediately for letting his gaze linger for too long on the maid.

"It would do well if your father could rest his leg as much as he can," Rahab said, looking to Sarah. As she glanced aside, she caught sight of a tall young man, tanned by the sun, his black hair touched with chestnut brown in the sunlight, broad shouldered and sturdy, yet fine of form and face. She knew of him and had seen him about the town, but had not seen him so close. Her mother, Fionnulagh, would have prompted her to put the lightest come-hither charm on him to close the distance between them, but she preferred to have him come at his own time and pace. To do otherwise would call too much attention to herself in this Puritan town, and she would not risk falling prey to the madness that took Salem to their south.

Even still, as she wound the bandages to bind the poultice to Goodman Jones's wound, she leaned closer to Sarah. "Who is the tall dark man in the fine cloak?" she asked.

"That is Major Nathan Stark, a nephew of Captain Winthrop Pickman, in Salem Town," Sarah said. "He took an appointment as a constable."

A man she would need to tread carefully about, she thought. Aloud, she said, "A well-placed man to tend to the local folk and protect them as they need."

In the further corner of her mind, she murmured the words of a healing spell, infusing some of her power into the poultice. "She has a gentle touch, she does," Goodman Jones said, looking to Stark. "Methinks she would make a good wife."

"She would, when her indenture has been fulfilled," Rahab said, softly.

When Rahab returned to the house, Goodwife Lynch had returned from tending Goodwife Kaine's house, and had started to mull a pipkin of cider for herself. "What drew you away from the house?"

"Sarah Jones called here. Her father had burned his leg in the smithy. I went to tend to him," Rahab replied.

"You could have waited for me, but with burns, time can make the difference in the healing."

"I did not mean to overreach my station."

"You did well, but you are still my servant."

"And a servant is not greater than her mistress." Rahab inwardly chafed at this stricture. She could forebear with some of the things her mistress required, such as attending Parson Horne's interminable sermons of a Sunday, and keeping her own customs to herself. Marriage could release her from her bond, but she would first need to find a suitable man who would have her hand. The thought of putting the come-hither upon Major Stark returned to her mind, but she would not stoop to that. Better for the man to court her attentions as he chose and as fate or providence or some mingling of the two intended, that she could raise her standing among the townspeople.

Later that night, when she lay asleep, she let her dreaming mind wander among the stars, till she gazed upon the cottage behind the town meeting house, where Major Stark quartered with Pastor Horne. Perhaps he, too, would dream of her.

***

Three days had passed, and on a fair day that felt more like late August than late September, the Lynch household turned out to gather the apples in the croft behind their house before the rains returned and the frost fell. Rahab wondered if such a glorious day served as a harbinger of things to come.

Old Goody Keziah Mason hobbled into the croft, her tatterdemalion brown cat with its weird face trailing her rundown heels. "Goodman Lynch! Goodwife Lynch! Goodman Jones has taken a turn for the worse. His wife is beside herself with worry."

Goodman Lynch climbed down from his ladder. Goodwife Lynch, at the foot with her apron open, emptied what apples she had into a bushel. "Has his wound soured? Has he changed the dressing and washed the wound?"

"He burns with a fever and raves that he has been poisoned," Goody Mason said. "Methinks he is bewitched."

"He might have been bewitched or driven mad if that cat of yours stared at him long enough," Rahab murmured, gathering apples from the lower branches of another tree, and raising a mental shield about her mind, against the darkness she sensed about the wild-looking older woman.

Goodwife Lynch glanced to Rahab. "I did not treat Goodman Jones. I had gone to Goodwife Kaine's lying in that day. Our housemaid tended to him."

Goody Mason looked to Rahab, eyes narrowed. "How then do you know that your tripping maid did not curse his wound? Do you know of all that she does when you cannot see?" Her gaze wandered to Goodman Lynch.

He blinked, shaking his head as if he cleared it, then looked to his wife. "Have you seen her going into the woods? Has she, to your knowledge, consorted with the French or the heathen savages when they came to the town?"

Goodwife Lynch looked to Rahab. "Nay, though I have not watched her every movement, certainly not in the night when she ought to be asleep. I shall see to Goodman Jones. Rahab, stay here and tend to my apples." With that, she went into the house, clearly to collect the necessary herbs. Goody Mason followed, leaving Rahab to collect the apples, while dodging the suspicious glances of her master and his children.

That night, over supper, the household exchanged few words. Goodwife Lynch looked perturbed over Goodman Jones's condition. They went to their respective beds, still ill at ease. Rahab, in her bed in the rafters of the house, extended her hearing as best she could, weeding out, as best she could, the house creaking and the wind in the trees outside. She decided that night she would not let herself stray too deep into the dreamlands of Arkham, lest someone with the eyes to see her venturing into the night.

***

That same night, Stark slept, though his mind kept watch, dreaming of a moonlit forest, a place he would not have ventured too far into at that hour in the waking world, and yet sleep drew him thither. He walked the path alone, desiring a companion to ward off the fear creeping into his heart, like ice slowly coating a wintry pond. *Where two or three are gathered,* he thought, and he caught himself wishing that he could see Goody Blackthorne's face in his dream.

He awakened in the morning, chiding himself for desiring a dream of a woman not his wife. *Or perhaps not yet my wife,* he thought with a secret smile.

In full daylight, at the request of Captain Hathorne, he brought one of his mules to the smithy to have it reshod. But as he reached the smithy, he found the doors closed and the windows shuttered, the chimney cold of smoke. No sign of Goodman Jones. A cluster of farmers and tradesmen, some with beasts wanting shoes, others with broken wheel rims or other tools for repair, had gathered before the door, the smith's apprentice beseeching them, even as they murmured. "Why is the smithy shut?" - "Has Goodman Jones's wound grown worse?" - "Boy, where is your master?"

"Begging yer pardon, good men, but the Lord took him to the reward or debt awaited him," the apprentice said.

The crowd murmured softly, some bowing their heads solemnly:

"Goodwife Lynch tended his wound, did she not?"

"No, it was Goody Blackthorne, the indentured maid, Goodwife Lynch's apprentice."

"The redhaired one?"

Goody Mason's voice rose from the midst of the crowd, "Aye, she tended his wound, and doubtless bewitched it."

The apprentice looked about him, eyes wide, shifting his feet like a wary colt. "She tended his wound with care. How could she witch him?"

"The worst of witches hide their sins in kindness. My kinfolk in Salem knew that well," Goody Mason said.

The crowd cried out:

"Boy, go to your master's wife and warn her!"

"The devil has fled Salem to find shelter in Arkham."

"Do not let this misdeed go unpunished."

"Let God's justice be rendered!"

The apprentice scuttled from the smithy and up the slope behind it to his master's house, his leather apron flapping loose. The crowd drifted away, murmuring among themselves. Stark guided the mule down the road to Salem, to the smithy there.

The smith, while filing the mule's front hoof, chattered of things at hand. The trials had wound down, but the talk of witches still occupied people's tongues. "Hope them witches ain't hexed the crops."

"I would hope that witches, if they must cast their spells, would focus on something less broad, for if they harm the crops, they would starve themselves as well," Stark said. "Or does the Black-Clad Man feed his minions as well?"

"Doubt it. He ain't done much to save his servants, seein' the ones we hung." The smith lowered the mare's right hoof and reached for the left. Stark's ears burned at these words, but he said no more.

When he returned to Arkham that afternoon, he found a crowd gathered about the meetinghouse, some spilling onto the green. Goodwife Jones stood in the midst, speaking with Parson Horne and Captain Hathorne, a nondescript small man, one whom few would suspect to look at him that he had tried and convicted so many cases of congress with the Devil.

"What goes on here?" Stark asked.

Old Goody Toothaker hobbled forward, shaking her bony finger at Rahab. "It was her doing, the shameless strumpet! Hugh Jones's shade came to me in the night and warned me of her. She cursed the poultice she put on his leg. She befouled his wound!"

"She lies. A want of cleaning the wound soured it. Goodwife Lynch said as much when she tended him," Rahab cried.

"Be quiet, woman!" Justice Hathorne cried.

The gathering surged in their seats, crying out:

"No witch may speak!"

"Her voice will bewitch us."

"Already I can feel her voice in my head!"

A few people clamped their hands over their ears. Others made the gesture against the evil eye toward her. Those did no good, for he saw in her eyes that she bore no ill will toward these people. The company surged forward, pushed and shoved against each other. A woman shrieked in startled annoyance as they pressed her against the end of a bench.

A child's voice cried out, the cry suddenly muffled. A woman screamed. "Felicity! Oh, my Felicity! She is crushed!"

The mass of people parted, stepping back from a woman crouched on the floor, cradling a girl of no more than two years. *Who would bring a child so young to these proceedings?* Stark thought. He stepped forward to hold back the crowd. As he did so, the prisoner – no,

Rahab – stepped forward. "The witch! The witch will harm the babe!"

The crowd cried out:

"The witch caused the crush!"

"The witch charmed the babe under our feet!"

Rahab reached her bound hands to the child, the mother not noticing through her shock. Rahab laid her palms on the greenish bruises already showing on the child's brow. The air vibrated, growing warmer. Rahab looked up, her eyes rolling back in her head.

The child groaned and twitched, as she opened her eyes. "Mama?" she said. Rahab took a step back and sank to the floor.

"She is healed. Felicity is healed! Goody Blackthorne healed her with a touch. She cannot be a witch. If she was, why then would she harm Goodman Jones?" the mother cried.

The crowd cried out:

"Her power comes from Satan, the father of lies!"

"She healed the child to deceive us!"

"She tricked us as her master would!"

Justice Hathorne looked to Stark. "Take the witch away to the jail."

"Begging your pardon -" Stark said.

"Not a word, Major Stark. See to your duty," Hathorne ordered.

Stark drew in a breath. *God, forgive me for what I am about to commit, for acting as the Centurions did to your Son*, he thought. Approaching Rahab, he lifted her, cradling her as he bore her from the hall, outside to the cellar stairs and thence to the jail cells beneath.

Halfway down the stairs, Rahab's eyelids fluttered open. "The child…?"

"You healed her, but the crowd would have otherwise," Stark said.

"Where are you taking me?" She gazed about them as they entered the dank hallway of the jail.

"They made me bring you here. I will return the first chance I get," Stark said. "Had I refused, they would have done to me what they did to John Willard in Salem, when he refused to arrest the accused."

"Understood," she said, leaning her head against his shoulder. How he wished the first time he carried her thus had happened on their wedding night as he bore her over their threshold.

He brought her to the first empty cell, a tiny one across from a larger one now occupied by three trappers arrested earlier for intoxication. One called out a lewd remark in French, directed at the young couple.

"Be silent, Du Roche, or you may earn yourself another day in the stocks when your case comes before the justice," Stark ordered. He laid Rahab upon the musty straw in a corner of the cell. To her, he added, "You have my word, I will come to you as soon as I can." He wanted to lean down and kiss her cheek, but not with the three louts across the passage. He hoped that she understood. She laid a gentle hand on his wrist, a touch that eased his heart. He returned the touch, his body shielding these tender gestures. He departed the cell, locking it behind him before he unlocked the three in the opposite cell, to lead them above for their hearing. Night's sheltering cloak could not fall soon enough.

***

In dreams that night, Stark walked the autumn woods he had seen before, the trees already bare of leaves, lifting scrawny branches to the waning light of a crescent moon. He sensed that presence which had hovered in his dreams. "Rahab! Rahab? Was it you who came to me in this dream world?" Even while dreaming, he wondered if he cried out this name in the waking world.

As if his word had summoned her, Rahab appeared, caged within a cell of woven branches bound with straw, her wrists bound with vines still bearing leaves. "Nathanael, I am here."

He ran to the cage, taking her hands. "So it was you all along."

"I kept watch over you and this town, keeping the dark things in the wood at bay."

He drew back. "Then it is true that you are a witch?"

She looked at him with pained eyes. "In truth, I am, but I am not as people believe. My powers come not from the devil, but within me."

"Where, then, was your power when Goodman Jones took ill and died?"

"I placed some of my power into the poultice, that he might heal more easily. That someone did not change it or cleanse the wound with care, that brought on the ill humors that took his life."

He wanted to disbelieve her, but he had seen her heal that child, leaving his mind and heart clashing. His hold on her hands trembled

She slipped her hands free of his and reached up to touch his brow with her fingertips. He felt her warmth, warmer than one would feel in a mere dream. He leaned closer intending to kiss her cheek, but she bowed her head.

He shook awake, his hand strangely warm. Listening, to make certain the household slept, Stark rose and dressed as quietly as he could. Carrying his boots to the door and wrapping his copy of the jail keys in a second cloak hidden under his own, he slipped out into the darkness. He took the long way around the meetinghouse, to avoid the stocks on the town common, where the drunken trappers remained for the night.

He let himself into the jail, feeling his way along the damp hall. Rahab huddled against the wall, an empty water bowl beside her pallet. He knelt beside her to nudge her shoulder. She gasped and jerked awake.

"Do not be afraid, it is I," he said.

"You came to me," she said.

"I promised that I would take you away. There is a place in the woods, which I found while hunting, a small cave in the rocks."

"I know of it; I found it when I was out gathering blackberries with the children." He offered her the cloak, helping her drape the folds over her shoulders before he let her out of the cell, locking the door behind them.

He lead her out into the night, behind the meetinghouse and then through the town, slipping from shadow to shadow. The windows of the houses showed dull light from the banked kitchen hearths, but no signs of any wakeful villagers. A few cows drowsed in the milking pens behind several houses. Rahab slipped her arm through his. The world blurred slightly around them. "What is happening?" Stark asked, pulling away from her without letting go.

"This is a veil. I have shifted what little light there is so that no one will notice us," she said.

"But this is a deception and it distorts nature," he argued, his feet slowed, but he could not let her go.

She match her steps to his. "Was it a deception for another Rahab to hide the Israelite spies under a pile of flax on her roof?"

He shook his head at her cleverness, but could not help smiling, the shadows hiding it. "Woman, I would say you are too clever for your own good, if I did not know of the powers you wield and the heart that controls them."

They reached the stockade marking the limits of the town. The guard at the gate, open in this peaceful time, when hunters or farmers coming to market might arrive in the night, took no notice of them as they passed through.

Once under the trees, their view cleared. She held out her hand. "Solas," she said. A soft blue sphere of light formed itself above her open palm.

"A will o' the wisp?" he asked.

"One of the truths behind the tales, and some of the light of my soul," she said.

He lead her down a path off the side of the road, the bracken and low branches brushing their clothes. The path grew less worn the further they walked. Owls called from tree to tree over their heads. Something small, likely a rabbit or a raccoon, rustled the bracken and brushed Stark's ankles.

"Did you feel that?" Rahab said, her light wavering. Something with golden eyes appeared at the edge of the light, which caught on the branching horns above them. A buck turned and bounded off into the depths of the forest.

"First a rabbit, then a buck. God's creatures are afoot in these woods," he said.

The ground turned sandy under their heels, and the trees opened up before a great rocky ledge. In Rahab's light and the thin moonlight, the cave mouth and two hollows above it resembled the mouth and eyes in the skull of some giant beast of yore.

He lead her into the cave. They clambered over the rocks that littered the floor. The shadows from Rahab's light wavered about them till they found a sandy nook among the rocks. Gathering the cloak about her, Rahab sank down and dimmed the light. He knelt beside her. With her free hand, she found his in the shadows.

"I cannot stay for long. Daybreak will come, and my superiors will miss me," he said.

"And they will search for me," she added. "What are we to do? We cannot linger here in the forest. They will thrash us out for certain." With the harvest in progress, the farmers would have their hands too full to hunt them, but the craftspeople and the merchant folk would have time to thrash the bushes and forests. "And we cannot stay in a town that would not have us."

"I know a man who may help us. I shall speak with him and bring him here as soon as I can."

She released his hand. "Lead him here at the first moment you can without being detected."

He wanted to lean down and kiss her. He wanted to take her into his arms and know her as Adam knew Eve in another forest so long ago. Instead, he leaned his brow against hers, feeling her warmth before he broke away.

He stepped out into the night, the sky overhead even darker and the cold starlight standing out as the daybreak approached, and picked his way through the wood.

A hint of cold dawn light showed in the east as he returned to the village. He walked straight to the village green, making a show of checking the trappers drowsing in the stocks. He cuffed their shoulders, awakening the men, who cursed him before dropping back to sleep.

Back at the parsonage, he found Parson Horne already awake and seeing to the cows in the byre.

"You have arisen early," Horne noted, looking up from putting fresh fodder in the manger.

"I rose early to see to the miscreants in the stocks. They are still sleeping off their indulgence, and I doubt they'll repeat that, at least in Arkham," Stark replied.

Horne turned back to his cattle. "God's justice has been rendered."

Stark went into the house, to his chamber, where he laid himself down long enough for a catnap. No dreams came to him in that brief time. With full daylight and feeling refreshed, he arose and descended to the kitchen where Parson Horne and his family broke their fast.

"Have you heard aught of what happened in the night?" Horne asked.

"I saw the trappers who were imprisoned for raising Cain at the tavern in the hollow, when I went out for my rounds," Stark replied.

"Did you see aught of the witch turning herself into a bat and flying between the bars before she flew across the moon?" Parson Horne asked.

"The last I knew, Goody Blackthorne lay asleep in her cell," Stark replied.

"Captain Hathorne and his men came to our door whilst you lay abed and informed us that Goody Blackthorne had vanished from her cell. He inquired among the folk who live closest to the jail. Goody Mason claims she saw the bat emerge from the jail window," Parson Horne said. "She happened to rise and use the privy sometime between midnight and the third hour when she happened to see this strange sight."

"There are bats in the woods and the rafters of the byres. Could it have been but an ordinary night flier?" Stark asked and hoped that his dissembling did not betray him.

'You are not familiar with the ways of this place and the things which lurk in the shadows among the trees and within the hills," Horne said. "You trust too much in the folk who do not join us at our meetings."

Stark wished to snap back a comment, but replied, "As you say, Parson."

He passed that day as he did on general days: patrolling the roads on one of the parson's mares, seeing that the folk of the village and the town mingled in concord. He intervened in a dispute between two elder women and a meek merchant's clerk in the dry goods shop. But all that time, his thoughts strayed to Rahab, of her lovely face and form as much as he thought of her kneeling beside the injured child, holding the poor creature in her gentle arms. He could not help but wonder if her thoughts strayed to him as she kept cover in the forest…

…Indeed, Rahab thought of Nathan. She barely dared to stir from the cavern, as she heard men moving about in the woods, cutting fallen trees for winter firewood, or shooting deer for venison to feed their families in the coming cold months. She could have raised another veil and moved among the trees, but she could not risk using the spirit, lest it fall by accident. Better that she lie quietly and wait till the air in the village cleared, though by now, half the town must have started to wag. She wondered what kept him busy and how he spent his time, though she know he could hold his tongue if anyone inquired of her whereabouts...

At the first chance he had, Stark rode into Salem Town, to seek out the one man who could help him and his beloved.

The footman admitted him to the study of Captain Winthrop Pickman. "Nathanael, what brings you here and what has you looking bothered?" the older man asked, looking up from the account books spread upon his desk.

"Captain, I have a dire problem and yet one of the most beautiful of dilemmas." Stark continued with the tale of Goodwife Rahab Blackthorne and her accusers, and the lengths he had taken to protect her good name.

"And you would take this young woman to wife?" Captain Pickman asked.

"To wife? I have only become acquainted with the woman in question. I wish rather to see justice rendered in fairness and so clear the good name of a woman." Even still, Stark felt his cheeks warm with more than ardor for justice and his duty to another child of God. He felt his heart stir in his chest and a soft warmth suffuse his flesh.

Captain Pickman sat back in his elbow chair, beaming as a proud father might on his son. "You may not say it with words, but your face shouts it from the rooftops, you would have to be blind in the heart not to see that this woman means more to you than fulfilling the duty to justice and charity."

"She is in truth a lovely woman, but my duty is to see that she is protected from false witness."

"Your eyes speak volumes more than your lips willingly confess," Captain Pickman said.

Stark allowed himself a small smile. "In truth, I would take her to wife, but not in this place where man and woman alike have sullied her good name with false witness."

"Then you would do well to draw her away from this place. You could not have come at a better time. I have a ship standing in Arkham Harbor, ready to sail on the morrow with a load of barreled cider and dry goods from England. I can ford some passengers if you have the coin."

Stark bowed his head in assent. "I would pay every coin in my possession to pay our passage. But for the moment I have her hidden in a hollow in Arkham Wood."

"Like two lovers in a ballad, fleeing the maid's cruel and capricious father," Captain Pickman said. "Show me where you have hidden her and I shall help you stow her away on my ship."

"You would assist in an elopement?"

"I would and I believe the good Lord would approve in aiding the happiness and good future of a young couple who circumstance and fate have pushed together."

Nathan rode back to Arkham and thence to the parsonage. He tended to his affairs with due diligence, but his mind tarried to Rahab, hidden in her forest covert...

...Night had fallen over Arkham Woods, with the mouth of the cave growing dimmer, till the patches of sky visible through the web of tree branches turned violet blue. She emerged from the cave and summoned a ball of witch light before venturing along a path to seek out a hazelnut bush she had spied.

Something rustled the undergrowth. The witch light glinted off two small points peering through the undergrowth. The intruder chittered and fled through the fallen leaves, likely a hunting stoat.

Once she had gathered a pocketful of nuts, she returned to her covert, smiling to herself that she had all but started to transform into a wood sylph.

A shadow darkened the cave mouth. She dropped her nuts and quailed back into her nook, making the witch light blaze up as a threat.

Nathan stepped into the circle of light. "Do not be afraid, it is only me."

She closed her hand slightly, to pull the witch light to a smaller orb. "I took you for an intruder."

"I came as I promised and I have brought help," Nathan replied. An older but hale man with a deeply tanned face stepped in. "My uncle, Captain Winthrop Pickman, has a ship that sails to Maine soon."

Captain Pickman bowed his head to her. "Goodwife Blackthorne, your servant."

She gave her hand to Nathan. "You are too kind. I would call it a foolhardy kindness, but I know what has borne it."

They lead her out of the woods and thence to the road. Under the thinning shadows of the maples, Nathan and Captain Pickman drove Pickman's gig down to Salem Town and thence to the wharf, Rahab hidden within a large basket in the well of the gig. As they had lowered the lid over her, she could not help smiling, thinking of another Rahab, Jericho's woman of the night who had spirited two Hebrew spies out of her lodgings by means of a large basket. She heard Nathan's voice above the basket as it jostled, lifting out of the cart, as someone carried it up a sloping path, likely a gangplank. The basket shuffled, descended, then settled. She lay still, till the lid lifted and Nathan looked in, his face pale even in the dim light of a lantern hung nearby.

"Will they mind our dwelling with them?" she asked.

"Nay, they offered me a place in their household, when they resume their claim in Maine. I declined his offer when I took my posting here, but he left his offer standing," he said. Overhead, the sailors and ship's men called back and forth to each other. Nathan clasped her hand. "Will you come above?"

"To take the air, at least. With all that has happened, I would rather stay below," she admitted. She rose and let him help her out of the basket.

The cries overhead grew to angered shouts. The noise hovered over the hatch leading to the hold. Nathan reached for the dagger at his belt. Hathorne's voice rose from the babble.

"Bring forth the witch!"

"We have no witch on board, only a load of flax and wool to bring north."

"What then is that beast?"

"The ship's cat, to hunt the rats that slip into the hold."

"Throw it here! It is the witch Rahab Blackthorne in another guise!"

A grey cat with long dense hair dove into the hatch, screeching in fear and hiding itself among the baskets and bales.

"Poor little malkin," Rahab said.

"Cast off the lines! Raise the sails, all sheets to the wind!" Pickman roared to his men. Footsteps thundered overhead and in a moment, the ship lurched from its berth, standing down on the open sea.

"We shall put Hathorne and his hoodlums behind us," he said, looking above them.

She arched an eyebrow at him. "Hoodlums?"

"I will have no quarter with them any longer, if they will hunt the woman whom I love."

"They would say that I bewitched you, that I put a come-hither upon you."

"If you have, I care not," he said. "I doubt that you have, even if you wished to. If it is bewitchment, I would embrace it as I would embrace you. You warm my heart as it has not been warmed in too long a time."

Fine words from the mouth of a fine man, and had they come from another man, she would have distrusted them. She reached to him, drawing him close, laid her lips against his. She felt him quiver and nearly withdrew, in case she grew too ardent for him. But rather she felt herself quiver with ardor.

"I know your heart, but what of your life and past? Whence came this powerful but kindly witch-woman?" he asked. "Who is Rahab Blackthorne?"

"You ask a good question," she said. "And it is not a long tale," she said. "I am the natural daughter of an English lord, the Earl of Clontarf, Lord Rupert Blackthorne, who owned the land which my mother's family farmed. My mother charmed him into her arms in a bid to lull him into lowering her rent. When he knew I had been born, he claimed me as his own. But I would rather till the earth or serve a family in the Colonies than serve as a companion to another lord's maiden daughter. I would rather sink my hands into the good earth and bring forth fruit than see them remain folded in my silken lap. And so, my mother and I rode the winds from Dublin to

London. I took an indentured position and sailed from London."

"Rode the wind… what do you mean? You haven't used that which makes a witch lighter than air?" From the look on his face, he had heard tell of the noxious ointment that her kind used to fly.

"It can be used, but any witch who does so will be outcast among our circle. We shun those who use their skills to harm or whose magick entails harming others. With the proper words and attitude toward creation, we can convince the forces of nature to heed our requests. Did not Christ rebuke the wind and waves and calm the storm?"

"But He was the Son of God."

"There is a tale that what folk call witches and what we ourselves call the Gifted or the Talented are descended from the children of the sons of heaven who consorted with the daughters of man, spoken of in the book of Genesis."

He took this in silence, clearly turning it over in his mind. "And who, then, is Major Nathan Stark? What brought him to this new world?"

"I? I was a younger son of a silk merchant. I had no head for my father's business, though I have a head for reading. Even still, my father bought me a place in the Kings Army, though I had little stomach for fighting and slaying, unless it involves protecting an innocent and defenseless soul. A call for constables to serve in the Massachusetts Bay Colony came, and so I shipped across the sea to Salem Town, then to Arkham."

"And has so handsome a man ever had a sweetheart of his own?"

He clasped her hands. "He has one now."

She dropped her gaze, glancing past the edge of her cap. "Never a lady love at your stirrup?"

"Not one who would wait for me, nor brave crossing the North Atlantic waves with me."

"I imagine you have had many towns men and farmers offer you their daughters' hands in marriage?"

He shook his head. "None that I could accept. I would rather have a woman who would offer me her own hand, over a woman who would let her father speak for her." He leaned in, reaching to stroke her hair. "Servant that you might be, I would rather have your hand, than the hands of a dozen shrinking highborn maidens."

She reached up and removed her cap, letting her red-black hair fall past her shoulders. He nestled his face in that silken cascade, and the shelter it offered for the tender moment that passed between them, there in the hold of the ship...

****

The following morning, after they refreshed themselves, they ventured onto the deck. Seabirds, gray and white with black tips to their wings, wheeled about the ship. "A sure sign that land is not far off," Captain Pickman told them, as he read the sky with his sextant. "You can rest your heads at an inn in Fairwater tomorrow night."

Rahab smiled at Stark. "After we have found a parson."

True to the captain's word, at sundown the following day, the ship pulled into the quay at Fairwater, alongside a sloop Nathan had seen in Arkham Harbor, a small craft that had often sailed to Boston. Pickman saw to unloading his ship, while Nathan escorted Rahab to the nearest inn, a grog shop with lodgings, under the sign of the Turning Wheel.

They stepped into the tap room, intending to order food and drink and ask the ostler for a room for the night and to point them toward the town parson. Stark lead Rahab close to the fire, where she warmed herself after the cold journey on the ship.

The ostler, a sturdy woman with work reddened hands, approached, her face oddly pale in the ruddy firelight.

"Begging your pardon, good folk, but I can't serve you," she said.

"What do you mean?" Stark asked. Rahab gripped his arm, staring past his shoulder.

Shadowy shapes moved in the darkness beyond the firelight. Captain Hathorne stepped into the light, his hand upon the pistol in his belt.

"Goodman Stark, Goodwife Blackthorne, this is a timely encounter," he said. Several Arkham men stepped up behind him, forming a half circle before the couple, closing them in with the fire at their backs.

Stark put a protective hand on Rahab's arm. "What brought you here?"

Hathorne fixed his cold gaze on Rahab. "I do not need to state my reasons. You know your guilt. The woman is charged with spellbinding Hugh Jones to death, with consorting with demons, and with bewitching an Arkham constable. And you, Goodman Stark, it will go easier for you if you surrender this witch that she may face her crimes."

"On whose word do you level this charge?" Stark asked.

Goody Mason stepped from Hathorne's shadow, pointing at them. "I saw you, Goodman Stark. I saw you spirit Rahab Blackthorne into the woods. I saw you take her in the roots of the witch elm as a bull takes a cow. I saw you and she dancing in the moonlight with the Black-Clad Man. I saw her convince you to sign your name in his black book with blood from your finger mingled with black blood from his red right hand."

That creature brushing his ankle in the woods. Goody Mason must have sent her dear familiar now perched on her shoulder, eyeing them with its too-human eyes narrowed and its thin lips curled in a smirk, to spy on them. He wanted to swat the creature away, but he had a sense this would gratify its mistress.

"You know this woman caused no man harm. And though I brought her to the forest, I did so to shelter her from the false accusations you laid on her. We took shelter in a cave, but no Black-Clad Man walks the woods," Stark said.

Hathorne stood up straighter, leveling his icy gaze at Stark and Rahab. "Then you have plead innocent?"

"We both plead innocent," Rahab said.

Hathorne's men stepped closer. "Then the both of you are under arrest, in the name of God, the Crown and the Colony -"

Everything blurred slightly. Stark raised his eyebrows at Rahab. "Take us from here," she said, softly.

Stark clasped her hand. Around them, the men looked about in clear consternation.

"Where did they go?"

"Where could they have gone?"

"She has bewitched our eyes!" One stepped aside, breaking the circle. Stark drew Rahab through the gap, careful not to brush against anyone.

"She is going for the door! I can see her fleeing this place, taking her lover with her!" Goody Mason cried. "I can see her true form, a creature like a woman with a goat's head and legs!" The veil around them wavered and the door blew open. Stark took the chance and dragged Rahab through the opening.

They ran up the sloping dusty track to the high road above, passing grog shops and chandler's shops, sailors' lodgings and counting houses, boathouses and fishing sheds, dodging sailors and shopkeepers and townsfolk.

The couple turned onto the high road, passing the cottages at intervals along it. Voices called after them. A shot cracked, winging past Stark's shoulder. Rahab cried out, dragging on his arm. He ran with her as best he could, with the passersby and carts all slightly blurred. Another shot cracked. Stark felt the bullet graze the side of his hat. The veil dropped. They ran full out, for the end of a row of buildings, around the corner of the last one, toward a rocky wall.

Shale rolled under their feet. Stark looked down, realizing they had run to the edge of a cliff. A cascade of pebbles clattered down, splashing into the breakers washing the base.

"In the name of God, the Crown and the Colony, I order you to come back!" Captain Hathorne roared from down the slope. One deputy leveled his musket and fired. The ball caromed off a rock close by Rahab's feet. She gasped, flinching against Nathan. He clutched her to him.

"There is but one escape," she said.

He looked over the edge. "Over the cliff? We shall be damned. But I am past caring. God gave me a heaven in your company." He leaned in and trembling, laid his lips against hers. She drew him close, slackening her knees so that his weight pressed against her till she heeled over the edge.

The world dropped from under his feet. She wound her legs around his thighs, holding tight, warm against him. The ocean rushed up to meet them. The wind rose, filling their cloaks like sails, slowing their fall. She released her knees on him, reaching down with her feet, touching down like a feather on the rocks at the cliff base. She drew Nathan down, steadying him om the damp stone.

A hollow showed in the rocks just above them, a smooth chasm carved out by the crashing wave. She pulled him toward it. Blinking, he divined her intention, and they ducked into the shelter.

Men shouted above them, words mauled into the cries of beasts by the distance and the roar of the waves. Captain Hathorne's voice rose in an impatient bark, clearly calling off his minions. The cries grew fainter, retreating.

"Where shall we go from here?" Nathan called over the surf.

"Come with me. The men who sought to take our lives have departed." She lead him out of the cave mouth. The wind rose, plucking them from the rocks and carrying them across the water. They flew some distance north from Fairwater, toward the lights from the windows of a small hamlet. The wind let them down on the dusty track through the center of village. The warm windows of an inn shone before them. He looked behind them, half-expecting to see his former comrades ride up from the gloom, then looked to the inn and back to her.

"What shall we tell the innkeeper?" he asked.

"We shall tell them what they need to hear. We are a young couple newly arrived from the south, seeking shelter while we seek work and a new home in which to start a new life. I can always find work as a servant."

"And I?"

"Every town needs a new constable who also knows his letters. All that we need is a parson to hear our vows."

He opened his mouth to question this, then paused, thinking before he said something foolish. "If this is your asking my hand in marriage, who am I to refuse the request of a woman of talent?"

She beamed up at him, the light of the inn windows warm on her face and gleaming on her hair. "Rather, who are you to refuse the woman of your dreams?" She drew him into the russet-tinted shadow of the oak tree by the inn door and kissed him, the waxing moon shining through the leaves as if to bless them…

…Since those days, the story grew in Fairwater, of a young witch who leaped to her death over the cliffs above the harbor. The site even garnered the name "the Witch's Cliff" or simply "Witchcliff". Some remember to mention her love, some even remember that he leaped with her. Few tell the tale as it happened, but time has worn away many of the facts behind it. Rahab and Nathanael did not mind, when versions of the story reached their ears. No one in the village suspected they had lived the story of Witchcliff.

Dedicated to my mother, Ida, a descendant of Hugh Jones, an ancestor who died under mysterious circumstances lost to history and whose name appears in the spectral evidence for the trials of Elizabeth Proctor and John Willard, during the Salem Witch Hunt; and to my dad, Michael, a romantic who wanted to hear this story when we saw a road sign in Maine bearing the name "Witchcliff".

Tall Glass of Water
Jarrett Mazza

SHE STARTED THE DATE BY asking me if I would please stop tapping my foot against the floor. She said it was starting to annoy her.

"So sorry."

This happened only a few seconds after I said that she looked like a tall glass of water, one I wanted to swallow up in one gulp.

Sitting at the table, in a fancy restaurant, I ordered the scallopini, with alfredo sauce while she ordered the salad. Mostly quiet, though nice, when she ordered, I told her she could have more than just a side dish. It was my pleasure, I said, to pay.

"I'm pretty sure I'm good."

Glaring, her gaze, so domineering and focused, it felt like she was trying to probe my subconsciousness using only her eyes. Liking it, actually, it seem as though she wanted to reach into my skull and pull out a big handful of my brains and squish it between her fingers like a heap of cold, succulent meat.

Who she was, how I met her, through a series of nonchalant interactions, it was all sent via her webpage, where I attempted to connect with her in ways she had advertised.

"You seriously trying to take this girl on a date, bro?"

"You never know."

Sending her several messages, her name, Cynthia W, an alias, she responded to each one I sent. Exchanging witty, playful banter, I sent her a variety of emoticons, and I didn't ask for her to send me the same lascivious pictures and videos that she did to her other followers. I asked her where she was from, what she liked to do, and eventually, whether she would be willing to actually meet someone who was paying a monthly fee to see her naked.

Playful, not insistent, she winked, and I told her she wasn't like the other girls I had subscribed to. I told her she was special. Cornily, and weird, I wanted to feel her body against mine, and it was weird to think of her as anything less.

Tits'n'ass, I hated that's what other people said she was.

So much more.

Indeed.

I didn't have the courage to ask to meet in person, but prior to asking her, I did make note of the fact that I was a journalist.

I would like to ask you a few questions, about the business.

Knowing nothing about the "business" and knowing even less about what I was going to say to her, I was buying all the time I could, and then telling her that I would love nothing more than to take her out on another date.

"Did you just ask out that model you follow, bro?"

Not really knowing how I was supposed to respond, the answer was yes, but the reasons for why had eluded me.

"Yes, I did."

"And what did she say?"

My roommate, Brian Evanson, a marketing coordinator at a tech start-up, knew all about this service, and had even subscribed to a few himself.

"She hasn't said anything, not yet, but she will."

"Sure."

Skeptical, all of this was a wanting dream; a weird possibility that may or may not come to fruition, and even so, I had faith she would say something.

"Enjoying yourself?"

Nibbling on the last bit of corn kernel, she kept the little pebble on the edge of her tongue, and circled it around her mouth, playing and then *drooling.*

Nodding, talking wasn't really her thing as far as I could see, but then why did she agree to meet me here?

Watching, my eyes always went to her chest. Shaking my head, ridding myself of the thought, I reminded myself that this was *not* the reason why I asked her to come, not what I wanted *this* to be.

"Yeah."

Answering in a rather passive-aggressive way, she sighed and slid her hand across her chest.

Never did I have a bad date, but then I never had a date with a girl I *didn't* want to have sex with right away.

The entire time, I felt so focused on her hands, so dainty and long, her fingernails were a series of perfect triangles. Like claws, she hadn't moved her hand since she brought it to the table and left it there. Scratching my chin, I asked her why she decided to start this platform, that is one that allows people to peer into her life, see her in all her disrobed glory. Yet, sitting in front of her, I began to see that the question itself, so utterly ridiculous, considering that the answer could well be one that predicated on the obvious notion that it was because of people like me she stayed employed.

Asking for the cheque, paying with my VISA, here was where we met, but said that she had taken an Uber to get to the restaurant.

Smart, considering she could leave anytime she wanted to.

"Wanna offer me a ride or somethin'?"

Forward, and bold, my heart skipped a few beats and my hand nearly slipped from around the cheque that was secured beneath my hand.

"What?"

Grinning, sliding her hands along the table, wrapped her long, perfectly painted fingers over mine, and just held them there, gently. Her lips, glossed beneath a fluorescent shade of pink, I could smell her perfume. She smelled as enchanting as she looked.

Like cinnamon covered in white frosting, she licked her lips, and then I felt a nudge in between my legs. Sharp, the sensation felt like it was coming from a pointed toe, like the edge of a heel, an appendage I could recall from how high it was upon first glance.

"Yeah," she said, her voice going soft, and her gaze deepening.

I thought she was trying to look through me, past me, or maybe into the heart that she was fully aware she was rupturing now.

The touch, a clear sign the date had ended, but the night was about to begin.

While sitting in my car, cross-legged, long legs, the entire time, I was glanced at her long, silky smooth skin. Like the restaurant whereby she was sitting plainly in her chair, she drank her wine, ate her food, and as I tried to ask her questions about her platform, my eyes were going straight for her breasts.

Round, voluptuous, she was mine.

All mine.

Scanning the interior of the restaurant, I saw other faces, some had glanced my- *our* -way.

I thought maybe they recognized her. Having amassed such a huge following, it was possible that they did know who she was, same as me. I did, however, doubt it.

What they were seeing was just an average man with an extraordinary woman.

So luscious, fine as leather, every part of her, so perfectly refined, how could they *not* be looking at her the way I was?

"Would you like to come upstairs?"

With my hand resting on the steering wheel, I felt flushed, with the blood racing straight through my legs. What I wanted was to put my hands on her, pull in nice and close, and just hold her there.

Worst date, or best one ever?

Grappling with the thought, I reflected on the idea about I had never been asked to "come upstairs", but of course, the implications of hearing such could have only one meaning.

"Yes."

Exiting my car, she walked across the stone path that led to the glass doors, the entrance to her luxury condo, and as I went with her, I stepped into the grand foyer, elegant and decorous, I knew her earnings greatly exceeded mine but not to this degree.

Stepping out, not saying a word, she marched forward.

Almost with a slight skip in her footsteps, I felt my heart beating in my chest.

Into the lobby, there was a doorman standing in a trench coat and with chapeau covering his head. Although an expensive residence, the man gawked at me as he watched me walk across. Listening to Cynthia's heels click the marble floor, she was going straight to the elevator, not saying anything, though she did expect me to follow.

"This *is* nice."

Waiting, I looked at her, hoping to catch a glimpse of her smile. Expressionless, however, she was forever displaying a vacant visage that made me think that every word I said only served to annoy her, and whenever I would think this, she would then smile later.

Was it something I said?

Dinging, the elevator opened, and I let her pass. Pressing the button to the seventh floor, we soared up into the complex, and I waited for her to go before me.

"After you."

Before I finished with my chivalrous invitation, and for that, she was already gone.

Strolling along, again she was always five steps ahead of me.

The door, poised at the end of the hallway, she pushed.

The door, swinging wide and hitting my elbow, it also bumped me on the shoulder as I moved.

Already inside, I was struck with cold. Like a refrigerator was just opened, the coolness gave me a shiver. Holding the door open with one hand, I peeped inside, and got a closer look at the interior of her condo. Gone, I couldn't see, for the room was so dark I could barely see the door that I was gripping with one hand.

"Hello?"

Silence.

Odd that she just walked in without waiting for me, or she just expected me to go with her, and like before I always would.

Why would now be any different?

As I made my way through the apartment, pivoting on my left foot, I tried to retrace my steps, only there were none to trace.

Vanishing, suddenly she disappeared into a haze of shadow and, while I was waiting for her to turn on a light, she insisted on keeping it dark.

"Hello?"

My voice, carrying humbly through the dim space, I saw outlines of furniture, some things were recognizable: a sofa, a table, but that's pretty much all there was. Stepping in slowly, minding my feet, the floor was a long blanket of blackness, and I still could not see or hear her.

She wouldn't just leave.

Perhaps she was going to turn the lights on, and until then, I insist on making too many sudden moves. Tripping on what was on the floor, it shoes and slippers, and I would hit something that would potentially crack my head wide open.

Why was she doing this?

"Cynthia?"

Her name, Cynthia W, on all her accounts, and even though I had taken her on a date, I had neglected to ask her what her last name was.

I was hoping to know by the end of the night.

Moving across the floor, my hand up, and I tried to find a light switch that would provide some amount of brightness capable of showing me the way. Whatever my hand was hitting, none of it felt in the least like it was a switch.

Pattering the walls, I felt something on the board, a picture frame, maybe?

Nicking the corners, it dipped off and the nail fell to the ground.

Shattering, I jumped despite not knowing at all what it was.

"Sorry!"

Feeling it against my feet, *didn't feel like glass.* Harder, allowing for me to pin down. I leaned forward. It was a picture, though not of her, not of anyone that I expected to find on her wall. Contrarily, what I was looking at now could have been a small mirror and it should have been…considering that the face I was seeing was indeed my own.

"What the…"

A snapshot, it was captured when, during one of her "exclusive" offerings, she would turn to the camera, and was able to see who was making all of her requests. In this case, it was me, at the computer, smiling as I waited.

Why did she have this?

"Cynthia?"

A cackle coursed through the apartment, hissing something that sounded like she was once again inviting me to find her. I couldn't find her because damn, I couldn't see, but in the end, what I had seen…was enough.

What was she doing?

As the cackles continued from the shadows, the farther I moved in, and the darkness that engulfed me.

Alone, left to scour the shadows, a cackle from an old woman began building in the dark. I passed more pictures; more candid shots of her paying clients, those who made so many requests.

Neither nefarious or perverted--perhaps only a little-- we were all just playing the game, giving her what it is she wanted, what it is she needed, and yet, she just kept laughing.

"Where are *you*?"

My voice, a whisper, my pace steadied, and I crept on as if stroking dark water. At any moment, the setting could change, at any second the world could change, and I could come face-to-face with something I never wanted to see.

Kill me?

I knew her, I said to myself.

We shared many moments and, when I asked if she wanted to join me for dinner, I let her choose the restaurant and I smiled, mannerly, and asked her questions about herself. Okay, yes, I was a little preoccupied with her body. I was obsessed, yes, and hoped- *prayed* - she would invite me back and give me what it is she knew I desired. Perhaps this was all part of her routine. Perhaps I was not the first. Seeing as how I saw her picture on the wall, one of me, and one of many others, nothing had changed.

There couldn't be.

I was only here because she wanted me to be and the lights were off, and I moved into the apartment- blind.

I knew her.

"Okay," I said, my frightened expression now amused, partially; a measly attempt to play off the occurrence like it didn't matter- didn't, because it couldn't.

"Very funny. Good joke. I get it."

Moving hastily, I felt something connect with my shoe. At edge of the carpet, I think, to my right, a tiny flicker from a light somewhere in the room.

Not a shadow but a figure, a person in a cloak, hidden as she gawked, and glared.

Once during Cynthia's sessions, she came out dressed in a robe; a hood draped over her face. She didn't need to tell us that she was naked, when she so clearly was. She asked what she wanted us to see, and read the suggestions made by her viewers.

Take it off. Take 'em out. Let us see.

Twirling playfully around, I thought it was a costume, and soon, she did remove the robe.

She was wearing it.

"Cynthia?"

With her head bowed, finally I came to see why the apartment was so dark, and the only light was cast from her room.

Throughout the space, there were candles poised on the dresser, on shelves, on the floor.

"Whoa."

With her head down, the entire room appeared decorated with candles, twinkling stars, great big bundles of hair, more photographs, so many, each one...*of me.*

"What the hell?"

Gulping, saliva gobbled back into my throat, and felt it pierce the inside of my esophagus, left a giant hole in my gut. Shaking, if this was a joke, I would have surely heard the punchline by now.

So far...*nothing.*

Peeling back her head, Cynthia W, the way she looked was still the spitting image of beauty, yet it was interrupted, severed as she uttered such incoherent demands.

Muddled, her voice unintelligible, she *was* speaking, but not *to* me.

Muttering a series of words that sounded like they were all connected; a batch of phrases and well selected consonants that hurt me as I spoke.

"Ya-dune-ya-malu-ny. Ya-dune-see-how."

"What?"

The door behind me, slamming a violent clatter, I whipped my head around, contorting my torso and feeling a strain in my ribs. What I did hear, I did not understand. Looking around the room for a place to crawl out of, I saw another window and then another fucking door.

"Ya-dune-ya-malu-ny. Ya-dune-ya-see-how."

Shaking my head, dubious, I stepped, and planned to blow right past her and leap out the window. Reciting the same phrase again and again, with each new syllable spoken, each weird word that she spoke in tongues, and then suddenly, I looked my hand.

My right hand.

"Wh…"

Tickling I held it, and then there was this burning, hence the reason why I brought it to my face to get a closer look. It didn't hurt, not initially, but when I saw it now, its shape changed. My fingers, elongated like they were being pulled, made of clay, my fingernails appeared hooked, and then curved my fingertips, and in front of me I could hear her cackle.

"Ah-ah-ah!"

"Guh!"

Horrified, I took another step back, trying to claw back the way I came.

By the door, I reached for the handle, I didn't bother to look behind me.

Gripping the cold steel, I turned it, then felt the bolt in the door.

Locked!

Strong enough to turn it, more than strong enough to open it, there was this sudden change in my hand: my bones, and my tendons.

Hurt, weak, her laughs amplified. Standing before me, her head dipped, and in the dark, a vengeful amused chortle hiccupped from the shadows.

"Hee-hee-ha-ha!"

"No!"

Yelling, I went for the door. Locked.

Against my chest, everything so brittle, flaky, and light, like spaghetti.

"You wanted *me*. Here I am."

Slipping off the handle, my legs folded into each other, and I fell into the hardwood.

My knees, jelly, everything became curdled cream. Old, not dead, I gasped and asked.

"Why? Why are you doing this?"

Leering, undressing me with her fixated eyes, she gave a seductive stare, for it wasn't just my clothes she was thinking of taking off.

My skin, riddled with goosebumps, now melted into thick globules, viscos as syrup.

Drawing in, her face looking aged, like she had stuck her head into a microwave.

Wrinkled around the ridges near her eyes, her cheeks so concave it looked like she was concealing a vacuum inside her mouth. Her eyes, now a shade of redness, her pupils oozed the colour as she licked each one of her teeth.

"They see you as something you're not, and never wanted to be. Do you know that?"

The door to her bedroom, right behind me, I remembered feeling it when I first stepped inside. With a sight turn, not even, I had a glimpse, a partial one, even I would be inches away, and thus, inches from the escape. Pressure on my knees, a marginal amount of pressure, it coerced them into buckling. As I turned around, again trying to make it to the door, the skin around my knees, all of it began to melt the same as my arms.

Quivering, and reaching back, fingers flapping, I slapped the wood.

"I always knew what it was like, to have people look at you like you're something so tasty that they just want to reach out…"

Lifting her arm, opening her hand, she did reach; her fingers long, nails pointed.

"And grab you right where you are. I know the feeling. I know… *hunger*."

"What?"

Vampire?

Cannibal?

Witch.

The narration, insinuating something that was to transpire right where I stood, what the hell did she expect? Her entire career was predicated on the idea that people would pay to see.

But that was the agreement.

Her idea, not mine.

"Why?" I said, my face now starting to droop, and the skin around my jaw beginning to feel like it was gazed with glue.

So sticky, it smelled of burning chemicals, the kind used to clean floors, and the entire time there was but only one question left for me to ask.

"Why," I said, my mouth drooping to the side, going numb, "are you…doing…this?"

Struggling to speak the last few words, my legs were just starting to buckle, and every last bit of energy I had stored had suddenly vanished, and I fell to the ground like my entire torso was reduced to fucking water.

It was.

"Because I wanted you to know what it feels like, to be thirsted over…and now…you do too.

Slovenly, transformed into a human laxative, and what once was…gone.

Bones, muscle, organs, face; eyes, nose, ears, all of it spilled and then suddenly, I was on the floor, as a puddle, as a mess of mush while above me, a woman grander than any one I had ever laid eyes on.

A date, that's all it was supposed to be, a chance to sit down and enjoy being with a woman who I wanted so badly I could taste her.

"Do you even know it's like?"

If I could speak, if I still had a mouth, I should have said that I understood, and I did know it was like to be thirsted, to be *craved.*

The last sight I saw, a witch in a robe, one my favourites, I asked her to take it off, to show me who she really was. Just trying to be playful, when she removed the robe, she was standing there, nude and lithe, and perfect. She smiled, and then she laughed, and then while ogling me from beyond the screen, she waited for more requests.

"Anything else you would like to see?"

Sitting before my computer, I thought of what to say, like something smooth, confident, I was trying to be like those who had impressed her: the ones that were tall, tall and handsome.

"I want to drink you like a tall glass of water, one I wanted to swallow up in one gulp."

Last message that was sent, I asked her if she'd ever dated a fan before.

She said she never had, but if she wanted to, I would make it worth her while.

REALLY?

It took her a few days before she replied.

When she did, I thought of the ways that I could impress her.

How many messages did she receive from people like me?

Kneeling, her hands plunging deep into the slick, my eyes bobbing in the pool, she scooped up what she could. Touching every part of me, I did know the feeling, to thirst for something you know you will never have, and yet you beg for it as though you will.

In Like Sin
Mark Mellon

Brrrr. Brrrr. Brrrr.

The phone's insistent buzz awoke him. He rolled off the couch with his usual easy grace and went to the mahogany side table. He ignored a slight headache and nausea's acid tinge in his mouth.

"Hello. Who's this ringing me up?"

"Errol, it's me, Bruce. You still among the living or did you start early today?"

"Bruce, old boy. How fabulous to hear from you. I did start early actually since I don't have to shoot tomorrow. But there's still some life in the old corpse. What's up?"

"Just this. I've got a line on three hot *señoritas*, all just dying to meet you. One says she's got a tattoo in a secret place she wants to show you."

"Ay yay yay and *Dios Mio*. You've definitely got my interest, Brucie."

"Meet us at this new joint on Cahuenga everyone's talking about. There's a big red neon sign. You can't miss it."

"And you'll be there, right? You've left me in the lurch before, Bruce."

"You're in solid this time, Errol."

"All right. Say fifteen minutes for me to shower and change and half an hour to get there. So, I arrive about nine, just in time for a champagne supper with the night still before us."

Bruce's laughter was loud and long over the phone. He went to the light blue master bedroom.

"Alex. I'll be dining out tonight, old boy, so let Marie know she can take it easy."

"Yes, Mr. Flynn."

He sweated off alcohol in the steaming hot shower. Still young and slim, he donned elegant, tightly cut evening attire, assisted by his Russian butler. A black fedora topped off his ensemble.

"Bring the car around."

"Yes, sir."

He walked over lion and tiger skins, past his Gauguin and the living room bar, and went outside. A low slung, creamy orange Packard pulled up, long with supple curves. Alex got out, held the door, and bowed with Old World courtesy. He got in the car.

"Don't wait up, Alex. You never know how an evening with Bruce will turn out."

Alex gave a knowing smile and returned to the house. He drove down the driveway. The grounds teemed with the animals he loved, ducks, geese, pheasants, cows, and, most importantly, dogs and horses. Well away from the house, secluded on the winding driveway, he stopped and took out a glass vial from a vest pocket. He uncapped the vial and inhaled, one nostril, then the next, long, deep drags.

Fifteen minutes later he drove through downtown Los Angeles, mind clear and focused, his unease from excessive alcohol consumption cured by cocaine euphoria. Crowded with traffic, rubbernecking tourists and elderly couples in flivvers, he slowly drove down Main Street, north into the city's crowded heart, past LA's endless sprawl of gas stations, bowling alleys, car rental lots, boarding houses, hot cot hotels, all night burger joints, oil derricks, and gaily lit nightclubs.

He turned onto Cahuenga, nerves alive with anticipation, mouth filled with a bitter, chemical aftertaste, every detail heightened to granular clarity down to the huge, red neon sign atop twin poles ahead on the right. On and off, on and off, a wide female bottom clad in flowered panties shamelessly flashed beneath a wind flipped skirt. A sign underneath blinked *The Wrong Way Inn* in curlicue letters.

He pulled into the lot. A parking valet strutted up in a Wild West outfit, complete with batwing chaps and a wide brimmed Stetson. He stretched out his hand to take the keys. His eyes went wide in recognition.

"You're- Oh, gosh, I'm your biggest fan, when you played Robin Hood-"

He smiled, shook the kid's hand, gave him an autograph, tipped him lavishly despite repeated refusals. Aura powerful as some ancient god, he entered the nightclub, confident, assertive, ready to fight, fuck, or frolic, to take on whoever came, friend or foe.

The nightclub was spacious with a lofty, domed ceiling and brightly lit. Scantily clad chorus girls capered in unison on a polished wooden stage while an enormous big band blared behind them. A young woman wailed into a microphone.

"So, you lie awake just singing the blues all night, goody goody!

And you found that love's a barrel of dynamite!"

"Good evening, sir. Do you have a reservation?" The maitre d' gasped in turn. "*Ouais, c'est Monsieur le Capitaine Blood.* Let me find you a table immediately."

He scanned the joint, looking for Bruce Cabot and his latest acquisitions. There was no sign of the high pompadour, the wide mouthed sneer, and nothing like a gaggle of eager, horny Mexican whores.

Instead, a tall, languorous blonde sat in a booth directly ahead, body juicy and ripe, eyes locked with his, the right tantalizingly veiled by long, lank, thick strawberry locks, bee stung, red smeared lips spread wide in a come hither smile.

"That's quite all right, old boy. I see my friend. Here, have a fiver."

"Ah, *quel noblesse oblige, M'sieu.*"

In his usual shameless, direct way, he walked right over and sat down. It wasn't like he had to introduce himself. She smiled with a blaze of perfect white teeth and held out a plump, jade beringed hand.

"How very nice to meet you. I'm a big fan of yours. My name's Damita Cameron."

He kissed her hand. Damita giggled. A waiter hovered.

"Two champagne cocktails and let's see the menu."

Damita leaned close to him. "Thanks for the drink, but the food here isn't anything to write home about. In fact, this whole joint is for the birds. Speaking of which, I've got fried chicken and cold beer at home. Why don't we just go there?"

Even for him, it had been a long time since someone offered it up on a platter, especially a cute trick like this. He licked his lips, raised his eyebrows, and gave a wolfish grin as he shrugged.

"Why not? Did you drive here?"

"No, I took a cab from my aunt's place in Pasadena. I was just sitting here bored, hoping somebody exciting would come along and take me home. And you sure did."

"You're certainly right on that point, darling."

He tossed twenty dollars on the table. "My car's outside. Let's go."

"I'll get my wrap."

In the men's room, he snorted from the vial again. She met him in the lobby. Despite the warm weather, Damita wore a heavy fur wrap over her gown, a dark gray, thick pelt.

"I say, isn't that a wolf skin?"

"Yes. Perceptive of you to notice."

"I hunted them in Canada."

Still largely sober, he drove away from downtown. Past Figueroa Street, Colorado turned into Route 66 and opened up. He accelerated, turned right on San Gabriel, and went into Pasadena. Damita led him deep into South Pasadena's well-trimmed suburbs. In the Oak Noll neighborhood, she told him to turn right into a cul-de-sac.

"Auntie's gone to Catalina on a cruise. She let the servants take their vacations too, so we'll have the place to ourselves."

"That sounds ideal, darling."

A three story, brick mansion was at the cul-de-sac's end, surrounded by a high granite wall. Iron barred gates swung open when the car approached.

"I thought you said no one else was here."

"There isn't anybody else, silly. That's just the electronic eye. Park in front of the house. I don't know how to get into the garage."

She fumbled in her purse until she found an old fashioned, brass key to open the massive lock. A paneled foyer opened onto a living room, filled with heavy, antique furniture, the windows covered by chintz curtains.

"Auntie's never bothered to update anything. Honestly, if you had to judge by this place alone, you'd think Teddy was still President and not FDR."

He laughed. "You've got a good sense of humor. That's just one thing to like."

She let her wrap fall to the floor, put one hand to her hip, the other to her hair. "Oh? And what else interests you?"

He drew her close and kissed her. Coty perfume, lipstick's strawberry taste, her hot breath in his ear, and a wet, yielding mouth and tongue melded with his own, overwhelmed his senses, drove him mad with desire. He fondled a breast through her clothes only to have Damita gently pull away.

"You are a fast worker, aren't you? That stands to reason though. We ought to have a little drink first. Auntie has some single malt scotch, pre-war stuff."

"You know me, honey. I'm always up for a drink. That and another thing."

He playfully pinched her ass as she passed by. Damita squealed in mock indignation. A cut crystal decanter filled with dark brown liquid stood on a heavy mahogany sideboard along with several tumblers. She filled two and handed one to him. Damita raised her tumbler in a toast.

"This is the real McMallachd, so drink hearty."

He smiled and knocked it back. There was a hint of oak and a warm glow in his stomach, just like good scotch should taste. Rather than drink hers though, Damita set the tumbler on the sideboard, a wide smile on her face. She pointed at him and burst into laughter, loud, unladylike whoops of hilarity.

"Mind if I ask just what's so funny, Damita, or is this a private joke?"

Damita fought to control herself. "It's no private joke. In fact, it wouldn't be funny if you didn't know. You see, I just slipped you a mickey. How do you like that, Mr. hot-shot movie star?"

He stood open mouthed. The walls swayed around him. Sweat burst from him. He pulled at his collar to loosen his tie.

Damita howled. "You're such a lush; you didn't even wait for me to drink mine. Oh, if you could just see the look on your pan right now. It's priceless."

"You rotten bitch. I'll kill-"

He staggered toward her. Damita calmly counted each faltering step he made.

"One. Two. Three. Four. Five. Si-"

He crashed to the floor, unconscious.

***

He came to in a subterranean chamber, naked and bound to an X-shaped, wooden cross on a high dais. A giant flambeau burned on either side of him. The chamber was filled with hooded, shadowy figures. They kept to the darkness, but there was no concealing the excited buzz among them.

"Is this supposed to be a joke? Well, I don't find it in the least bit funny."

Silence.

"All right. Fine. Now you've got me here. Go on and take your pictures for your rotten tabloids. I'll sue you for everything you're worth the moment I get home. You know you're guilty of kidnapping."

"You think you're under the law's protection?" A deep, silky voice asked. A tall man strode into the torchlight, face hidden by his hood.

"Why should petty, human law interfere with our Master's rites?"

"Master? What in God's name are you talking about?"

The man pushed back his hood. His jet black, dyed widow's peak and pointed beard were thick and lush. He bared yellow teeth in a grin, wide spaced brown eyes alive with mischief.

"Our Master, Baalzebub, Satan, Lord of the Flies. And the God you cry for has no authority here."

Dim lights brightened. The chamber was revealed as a Gothic shrine, heavy arches supported by crude, Romanesque columns. The other attendants slipped off their robes and stood naked, men and women, Damita among them. She laughed and pointed in derision. Some faces looked familiar, possibly extras from crowd scenes. Everyone had a malicious, anticipatory grin. The high priest dropped his robe. Except for a pot belly, he was lean and muscular. He held a short sword.

"In this city, Los Angeles of the Damned, we are sworn to our Master, to work mischief in his name, the Prince of Evil. And you are notorious as being the most evil man in the world, a rake, a womanizer, and a debauchee, sworn to passion, drink, riot, and violence. Who else would make a fitter sacrifice?"

"Sacrifice? Me?"

They laughed.

"Yes," the high priest said. "Slowly and methodically, we'll cut you to pieces. We'll take drugs, your favorites; cocaine and even heroin, the big H. There'll be sacred sex before your eyes, but you'll be in far too much agony to enjoy it, Mr. Flynn. And every moment will be filmed."

Cameras' familiar whir. Banks of klieg lights snapped on, necessary for interior scenes. A mike on a dolly swept down low. The high priest took his mark. In the shadowy background, a man wearing a beret sat in a canvas director's chair, intensely smoking.

"Your last and greatest role, Errol, something I and my brethren will cherish in secret for decades to come. Too bad your adoring public will never know what a performance you put on."

Men played music on bizarre stringed instruments, strange, droning, atonal Middle Eastern noise. Damita and the others went into a choreographed routine, a movie harem dance only with naked men and women. The high priest advanced, short sword held high.

He looked wildly around him, shook the cross with his arms. It was loosely fitted, the bolts worn and buckled from long use as helpless victims shrieked and writhed. The only way he'd ever won in life was by taking chances, by looking fear in the eye and saying go fuck yourself.

The high priest put his foot on the dais's first step. "It's easier if you don't watch."

He heaved himself to one side.

"No. Hold still," the high priest cried.

The cross fell with him. It hit the stairs, snapped in two from the impact. He slipped free from his leather bonds, jumped up, and snatched the sword away from the high priest.

"Here."

He ran the sword through the high priest's concave, hairy stomach.

"AAAAAAAAAAAAUUUUUUUUUGGGGGGGHHHHH."

He pulled the sword out, the blade covered in scarlet. The high priest fell to the floor. He writhed and moaned, blood and viscera pouring from him.

"Cut. Stop the cameras," a man screamed.

Eyes wild with energetic fury, he assaulted everyone around him, stabbed and thrust. Damita was close, eyes wide with fear, mouth open in a piercing scream, inaudible over the general din.

"You set me up. You slipped me a mickey."

He raced toward her, sword high. Damita sensibly fled, only pausing to snatch up her robe. Men made bold by drugs and devil worship tried to rush him, but he had a sword and the element of surprise. He hacked people down left and right. Men and women shrieked. They fled from his murderous onslaught.

Covered in gore, his bare feet slipped in greasy blood as he ran down a corridor after Damita. A door slammed at the corridor's end. He opened it and went through.

Outside, the night air was cool on his blood drenched body. There was no sign of Damita. The Packard was parked nearby. He kept a spare key concealed behind the back license plate, just to be careful, never once anticipating he'd get in a jam like this. He got the key, jumped in the front seat, and started the car.

Two men ran out, hastily attired in slacks and t-shirts. Both held guns. He slammed his foot on the accelerator. The Packard roared toward the gates, but they'd already started to close. Pistol shots rang out behind him. A bullet put a neat hole through the front windshield. He slammed through the partly open gates with a great crash of metal.

Naked and befouled, he drove through LA. Sweat cut rivulets through the dried blood on his face. He could only crouch low, drive as fast as possible, and hope the night shielded him from prying eyes (especially policemen's) until he got home. After what seemed an eternity, he reached Mulholland Drive and turned onto the driveway to his home.

He stopped the badly mangled car, got out, and went to the front door. Alex opened it in his bathrobe and pajamas.

"Rough night, Alex."

Like the experienced gentleman's gentleman that he was, Alex said nothing. He showered and went to bed where he passed out, exhausted from the ordeal.

***

Brrrr. Brrrr. Brrrr.

The telephone's ring awoke him. He had a headache and dim, dreamlike memories of the night before. A beautiful woman. Blood and guts. Devil worship?

He picked up the phone. "Hello."

"Errol. Where the hell were you? We waited until midnight. The girls were really mad at me."

"Bruce, you son of a bitch. You set me up. I almost got killed last night on account of you. Why did you send me to that nightclub where that bitch was waiting? I thought we were friends."

"Wait a minute. Whoa there. What nightclub did you go to? I said the new place on Cahuenga with the big neon sign."

"Yeah, and I went there. *The Wrong Way Inn*."

Bruce laughed. "No, Errol. I never even heard of that joint. No, I meant *The Liquid Lunch Cafe*."

"So, it was just a mistake?"

"Sure sounds like it. Look, the girls were mad, but I made excuses and I know I won't have any trouble setting us up with them again tonight. Sort of like a second take, you know? Are you up for it?"

It was foolish for Bruce to even ask. He was always game, ready to take a chance on women, alcohol, gambling, drugs, a fistfight, to dice with his own life until even his prodigious vitality was entirely consumed, a glorious, sinister, flaming Roman candle of a man.

"Of course, old boy. Just name the place and time."

Hot-driving the Pot
J.J. Camberwell

I met Anna in *Lantana,* a trendy little Australian-style coffee shop in Camden. 'Can we get together somewhere near me, is that OK?' she'd asked over the phone. The phone call was her idea. 'Just checking you're not weird, sorry, but I'm sick of meeting strange guys,' she'd said online.

I didn't much like all the conversational pre-vetting women were increasingly doing these days, but I agreed instantly because Anna's profile pics were amazing. Perfect white smile. Incredible figure. One photo must have been taken in a yoga studio with fading light or something, and at first I thought the picture had been loaded the wrong way around. Then I tilted my head sideways and realised that Anna was in this incredible pose where, by core muscle strength alone, she'd managed from a seated position on a mat to get both her legs levered back behind her ears. Whether she'd intended it or not, the part of her body closest to the camera were her slim hips, wide-open, under the thinnest, tautest layer of green lycra.

"This coffee place suits me, sorry to drag you out so far," Anna said when we greeted each other. "I hope you don't mind. The people are friendly and none of the food is expensive."

"It's great," I said, assessing her.

She wasn't quite the foxy eyeful I'd been expecting. Older than her profile pics. Distinct crows-feet. And what was this annoyingly flouncy dress she was wearing? It entirely covered up her legs and arms, making it impossible to properly gauge her figure. The dress design was seriously bonkers as well, with not just real flowers sewn into the seams but herb tufts and twigs.

"What are those?" I asked, pulling a face at the dead-looking blossoms.

"Hibiscus, valerian, yarrow and mugwart mostly," she said. "Want a whiff?" And before I could say no she bent forward to offer me a noseful near her left breast.

What I inhaled smelled so damp and pithily earthy that it made my head swim.

Anna smiled sweetly at me.

"Want a coffee?" she asked, and I nodded automatically, but I was already planning my exit. Only the promise of that yoga photo had kept me here this long, but the pic was obviously years old. She'd arrived late, too. I fucking hate being kept waiting by a date.

"Sure is warm in here," she said, ordering me a latte from a passing waiter and at the same time untangling a gauzy yellow neckerchief in a slow, complicated way from her neck. I watched it uncoil, mesmerised by the drifty way the material seemed to unwrap itself. "And how about some carrot cake?" she added. "The version they do here can divide a nation: it contains pineapple. But you know what, it tastes damn fine."

I blinked, still staring at the neckerchief now being tucked into her bag. "Sorry?"

She pointed at one of the blackboards on a nearby wall, which stated as much.

"Actually, I'm just going to have water, not coffee," she said, reaching for the carafe on the table.

When she leaned down to pour it I flinched. There was a boil on her neck. A greasy, angry red eruption bigger than my thumbnail. She hadn't even made an effort to cover it up. Didn't she know it was showing? The way it was pressed up against her collar she had to be able to feel it, didn't she? Then a creepy tingle shot through me. What about other spots or sores? Were they hidden under her clothes? Was that why she'd worn such a concealing dress? I tried to think back to her profile pictures, recall which parts of her body had been hidden, which on show.

Anna noticed me checking her out.

"You look like you've seen better," she said, staring directly at me. "Are you disappointed, David?"

"What ... no no, of course not," I said blushing at being caught out. Next second I was seething, though. Her calling *me* out, when she'd turned up like this?

"Ooo, you look mad as hell," she said, throwing her head back and laughing.

I'd had enough of this. I was getting up to leave when Anna felt quickly for one of my hands. Traced a whorly pattern on my thumb. "Sorry, David," she apologised. "I get jitters on a first date, that's all. Sometimes let my thoughts spill right out instead of keeping my mouth shut. Shall we start again?"

I didn't know how to react to that. How were we supposed to start again? Besides, I didn't want to. This sarky, spotty woman didn't come as advertised. I'd had way better. In fact, since I'd moved to London when I was twenty-one, I'd had a good level of trim basically available on tap whenever I fancied it. If I'd been desperate to get my end off tonight I might have persisted with Anna, but I already had Nikki, san spots, lined up for the weekend. Nikki was a twenty-two year old trainee architect I'd met at Electric Brixton. We'd already had straight sex once, and at the end of the night I'd asked her if she'd shave next time. When she hesitantly said yes I knew from experience that within a few dates I'd be able to do her any way I wanted with few objections raised.

Nikki was the lonely, pliable type I generally went for. At thirty-one years old she was the perfect age, too – a tad older than me. In my experience when women reach their thirties they often worry you might walk away if they don't put out early. Last month I'd met this incredibly anxious, stuttery anthropology MA student called Suzie Chang studying at SOAS. She was almost too easy: so grateful for the attention of a decent-looking guy that I only had to buy her a cappuccino and a single slice of carrot cake (total cost of date £4.20) to get her to open her legs at her flat around the corner. I just shagged her as well, no frills. I barely even said good-bye. She still followed me to the door. Padded as fast as she could in her pvc yellow slippers, with an outpouring of appreciative smiles, asking when we'd see each other again.

Point being: I didn't need any hassle or awkwardness.

"Would you like to excuse yourself and go to the counter on the pretext that you're studying the menu, but actually to get your shit together and decide how you want to handle me?" Anna said cheerfully. I realised she was still holding my hand, rubbing my thumb in an intricate, soft way.

"What the fuck?" I said, so loudly that a couple on the next table heard.

Anna didn't react. Just released my thumb and *tucked* into her glass of water – and when I say tucked I mean that literally; her hands were abruptly all over as well as inside the rim of her fluted Picardie tumbler, an elaborate octopus-like wrapping and unwrapping and re-gripping that was off-putting but also oddly sensual.

Until, that is, my eyes were led to her fingernails, and I couldn't believe the state of them: not just bitten-down and chipped, but *dirty*.

"What the hell have you been doing?" I grimaced. "Gardening?"

"I get nervous before a date," she answered. "I pick at my skin. It's congealed blood. It goes this colour when it's dry." When my mouth fell open, she chuckled. "Hey, chill out, will you? I'm only joking."

She found my hand again, ran her index finger in a percussive skate over my palm.

I swayed, feeling fractionally dizzy. "I think I need to go now," I said, the words not even chosen by my brain; they just shot out.

"Don't be silly, we just got here."

I was up and standing, grabbing my jacket and ready to leave when Anna whispered in my ear, "I'm dying for a shag, please don't go." She squeezed my hand. "Really, I am. I'm gagging for it. Haven't had a fuck in ages. I'm just a bag of nerves, OK? You're so gorgeous. I'll let you do anything you like to me. Anything."

Before I could answer she used my crotch to gently push me back down onto my stool and re-filled her tumbler with more water. My latte arrived.

"What do you do for a living?" Anna asked, playing with the coffee's frothy rim with her fingertip. "Only on your dating profile you say virtually nothing about yourself, David."

I blinked, peered down at my hand. It was back in hers again. When had that happened? I withdrew it. At the same moment all the colours in the room brightened, and I felt the belt of my jeans pulled forward, everything hitched closer to Anna.

"There, that's better, isn't it?" she said. "Everything more ... *present*. More immediate. Did you like my *yoga* pic, by the way? You'd be amazed how wide my hips open when I'm really motivated." She grins, showing teeth less white than they should be, and suggestively rubs my forearm. "Tell me about yourself, David. The real you."

Blinking a few times, I notice she's begun stirring my latte with a brown twig, a stick plucked straight off her dress.

"Is ... that hygienic?" I ask, shaking my head, trying hard to clear it.

"Probably not." She removes the twisted thing, licks the tip. Playfully taps my nose. "Just ignore my antics, David. My hands are a nightmare. Always on the go, stirring something." She laughs. "I was taught how to stir professionally by someone, actually. You want to meet them?"

"What?" I say, feeling weirdly drowsy.

"Never mind. We can talk about that later. Your profile said you're a broker for a top 100 insurance company. That's fascinating. Tell me more."

"Yeah ... um ... investment decisions, capital into the tens of millions," I trot out, glad for some secure territory I can grasp onto for a moment. I give her my standard flannel. "... deep-sea oil exploration. Logistics around that. I take a commission."

Anna smiles. "And how much money do you make, once you've taken your *servant's* cut, David?"

Fuck! I can't believe this. The condescending bitch is mocking me.

I break eye-contact, assess the woman in front of me afresh. She's confused me so far, but I think I've finally got her figured. She's a feminist ball-breaker, one of the clever-bitch variety. Often the hardest types to engineer into bed, but if you get them there it's especially sweet to do them up the ass. From the crazy look of her home-made dress she earns jack shit. Has to be unemployed. Let's see if a suggestion of real wealth makes our acerbic Anna more pliable.

"I make millions on some individual deals," I tell her, and let those words sink in. "What about you?"

She smirks. "Pfff. Me? Almost nothing. This morning I barely had enough cash on me buy a pack of nappies for my sprog."

I'm sipping water when she hits me with that – and splutter.

"Your face!" she hoots, again grabbing my right hand. "Priceless! Don't want kids, huh? Well, don't worry, I haven't really got any." She glances around to make sure no one's listening on us, murmurs, "Can we have sex soon? Unprotected sex, if you like. That's always a risk, but I prefer the feeling, you know? You can watch me take a morning-after pill once we're done, if you want to be sure nothing happens. I saw your pictures online and ... well ... fucking hell! I could just imagine you inside me, you know?"

Anna folds her hands like two elegant wings over mine. Waits for my reaction. Is she serious? If this is a come-on it's the weirdest I've ever heard. But what the hell? I didn't get to screw as many women as I have by missing out on an obvious opportunity when it presents itself. What's the worst that can happen? Even so, unprotected sex? How do I know the pill she shows me isn't fake?

"I have ... condoms on me," I say.

"Really?" Anna's thick, curved eyebrows arch. "You carry them with you on every first date, do you?"

"Well ..." I mumble, "you know ..."

"No, it's OK, no need to explain," she says, then surprises me by stretching across to nibble my earlobe – and I gasp. Normally I hate it when women touch my ears, but with Anna, desire spasms through me. Her tongue is strangely cold as its tip lifts away, and I pant, my head trying to follow it back to her mouth.

Anna watches me aim for a mistimed kiss, seems satisfied. Then she takes hold of my thumb again and stirs the soft tissue part in a much more insistent, jerky way this time. Adjusts the speed up and down, minutely watching my reaction.

"It's OK," she murmurs, and suddenly I'm lost in her eyes. "Just relax, David. Anna will take of you."

I swallow, not knowing what to say next, not even quite sure I can answer at all. My lips feel numb.

"Let's see if you're ready, shall we?" she says, touching her index finger to the spot on her neck, then popping the same finger into my mouth.

I don't object. I know I should, but it doesn't feel invasive.

"Oh, you're fully dilated, aren't you?" she says, opening out one of her armpits beneath my chin. I find myself burying my face into it. The pit reeks of ... what is it? Stale sweat? No, something worse. The same putrid scent that's concentrated in her fingernails. It's disgusting but, like a sleepy python following a snake charmer, my head sways towards the nails rather than away.

"What are you feeling like now, little man?" Anna remarks tenderly, and I'm filled with a sudden childish happiness because this is a question I feel I can finally answer.

"I'm feeling ... wow, really good," I say, with absolute honesty, and she walks her nails across my lips.

"It's not the sex act itself that I really look forward to," she tells me. "It's more the anticipation. It's everything surrounding it, isn't it? Would you agree?"

I have a desperate desire to impress her suddenly, but what's she implying? "You mean foreplay?"

This time she cracks out a laugh, a cackle drawing the attention of half the café.

"That's funny, David. Foreplay is about as far as your limp imagination can extend from pure sex in terms of intimacy, isn't it? But it's OK, I know you're only trying to figure out what I want." She gazes deep into my eyes, and my heart flutters. "A lot of women have been hurt by you, my friend. A great multitude. Remember Dominique?"

I frown, trying to recall a woman with that name. "Was she Belgian?"

"No. From Marseilles."

I try hard, but still can't bring her to mind.

Anna sighs. "I know. After you ball them, they vanish right from your head, don't they? What can you do? She had hip arthritis, nothing you'd have noticed in the sack, though she talked about it, asked if you'd avoid certain positions. You couldn't resist once she explained, could you? Broke her pelvis."

I remember now. Green dress. Chameleon pet.

"All those successive humiliations drove her to suicide a few weeks ago, David. Shush now." Anna covers my mouth when I go to speak. "I understand you better than you think. I'm cursed by my own sins to be able to read your heart. There's not much to it, but" – she touches my chest – "what little resides there belongs entirely to me now."

She pulls back when I reach for her hands.

"Listen, David. I'm due in several cities over the next few weeks. Istanbul. Seoul. Gdansk. You can accompany me as my sex-slave, the way Dominique accompanied you on your business trips. I will have to rape you, obviously. Rub shit into your mouth a few times."

She digs a broken nail into my chin, making my eyes water.

"I ... I don't want to be a sex slave," I croak.

"No, of course not," she agrees, patting my wrist. "So we'll go straight to the end-game. You get to meet my friend a little sooner. Does the word *uncoagulated* mean anything to you?"

My eyelids flutter, lost in her gaze. "No, Anna. I don't know that word."

"Shall we find out together then?" She stands, and for a moment a hint of self-preservation kicks in, and I shake my head.

"Too late. You've made all your choices, David," Anna says, and reaches below the table to stroke the denim directly over my cock. It goes instantly rock-hard, and automatically, stupidly, I look around to see if anyone's noticed.

No one has.

Anna winks at me, licks her hand and this time cups my balls. I didn't think it was possible to be stiffer than I am, but it is, I'm way too stiff, and it's all I can do to stifle a scream of pain.

Here's the revelation, though. I don't care. I realise it doesn't matter to me what my cock is up to. It's just a weight, a lump of flesh. What matters is this tide of emotion sweeping through me for Anna. Incandescent feelings collect and gather inside me, and it's such a profound relief to be held within their intensity. They overwhelm me. Feelings I never knew I could have for a woman – or anyone else for that matter.

Transfigured, rooted in my seat, my mouth flaps open like a love-sick dog.

"Are you crying, David?"

"Of course not," I whisper, looking away.

"Oh go on." Anna smiles. "Let them flow. Real tears. Even if there's only space in that narrow, pipsqueak soul of yours to weep for yourself."

I know she's demeaning me, but still feel compelled to do as she asks. So I weep. I do more than just weep, actually. I make a performance of it. "Keep it silent," Anna hisses, amused. "We don't want any social awkwardness, do we?'

"OK," I say, choking back the sounds. It's incredibly hard not to make any noise as the small rivers stream silently down my cheeks.

"Now that's love." Anna scratches my wrist. "That's a bloody hard thing to achieve without opening your mouth. Come on. Time to go."

"My card? My jacket?" I say as she propels me towards the café door, but Anna shakes her head and no one notices us leave, not even the staff.

"It's a new life," Anna promises, winking at me, and suddenly the two of us are striding together like lovers down Camden High Street. She leads me past the NatWest bank onto Greenland Street where the houses are very tall. Heavy, noisy traffic hems us in, but I don't care. All that matters is that Anna's holding my hand. I don't know where she's taking me, but there's a lightness in her step and mine.

A tabby cat sidles up, rubs against her black boots.

"You're an animal person!" I say.

"Actually, it's more of a hair thing for me." She stares at my groin.

"Down there?" I ask. "You like hairy men?"

"I like it to start down there, but then sort of go everywhere, lots of matted curls," she says, and for some reason my stomach swoops with fear.

"Where are we going?" I ask.

"Does it matter, as long as we're not parted?"

I realise it doesn't.

I follow her over a zebra crossing, feeling the bond between us tighten. It's love I'm feeling. I've always had a sexual agenda with women until now, but that's not what love is. Love is floating. Love is being like this, I finally understand. Just trusting. I glance across at Anna and when she flashes a smile back at me my heart nearly bursts.

Then abruptly she lets go of my hand, vanishes around a bend in the pavement – and I feel devastated. In sheer terror, I hurry around the corner after her.

"Feels horrible, doesn't it?" she says, waiting there for me. "Being abandoned, that is. Come on, silly. This way." Her fingers enclose mine again, but the grip is fiercer than before. "Man up," she mutters, when I wince. "I need a proper partner in my life, not an emotional wreck." And though she's laughing as she says it, aren't those the words I used with Dominique?

"Hey, your hand is freezing," I say, desperate for any conversation between us that sounds vaguely normal. Only October, but her skin feels icy.

"Ah well. You know what they say about cold hands, don't you?" She hustles me through the greenery of St Martin's Gardens.

"Warm heart?" I manage.

"Big cock," she says – and I explode with laughter. It's one of my own chat-up lines, something I use to test the boundaries.

"Hey," she whispers. "Would you really mind if I did have?"

And I think about that. Try to put it in some sort of practical context alongside my feelings for her. Is Anna a transvestite? Or maybe someone half-way through a sex change? A transition point still with both sets of organs?

"Confusing, huh?" Anna says. "You saw my yoga pic, though. That's the real thing, bud. But they're both there when I want them to be. A gift from my friend, whether I want it or not." She's laughing at my totally puzzled face now. "I believe in you, David," she whispers, and my heart thumps with pride.

We stop. We're standing outside a four-story terraced house on Bayham Street.

I peer up at the crumbling brickwork. Black-framed, shuttered oval windows that look very old. "In we go," Anna says, opening the front door with an ornate brass key.

The long shadowy hall is wallpapered. Dark blue patterns seem to be writhing: swirly drawings of goats rutting with men and women.

A cold sweat slides down my spine, but Anna smiles and that's plenty enough to get me to follow her to the hallway's end. A rough set of stone steps lead down from it into a large basement. As we walk down them I realise this part of the house is warmer than the rest and illuminated in darkly orange light.

"He's on his way," Anna says.

She tilts her head towards seven cats who've abruptly appeared, lined up in a row along one wall of the basement. The cats are all tabbies but bigger, chunkier, than standard tabbies, with curiously flat-ended tails.

"Seven?" I inquire.

She gives me an indulgent smile. "Common tabbies raised up to greatness. As you will be, David."

An inchoate fear is beginning to jiggle about inside me now, but Anna seems fine, and remembering what she said about manning-up I suck in a deep breath.

"Take off your shoes and socks," she says, and I do, without feeling the need to question the order. An uncomfortable heat immediately radiates through my toes. Where's it coming from?

Anna asks me to enter a circle in the middle of the floor with a gold star and other markings, and while I'm doing so she rubs her armpits and face thoroughly with a bar of something black that stinks like a long-dead animal. I gag as she lifts her dress to give her groin several more long thorough rubs with it.

"He sometimes ... makes mistakes," she says, at my bewildered glance. "He's old. Doesn't see too good any more. This way he won't mistake me for you." She sizes me up, pulls on her lip. "Take off your clothes, including your underwear."

"Will you take yours off, too?" I ask, as I'm kicking off my boxers.

"In a moment, yes. Kneel down, David, and bend your head forward, like this."

Anna folds me into a supplicant pose, then reaches down for the buckle of her own dress. The room is infuriatingly dark, so I can't quite see what she's doing. I can tell she's taking off all her clothes, but everything is so dim.

Then something long and thin like a whip swishes in front of my face, and I yell out in surprise.

Anna puts a finger to my lips. Points out that the nail is attached to one of her own toes; its hers. She cracks the toenail a few times to loosen it, then flagellates not me – I'm expecting that for some reason – but her own breasts with the barbed tip multiple times, each lash cutting deeper.

"I don't get to see Him without paying a penalty," she chokes out, clenching her teeth. "No one does." Her fingers travel to her dripping breasts, and from their wetness to my lips. "Don't say anything," she says, then backs away into a pool of slightly improved light so I can see her. Fully see her, I mean. Her vulva.

Moments later, with an improbably hard thump, a penis drops out of it. It's a normal man's penis as far as I can tell, but very withered and sliced off at an oblique angle near the base.

"I'm not going to do that to you, if that's what you're thinking," Anna says, when I shout out. "I can't touch you, actually. Not now that He's decided He wants you. You have strong legs." She admires them a moment. "He'll like that."

"Anna," I croak, pawing at her breasts.

"No, no." She slaps my hands away, but without venom. "These aren't for you." She sighs, a brief look of true pity in her eyes. "I have a deep belief in you, David," she says, kissing my forehead a moment. "In your instinct for self-preservation, at least. I really think you're going to last longer than you expect. I'll be here the whole time willing you on, my breasts on show, my vagina as well, naked, unshaven, the way you like it, yes? Just look in the left corner of the basement when things get really bad."

I'm crying now but I don't understand why.

"It's alright," Anna soothes me. "It won't be long now. I can't be here myself in this space with you when He arrives but my cats can be. They'll keep you company until He gets here."

"Anna, please," I murmur, tears shooting out of me as she retreats into the shadows.

I try to follow her, can't. The boundary of the circle I'm inside contains me.

As I reach desperately up higher and higher, trying to claw my way out, all seven of the tabbies leap on me. Collectively they truss my pelvis in complicated ways, tightening, twisting and puckering the skin with their teeth and claws, while I scream.

Across the room Anna's breasts re-appear. They loom like two pale pendulous moons above what I eventually make out to be a round-bellied black cauldron.

"My pot, corny I know," she says. "But this brew's been simmering ordure and worse for thousands of years, and the promise of a cup of it is about the only thing that'll bring Him here. My grandmother was the first witch to call Him up with it, and ever since then He expects it. Comfort food, I suppose. He's set in his ways."

"Anna ..." I whisper, but she's sitting on a stool behind the cauldron now, working her inner thighs around its belled curve. An audible pop follows, twice, and I see with horror she's dislocating her hips to get them wide enough for her knees to slide around the barrel of the pot.

"Stir, stir, let the cats purr," she says, once her kneecaps are snugly aligned, and begins stirring the pot. Naked and earthed, her slim arms pump the liquid around, delving up and down, swirling thick contents I cannot see, only smell – and suddenly a stink wafts across me so overwhelming that I empty my stomach.

Two of the cats catch my vomit on their uplifted tails. Padding across the cauldron, they fling it in.

"What's about to happen?" I whimper.

"Who knows?" Anna shrugs. "I'm not even sure how He found out about you. Perhaps He'll let you live." She digs hard into the pot, tunnelling deep into the ordure with her elbows this time, and I puke again. "Down here it's all inhuman activity, David," she tells me, panting with the effort to keep the mixture churning. "It's all High Witchery, crunching bunions and the juices of Man."

She stops briefly, standing up high enough to dab her vagina across the lip of the cauldron. Then she nods at her cats, and all seven of them lift and carry me on their raised flat-ended tails and tip me like a giant mouse into the cauldron.

I scream as I splash and land, but I don't go under. The fetid liquid is so solid that I only bob around on the meniscus.

Anna pushes my legs beneath the surface, then begins to hot-drive the pot. Around my calves she stirs, her cats' wild-gusting tails working in feline symmetry, while Anna, wildest of all, digs deep below me at the sludgy pot-base with her nails. I hear her scratching symbols that then appear in sharp pentacles across my own chest.

I'm terrified now, I'm shitting into the pot, with Anna's hand suddenly pressing my buttocks from below, encouraging the flow.

"Let it go, let it go," she sings, in the style of the Disney song. "Because all this is a ritual," she shouts, drowning out my screams. "It's all a study, all very formal, David. It has to be in the right order, because He's so bloody fussy. He's like a nerd with his train-timetables. And well ... here He comes. Gird your loins."

"Wait," I say, as she backs off, her breasts withdrawing into the darkness. There's a final hint of her face and neck, bowing deep and long towards the floor at ... at what?

He uncoagulates though the hot floor underneath me.

He comes straight through, as if an elevator shaft from a furnace delivered him. He's three times my height, four times my girth, and what swings between his legs is thicker than my shoulder. Whorl-horned and crimson-skulled. Yellow-eyed, vertically-slitted, and under those eyes a body hewn in black, as if from granite, all edges, stinking of goat and tombs and dead children.

His hooves, prodigiously cloven, splay unsteadily as they make purchase on the slippery floor. The whole room rocks under his weight.

He glances across at Anna and she walks out of the darkness, eyes down. Kisses under his tail.

He nods acknowledgement, then drags his ancient body towards the cauldron. Scoops two muscular hands into the pot and drinks greedily. His body is part-animal, part-man, part-magic, part-prince.

He finally spots me floating, slippery-arsed, amongst the faeces. Frowns. Wipes His mouth. Seems to register who and what I am, but with effort. Then a little smile, an imp's smile, a boy's naughty smile, and He raises a single encrusted, noduled claw – and I yell out as something lights up behind my front teeth, my whole mouth glowing a sulphurous yellow-orange.

He reaches into the pot. With one hand lifts me out and places me, basted and sticky, onto the floor.

I scream and feel my bowels loosen again as he tightens one clawed hand into a fist like a boxer's glove and punches me – rather delicately – on the nose.

The blow makes me gasp, and while my mouth is open He stuffs his black claw all the way inside my mouth – and stirs. My jaw cracks and breaks, his nails and knuckles knocking away my teeth, slicing away gums, my tongue, the palp of my tonsils. And all the while He's grunting and snuffling in quiet satisfaction to himself. He's happy. Holding my neck stiff as I buck, He rummages ever deeper clockwise and anticlockwise, probing, making incisions, until the last of my back molars pops out, my throat fully hollowed out now, a circle made smooth and wet.

Briefly He lets go of me then. Seems, in fact, to forget about me. Slouches uncertainly across to a wall. Idly examines his own belly. Looks for and finds his belly-button hiding under the matted hair, like a child might. Bats it idly back and forth. *He was born from something else*, I realise.

Then He turns back towards me.

I bring my hands up to cover my face, hoping He'll forget about me again. But no. He follows the smell of fresh shit until He finds me.

Once his rheumy, goat-eyes focus again he sharply snaps his claws in front of my face to distract me, then swings his barbed tail in secretly behind my back to penetrate my anus.

He waits until my eyes go white with pain before he stops shoving it upward.

Then, bouncily testing my weight on its end, he brings me around so he can to get a good long look at me. My hands automatically come up to protect my mouth, but He seems to know that's going to happen, catches my wrists and breaks them. Twists them off as effortlessly as decapitating a chick.

He doesn't do anything for a moment after that. Just enjoys listening to me shriek with the shredded remnant of my tongue. Then He brings me closer. Peers thoughtfully inside my throat, like a tradesman checking out his own professional handiwork.

Long, pensive and dreamy he looks. Rheumy-eyed, with triangular ears folded back. Drawn out of Hell, but not yet fully present. His breathing is surprisingly tentative, as if He's still not quite adjusted to this non-sulphurous air.

But the next moment that changes. His eyes flash with Hell's gleam, the seven cats all simultaneously bay like dogs, and Anna bays with them, bays loudest of all, prostrate, whispering, *Abadden, Amon, Asmodeus, Baphomet, Chemosh, Marduk, Satan, Sedit ...* '

He seems to like this roll-call. His eyes ripple with intelligible delight. Then he gets my attention again. He's pointing. At his loins. He gestures for me to look down and up at what is rising from there.

It's a fresh thing and a pink thing. Newly-shed skin.

"He's honouring you," Anna tells me. "Dawn-fresh."

The huge blunt head dances in front of my face, coated in delicate hoar-frost at one edge of the glans, deep red fire at the other. "Hurry. Choose which end to start with or He will," Anna tells me.

When I can't He sniffs my face, decides I need another pot-dunking.

While I'm being dipped all over again He muses. Drinks a little more from the cauldron. Watches me rowing my arms, trying to get as far across the pot as I can from him. His claws copy me. He smiles with black teeth. Makes the same rowing gestures.

"*Whither away, small bird?*" he says, his voice both beast and god, and now he's lifting me out again, his crisp-clattering hooves suddenly eager, all drowsiness gone.

I look for Anna, but she's no longer here. Nor are the cats.

Squeezing my face a moment, He lifts me up – but carefully this time, just enough to dislocate the last ligaments and sinews hinging my jaw together. Then, hawking up a mouthful of phlegm, he spits into my slack open lips and I feel him bellow and stiffen, nostrils distending, yellow slits slanting to cock-eyed, as he lowers my mouth to his groin.

The Poetess
Doug Dawson

I thought I was smart - 39 years old and still running around - a sexual libertine who loved wild women and sexual conquests. Over the years I'd cut a swath through the arts community and in my spare time dated love-starved ex-nuns, socialites, cheating housewives, well-padded matrons, a swimsuit model, a 19-year-old college cutie and if I hadn't been afraid of catching a disease I would have tried every fornicatrix, trollop and strumpet out there. What I hadn't done I'd imagined, like being attended to by randy female boxers and exponents of the flying trapeze, lady doctors, lawyers and Indian chiefs, salacious sky divers and astronauts. I mean, why not have them all, at least in your dreams? I had a good sex life and imagined a better one, the kind few people have ever had. But that was B.P. - Before the Poetess. Now it's A.P. (After the Poetess, if you hadn't guessed) and nowadays I prefer a female personality as calm and mild as tepid bathwater.

Now who could take a bon-vivant like myself, full of bonhomie and good will and reduce him to a cross between a bitter, burned out shell of a man and a sexual milquetoast who craves nothing more than platonic dating, a little high-minded, missionary-position-only sex and overall a life without drama? I'll tell you who: a woman of impeccable face and form, an artiste and a gifted poet, and what's wrong with that, you ask? Give me a few minutes of your time and I'll tell you.

It started six months ago. My artist friend Sharon invited me to a cocktail party for singles of the artistic persuasion. These artsy crowds can be just a bit pretentious and to be on the safe side I wore my beige dress pants, yellow turtleneck, navy blazer and burgundy penny loafers and wondered if a beret would have been too much. When I arrived, I did a quick look-around, noted the usual crop of writers, poets, sculptors, classical musicians and painters - me being one of the latter - and decided my careful outfit selection had rendered me more college professor than painter. *Oh, well, I thought. At least I'm not smoking a pipe or a Du Maurier cigarette.*

A veteran of such soirees, I had my eye on a Thomas McKnight hanging on the wall, wondering if it was a numbered print or even an original - our host was a man of considerable means and hanging a humble poster on one of his walls would be, well, not only déclassé but completely out of the question.

I was thinking this party could hold no surprises for me when Sharon walked up and interrupted my reverie. "There's somebody I want you to meet," she said.

Suffice it to say I almost dropped my Dubonnet with a twist of lemon in it when I took a gander at the somebody I was to meet.

"Harry, this is Mindy Mink," said Sharon. "She's new in town. I told her all about you."

I delivered the obligatory, "Don't believe a thing she told you," line then gave Mindy as subtle a once-over as I know how and I'm not ashamed to say it wasn't so subtle.

If I could have commented out loud without sounding like an uncouth dullard, the first word out of my mouth would have been "Magnifique!" the second, as I noted her bust, would have been "Incroyable!" and I might have followed up with "Cherchez la femme" or even "Sacre Bleu," whether it fit the occasion or not.

Forgive me for being blunt, but I'm a breast man and this woman was one of the finest specimens of feminine pulchritude I'd ever had the pleasure to admire. You are speaking to a connoisseur of all types of décolletages and breast size, from the tiny, with protruding nipples, to the heavy hangers, with flat nipples and wide areolas so big you can't get your mouth around them. Nothing gets my attention faster than an ample bosom, but what was before me was simply … stupefying. Mindy "pulled the hat trick," as I refer to it on the rare occasions when it happens; she was beautiful, with a concomitant figure and far more important, she completely filled out her blouse, discreetly covered as it was by a jacket-like top which matched her skirt. In fact, it wasn't just Mindy that got my attention, for her clothing reminded me of those girlish Octoberfest outfits redolent of Old-World Europe. Her blouse was white and frilly, her matching skirt and jacket, an ochre of the kind Rembrandt often used in his chiaroscuro paintings. She even wore baby-doll shoes with lots of toe cleavage, complementing her ensemble, completing the picture, so to speak and causing me to conclude: "Simply smashing," - to myself, of course.

Back to cases, for when I say Mindy filled out her blouse, I am understating the matter, but that's not the salient point, for it's the way she filled it out that took my breath away. Most well-endowed women sag and that's no fault of theirs, for gravity has its way with all of us and in any case such women just don't have the shape of women who are more modestly endowed.

"Mindy's got them," I thought, almost exclaiming it out loud, "bodacious ta-tas!" Please forgive this crude expression which probably came from some lout in a bar (yes, bar - lots of women in bars, that's why I go to them). What shocked me was not their sheer size - all right yes, their sheer size, but also their shape, as best one can tell when a blouse and brassiere are in the way, and the way they projected forward like twin torpedoes on their way to sink a battleship. Already plotting my strategy to get at her, I tried to imagine his Mink woman topless and the thought that I could never be that lucky stopped me from forming a clear picture in my mind - the first time my powers of visualization ever failed me.

I didn't say anything for what seemed like a full minute, as I was a little taken aback and it felt like all the words had run out, so to speak. By the time they came back, Sharon had left us alone and Mindy was talking to me like I was the only person in the room. She's a poet and that turned me on too. We talked for what seemed like an hour then, just to be polite, we made the rounds side by side, talking to the others at the party like we were a couple of long standing.

Mindy made me feel like I already meant something to her and I was quickly finding a niche on cloud nine when she pulled me aside and asked, "Why don't we go back to my apartment?"

I didn't need any convincing and never stopped to wonder if we were being obvious, meeting for the first time and taking off together like that. Mindy lived in an expensive-looking apartment building on the prosperous north side of town and the lobby was what I'd call sort-of-opulent, with marble floors and lots of stuffed sofas with pillows. We took an elevator ride up to the thirteenth floor and she held my hand the whole time. If I'd been asked to pick a dream date - something wonderful to imagine, but that doesn't happen in the real world - this would have been it. How could I know that things were soon to get much better?

Mindy's apartment was quite spare and by that I mean very little furniture. The place seemed to be just one big living room. There were shelves along the walls, all of them full of books and papers, some chairs and a long table full of more papers, like they were all works in progress. There was a litter box under the table but no cat in sight, a small couch and a baby grand piano. It was the latter than got my attention, not for itself, but for what was under it: several cat turds. The latter could have meant several things and I didn't want to jump to any wrong conclusions, not with a bust like Mindy's at stake. For one thing, her cat may have simply "missed the litter box," but what cat is that clumsy? It also could have meant that the cat had done it while Mindy was at the party and the poor little thing may have suffered dyspepsia, "gasid indigestion" or even some feline sort of explosive diarrhea. The other possibility was that things were always like that in this apartment and that wasn't a possibility I found comforting, so I ignored it.

Mindy worked fast and she wasted no time with me. She carefully placed me on the couch then sat in my lap, close enough for me to feel her body heat then removed her jacket-like top. I figured she was just warm but then she removed her blouse and my pulse raced in a way that scared me. To this day I've never seen a more wondrous cleavage and I truly admired her bra for being able to support her the way it did. Next the bra came off and Mindy put my hands on her breasts - not just on them, mind you, but under them, like I was now her bra, supporting their full weight and girth. Then she wrapped her arms around me. I must pick my words carefully here, for trite expressions like "great rack" and "played with her tits" merely diminish me and the experience. What I can tell you is that my first bust-busting-out-of-blouse impression of Mindy was not disappointed. Now I'm "talkin' to ya plain," as my uncle used to say to me, so let me continue in the same vein: her tits were soft, all right, but firm and my God, how they hung - forward and out like the two zucchinis I should have been able to imagine at the party. I've never had a feel like that in my life and was thanking my lucky stars and meanwhile she was kissing me to beat the band. Well, my trousers were getting tighter by the second and I was starting to hope old Mindy was about to top the hat trick I referred to earlier and complete my sexual bliss when she stopped me, just like that.

"I have to take a nap," was all she said. She just put her bra back on, then the blouse, buttoned up and was off to the bedroom.

What's a fellow to do in such circumstances? Rush into the bedroom and "possess her," only to be later accused of date rape? Then again maybe she wanted me to follow - perhaps that was her way of seducing me, I mean you can't say I wasn't encouraged. I want you to think that I am a gentleman and dammit, I am, but all's fair in love and war and I felt I couldn't let things stand as they were, especially my throbbing manhood, so I tip-toed after her. The bedroom door was left ajar, so I peeked in and by that time she was already asleep, a fact confirmed by her snoring. So, there I was, boner-in-trousers - do I have to tell you how uncomfortable that is? - my heart racing and nowhere to go but to the bathroom to relieve myself, out the door and home or back to the couch. I chose the latter and forty-five minutes later my pants felt a lot looser and Mindy was back on the couch talking to me about her poetry, but this time no bare titties, no feel and no kissy-face. Now you've just been privy to some frank, hard-hitting talk about my sexual feelings, but lest you think I am merely some sort of one-dimensional walking phallus, let me remind you that at heart I am an artiste and really wanted to hear what Mindy's poetry was like, so I asked her to read it.

She went to her long table and pushed the papers around until she found the one she wanted. "Here's one of my favorites," she said. "It's called 'A Poet's Life.' It went as follows:

> *How do I write for thee?*
> *Let me count the ways: a poem, a sonnet, a verse, an ode!*
> *I shout, I scream, I yell to all creation what I have to say and here it is:*
> *How do I find the words? I fear I shan't - then again, I shan.*
> *See this typewriter before me - well, do you?*
> *Each key has its own ambidextrous arm attached,*
> *Each shaft a lethal lance with a letter,*
> *Each alphabetical appendage a phallus, raping the white paper below,*
> *Each key expressing genius with a furious, belligerent puddle of ink,*
> *Raining down dank ruin on porous paper, creating a floodtide,*
> *Portending the End of the World, smashing all that is, as I*
> *End it all with the might of the terrible, swift sword that is my*
> *typewriter;*
> *Do you see it now?*
> *Fear it!*

She turned to me and asked, "How do you like it?"

"It's remarkable," I answered and really thought it was, though what else it may have been I couldn't say. I couldn't even decide if the obvious borrowing of Elizabeth Barrett Browning's *How do I love thee? Let me count the ways,* was plagiarism or brilliant parody. And *shan* - is that even a word?

"I'll read another," said Mindy. "This is called 'Express Elevator.'"

> *I'm thirteen stories up and thinking about taking the Express Elevator.*
> *I'd parachute, but there's no time for the chute to open.*
> *I could lower myself down on a rope, but I'd probably slip.*
> *Or shimmy down a drainpipe, but the neighbors might laugh.*
> *I always told my parents I'd make a big splash someday.*
> *I'll take the Express Elevator, straight down to the pavement below.*
> *It'll be a mess, all right, but it will end this tormented train ride of*
> *terror I've been taking for thirty-three wenching, wrenching years.*
> *No more waiting for the checks from my parents,*

No more men staring at my tits,
No more gnarling and washing of my teeth,
Or should that be wailing and gnashing of my teeth?
I'm no Bible scholar, you know, so what the fuck do you want from
me?
At any rate, I scream, I fall, I turn into a bloody pool, in a love-death
embrace with the pavement below.
It was quite a ride, the Express Elevator. Care to take it with me?

"Well," she said, "how do you like it?"

"I'm ... stupefied," I answered, quite correctly.

"Here's one more," she went on before I could stop her. "It's about this kid. I call it *Crucifixion.*"

I was truly afraid of what I might hear, so I stood up and practically shouted at her: "My God! The time! I just looked at my watch."

"Oh, you have to go," she said, not even a little annoyed.

"Yes, I do."

"You'll have to come up and see me again. I'll call you - you did give me your number, didn't you?"

I nodded then headed for the front door. She followed me to the door and stood close, like she expected a kiss goodbye, so I turned to face her. She turned her head sideways and allowed me to kiss her on the cheek and I left. I was still plenty turned on and impressed with her considerable, if bizarre, powers of poetic description. Still I was disturbed by it, not to mention the pile of cat shit on the floor, but felt I needed time to digest it all, in a manner of speaking.

I thought about nothing but Mindy the next few days as I worked on a painting, talked to potential customers and made the usual rounds of galleries, bars and taverns. I couldn't decide if she was a little loco or just an eccentric artist. When I talked to my poet friends Mindy's name came up several times, for she is known both for her poetry and performance pieces, which I took to be some kind of multimedia art, involving avant-garde theatre, music and poetry. I came to the conclusion that my first judgment of her had been hasty, that I ran out of her apartment because I'd experienced something I wasn't prepared for. It crossed my mind that artists are unusual people and consequently misunderstood, that I'm unusual. I recalled the sad story of Sylvia Plath, which made me feel sympathetic and legitimized the whole suicidal-poet thing. I began to see Mindy's poems as attempts to reach out with her deepest feelings, something most of us, including artists, are often too "sophisticated" and guarded to do. Then again, there were her alluring looks and sumptuous body to consider, so I called and asked her to visit one of the local art galleries with me.

When I picked her up, she looked even more appetizing than previously, even in her simple pants-and-blouse outfit, over which a coat hid her ample assets. *It can't be her clothes, not this time, I thought.* I realized the date was a test, a sanity check, to make sure she was safe and sane, but that didn't stop me from having little pangs of yearning. Let's face it, when you've been single all your life, you're missing something - call it closeness, bonding or whatever you want to. We walked around hand-in-hand, enjoying the art and each other's company. On the way back we stopped at a little Italian restaurant, where she seemed to like the food and our talk about the arts. When I walked her to the door of her apartment, I was hoping for a close encounter of the first kind – from the first time I visited her apartment, that is, but she said she needed to rest. I told her I'd call her in a few days and she said that would be fine. If the date had indeed been a test, she'd passed it with flying colors. Maybe it took physical attraction and an enormous pair of tits to bring it out of me, but I was starting to want her in a way that was more than sexual.

When I called a few days later Mindy sounded like she was in good spirits and I was ready for her. I'd found out about a cafe where they had poetry readings of the type known as "slams" and asked her to go to one with me. The reading was at eight o'clock the following evening.

We arrived at seven for dinner and Mindy said, "I don't drink," when queried about wine or cocktails. She seemed to like the place and the food, so I felt that whatever else happened that evening, I was racking up some points with her. When it was time for the slam to begin Mindy seemed energized. Trained in academia, she had little familiarity with street talk and culture but nevertheless seemed to enjoy the animated poets, who punctuated their rhyming, rap-like personal stories with aggressive gestures that reminded me of karate chops and punches. Whatever she thought of it all, she paid close attention.

When the last poet finished, she looked at me as if she'd had a revelation.

"Hope you enjoyed it," I said and she responded by holding my hand.

When I escorted her to her door, I had my hopes but settled for a goodnight kiss, as it was late and she was tired.

She went inside, started to close the door, then turned and said, "I'm having a get-together in my apartment next week - would you like to come?"

"Of course," I answered.

She explained it would be a poetry reading and a rehearsal of some sort. I was glad to be invited, both for my own curiosity about her work and mostly just to be near her.

A week later she called to say she wanted me to come over the next evening at 6 o'clock, at which time she'd have a wine and cheese gathering, followed by a rehearsal of her latest performance piece. I showed up fashionably late and walked in to find a group of about fifteen people, some standing and talking, others on the floor, performing motions which made me think some were doing yoga and others Pilates. I guessed they were warming up for some sort of dance. I poured myself a glass of wine, had some cheese on a cracker and tried to talk to Mindy, who was occupied with planning the rehearsal of her piece. I stood next to a very short and slightly stocky fellow who appeared to be a few years younger than me. We got to talking and he seemed a bit odd but was nevertheless very friendly.

"This is Frank, my boyfriend," said Mindy, as she turned and stood next to the young man I'd been speaking to. As Mindy was rather tall, they made a true Mutt and Jeff team, not to mention the fact that on my scale she was a ten and he didn't register anything at all. I continued to drink wine, eat cheese and crackers and talk to this fellow Frank, for I wondered what he had, if anything, that made him so lucky as to be designated *her boyfriend* and what exactly the latter term meant. Finally, Mindy and her friends were ready to begin.

"This piece is accompanied by the reading of my poem," said Mindy, as everyone stopped what they were doing to listen. "Now you all know my style, but this one's completely different - it's my very first rhyming poem. I call it *Crucifixion*."

This red-haired kid who lives nearby
Does all he can to make me cry.
He calls me "douche bag" and "big tits"
I guess that's how he gets his kicks.
I made a fist and tried to hit him,
Even tho' he's mighty quick.
He went and told his parents on me -
Dirty, rotten little prick!
This vile little sack of sin,
I'd find a bag to stuff him in.
But I decided how to fix him -
We will have a crucifixion!

In Mindy's new rhyming style I sensed connection to the poetry slam, though I didn't say anything about it.

"All right, everybody in their places," ordered Mindy, who stood in the center of the room, hands raised like a symphony conductor, waiting for everyone to get ready. All seven players found their places on the floor and looked up, waiting for Mindy, who started waving her hands as if directing an orchestra. The players all went into bizarre, helter-skelter motion, rolling on the floor, flailing arms and legs and making facial contortions. One fellow stood on his head and pretended to scream, though he uttered nary a sound. Another stood behind the couch, making grotesque faces, then all at once tumbled over the back of the couch, onto the couch itself and then onto the floor, muttering "oh, my God," the whole time.

"This makes Theatre of the Absurd seem logical as hell," I thought.

Somehow Mindy found fault with the studied chaos around her and shouted, "Do it right - you're losing the meaning of the play!" She stopped her conducting and all the players became motionless.

"We'll start again," commanded Mindy, raising her arms and directing everyone in what appeared to be the exact same frenzy as before, including the upside-down fellow who pretended to scream. This time it was acceptable, apparently and the contortions and flailing went on until Mindy pointed to one of her male players, who was writhing on the floor, in apparent agony, or ecstasy - I couldn't tell which. This player stood up, went to the wall and stood, head hanging forward, arms stretched as if on a cross, at which point the other players stood, approached him and pretended to nail his wrists, beat him and apply a crown of thorns.

Mindy stopped her conducting and read aloud:

> *Snap! Crack! Go the lovely lashes from a red-hot whip*
> *That rends the flesh 'till white bones show.*
> *Nine-inch nails, pounded through stinging wrists,*
> *A crown of thorns that feels like fangs*
> *The agony of the damned, who suffers the longest day of his life,*
> *Each second an hour, each minute an eon*
> *Swells to a white-hot crescendo as the end draws near.*
> *The essence of a callous wretch spills out*
> *Like the crimson juice of a beet, squashed by the boot of righteousness,*
> *Like the evil red of his heathen hair, set afire by angels of vengeance.*
> *Nothing more to say, nothing more to do, for he is no more.*
> *His suffering ends in this valley of the damned - so be it.*

Mindy stopped and took a deep bow and everyone there applauded.

"Surely it's a joke," I thought. Everyone went back to drinking wine and munching cheese and crackers and I indulged in small talk with several of them, who were local actors. Finally, it was nine o'clock and Mindy announced it was time for her nap. Everyone left but I stayed behind.

"Want me to wait up for you?" I asked, sounding as innocent as I knew how.

"Why?" she replied.

"I have to be honest, Mindy," I nearly panted, for this woman, despite her wacky poetry and performance piece, really got to me. "You knock me out, your company, your poetry ... everything - I think you're fantastic. You nap as long as you want, I'll watch TV or something and when you're up we can hang out - sound good?"

"Not tonight," she protested. "Maybe some other time."

"I'm only trying to be closer to you," I whined, sounding more than a little desperate, I'm sure.

She just smiled at me and I almost thought I perceived a smirk, like she'd been through all this with men before, like she was laughing at me. I decided to take my losses and get out of there.

"G'night," I said as I walked out the door.

Once again I rationalized away everything I'd experienced in Mindy's apartment with thoughts like, "Hell, can't condemn every controversial author or artist for their work or you'd have to censor Bret Easton Ellis for writing *American Psycho* or jail every sculptor whose work created turmoil at the Brooklyn Museum of Art." I pictured the target of Mindy's ire as a teen-ager, like some I'd known in school - never happy unless they're breaking something or hurting someone's feelings. I recalled high school jocks who thought anybody with artistic talent was not only gay but a wuss and even though they didn't beat me up I despised them. With such thoughts in mind I smiled at Mindy's reaction to an obnoxious kid and giggled at the theatrical torture she meted out. It was all just a little theatre piece; she didn't advocate really hurting anyone, did she?

Over the next two weeks I talked to Mindy on the phone several times. Each time I tried to ask her for a date something got in the way, like going away to visit her parents and the various things she had to do when she got back. I don't know if she sensed how badly I wanted her but finally she called me. Her alleged boyfriend had just died and she needed some company. I was elated - not at someone's death, of course, but at the chance to comfort her in her hour of need, to succor and support her. I was already giving up hope of "getting any" and by now was just grateful for the chance to be near her again. We made a date for the following evening.

When I arrived, Mindy came to the door in tears. I could see she was really shaken up, so I hugged her then we sat on the couch, but not too close.

"He jumped off the balcony," was all she said.

I held her hand, not knowing what to do. If the expression "In for a penny, in for a pound" has any meaning at all, it tells how you'll start with something small and fleeting, like my selfish desire for Mindy's body and end up wanting to hold on and not let go, for after only a few weeks of knowing this woman I felt I'd do damn near anything just to be with her, wacky poetry or no.

"I'm sorry you lost a friend," I said.

"It's all right," she answered. "He didn't really support me or my poetry anyway."

"But I thought he was your ..."

"And I don't think you do either."

I didn't like the way this conversation was going and so I said, "Let's get out of here."

She looked at me for a moment as if puzzled and finally said, "All right."

I said, "I know a movie that's playing - it'll help get your mind off things."

She smiled at the idea, got up and grabbed a stack of her poetry and said, "Let's go."

On the way out the door my eye caught sight of a little boy, sticking his head out of the apartment next door. He appeared to be about nine years old, with bright red hair. He looked at Mindy like he was afraid of her and I guessed he was the guy she'd crucified in effigy. I did wonder why Mindy needed to carry her poetry around just to go see a movie, but I knew better than to protest and a few minutes later I was parking my car down the block from a local theatre where "indie" movies played. Trying to be the perfect gentleman, I walked curbside of Mindy and wanted to hold her hand all the way to the theatre but the hand and the arm I wanted was firmly curled around the stack of poetry, which I decided must be a kind of emotional security blanket at a time when she'd just suffered a loss.

I am still trying to figure out what happened next, or at least why it happened. There was a line at the box office and people were converging from all sides when Mindy seemed to come unglued. She looked at me wild-eyed, pushed me away and made erratic gestures with her free hand.

"C'mon honey," I said, "everything's all right, you've just had a shock ..."

She pushed me away harder and I blurted, "Mindy! Don't have a fit! We're just going to see a ..."

At the word "fit" she must have started swinging but I didn't see it coming. Her closed fist hit me hard in the right eye before I could utter the word "movie" and next thing I knew I was holding both hands over an eye that was gushing big tears and hurting like hell. Mindy then screamed "Help!" like I was the one who hit her and she started running. Where she thought she was going I'll never know, but there were so many people on the sidewalk she kept colliding with them, yelling "Help" at each encounter. Within seconds every eye within two blocks was focused on Mindy, who reminded me of one of the little steel balls in a pinball game, bouncing off the electric targets, each of which sends it careening in another direction. Finally, she made it through the crowd, down the block, toward a bar and disappeared inside. With my one good eye I strained to see and a few minutes later a taxi showed up and she ran out, got in and took off. I could only surmise the proprietor of the establishment called the cab to get rid of her - Mindy - the woman I wanted so badly— wanted her before she hit me, that is.

My damaged eye required me to wear an eye patch and take pain killers, but eventually it healed.

It seems funny, now that I look back, that my friend Sharon introduced me to Mindy but had no idea we were dating, as I hadn't talked to her since the cocktail party that now seems a lifetime ago. She called to say hello about two weeks after my last outing with Mindy. I was finishing a painting I'd been commissioned to do, one that I was very proud of, not least because I'd completed most of it with only one good eye, when the phone rang. I hate being interrupted when I am applying the last few brush strokes and normally wouldn't have answered, but something told me this call was important - it was.

"Hello?"

"Harry! It's Sharon. Haven't spoken to you since the party. People have been asking about you. Where've you been?"

I hesitated before answering then blurted out: "I've been seeing your friend Mindy, as much as she let me, that is."

"Mindy? Oh my God, I didn't know ..."

"Now you do."

"You should have told me."

"Told you what, that I was seeing her - why?"

"Sweetheart, you must know by now if you've been with her."

"Know what?"

"She's schizophrenic."

"What?"

"She's been ... you know, locked up in the past. She takes strong medication; she has to ... to keep her sane. I don't know her well but someone who does told me she's one person half the time and when she's writing her poetry or doing one of those performance pieces she doesn't take her medicine because it stifles her creativity - she becomes a different person!"

I wanted to say, "Now you tell me," but I just thanked Sharon for the information and hung up. What she told me explained a great deal, like the fact that I'd fallen for the woman at the cocktail party, the one who turned me on that first time in her apartment as I've never been turned on before or since. That was the Mindy I took to the art museum and the poetry slam, while the woman of other-worldly, frightening poetry and unfathomable performance pieces was a dark abyss I'd come too close to and paid a high price for it. I'd loved a female Dr. Jekyll, who turned into Ms. Hyde in front of my very eyes.

I never saw Mindy again, save one time I was shopping. I was looking at leather jackets and who walks in but The Poetess. She seemed slightly unsteady on her feet, like people who take certain anti-psychotic medications. I didn't know what I'd do or say if she approached but I didn't have to worry, as the instant she saw me she turned around and ambled out as quickly as she could. I don't know why, but by God a part of me wanted to follow her out and beg her to let me into her life again. Perhaps my subconscious mind felt that with a football helmet and some anti-personnel devices I'd be fine around her, but I guess I was still in love with the sane half of her, the only woman who'd ever pushed all my sexual buttons at once. What I felt the moment she hit me and when she walked out of that store can only be understood by someone who's suffered a sudden and permanent loss, like a close relative in a fatal car crash, where one second they're there, the next second they're gone.

So that's my story about a self-indulgent, womanizing painter with the hots for a crazy lady. The heart's a strange place and it does strange things to us: what it's done to me is that I've started writing poetry and tried to write one about my brief affair with Mindy. As far as I know how to make it so, it's in her rhyming style - without the suicide and the violence, of course.

Horny Harry had a hard-on
He still has it to this day,
Never got to first base, so he
Paints to while his time away.

Horny Harry misses Mindy,
Even though she's gone away.
You see, he's lost his love and now he
Wishes it were yesterday.

To this day I can't forget that first time in her apartment and no woman I meet begins to turn me on like she did. I feel like the cocaine addict who said the first time's the greatest rush of your life and then you spend the rest of your life trying to get it back - and you never do. Did I learn anything from all I've been through - the womanizing, Mindy, the damaged eye, the loss I feel I suffered? Maybe the following poem will tell you; it comes straight from the heart.

The immature and callow man, who thinks he's learned the most he
can,
Will find a red rose oh so sweet he'll rush to grovel at her feet.
Then finding her mirage and sham, an empty pearl within a clam
Becomes a sadder, wiser man - but do you think that's what I am?
For I, my friend, am hardly wise - I loved a lady with two sides:
One side was a rose's petal, the other twisted, jagged metal.

Thanks for listening - I'll trouble you no more, for I have another painting to finish.

Inheritance
Ksenia Murray

Leo and Oliver Vasquez moved into the house on a Saturday in the dead of winter. It was their first home together and they were enjoying every minute of it. They lapped up black Friday shopping for furniture, their choices a mix between modern and vintage. The house was four stories tall, including a basement and an attic, situated at the end of a cul-de-sac in a large gated community.

"We finally made it," Oliver said as he leaned over and kissed Leo on his cheek, the red stubble scratching his lips.

"Indeed, now we can actually relax and not worry about anything, except maybe some travel once COVID is over."

"I don't think COVID will ever be over, we'll probably have to get yearly shots."

"Gross," Leo said and shook his head. They were sitting in their living room; their black sectional couch situated in front of the large fire place. Leo laid his head on Oliver's bare shoulder and cuddled up against him; the fire being the only light in the room. The air smelled of burning wood; smokey and comfortable. Oliver wrapped an arm around Leo and kissed the top of his head.

"I actually really enjoy working from home. I don't think I can go back to getting up at five in the fucking morning and driving to work ever again," Leo said as he stared into the fire.

"Of course, you wouldn't. If you could never work again, you'd jump right on that opportunity," Oliver said while he caressed Leo's fiery orange hair.

"I'm ready to be your sugar baby."

"You're older than me, dumb ass, I'd have to be the sugar baby," Oliver chuckled.

"That's just semantics," Leo said as he waved his arm in the air.

Oliver laughed and kissed his husband deeply. The kiss started slow and moist, then grew hotter with every second that ticked by. Oliver reached up to pull off Leo's flannel night pajama shirt. He ripped it up and over Leo's head with vigor. A moan came from Leo as he pushed Oliver down onto the couch. Leo climbed on top of him and pulled on Oliver's black hair while he kissed him. Oliver moaned and grabbed at Leo's hard cock underneath his matching pajama bottoms.

As the men grew more passionate with every breath, a tumble was heard above them.

Oliver pulled his lips from Leo's. "Did you hear that?"

"Yes, but just ignore it," Leo said and kissed Oliver along his jawline.

"No, I'm serious, I think someone might be breaking in," Oliver pushed Leo off of him and sat up.

"We live in a fancy white people neighborhood now. We don't have to worry about things like that anymore," Leo said as he grabbed Oliver's large hand.

"I'm going to go and check it out," Oliver said. He stood up and wrestled his hand away from Leo.

Leo smirked and bit his bottom lip, "Come here baby, I've got something here for you that's more important than a burglar," he pulled his cock out from his pajama bottoms and motioned for Oliver to get on his knees.

"Well, if you insist," Oliver mumbled as he dropped to the floor in front of his husband. He looked up and into Leo's bright eyes, wide smile, and muscular form. Leo kicked off his pajamas and stroked his member in front of Oliver's face. Oliver grunted and slowly enveloped Leo's cock with his wet and warm mouth. He sucked gently at first, then rougher and faster as the seconds ticked past.

"Oh, fuck yeah," Leo moaned and relaxed against the couch. He grabbed a tuft of Oliver's hair and forced him to gag on his cock. Oliver whimpered and tried to pull away but Leo's brute strength stopped him.

"Stay right there, you little bitch," Leo commanded. Oliver did as he was told and took the cock as far as he could into his throat. He was gagging loudly and almost lost consciousness from breath loss right before Leo blew his load into the back of Oliver's throat.

"Mmm, that's a good boy," Leo moaned as he came, his salty yet tasty cum dripped out of the sides of Oliver's mouth. Oliver fell backwards and gasped for fresh air. Oliver tapped the spot next to him on the couch and Oliver crawled over and sat down next to him.

"Take off your pants and bend the fuck over," Leo commanded.

Oliver smiled and did as instructed; slowly pulled his pants down and tossed them across the room. He bent over the back of the couch and spread his legs. Leo reached over to the wooden coffee table and opened the door quickly. He grabbed a spare bottle of lube and popped the cap open. Leo dripped the cool liquid onto his still-bulging cock and smeared it on. Once his dick was thoroughly drenched, he squirted a few pumps into the palm of his hand and glided it onto Oliver's waiting asshole.

"Oh yes, Daddy, that feels amazing," Oliver moaned and shut his eyes. Leo grunted and slowly inserted two large fingers into Oliver's pert butt. He moved his fingers in and out to a rhythmic beat; his fingers tickled Oliver's g-spot. He moaned in extreme ecstasy and rocked his ass against Leo's hand.

"Woah, not so fast, babe," Leo said and pulled his fingers out of his ass. He grabbed Oliver by his tan hips, stroking his tiny ass cheeks gently. "Ready?"

"Yes, Daddy," Oliver moaned as Leo shoved his dick into his ass.

Oliver screamed in a blissful mixture of pleasure and pain and bit down on the back of the couch. Leo moved vigorously in and out of Oliver's tiny and perfect asshole. He reached around while pumping and started stroking Oliver's humble cock. Oliver moaned into the couch and bounced his ass against Leo's cock, rocking in quick motions to up the speed of the pounding. Leo grunted quietly as he continued to jack off Oliver and pound into him at the same time. Without a moment to ask for permission, Oliver came hard and fast all over the couch as well as Leo's hand. Oliver collapsed but Leo kept battering Oliver's chrysanthemum for a few moments until Leo came robustly for the second time.

Leo pulled out of Oliver and grabbed a tissue from the coffee table and wiped Oliver's jizz from his hands. Oliver sat up and plopped down onto the couch, letting the jizz drip from his ass and into the fabric. They collapsed against each other on the couch, entwining their legs together like a fresh pretzel from a bakery.

"Oh God, I love you so much," Leo whispered as he nuzzled his head into Oliver's neck.

Oliver giggled, "I love you too." Just as the men were beginning to relax, another crash from upstairs broke the moment.

"Did you hear that?" Oliver perked up and stared at the ceiling again.

"Are you fucking serious? It's nothing, probably just the house settling."

Another tumble was heard upstairs. This time, it was louder and shook the house.

"Really? Was that just the house settling?" Oliver's dark eyes looked intensely into Leo's blue eyes.

Leo rolled his eyes and stood up, "I guess I'll go with you then, put your pants back on just in case. I don't need no burglar taking a gander at my man."

The men dressed quickly and then climbed up the stairs to the second floor. "Do you think it was here or up in the attic?" Oliver asked.

"Not sure. Let's just check every room first," Leo whispered.

They reached the top of the stairs. Leo motioned for Oliver to check out the bathroom while he headed into their guest bedroom. Oliver walked into the small guest bathroom and peeked around. The porcelain sink glittered in the moonlight that shown through the bathroom window. He took a deep breath and grabbed the clear plastic shower curtain and moved it aside. The small bathtub was empty.

Leo walked into the guest bedroom, which as of right now was piled high with boxes. The queen-sized bedframe sat against the wall with no mattress and dingy boxes piled on top of it. The room was pitch black due to the boxes piled up against the window. Leo flicked on the bedroom light; it flickered a few moments before it illuminated the guest bedroom with a yellow light. Leo looked around and shrugged. He walked back out of the room and shut the door behind him.

"See anything?" Oliver asked while he shut the bathroom door.

"Nope."

Oliver grabbed Leo's hand and squeezed. They walked into their bedroom, the master bedroom, and Leo opened the door. He pushed it open slowly, the old door made a squeak. Oliver flipped on the light and they both looked around. Their king-sized bed sat against the wall in the corner of the room. The purple duvet covered in white flowers and matching pillow cases sat neatly made without a wrinkle in sight. Their black nightstands sat on either side of the bed with nothing but their cell phone chargers on them as of right now. Their brown walk-in closet door was wide open, filled with all of their clothes and boxes that need to be unpacked.

Oliver walked toward the closet and peeked in. He squinted his eyes and walked inside. While he looked around the boxes, Leo crouched next to the bed and lifted the duvet.

"No one is in here," Leo said.

Oliver nodded and walked back out of the closet.

Leo went into the master bathroom and turned on the light switch. Their in-ground jacuzzi bathtub against the far wall and their double-sink cluttered with the essentials.

"No one is in here either," Leo called out.

"Good," Oliver said.

Leo walked out of the bathroom and didn't shut the door behind him. He grabbed Oliver's hand once more and they walked out of the master bedroom.

"Only one more place to look," Oliver said, his voice cracked.

"Don't worry babe, there's no one in the attic. I'm not even sure how someone could get in there without us knowing anyway."

Oliver nodded and Leo opened the door to the stairwell. The door opened with a loud creak. He stepped onto the first step, a loud groan from the old wooden staircase echoed in the tight hallway.

"Well, if there is someone up there, they definitely know we're coming," Leo laughed.

Oliver didn't respond as he followed suit. The men climbed up the stairs one by one, the steps sank a bit as they did. They made it to the top of the stairwell and Leo opened the door. The stench of mold, dust, and musk wafted up into their faces.

"Jesus, I don't remember it smelling this bad. Dear God, we'll have to hire a cleaner or someone to fix this up," Oliver said while he covered his nose.

Leo nodded and sniffled. He reached over to flick on the light but nothing happened. There was a buzzing sound and then silence.

"We'll need to hire someone to fix that too," Leo said.

They walked into the attic and looked around. "Go and grab one of our phones so that we can see." Oliver did as instructed and trudged downstairs.

Tap tap tap.

Leo stopped moving and held his breath.

Tap tap tap tap tap.

He walked forward into the attic, and peered over the boxes. Oliver appeared behind him with his own phone and turned on the flashlight app. It illuminated the room and highlighted the dust and dirt that covered everything in there.

"I think someone is up here," Leo whispered.

"What?" Oliver gasped.

"Shhh," Leo said as he brought a stubby finger to his lips.

Oliver grabbed Leo's arm and they walked forward. He moved the phone all over the attic. The boxes that were up there didn't belong to them. They were molded and damp. Some boxes were almost rotted away completely. There was an old acoustic guitar sitting on top of a box and an old street piano propped up in the corner. It was black with yellowed keys. They crept closer to the piano as it wasn't sitting directly against the wall. There was a large space behind it. A shadow skittered across the wall while they stared. Oliver jumped and Leo held firm.

"Shine your flashlight underneath the piano," Leo commanded in a deep voice.

Oliver did as he was told and shined the light over to the piano. There was no one standing up behind the piano. Leo grabbed the phone out of Oliver's hand and crouched down, shinning the light onto the floor. There was something behind the piano. Definitely not a human lurking up there. Leo watched as a gnarly shadow outlined two sets of four legs. They were hairy and pointed black at the end. Dark brown fur covered each leg. When it moved it legs, the tapping noise echoed within the room.

"What the fuck was that?" Oliver asked in a hushed whisper.

"We need to get the fuck out of here!" Leo screamed as he stood up.

The creature then jumped onto the piano and stared them down with eight large eyes. Its face covered in dark brown fur, fangs as long as a man's forearm. It was ginormous, about the size of a six-year-old girl. Droplets of saliva mixed with venom dripped from its moving fangs and onto the piano. A puddle of drool coated the top of the old and dusty piano. The fangs moved in a rhythmic fashion along with the tapping of its legs. The air turned a vile shade of decay with every breath the spider took. Oliver backed up slowly and Leo turned to run when the spider pounced. It jumped from the piano into the air, across the room, and onto Leo. Oliver watched with wide eyes while his lover was being attacked. Leo screamed, a high-pitched wail that one should never hear in their lifetime, while the spider clung to his back. Oliver was frozen with fear.

"Oh my God what the fuck?! Help me, Oliver!" Leo wailed and stared right at Oliver. The spider dug its legs into his bare chest and drew blood. Leo's once pale and freckled chest now a deep shade of crimson. It clung to him while its body shook with intensity, a low growl of sorts emitted from its mouth.

Oliver shook his head and looked around, and noticed an old wooden bat propped up against the wall. He grabbed it and squeezed; his knuckles turned white. The spider bit into Leo's neck and sucked. Leo gurgled and turned a disgusting shade of grey. Blood poured out of the wound with the same intensity as a flowing river. Leo's screams turned into grunts and sighs. Oliver swung the bat at the spider, missed, and hit Leo in the head; knocking him out cold. Leo's body fell to the ground with a thud. The spider let go of Leo and hopped off of him before he hit the ground. It bounced backwards and away from Oliver's swinging bat.

"Oh fuck! I'm so sorry! Jesus Christ!" Oliver cried. His hands shook as he held the bat, tears endlessly flowed from his eyes and blurred his vision. He swung at the spider again. It jumped backwards and rocked back and forth on its legs. He stepped closer to the spider, his hands sweat and his knees shook. His breathed deeply and stared at the spider. It leaned back onto its hind legs, its abdomen a deep shade of blue. A wicked voice could be heard within Oliver's head.

Come now, you do not want to hurt me. I can help you.

"What the fuck? Shut the fuck up right now!" Oliver screamed and swung the bat, missing again.

I can give you everything that you need, everything that you have ever asked for.

The spider moved its front legs in a triangular pattern. It swayed back and forth, its beady eyes never leaving Oliver's. He stared right back at the spider and swayed with it.

Drop the bat and come to me my child.

Oliver did as he was told, the bat echoed within the attic. He walked toward the spider, his steps quiet and his feet sluggish. The spider opened its legs for him. Oliver reached the spider and got down on his knees. He laid his head against the spider's abdomen and sank against it. The spider enveloped Oliver as if he were a baby. Oliver was held tightly against the spider and was unable and unwilling to move. The spider rooted its fangs into Oliver's skull and sucked the life force from him.

Once the spider finished devouring both Oliver and Leo, it crawled back into its disgusting damp hiding hole and waited for new home owners.

Young Love (With Hacksaws)
Daniel R. Robichaud

Mouse fell in love with the blonde the first time he saw her behind his warehouse home. Moonlight and a nearby security lamp cast her in a romantic glow.

At the time, she was too busy taking a hacksaw to a tough looking man with biker's tattoos to see the smitten hunchback, but Mouse planned to change that. After she was finished, of course. No sense disturbing her while she was obviously concentrating.

Mouse watched her work. Every stroke made her tight bottom wiggle, made her firm legs quiver. She was a tall woman with strong arms. Bodybuilder strong.

And she was naked.

The woman arrived wearing a purple dress, matching undies, and knee-high boots, but, after yanking boyo from the trunk of the sports car, she stripped out of these before getting down to the dismemberment business.

The blonde paused to wipe a hand across her brow. Mouse empathized: sawing *was* tiring work. Then, she went back to cutting through the meaty thigh of her fella.

Even her voice was lovely, Mouse discovered, when she snarled "Dammit!", tossed the saw aside, and started hopping around holding her left hand in the universal "owie-owie-owie" dance.

Had she cut herself?

"Are you all right?" Mouse asked, and then clamped both hands over his mouth. Momma had always said Mouse was so helpful he'd pull the cord on his own guillotine if he could. She was right, again.

The blonde heard. Stopped dancing.

In the moonlight, the dead man's blood gleamed dark on her torso and face. It made her bangs look dyed. She did not appear to be bleeding, so maybe she had twisted funny during the cutting.

She spotted him easily enough.

"How long you been there?" Her voice had an exotic drawl--maybe from Texas--and this charged her demand with an undeniable energy.

Terror twisted inside Mouse's belly, but he felt tingles, too. He could not help but stare at the tops of her thighs, the rock-solid stomach, the soft looking flesh between and beneath her breasts, her private places...

"Hey, are you retarded?"

Despite her tone, Mouse could not feel offended. "No," he said, "but I'm strong. I can help with your fella."

Even suspicion looked luscious on her features. "And why would you want to do that?"

"Because you're so beautiful," Mouse said. "Pretty people do no wrong, my Momma said. It's the ugly folks who are evil." Momma hadn't quite said it that way, but it was close enough, and the sentiment made the blonde's defensiveness melt a little bit.

"Well, come on over," she said. "Sawing bones has never been my forte." This last word, she pronounced *fort*.

Mouse emerged from the shadows around the Dumpster and the blonde's lips drew into a haughty sneer. "You're a hunchback cripple," she said. "Like that cartoony guy in the French place. You know the one. With the bells?"

Mouse shook his head, but he knew all right.

Momma had bought a Happy Meal when that Disney movie had been released, and it included a toy version of the Hunchback of Notre Dame. "They made a puppet of my Mouse," she'd said and danced the toy around the table. She stuffed her hand up the toy's shirt and made it say, "Mouse is a movie star." Sure, its lips didn't move, but Mouse could not stop staring at it. Its distorted facial features unnerved him. "Why'n't you bring some of that movie money home, Mouse?" Momma'd asked when she was done playing. The question vexed her because soon enough she repeatedly screamed it and swung the toy like a flail upside Mouse's head. Its plastic, bulging eyes scraped his cheek and nose and ear and temple. Soon enough, he shrieked apologies for not bringing home movie money or any money, for that matter, and she sent him to his room to pray to Louis Whiffle, Mouse's dear departed Da, for forgiveness.

Oh, yes. He knew that movie all too well.

"I guess they don't let retards see movies," the blonde said, "only make 'em." She giggled for a while. When she'd pause for a breath, her eyes would widen and she'd make a tiny snort sound. This added to her loveliness.

"I'm not retarded," Mouse said, "or a cripple." He tried not to be defensive, merely to state the facts, but her face screwed up with irritation, and then Mouse felt like he'd wolfed a whole tray of ice cubes: unspeakable cold filled his head and bowels.

"Whatever," she said. "You going to help me or what?"

"Sure," he said and got to sawing.

The fella's bones were strong, not at all brittle like Momma's, but Mouse did not stop until the man had been reduced to eleven messy pieces in as many black, plastic garbage bags. By that time, Mouse felt sore and tired but, nevertheless, deliriously happy because that gore-streaked blonde was smiling at him.

"You *are* a strong fella," she said.

"I did all the chores for my Momma," he replied, turning sheepishly in place.

"And I'll bet you're good to your Momma."

"While she was alive, I tried to be a good son," he said. At the end and afterwards, well, that was a different story, but he'd apologized to her spirit a lot and never heard back that she was still angry, so he took that as a sign of forgiveness.

"All alone in the world?" she asked.

"Kind of, yeah."

"Well, you were my white knight. All you need is a horse and some armor and a sword. Kept little old me safe from that mean old Dragunov."

"You mean dragon?"

"No, I mean Dragunov." She kicked the garbage bag with the fella's head. "You know, like the sniper rifle?"

He shook his head. This time, he really had no idea what she was talking about.

"Well, I suppose I should get dressed," she said.

"Why?" As soon as he realized the question was out of his mouth, Mouse felt his face catch fire with scalding embarrassment. *She's going to hit me. Real hard. Leave a mark on my face.* He suddenly wondered if that might really be so bad.

She didn't hit him, however. "You're cute," she said, instead. "Say, handsome, I hate to get my dress all messy. Is there a place to clean up around here? Bathroom or something?"

"Uh, there's a shower." He cocked his thumb back to the warehouse.

"A shower in there? With running water? I thought this place has been closed for years and years."

"Well, sort of," Mouse said. "My Momma owned it. Fixed it up as our home."

"You live here? Way out here? Spitting distance from the harbor?" She seemed pleasantly surprised. "Alone?"

He became glum and nodded.

She held out her hand to him. "Show me?"

Mouse stared at that outstretched hand like some folks might stare at the Mona Lisa or Dogs Playing Poker.

After a moment, she made grabbing motions. "It's all right, you can touch me."

He reached out and did just that. Her skin was sticky with gore but soft, too. Mouse felt a new tingle in his chest when she squeezed him reassuringly.

"You never been with a woman before, huh?"

"I been with my Momma."

"Not what I mean, handsome. I mean..." She ran her free hand between her breasts and down her stomach to the top of her left thigh. "With a woman. You know, a girlfriend?"

He shook his head like an Etch-a-Sketch. "Nuh-uh. No, ma'am."

"I'm not old. Don't ma'am me," she said. "You can call me Dixie."

"Dixie." That word tasted better than chocolate-chocolate chip ice cream, and Mouse really liked chocolate-chocolate chip ice cream.

"How about you, handsome?"

"Me?"

"Yeah, I can't keep calling you just 'handsome' can I?"

Why not? Secretly, he felt a thrill every time she said it. Not even Momma had ever called him handsome.

Should he make up a name? Hank was good. It sounded really tough. Or Richard. Yeah, an everyman's tough guy. "Momma called me Mouse," he said and wrecked everything. *Nuts*.

Her giggles made her breasts bob like beach balls on a stormy sea. "Mouse?" she said. "That's cute. All right, Mouse, won't you be a gentleman and show me this shower?"

A gentleman? Wow! "Sure."

The bathroom had a full-sized bathtub in it. When Dixie saw that it included shampoo, a cake of soap, and a set of only slightly mildewed towels, she said, "Why, Mouse, you bring me to the classiest places."

Brown water chugged out of the showerhead for a few seconds but soon cleared up. "And hot water, too." She waved her hand through the spray.

Mouse said, "I'll leave you be."

"I won't hear of it. Get these things off." She tugged at his blood-soaked shirt. "Get in here with me."

"Get...in?"

"Mmmm-hmmm. Can't have my white knight smelling like an abattoir, now can I?"

He shucked his clothes faster than he ever had before. She eyed him appreciatively. He covered up his pee-pee, but she pulled his hand away and clucked her tongue. "Now, now, handsome--I mean *Mouse*--there's no need to be shy. Oh, now isn't that the cutest thing?"

Mouse felt certain he would die straight away.

"Oh, it's twitching." Giggle-snort-giggle. "Like it's saying 'howdy.'" She curled her fingers in a cutesy wave.

"Hello, fella," she said, and Mouse's pee-pee did a very nice imitation of a Morse code response.

The water was warm on his skin, but Dixie's touch was hotter still. She lathered his hunch. He worked up foam in his hands and gingerly applied it to the smooth flesh of her back. "Scrub harder," she said, "Don't be afraid to really get in there. Oh, yes. Like that." She was practically purring.

Mouse's pee-pee got stiff as a toothpick and twice as long.

Would she scrub him down there? He couldn't ask. No way those words would flow out of his throat. If, on the off chance they did, he knew he really would die.

"Oh, Mouse. *Yes*..."

She didn't *need* to touch him down there. Every syllable she spoke was charged enough that they affected him like playful fingertips. Brushing. Stroking.

With her next, gasped "Yes," he felt something slip inside him and then realized he was peeing on her. But his pee was all funny and lumpy and white. Had her words done something to his--

She saw what he was doing and started screaming at him. Cussing. "You stupid fucking retard! Don't you know better than to spray your jizz-juice all over a girl when you're showering with her? Get out! Get out of this tub! This room! I don't wanna see you!" As though this weren't clear enough, she shoved him. "I'm too young and too pretty and too busy to be having hunchbacked babies, you perverted little bastard!"

Mouse splashed out of the tub, across the linoleum floor, and tried to turn for the door, but he kept moving in a straight line. His feet slipped. He hit the floor and twirled in a nearly full circle.

He tried to push himself up, back onto his feet, and only succeeded in spinning in more circles.

All the while, his pee-pee never stopped pumping out the sick looking white stuff. *Oh no,* he thought, *Momma always said that bad thoughts were a curse, I must've cursed my pee-pee*! He cupped his privates and wailed for them to stop, but they wouldn't, so he was spinning on the floor and pleading, and it just kept firing, and--

Dixie started laughing. It was the meanest thing Mouse had ever heard, and he'd heard some doozies. Even the little piglet snorts couldn't stop her from sounding cruel. More than sound. It was the way her face pinched. It was the way she pointed at him. It was--

He clawed at the tiles. Still no luck getting to his feet. The efforts only made her laugh louder. He ended up dragging himself out the bathroom door.

Her malicious glee followed. Hounded him even after he found a dark, empty space between his Momma's bed and the closet and shivered in miserable silence.

Dixie came to him. The trail of wet over which he'd dragged himself was pretty obvious.

She had stopped laughing, but for some reason, he could still hear those awful chortles and snorts. They couldn't be echoing from the walls. Were they in his head? That's the only thing that made sense.

She hunkered, naked and dripping before him. The side lighting from the bathroom did little to reveal her features, actually it deepened the shadows on her face. However, when she spoke, her voice was calming. "You okay, handsome?"

"I'll just stay here," he mumbled, "I'll leave you be."

"Don't be stupid," she said. "I got mad because I don't like fellas I only just met unloading their protein bazookas all over me like I'm some porno whore. Everything I said got you to quit shooting off your baby-juice soldiers, didn't it?"

"Huh?"

She was quiet a moment. "You don't know nothing about what I'm saying, do you?"

Mouse shook his head and then realized she wouldn't be able to see the motion in the dark. "No."

"Haven't you ever used the Internet?" she asked. "Taught me everything I needed to know about sex. And a bunch I didn't need to know. Or want to know."

"I know about sex," Mouse said. "Men and women who love each other very much and don't want to have lives no more have sex. And eight months later babies are born. My Momma told me all about that."

"So, why'd you try to hose me down with your solid spunk dancers?"

"Huh?"

Dixie said, "Your Momma. Did she tell you what sex is?"

"Yeah. What men and women who have--"

"Blah, blah. Don't want lives. Babies. Yeah, I got that. Did she go into mechanics?"

"I don't know nothing about cars."

"No, I..." Her shadow shape shifted with a giggle-snort-giggle. "How cute. Why don't you come out of there?"

Mouse did. She looked at him and clucked her tongue. "You're all messy again. Go clean up."

"Will you--"

"I'll get dressed and wait by Dragunov. I want to tell you a few things."

Mouse had the unshakeable belief that she was lying, but he could not argue. He dragged his feet but did as told. Washed, though the water was cold. Dried himself on the moist towel Dixie had used.

She waited for him as promised. Even in her purple dress and tall boots, she was gorgeous.

The garbage bags on the floor were lying open. Dixie was holding some of Dragunov's parts. His pee-pee in one hand, his severed head in the other.

"Feel clean?" she asked.

He nodded. "What are you doing?"

"Educating you," she said. "Hopefully, you're not so retarded you'll forget." She held up Dragunov's pee-pee. "You seen this before, right?"

"Uh-huh."

"Good. All fellas have one. Girls don't."

"Girls have innies," Mouse nodded sagely.

"Your Momma teach you that?"

"Uh, yeah."

Actually, he'd found out when he was cutting her up. Momma didn't have a pee-pee at all, just a hole. Not her butthole either; Mouse checked. He reached up her non-butthole, to see if her pee-pee was hiding inside, retracted like a lipstick into its tube, but if so, it was too far in there for him to reach. Then he remembered how bellybuttons worked. Some folks had innies, some outies. He decided that pee-pees must be the same way.

"Good," Dixie said, "Well, we don't have one for demonstration purposes, but suffice it to say Dragunov's neck is a girl's 'innie'." She held it up. "Now, when a boy gets happy to see a girl, his pecker gets all stiff."

Yep, Mouse was familiar with that.

"And when a girl's all happy to see a guy, her hootchie-hole gets all wet. If the boy's got enough money or looks to make it worth the girl's time, they..." She fitted the pee-pee into Dragunov's throat and worked it in-and-out. "Now, if the boy doesn't have enough money or looks, but he's still got some, he might convince the girl to do this..." She pulled the pee-pee out of the neck and shoved it into Dragunov's mouth, repeating the in-and-out motions.

Mouse had to admit it was all very mystifying and exciting.

"But that boy should *never* blow his wad this way," Dixie continued, "cuz there's not enough money or looks in the world to compensate for a mouthful of swimming sailors, got it?"

"So, that's sex?" Mouse asked.

"No, this is down and dirty fucking," Dixie said. "Sex is what your Momma told you about. Mechanics are similar, though." She played with the parts for another minute, then tossed them into the garbage bags. "Gotta wash my hands. Then, I need to go."

"Go? Can't you stay?"

"I need to get rid of Dragunov."

"Oh," Mouse said. "Will I see you again?"

She considered this, briefly, and then nodded. "Next time someone blows his wad in my mouth, I'll come back. I need a white knight with strong arms."

Embarrassment burned on his face, and he shuffled his feet. After she washed her hands and tossed the garbage bags in the trunk of the sports car, Mouse waved bye-bye and watched her taillights vanish into the night.

***

As it turned out, more people blew their wads in Dixie's mouth than Mouse had believed possible. It started out that he saw her once a month. Then twice. Then once a week. Then every few days. Manners were on the decline.

She must've been rich because she drove a different car every time he saw her.

Her friends all had exotic names: Colt, Magnum, Heckler, Koch, even Lady Smith. He worked hard to chop them all up. Dixie would pat his hunch and call him sweet names and occasionally wash his back when he was done.

It got so that Mouse longed to put his pee-pee in Dixie's innie or her mouth.

He didn't have looks, but maybe he could get money? He didn't see how. Momma hadn't left much but the warehouse and an automatically deducting back account for utilities. None of Dixie's boy or girl friends ever had any money that Mouse could steal . . .

When Dixie was around, he mooned away the time. When she wasn't, he pined for her.

***

Mouse wandered the waterfront, kicking cans and strays off the pier to help keep it clean. It was as he leaned against a guardrail, chin braced against the steel, that he heard the angry cat coming up behind him.

Terrified, he glanced around. It was no animal of any kind. It was the engine of a cherry red Corvette, which was shrunk down to only two-and-a-half feet long. Not a radio-controlled model, however. This thing was real.

A small man was in the driver's seat. When he got out, Mouse saw he was no taller than one of those Barbie dolls. He wore a business suit made of shiny black leather cut so as not to pinch, bind, or otherwise hamper the wispy tail poking out of his bottom.

"Evening," the little man said. "D'you need the whole pier or do you mind sharing some space?"

"No, I'll share."

"Thanks, buddy." The little man went to the tiny car's trunk and pulled out a small glass bottle. He glanced Mouse's way. "You look miserable, chum." Then, he asked something that sounded like, 'Do you wanna fuck 'em?'

"Huh?"

The little man held up his bottle. "It's beer from Thailand. I guess the proper pronunciation is 'fo-kim' but it's spelled P-H-O-K-E-M, and how's that look?"

"Uhm, okay, I'll try it."

The little man pulled out a second bottle, popped the top, and then walked it over to Mouse.

Mouse had to hold it between his thumb and index finger, making sure not to squeeze too hard. He didn't want to break the bottle and wreck the little man's refund. "Thanks."

"Don't mention it," the little man said, then went back to close the trunk.

"Where do you find such small bottles?"

"Thailand's good to the little people." The small man took a pull from the neck. "The flavor's weird the first time, but drink enough and you'll acquire the taste. Check out that moon." He pointed out over the water. The full moon hung over the horizon. The reflection of its enormous, milky face rippled in the bay.

"Pretty," Mouse said.

"Reminds me of a woman I knew in San Francisco, though there should be a big old Chinese character tattoo overhead that translates to 'aim here,'" He giggled like a monkey. Mouse wasn't sure why that was funny, so he stayed quiet. "What's a matter with you, kiddo?"

Mouse shrugged.

"I'm betting girl trouble."

Reluctantly, Mouse nodded.

"With or without?"

"Huh?"

"You either got a girl you'd rather not have," the little man said, "or want one you haven't got. Those are the only two real problems I know about. Anything else is bullshit window dressing."

Mouse dumped the bottle's contents into his mouth and winced. It was kind of bitter and foamy.

"Like I said, it's an acquired taste."

"Maybe I should acquire it."

"Maybe." The little man stuck out a hand. "Name's Gordon."

Mouse took pains to accept it delicately, only to find the little man had a strong grip. "Mouse."

Gordon's grin got tight, and his handhold got uncomfortably firm. "I hope that's not some kind of joke."

"No, no. *My* name's Mouse. What my Momma called me."

"Well, you ain't one of mine, so I guess that means your Momma was just cruel."

"No, she was all right." Or was she? Mouse had really started wondering. "So, you got a girlfriend in California?"

"I got girls all over North America." The little fellow started singing the chorus of "California Girls" off key, and then he pitched his empty bottle into the wharf.

"What about your deposit?"

"Fuck 'em," Gordon said. Mouse wasn't sure if he meant 'fuck the deposit' or he was disparagingly muttering the beer's name. "Want another?"

"Sure."

The little man retrieved the rest of the six-pack from his trunk and popped the caps off two more. "Provost," he said, and they clinked bottles. After a long drink, he added, "One girl isn't worth getting miserable about. There're a lot of them around."

"But I want this one. I think she likes me. She's always coming to me for help."

"Oh no, buddy! You've got a leech! She ain't worth it, I don't care what she looks like."

"But all I want is for her to like me enough to let me put my pee-pee in her mouth. She lets other folks do that. Boys *and* girls."

"Whoa," Gordon's eyes got wide enough to show their full circumference. "Well, she's probably still not a keeper. Ain't so easy to get the freaky stuff, but it's not impossible." He took a long pull off the bottle and then pitched it into the water. "So what's this kinky leech called?"

Mouse said, "Dixie," and then glanced at Gordon suspiciously. "You're not going to try--"

"Mess on your turf? Nah. I've had more than my share of leeches, thanks. As for kink?" He motioned as though plucking lint off of his leather suit. "Well, I'm no stranger to it, but I usually aim for something different. Like last spring? I took this fine young thing to her prom. Afterwards, we rocked out in my 'Vette. Had that little one singing 'Gitchie-gitchie-yaya-da-da.' A fine night." He sighed nostalgically.

"There a lot of folks like you in the world?" Mouse asked.

"You mean handsome?" Gordon laughed; Mouse grinned.

"I mean girls?"

"Not too many. I usually go for normal chicks. Well, normal babes, anyway. Still, I've been known to dip my toes in the freak pool from time to time. Like that prom girl. A finer piece of tail I haven't had in a god's age." He popped the cap off a fresh beer. "Women love the exotic," Gordon said. "They equate it with romance. Folks like us, if we're smart, we can use that to our advantage." He drank half the Phokem and then pitched it into the water.

Mouse asked, "Gordon? Why are you being so nice to me?"

The little man belched and smiled. "Don't you know, buddy? This is Freak-o Pier on Monster Wharf. Don't bother looking for a sign. We all end up here one night or another. Twenty years ago, I was where you are now.

Down and frustrated. Well, another fella--an outsider like us--showed up and talked to me. It's nice to know you're not alone. So, tonight, I was jamming with a couple of catty Gothic babes--and I mean *meow*--when I felt the tug to come back here. Figured it was time to pay my karmic debt."

"I don't understand."

"I can't help that," Gordon said. "Well, for what it's worth, here're two things to keep in mind. Pay attention, buddy, I'm imparting wisdom. First, if you can use it, play the exotic card to nab as much as you can. And if you can get two? Twins or sisters or something? Then do it. I mean, *damn*.

"Second, don't let this Dixie-leech ruin your life. Get her first. Fuck her sister or something. Trash her credit. I mean really demolish her life. Don't let your heart get broken. Instead, rip hers out of her fucking chest. Great place for your pee-pee. Then, get out of town. See the world. It's a big, beautiful place." He gestured to the last bottle. "You want it?"

"I'm not done with this one."

"Keep it anyway. See you around, buddy." The little man walked to his Corvette and then drove off. He tooted the horn when Mouse waved.

The hunchback had a lot to think about.

***

The next time he saw her, Dixie was driving a beat-up station wagon. The back windows were covered with aluminum foil and duct tape. This, Mouse soon discovered, was to keep the family out of sight. A Dad, Mom, teenage son, elementary school aged daughter, and a golden retriever occupied the car, too. They were all dead.

"Lots of work, tonight," Dixie said in way of greeting.

"I want you to let me put my pee-pee in your mouth," said Mouse. This stopped her cold.

"Is this because of the dog?" Dixie asked. "Because, let me tell you, this sick bastard," she waved toward the Dad, "He blew his wad in my mouth and had that mutt blow its wad in my asshole. And those kids? Sure, they look angelic now, but they were as bad as their Daddy. Dirty, evil little spawn. And this Momma? Well, she was pretty much an innocent soul, and I wish I didn't have to, but she was screaming and it got on my last--"

Mouse said, "I know I don't have looks or money, but I've been doing tons of work for you and if you were paying me, I could put my pee-pee in your innie, but all I want to put it in is your mouth."

She asked, "Who's been putting these ideas in your head?"

"No one. I've--"

"Bullshit. There's no way a retard could come up with this on his own."

"I told you," Mouse said, "I'm not retarded."

"Fine, whatever. Let's just call this whole thing off," she said. "I was only coming around here because I felt sorry for you. This was for charity-like."

"What's wrong with my pee-pee? You take everyone else's. Even girls' and dogs'."

"Don't you judge me, cripple!" Dixie snapped. Her face was wild and angry, but Mouse wasn't afraid.

"Then, don't judge *me*."

"Oh, to hell with this. If you think I'm gonna stick around here with a horny hunchback, well--"

"You are a leech."

"A leech?" Her laugh was shrill and verging on maniacal. This *did* frighten him. "Well fuck you, retard. Yeah, I used you, and you know what? After a month, a week, you'll be begging for me to use you some more. To let you touch me with your deformed hands or have me scrub that disgusting hump of yours. But it isn't gonna happen, handsome. Or should I say mule-ass-ugly? Because that's how foul you are. Listen, Momma's boy. No one who looks like me will ever want something as repulsive as you, much less let you stick your pee-pee, wee-wee, love pickle in their mouth."

It's impossible to say when misery transformed into pure rage, but that's what happened.

He lashed out at her. Clawed her throat. Started squeezing. "*You're* ugly!" he shouted. "Ugly like me!"

She scratched his face, actually dragged a fingernail across his left eyeball. Mouse screeched like a tropical bird and threw her back.

She came in swinging, and her mighty arms drove fists against his torso and face so hard Mouse thought he'd break to pieces. Something cracked inside his chest, and pain flooded his system. His eyes filled with tears.

Still, he stomped on her foot, felt something break from the blow. She let out a squeal of pain and collapsed backward onto the rear bumper of the station wagon.

Mouse leapt forward. Grabbed the car's rear door and slammed it hard. Steel and faux wood paneling rebounded off her extended arms, but the blow shoved her upper half onto the bodies. The rest of her was dangling out of the wagon's rear.

Faster than she could pull back, Mouse slammed the door, again. It crunched when it hit her thighs. A piece of the faux wood went flying. She yowled like a cat with its tail caught in a meat grinder.

When she tried to get her feet, he knocked them out from under her and slammed the door across her pelvis. This time, the crunch he heard was not the faux wood paneling. It was bone. Sounds of breakage and pain intoxicated him.

Mouse kept bouncing the door off her, discovering strength he never knew he had.

Soon, her screams became whimpers.

The steel bent all out of shape and so did Dixie's body.

Mouse yanked the door open, let her slide awkwardly down onto the floor. Her spine, thighs and pelvis made awful crunching noises as she dropped. Her legs didn't seem to work right.

She seemed barely cognizant of her surroundings. Didn't respond to her name.

Mouse felt his ribcage flood with the worst levels of pain he'd ever experienced. He knew what it must be. He pawed his chest, weeping, and whispered, "You broke my heart."

When he used the saw to open her rib cage, Mouse accidentally ripped her heart. However, that gouge let him fit inside easier than any of the tiny holes at the top.

The little man in the Corvette had been right. Walking around with his pee-pee inside Dixie's heart and the heart making a large bulge in his drawers, Mouse felt lots better. Not completely healed, maybe. But better.

It turned out Dixie didn't have either credit or a sister, but she did have a stepmother. Would that be good enough?

The Right Social Group
Tom Fegan

He lay motionless, non-responsive and helpless on my couch of the two-bedroom house I was renting along with my girlfriend; Rick Stacy-first class jerk and manipulative genius was down for the count. His one weakness was Chivas Regal which I laced with muscle relaxers; two stiff belts were all it took. Stacy had the clothes, the car and the money. His inheritance from a rich investor dad supported his lifestyle. His father's investment was outside the U.S. as a dodge for IRS investigations; a well contrived family secret they hid; they lived well but not high.

His parents were over indulgent. His father died suddenly and his mother grieved into her own early grave. Thusly, Rick lived high and above most single young adults. We were dragged up together more as brothers than friends. My dad was a butcher and my mother a schoolteacher. Our families were friends which began as Stacy and I started kindergarten together. I was stuck with him.

My two older siblings included a brother that became a lawyer and moved to Chicago and a sister: a Presbyterian minister. School was never my priority and I skated through junior college and managed to attend North Texas University in Denton, Texas. Stacy followed.

At my parents' insistence in early years I had to drag him along wherever I went. It was always his manipulation that buried me in any social group, even as a kid. When I was silent about my whereabouts with a new group; he found me.

We pledged the same fraternity. I was blackballed; he wasn't. His subtle remarks ruined it for me whispering in someone's ear. It never stopped. Bible study groups, academic groups, or intramural sports offered on campus; Stacy succeeded and I didn't. I consistently searched for the right social group that would disable him from joining. I felt like a loner in that I felt apart from not a part of most groups, with his presence. Socially awkward Stacy claimed of me to others. The military kept him away as I was a U.S. Marine Corps Reservist. It was perfect as a means of financial support and patriotism in college.

Folk Dancing Class offered me a social access; fortunately it was too nerdy for Stacy; he stayed at bay. Myra: a psychology major became my dancing partner. Her slender figure and tallness intrigued me as her dark hair flowed past her shoulders to the small of her back. Her energetic smile and dark eyes that glistened as she laughed displayed her inner charm. She had a compassion for people that encouraged my attraction. It was a fast hook up.

We became inseparable. She had an apartment and I resided in the dorm but nights were spent with her; dinner, studying, television and sex as well as night outs for a movie or other fun times. My weekend excursions with the Reserves did not interrupt our time together; even when I was on an overnight maneuver. Trust was never an issue. Myra was the woman I had dreamed of from the time puberty struck. Our bond was solid. She was there for me anytime. Also, Stacy was out of the picture.

One morning at the Student Center I approached the booth Myra and I met for coffee and witnessed Rick pushing himself out of the bench across from her. "Okay," he replied, "I'm outta here." His gestures were animated and assured Myra's rejection. I watched as he left and joined a blonde named Mary Callahan at a table.

I glared at him for a moment and was interrupted. "Well," Myra teased, "Are we going to have coffee or are you going to watch him all day?" I smiled and sat across from her as she handed me coffee purchased for me. We didn't banter about trivial matters of who bought what; we were comfortable with each other.

I jerked a thumb over my shoulder, "What does she see in him?"

"Friends, she claims," replied Myra. Mary, a fellow psych major that Myra considered a close acquaintance she studied with. I was assured from the beginning of our relationship that when I was out in the field if she spent any time with anyone besides me it was with Mary for studying. "She's about to fail statistics. I've been helping her. I am the only one in the class that gets it," she claimed. I nodded assuredly. Myra was smart and grades seemed easy for her. I had to struggle; she kept me motivated.

"It seems every psych major fear statistics," I observed heartily. Myra laughed and nodded. Unknown to me; this would be our last coffee together. It was Friday and I would leave for weekend field duty and return to heart break, which happened after drill ended and I arrived at her apartment door.

My heart pounded hard in my throat as I peeked inside the window in her sparsely furnished apartment. I could not see any movement. No lights were burning. "She didn't come home last night." Startled by the verbal intrusion I spun quickly and spotted a portly middle-aged man and apartment manager and owner Max Burn. "I saw her leave on foot last night," he began. "I was replacing a window someone threw a rock through. We waved and haven't seen her since."

"Maybe we should call the police?" I asserted.

"Maybe," nodded Max. We did. They arrived and information was exchanged. Mary Callahan claimed Myra left around nine o'clock Saturday night. Daily I dropped by and inquired with Max about her. One day he gave me an envelope with my name on it in her handwriting. I rushed back to my dorm room and ripped it open. Shock overwhelmed at what she had written. Myra stated due to medical problems gone home to Houston. An apology was made along with plea to move on with my life. I placed the letter in my Bible.

Tears followed for several nights as I tried to sleep. It was as if part of my soul had been shredded. A period of mourning began that never ended through my academic career. I passed by Mary and Stacy. They asked about her absence, their phony concern apparent. I moaned to them I knew nothing and stayed clear of them.

I struggled through final exam week and passed; returned home for the summer and did my two-week active duty plus a semester at the junior college. My parents were supportive in my dilemma of Myra's absence. I seldom dated during the rest of my collegiate tenure as I trudged towards completion of my degree.

After graduation I secured a job as a Purchasing Expediter for Texas Star Steel in Dallas, Texas. Stacy took a government job in the Social Security Administration and would call me from time to time with his nosiness. My aloofness prompted him to investigate my social group status. I had joined Dallas Professionals Single Society. Like most everyone else I was there to meet the proverbial right person and scram. Monthly meetings occurred in a rented banquet hall at the Mockingbird Inn. This provided us to gain insight into monthly activities as well as each other; mostly the latter.

Snacks were provided as a bartender served drinks. I was sipping club soda with lime and my eyes met Stacy's predatorial nuance. He defiantly waved and approached. "Hey Bud," he greeted, "Nice looking crowd." A few of my acquaintances were drawn towards him as his charm spilled with humor and history of our relationship. This perfect launch for him ended my dating career with Dallas Singles that night. Those mesmerized by his gleeful manner welcomed him. His transparency no one noticed.

Stacy slapped me on the shoulder as he reminisced our years together. I tried to break away. "Where you going?" he asked, "Party pooper?" With my back turned I overheard, "He's kinda quiet. Likes books though." The group was his; Rick Stacy had arrived.

As kids his father took us skeet shooting along with other outdoor activities. Other activities were what boys normally did as little league and pee wee football but Rick always had his mind on girls, even in elementary school. However, his presence always disrupted my chances at meeting others. My fun was over when he appeared. A master manipulator that seemingly had has parents in control that believed whatever he told them. He knew what buttons to push for control. His absence in my life was needed and told him to stay out of it after I left college, to no avail.

I desired meeting others and after Dallas Singles; Dating Gate an online service was next. I put in my personal info along with a recent photo; hit the button and checked my e-mail regularly. The encounters remained on the net. We would trade messages and when I invited one out for a mutual meet at a safe place; I never heard back. What did they want? A question I continually asked myself. This did not dismay my efforts; I continued.

The payoff came on evening. My jaw dropped; with shock struck eyes I studied the photograph and nervously typed a message. It began 'Where have you been, Myra? I have so missed you!' She was not on to answer but with that message; I shut down my computer and prayed for a response.

An hour later I nervously checked and she had responded. "Missed you," it began and followed by her address; a cell number and ended with, "Busy tonight? Come on over." I quickly responded and hurried to her apartment as my soul foresaw a reunion of hearts. There was no fear of changes in our relationship. She lived in the center of Dallas and as I wheeled into her complex I saw her waving to me from a second story floor. I ran from my car to her and we embraced and held each other as tears flowed down our cheeks. I felt whole again and our bond felt as strong as it ever.

It was Friday evening; I stayed with her most of the weekend. Although fall was the season; my reunion with her seemed like spring had arrived. As she took me by her hand and lead us inside she smiled, "Let's see if you remember all I taught you." I had not been her first but she had been mine which made me more valuable to her to keep her sexual pleasures insured.

Later as we lay next to each other she spoke, "What have you been doing?" It was Sunday morning and we hardly left her apartment. I told her about my history with various groups and included Dallas Singles. She rolled her eyes. "Bunch of losers who look for commitment but are afraid to commit; lengthy conversations of what they each do and feign being impressed," she commented, "Nothing has worked since we parted."

"We're back together and I want to keep it that way." I kissed her. The conversation later shifted to Stacy. I had checked Dallas Professional Singles website periodically and seen his ascension up the ranks to Social Chairman and hoped his character would be exposed. I groaned to Myra of him and his status; she turned away suddenly.

"What?" I exclaimed. She shoved herself out of bed and grabbed a robe from the closet and sulked away. Noise from the kitchen began as I pondered what upset her. I pulled on my underpants and met her at the dining table.

"Coffee's on. Get a cup and join me," she blandly invited. A mix of anger and pain displayed her demeanor as I returned and sat with her. Tears welled up and flowed from her eyes as she placed her forehead in the edge of her hand and spoke, "There was another reason I left North Texas." My heart throbbed hard in my throat as I feared what was to come.

An intense recollection volleyed forth; she unraveled an incident that had separated us. I was on weekend drill in the field with the Marine Reserves when it happened. Mary Callahan a friendly acquaintance and classmate invited Myra to spend Saturday night to help her with Statistics assignment. "Cancelled my social engagements to try to understand this, Myra," she paused. "I need your help." Myra never could walk away from a person in need whether it was a panhandler or a classmate.

A short walk through the cool spring Texas sunset placed her at Mary's apartment and as the door opened; Mary greeted giggling as she sipped a glass of white wine. "You wanted to study?" Myra skeptically inquired. Mary waved her in.

"Like a drink," she offered. Myra declined and disgustedly dropped into a chair. Mary offered her tea which she accepted. "Sorry," she began, "Sometimes I study better relaxed." Myra shook her head in disagreement. "Drink your tea and I'll cook us something. A little food in me and I will be good as new and willing to study." Dizziness from the tea struck Myra; she placed a hand on her forehead as the tea spilled. The surroundings of the apartment spun as a door opened from the bedroom and Stacy appeared.

"I woke up in a hospital bed," she grimaced, "My vagina sore and only a dim memory of Mary laughing, the smell of pot and Stacy on top of me." She couldn't remember how she arrived at the hospital; a nurse stated she was discovered in its parking lot. My face reddened with rage. I wanted to kill him. Nothing I could say would sooth her; I clutched her hand and she squeezed it. We stayed at her place the rest of the day and I held her most of the time whether we slept or sat on the couch. My mind cluttered as Stacy walked away from a crime of revenge due to rejection. Years she and I could have been together destroyed.

A phone call interrupted lunch as she answered, "Sorry I missed it. Sure. I'll be there. I am bringing a friend with me." She ended the call and winked, "Wanna play Cricket?" By Sunday evening we were more relaxed; even gleeful.

"Cricket?" I responded surprised. Myra sat and enthusiastically explained her social group their team name, practices and games. "We always have a monthly sleepover party at Bob Martin's place out in the country. It is fun." Her eyes widened as she described events. I accepted the invitation to participate in the next practice generally held on Saturday afternoon. Whether I liked it or not did not matter, it was an outside activity we could do together.

The group enticed me. All missed Myra at the last practice but warmly welcomed me. There were young couples along with older ones. Race, age, religion, married single, gay or straight did not restrict membership. Bob Martin, the undeclared leader; a tall, solid built man with a weather-beaten complexion bestowed a West Texan cowboy under his Stetson. A warm handshake and a "howdy" he offered me.

Martin owned an auto body parts business he joking referred to as a junkyard. He lived on the property with his pet hogs. His wife Marta sat on the sidelines. "Heart condition," he whispered, "Fine gal though. Our kids moved out of Texas." Martin shrugged, "We hear from them once in a while."

Another man approached named Calvin Jones, a black man with a butcher shop in a neighboring town near Martin. We were introduced. "Raised by a butcher and took the family business over," he grinned, "Even Klan members bring their deer meat to me to process for them." He laughed heartily at the fact. "If you're the best at something it doesn't matter what your color is," he added and boasted of his son that was a Doctor in Chicago. "He had his reasons to leave," Jones remarked, "I didn't put up a fight." Jones was widowed.

Martin would later confide wryly that some of the wives of those Klan members visited him on meeting nights. I laughed out loud and shook my head. I mentioned it to Myra. She snickered and nodded knowingly. At the edge of West Texas where he and Jones lived the KKK was still active. The nearest city was Weatherford which made the drive to Dallas cumbersome. "I love this group," grinned Martin, "It is worth the drive over."

Practice began and I found this sport easy enough to participate in especially with the jovial teammates. Winning of or losing was not the goal; fun and fellowship was. A lot of laughter, gentle teasing and joking. I liked it. The group was more tribal than others I had encountered. Myra was their ombudsman. Doctors, lawyers, teachers, CPA's, and a couple of pharmacists formed this team with a few business people like me. They were there for each other outside of practice and games and I was blessed to be one of them. My parents applauded my new found happiness and were overjoyed that Myra and I had rekindled the relationship.

The game schedule was monthly Sunday afternoon games and the following week a sleepover party at Martin's. Many shared travel trailers, some came with pup tents, others in their pickups with a camper but everyone showed. Martin hosted BBQ, baked potatoes, salad, and booze. Tea and coffee served to non imbibers. Children were left to friends and family for sleepovers. In the center of his back yard was a pit filled with small logs and other items that would burn. The post game party began.

As darkness covered the country sky; I experience the still peace of the area. Stars filled the sky and I envied Martin's lifestyle. My meditation was disrupted by the melodic tune from a wood flute and rhythmic pounding of a large hand drum. All stood silent in the moment.

The drum pounding got steadily got louder; suddenly it broke into a rapid beat as the flutist followed. The crowd began to shuffle and bounce to the music; a line was formed as clapping and cheering began. Myra and I joined as the line danced by a trash can full of ground meat; each person grabbed a handful and ate.

Myra ate and so I followed her in the rite. The dance continued and when all had been served; Martin tossed the remains to the hogs. The dance went on. I felt inspired by the camaraderie. I laughed heartily and jumped gleefully. The music stopped and we paused and soon were laughing and hugging one another.

In our pup tent as we curled next to each other I asked about the raw meat and how the entire experience appeared ritualistic. She pressed hard against me, "I hope you are ready for this." A kiss and she pulled me close to her and our naked bodies embraced; she spilled the facts. I was shocked, appalled and then we both began laughing. I was with the woman I loved and a group that suited us.

Months passed as I anticipated time with the Cricket team. One weeknight Stacy called, "What have you been up to?" I muttered routine. "Saw you playing Cricket? You're really the athlete now," he joked. He didn't mention that he spotted Myra although she wore thick sunglasses and a wide brimmed hat with her hair up at games and practice. I changed the subject and asked about Dallas Singles. "Well," he began, "I am the Social Chairman and am constantly looking up activities for the group." I smiled. It was the shapely twin blondes he was interested in that played on our team I guessed. They were Wiccans and were funeral directors. I waited for his pitch. "Tell me more about this Cricket team." I explained I couldn't over the phone and invited him to my apartment with the promise of Chivas Regal. "You don't drink," he remarked. I explained it was a peace offering and he accepted.

My consternation of his prostrate body was interrupted as Myra used her key to enter our home. She closed the door and paused to stare at Stacy's helpless state. "We got him," she grinned. I nodded.

"Martin will be by with the van and help us roll him in the rug," she reminded me.

"Too bad Mary Callahan can't join him," I chuckled.

"Yes," she giggled, "Too bad."

"I thought she was a bit stringy," I joked and added, "It was our team name that caught Stacy's curiosity."

Myra tossed her had back with laughter, "The Cannibals!"

OTHER HELLBOUND BOOKS

The Toilet Zone: Number Two
"Restroom reading at its most terrifying!"

Imagine, if you will, you're traveling through the unknown, hellbound, with no roadmap or stars to guide you. The light fades as you descend into a shadow realm where supernatural terrors make their lair and evil lurks at every turn. Here, dead things don't always stay dead, for this is a world where things that shouldn't be… *are*, and things that should be are not.

In this world, it takes between 2,500 and 4,000 reading words to pay a visit to the smallest, but terrifyingly necessary, room, and stories are written precisely to chill the bones as you wait for nature to make its call.

You open up the book, and one of the 32 tales skulking within its hellish pages chooses you…

It's too late to turn back now. You are about to set foot into another dimension, so best watch out for that signpost up ahead...You've just crossed over into... The Toilet Zone

Blood and Blasphemy

If you enjoy your horror dipped in buckets of blood and sprinkled with generous amounts of blasphemy, then you've come to the right place!

Blood and Blasphemy is a collection of over thirty of the most sacrilegious horror stories ever written.

Within these irreverent pages, you will encounter a priest that keeps his deformed spawn chained in a root cellar, a convent where a poisonous species of salamander is worshiped, a demonic altar boy, possessed religious relics that kill, blood-drinking clergymen, a Son of God who feeds on sin, an unsuspecting couple who run afoul of religious lunatics in a small town, the divine (and deadly) turd of Christ, and other terrifying tales guaranteed to make church ladies faint and nuns clutch their rosaries.

Schlock! Horror!

An anthology of short stories based upon/inspired by and in loving homage to all of those great gorefest movies and books of the 1980's (not necessarily base in that era, although some do ride that wave of nostalgia!), the golden age when horror well and truly came kicking, screaming and spraying blood, gore & body parts out from the shadows...

This exemplary 80's themed/inspired tales of terror has been adjudicated and compiled by one Mr Bret McCormick, himself a writer, producer and director of many a schlock classic, including *Bio-Tech Warrior*, *Time Tracers*, *The Abomination*, *Ozone: The Attack of the Redneck Mutants* and the inimitable *Repligator*.

Featuring stories from: Todd Sullivan, Timothy C Hobbs, Mark Thomas, Andrew Post, James B. Pepe, Thomas Vaughn, Edward Karpp, Jaap Boekestein, Lisa Alfano, L. C. Holt, John Adam Gosham, Brandon Cracraft, M. Earl Smith, Sarah Cannavo, James Gardner, Bret McCormick, and James H. Longmore.

Graveyard Girls

Female authors + Horror = something spectacularly terrifying!

A delicious collection of horrific tales and darkest poetry from the cream of the crop, all lovingly compiled by the incomparable Gerri R Gray! Nestling between the covers of this formidable tome are twenty-five of the very best lady authors writing on the horror scene today!

These tales of terror are guaranteed to chill your very soul and awaken you in the dead of the night with fear-sweat clinging to your every pore and your heart pounding hard and heavy in your labored breast...

Featuring superlative horror from: Xtina Marie, M. W. Brown, Rebecca Kolodziej, Anya Lee, Barbara Jacobson, Gerri R. Gray, Christina Bergling, Julia Benally, Olga Werby, Kelly Glover, Lee Franklin, Linda M. Crate, Vanessa Hawkins, P. Alanna Roethle, J Snow, Evelyn Eve, Serena Daniels, S. E. Davis, Sam Hill, J. C. Raye, Donna J. W. Munro, R. J. Murray, C. Bailey-Bacchus, Varonica Chaney, Marian Finch (Lady Marian).

A HellBound Books LLC
Publication

http://www.hellboundbookspublishing.com

Printed in the United States of America